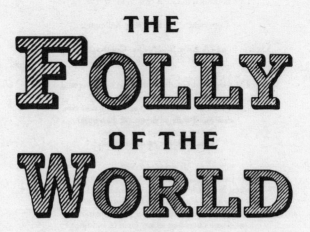

THE
FOLLY
OF THE
WORLD

JESSE BULLINGTON

orbit

www.orbitbooks.net

ORBIT

First published in Great Britain in 2012 by Orbit

Copyright © 2012 by Jesse Bullington

Excerpt from *The Fallen Blade* by Jon Courtenay Grimwood
Copyright © 2011 by JonCGLimited

The moral right of the author has been asserted.

*All characters and events in this publication, other than
those clearly in the public domain, are fictitious
and any resemblance to real persons,
living or dead, is purely coincidental.*

All rights reserved.
No part of this publication may be reproduced,
stored in a retrieval system, or transmitted, in any
form or by any means, without the prior
permission in writing of the publisher, nor be
otherwise circulated in any form of binding or
cover other than that in which it is published and
without a similar condition including this
condition being imposed on the subsequent purchaser.

A CIP catalogue record for this book
is available from the British Library.

ISBN 978-0-356-50088-1

Printed and bound in Great Britain by Clays Ltd, St Ives plc

Papers used by Orbit are from well-managed forests
and other responsible sources.

MIX
Paper from
responsible sources
FSC
www.fsc.org   FSC® C104740

Orbit
An imprint of
Little, Brown Book Group
100 Victoria Embankment
London EC4Y 0DY

An Hachette UK Company
www.hachette.co.uk

www.orbitbooks.net

This novel is dedicated to brave little Holland,
for all she taught me.

...Not nearly enough, some will inevitably suggest,
but I feel well served by her instruction. Proost!

Author's Note

A very long time ago, the peasant-happy painter Pieter Bruegel the Elder crammed an impressive number of personified proverbs onto an oak panel. This painting, *Netherlandish Proverbs*, which is now housed at the Staatliche Museen in Berlin, allegedly bore the original title *The Folly of the World*. Bruegel's masterpiece inspired the title of this novel, as well as providing the proverbs with which I have begun the various sections of the book. Those who are inclined to find significance in this are encouraged to do so; those who would rather not are invited to forget this prelude at once and get on with the story.

Feast of the Annunciation 1422

"The Topsy-Turvy World"

The little boat slowed, both rowers setting their oars and kicking up amber water as they came to the willow wood bordering the village of Oudeland. In all directions the meer stretched flat and cold, but here at last the smooth expanse yielded to what lurked beneath it. The craft brushed the treetops, the few dead willow shoots that broke the filmy surface snapping like old rushes as the boat drifted through them. The two men peered over their respective sides, murmuring to each other where larger boughs threatened the belly of their vessel. Gray bream huddled in the rotting nests of their former hunters, eels festooned through the branches like Carnival ribbons.

The boat slid between the last fence posts of dead limbs, and then the town itself was beneath them. It was a shadow village, without thatch for its roofs to keep out the wet and the cold, without paint or color for its disintegrating shutters and doors, without any sun at all, only a vague, shimmering moon, never waxing, never warming. The mill had kept its blades but the great fan felt no wind in the ever-gloaming depths, yet all clothes-lines and carts and even the well house had long since blown away. The boat scudded over Oudeland, quiet as thieves in a church or leaves on a lake, and there at last rose the old elm, what had once been the tallest tree in thirty leagues now only a tangled, naked bush pushing out of the water like a mean clump of blackthorn on the edge of a canal.

It had been a grand tree for climbing, if one could get a leg up to the lower branches, and one of the two men recalled the feel of rough bark against rough palm, the sound of laughter above and below, as close to flying as any could come in this life. Yet here they came, like unquiet spirits returning through the air, and with wonder they saw a figure balanced there in the boughs of the elm, waiting. They coasted past the bell tower of the church, a wide mooring post with a thorny crown where four herons had recently come of egg and age, and then the nose of the boat nuzzled the branches of the elm, the men staring at its keeper.

Much of the ram's hide had come away in greedy beakfuls, but enough had hardened in the sun to lash it to the boughs, a sunbleached and waterworn puppet tangled in the treetop. Its bare, eyeless skull was tilted upward with jaw agape, like a child catching snow or rain, and its forelegs were spread and caught amongst the branches, as if it were falling into flight or rising to crucifixion. The two men in the boat stared in silence at the ram, the vessel motionless upon the face of the deep, the moment seeming to stretch on and on, longer than all the roads and rivers in the world, and behind them, beneath them, the wheel of the mill mutely turned, kicking up silt as a great shadow slid past its mossy blades.

All Saints Day 1422

"Shitting Upon the Gallows"

Heaven bled when they took Sander from his cell, the condemned man scowling into the East as if offended by dawn's decision to attend his execution. In Dordrecht the harbors would be turning to molten gold, the walls of the city transforming into the gossamer white robes of angels, but here in Sneek the first light of morning shone only on shit, and all the alchemists in the witch-riddled West couldn't turn a turd into more than what it was. These were the thoughts Sander harbored as the cart he stood in squelched through the muddy square to the gallows-tree, and not even the rotten apples and clods of filth the mob hurled at him could detract from the thrill of anticipation. They were going to hang him, and Sander grinned as he spied the thick hempen rope. A ball of horse dung struck him on the teeth, the thankfully dry clump leaving an earthy taste in his mouth as he spit into the cheers of the crowd. He focused on the noose, trying to secure the burgeoning erection already firming up in his breeches—he was going to enjoy this.

Sander assumed that most people in his circumstance dreamed of escape, reprieve, *something*, but he would not allow himself the indulgence. Nor did he dwell on the life that had led him to this doomed place as surely as if he had followed a path without fork or intersection, much as men in his place are thought to. Were he to hang, the vast conspiracy he had carefully navigated, like a man creeping over an uncertain fen, would never be fully understood; the countless secret enemies who had orchestrated this farcical display would go unpunished ... but he did not deign to give them his ruminations. No, Sander thought only of rope, coils of it wrapping around his ankles and thighs and balls and waist and chest and arms and elbows and wrists and, especially, his neck. Itchy, tight, sinuous rope constricting him until there was nothing left but braided, bloody knots.

That thought was what helped him fall asleep on nights when the dream-countries proved elusive, but now was not the time to linger on such fantasies, and he knew it. His heart beat faster as he looked around the town square, saw the hundred contorted faces of the crowd, lit for a moment on the desperate thought of *Escape*! like a horsefly flirting with a butcher's apron, and then settled back on rope. Cord was what bound his hands behind his back—also hemp, thick as his thumb, tied in his cell before they led him to the wagon. Sander flexed his hands, confirming the make of the knot he could not see and smiling all the wider. He let his fingertips curl up to stroke the knot a single time and then spread his hands again; a gull's wings taking flight, an over-bloomed rose falling apart.

A pair of guards with crude pikes waited at the stairs of the gibbet. As the wagon jerked to a stop, each hopped into the bed and grabbed one of Sander's elbows. He thought he recognized them as militiamen from some other town, some other setup, but quickly calmed himself. Bland, halfwit boys like these were a pfennig a bushel, and so odds were they were local muscle, which would legitimize it all as far as Sneek was concerned. Fools. A priest and the hangman waited on the platform, and the guards brought Sander forward, their tugging on his arms causing the binding cord to cut into his wrists. His cock throbbed from the sensation.

There was no trapdoor awaiting the convict, only a shove off the edge of the cramped platform, and the guards stayed on the final step as they delivered Sander to his death. The hangman wore no hood, only a stupid-looking feathered cap, and the edge of the priest's habit was powdered with dry dust instead of wet muck—he must have raised it like a noblewoman careful of her skirts when he left his church. A man in the crowd swallowed from his bottle too quickly and choked on it. The things Sander noticed as the hangman slipped the noose around his broad neck and yanked it tight.

"Sander Himbrecht," the priest said without raising his voice, and it took several moments for the tide of elbows and hisses to work its way back through the crowd until the morning was as quiet as it should have been had men never learned to speak. Sander couldn't properly converse in the garbled garbage-tongue of the Frisian, but like many people of the South, he usually got the thrust of what was barked at him by the stiffheads. The priest said something like, "Sander Himbrecht, you stand here a dead man, but need not fall a damned one. It is established you shall serve as an example to what wages a blackguard and killer is paid in Sneek, but here at last is a chance to also demonstrate the power of repentance, of salvation at the cusp of ruin."

Something like that, only like as not less pretty-sounding—priest or no, Frisians were not known for their eloquence.

"Hang the dicksucker!" said a straw-haired, wheat-mustachioed man at the front of the crowd. Sander understood that bit perfectly. "Don't let 'em off, Father!"

Sander licked his lips, the man's outburst a confirmation that they knew much more than they should, each and all of them. That this was inevitable as sin, that he was flat-out lucky they weren't having him quartered instead. Sander rubbed his wrists against the rope, eyes flicking to the blond heckler and back to the priest, breathing deep to better feel the noose against his throat, his cock positively aching up against his breeches like a drowning man kicking his last to break the surface of the water. He knew the priest was waiting for him, but he also knew the hangman had an unobstructed view of his back, and so he turned a bit to better put the clergyman between himself and the executioner as he stalled. The old boy had a strip of red cloth in his shaky hands, and Sander smiled at the realization that in Sneek they must have the priest do the blindfolding after the last rites and all—funny, that, and a far cry from the communion he was expecting.

"It's like this," Sander said quietly, not even trying to ape the stiffhead dialect. "I would if I could, but I'm not, so I can't, yeah?"

"Not what?" said the priest in proper-talk, evidently a learned man who knew a real language when he heard it.

"Look." Sander nodded down. Behind him, he relaxed his aching wrists from the strained position he had held them in all morning, before they had even bound him. If they had used baling twine or something thinner, he might have been in real trouble, but—

"What is it?" The priest blinked at the condemned man's damp, diaphanous tunic, as if Sander were trying to point out an especially interesting stain. Then Sander knew the older man had found it, his eyes opening wide as silver double-groots, his lips pursing tighter than the strings on his purse. To seal the deal, Sander bore down a little, making his cock nod upward at the priest through his thin breeches and thinner tunic. There was a moment of silence on the platform as the ancient stared at Sander's unmistakable bulge and Sander grinned over the priest's shoulder at the hangman.

"He's getting loose!" someone in the crowd with a vantage of Sander's back shouted.

In response, Sander bit the priest on the face.

Brown teeth met brown stubble and were proved the victor, bumpy cheek yielding to smooth enamel, and Sander tasted blood. His left hand came free of the amateur knot, loosing its twin in the process, but before he could properly grab hold of the priest, the hangman lunged forward and shoved Sander. A lesser executioner might not have dislodged him from the priest, but the hangman had a smith's arm, and Sander came away with but a flap of skin and meat as he pitched from the platform.

Sander's left hand caught the rope as he fell, and an instant before it went taut, he flexed all his muscle, saving himself a snapped neck at the cost of a dislocated elbow. His arm immediately dropped limp and the noose clamped tight around his throat. Sander did not let the glorious distraction of being hanged consume him, and as he was strangled, he kicked his legs in the air to spin around. It worked, and he twirled in the air almost too quickly.

Almost, but not quite. As the chest-level platform swung into his tear-blurring vision, he saw the feet and hands of the sprawled-out priest. More importantly, he saw the hangman's heel coming down to stomp his shoulder and affect what the drop should have, had he not caught the rope in time. With his right arm Sander snatched the hangman's boot and jerked him downward, which tightened the noose even more. The startled lummox tumbled from the platform, lamely slapping the air as he fell past the still-spinning Sander. The familiar black wheels were spinning larger and faster in Sander's vision, and though it pained him, he reflexively heaved his injured left arm to his crotch and rubbed himself as the platform came back around.

Slapping his right arm down beside the half-prone priest and focusing all his strength, Sander arrested his spin. Clawing his arm forward, he dug his fingernails into the platform until he could verily taste the oak splinters through his quick. His right elbow set beside that of the doubled-over priest, Sander heaved himself onto the platform. The hangman knew his business well, however, and so the noose did not relax even as Sander scrambled to his feet on the wooden deck. Before he could get his fingers under the rope to save himself, the two guards on the stair shook off their shock and rushed forward, jabbing at him with their pikes. Sander hooked the elbow of his good arm under the now-wailing priest, hoisting him upright in the nick of time. The clergyman accepted both spear points in his chest as easily as he accepted the more exciting confessions from the young women of Sneek. One pike became entangled in the priest's ribs, but the other broke clean through the man, nicking Sander's left shoulder.

Even without the dying priest grinding against him from the

impact Sander would have come then, the noose too tight, the hemp too coarse. Delicious. Even as he grunted his satisfaction, he got his fingers under the rope collar and jerked it loose, gasping like a landed herring from more than the release in his breeches. He had dropped the priest, but the guards still held the man aloft with their weapons, neither sure what to do given the circumstances.

The tunnel of Sander's consciousness expanded to take in exactly what had happened, and he tried to laugh but gagged instead. Pulling a face as he widened the noose, he slipped it over his head just as several crossbow bolts whizzed past him and the fallen hangman regained the platform behind the horrified guards. Sander kicked the priest in the back, driving him deeper onto the pikes and managing an actual laugh through his dry retching fit. He had known it would be a grand day but could never have anticipated such a glorious fiasco.

That said, getting out of the ropes was the easy part; getting out of town was where things got tricky. What kind of savages held their executions in the main square, instead of outside the village walls like civilized folk? *Stiffheads*. Going on the wave of furious peasants crashing below him at the edge of the platform, his killing of their priest was not liable to make his escape any easier—even those who hadn't been actively involved in the plot to hang him would certainly want him dead now. There were only a few streets leading out of the thronged square, and even the one behind the gibbet was a good fifty paces off. Tempting though it suddenly was to simply give up, Sander knew they probably wouldn't still be satisfied with a hanging given the recent turn of events, and he would be damned before he went to his maker in any other fashion.

Well, then, he had to do something. Sander jumped from the platform, landing feetfirst on a fat man. They both hit the ground hard, but Sander rolled forward and onto his feet as his human cushion spit blood and teeth.

They were on him then, the edge of the mob washing over

him, but Sander was a dirty son of a bitch's bastard's whore, and what's more, he knew it. The citizens of Sneek should have suspected that a man willing to bite a priest would not shirk from snatching a scrotum or poking out an eye if he could, but in their fury to catch him they failed to consider this. Thus, the first man to lay hands on Sander had his testicles crushed and twisted by thick fingers, and the second had his left eyeball hooked viciously with a thumb, the entire orb popping loose of its socket and bouncing against the poor fellow's cheek.

Three fists and a knife connected with Sander. The knuckles bounced off his leathery skin, but as he twisted away, the knife carved a neat little flap in his already bloodied, dangling left arm. Then he saw it. Saw *her*. The pommel of his beloved had appeared just beside him, and he caught a glimpse of brown hair and brown eyes, a handsome face he loved more than jellied herring or fresh beer materializing from the mob—

—But then the weapon was in hand and her hooded deliverer swallowed back up by the crowd, and Sander howled with joy to once again wield Glory's End.

Her blade had been recently whetted, and in bringing the sword up to put her between himself and the crowd he clipped off three of a man's fingers. Before Sander could get a proper swing across, the crowd had already fallen back, and he used the moment to catch his breath. He had a clean break to the side street he had been making for, but then he saw three militiamen with crossbows atop the platform, their weapons leveled at him. Before he could blink, the bows fired.

And, incredibly, all missed. One quarrel whipped through his long, manky hair, the other two splashing into the muck at his feet. Sander stared at them for a moment, grinned, and ran away. The crowd recovered its courage at the sight of his back and followed after.

Sander gained the side street…and ran directly into four more militiamen, likely shirkers late to the execution. Their

pikes were not leveled, praise to the appropriate saints, sparing
Sander an end similar to that of the priest. Glory's End flashed
in the shadows of the alley, and before the first man realized he
was disemboweled, the second was hacked to the collarbone,
both falling in a welter of gore and blood as their stunned com-
patriots stumbled back. Sander kept moving, tagging another on
the knee as he fled down the street. The man shifted his weight
the slightest bit and immediately pitched forward, gasping as the
thin red slit in his beige leggings split into a yawning fissure of
wet muscle and exposed bone, and the fourth militiaman stared
aghast after the demon who had butchered his friends.

The alley opened onto a lane between rows of squat, tightly
packed houses, and glancing back over his shoulder, Sander saw
the mob only half a block behind him, the hangman now leading them. Sander turned left, booking it for all he was worth
down the narrow street. Left turned out to be a rather poor decision, as another group of militiamen rounded a bend before him,
but he only ran faster, making it to another alley just before the
new crew reached him. This avenue was clogged with low-
hanging laundry, the lines of which Sander cut as he ran to bring
the drying clothes down on his pursuers. Sander laughed to hear
the shouts behind him become angrier still, and then burst
through the last row of dangling sheets and toppled into the
canal into which the alley terminated, Glory's End flying from
his hand as he struck the gray water and sank like a millstone.

Spring 1423

"Catching Fish Without a Net"

I.

A hush fell over the dingy, cramped tavern. Such an occurrence was not particularly rare, requiring little more than a dirty joke, even a bewhiskered one, but quiet the place did, and the handsome stranger smiled at the staring faces surrounding him. The fisherman he sat across from smiled back, an easy, dangerous sort of smile, and nodded.

"Settled, then." Pitter extended his hand. "A double-groot."

"One double-groot," agreed the handsome man, shaking on the wager. It had taken them longer to come to terms on how many Brabant mites and Holland pfennigs added up to a Holland groot, and from there a double-groot, than it had for the stranger to make the acquaintance of Pitter, get him drunk, and share a plate of early chèvre with him. As they ate and debated currency with the unsolicited help of their fellow patrons, the barkeep apologized for the ferocious saltiness of the cheese—the kid had been born too early and lived but a week, and the tears of its mother must make their way down through her teats. The stranger was the only one who laughed at this, and he quickly withered it into a cough under the dour stares of the locals.

The handsome stranger's name was Jan and he was from the Groote Waard in southern Holland, but he had told everyone he was a riverboat pilot named Lubbert down from Sneek. This deceit had instantly endeared him to the tipsy Friesland transplant Pitter, who had bought him a drink. The local beer tasted like a respectable brew Jan had sampled in Haarlem, if said beer had been filtered through a drunkard or two and returned via piss-stream to the barrel, but then Jan had not come to Aalsmeer for its ale.

It was a pretty enough village, small groves of alder and willow spotting the outskirts like patches of peach fuzz on the cheeks of a young man impatient to grow a beard. The quality of the lakes had inspired Jan's decision to try the place instead of pushing onward to the sea, for they were dark, muddy pools carved from the peat by villagers in generations past and left to languish like bloody gouges in the earth that would never clot. The water might not burn the boy's eyes the way the sea would, but Jan knew from experience a peat-pool would have enough silt swirling around to make things comparably difficult, and if he never had to ride his horse over another dune he would die a happy man.

The wager set, Jan followed Pitter out of the smoky common room and through what passed for streets in Aalsmeer to the fisherman's house, half a dozen of the patrons accompanying them. Pitter had told him to leave his horse at the tavern, but Jan had insisted, his Frisian stallion clopping along beside them. They came to the willow-and-mud hovel Pitter shared with his family and an Urker down from the islands to visit kin, and Jan waited in the alley with the other tavern-goers while the strawberry-nosed gambler went inside.

The huddled locals said nothing, which suited Jan just fine. He had not come to Aalsmeer for the conversation. Pitter soon emerged with his eldest boy. The handsome stranger nodded at the youth, whose gangly arms and legs reminded Jan of a willow's shoots, his olive eyes bringing to mind a certain stream outside of Papendrecht—if ever a lad symbolized the harmony between water and land it was young Wob. Besides that, his face was not as bad as his father's, and Jan allowed himself a slight smile at the boy, now hoping more than ever that he would soon be out of a double-groot.

The procession traveled the rest of the way through town, picking up a few more spectators, which displeased Jan but could not be helped. If a next-time proved necessary, he would adopt a different strategy. Pitter blathered on about his son's prowess, comparing him to an otter, an eel, a fine, fine fishy; father's furry hand on son's bare shoulder. Jan admired the sleek, bronzed skin of the lad, whose chest was only just beginning to show a few pinfeathers of hair; his chin smooth; his eyes, green as catkins, refusing to meet Jan's bark-brown ones. Jan imagined those eyes brimming with tears, those tan cheeks roasted to a fine pink, and nodded to himself. The tone of the group had become celebratory now that young Wob was with them, the double-groot good as won.

Heaven burned in the west, as is its custom, and the merry troop came to the largest of the lakes nudging the outskirts of Aalsmeer. The water shone the color of cider before them. Jan tied his horse to a post set in the shore, and they marched onto a long dock jutting over the meer. Father slapped son lightly on the back and arms, Pitter's face beaming with pride and eagerness. Well he might, reflected Jan; he wasn't the one to be diving into a lake at sunset with the blooms of water lilies still only a promise of the pad-scaled shallows.

"Da," Wob said, "are ya sure—"

"Good lad," said Pitter, cuffing his son. "The sooner you're in, the sooner you're out, eh, Lubbert?"

"Hmm?" It took Jan a moment to realize he was being addressed—bitter the beer might be, but strong. Not unlike old Sander, whose ill-executed escape attempt in Sneek necessitated the whole affair Jan was currently undertaking. "Aye, that's right, boy. Your father's staked a double-groot you can win a swimming trial, and I'll tell you here in front of all that if you win, I'll give you a few mites yourself for the trouble."

That earned a few huzzahs, and another one of those dangerous smiles from Pitter. The boy still would not meet Jan's eye. He wondered if young Wob was a virgin.

"Now, Lubbert, we said he's to dive for a shoe, then?" Pitter took an old iron horseshoe from his pocket and held it up, the rusty metal dull against the shining water. "You want to toss?"

"Indeed," said Jan, taking the shoe and drawing the dagger he kept at his belt. The way Pitter's lip twitched as Jan began scraping several bands in the rust confirmed that the fisherman had meant to cheat him. He wondered where the boy had secreted the shoe's twin, or if one of Wob's siblings had run ahead and dropped the double off the end of the dock. No matter. The shoe was soon striped, and Jan winked at Pitter. "Just so the boy's not confused by any old piece of metal he feels down there. This one's rough then smooth then rough again from the rust, aye, Wob?"

Wob looked even less comfortable than he had before, a light breeze skating across the water, and Jan stepped forward, making a show out of hefting the horseshoe. Then he slung it sidearmed, the shoe skipping across the surface four, five, six times before sliding into the water. One of the tavern-goers whistled, another sighed, and a third spit. Pitter opened his mouth to speak, but then Wob was in after it, and seeing him come up a short way out, Jan chided himself for letting the boy strip unnoticed. Wob treaded water, gasping and paddling and looking as if he were trying to crawl out of the lake, up into the air.

"Farther on, yet," Pitter called, but his son did not immediately proceed. "Go on, then, you'll warm yourself directly!"

Wob threw himself ahead, the slapping of warm, hard skin on cold, hard water bringing a prolonged wince to his father's face. Several of the spectators came forward to stand at the edge of the dock with Pitter, and Jan let them by, content to move backward on the pier. It was not as if his watching would impact the search, and he was happy to stand in the rear as useless suggestions and encouragements were cast out after the boy. It was growing dark, and the wind was picking up. Jan frowned.

Two of Pitter's friends went back to the tavern, neither congratulating Jan on his impending victory as they passed. Again and again Wob surfaced, sometimes spitting, sometimes coughing, but always diving back down. Jan imagined that the boy's skin was quite numb by now, and that must make it even more difficult. Worst of all, any light that might have stretched to the bottom would have long since been reeled in, leaving Wob blind and fumbling through the muck for a horseshoe that would have instantly sunk into the mud.

"The devil you will!" Pitter shouted. "Go back a bit, then, I told you, farther back!"

Wob's voice came again but Jan could still not make out the words, warped as they were by wind and water. Pitter might have heard and answered with his shaking head, or perhaps his gesture was based on intuition for what complaint his son would lodge now that the sun was nesting in the cattails. Perhaps he was simply mourning for coins lost.

"If we come out in the morning—" One of the other men spoke for Pitter, but Jan cut him off.

"The bet was what it was. Was it not, Visser?"

"Stay the fuck where you were!" Pitter shouted again. "There, right there! Again, lad, again—that's the spot!"

Squinting between the capped heads of the Aalsmeerers, Jan saw Wob gulp the air and sink again, bubbles rising to mark his descent, and Jan wondered if there were weeds down there, the sort that are both slimy and scratchy. He hoped so, envisioning the boy snared in long emerald strands, his hands digging in the lakebed for an arc of iron, eels weaving between his fingers, a faint glow shining on his bare skin from some sunken moon...

"Been down too long," one man said, and Jan realized he was right.

"He's got it now, is what," said Pitter, but his voice was strained, a fishing line about to snap.

The surface of the lake was still save for the wind scratching along it. Pitter began to strip, but by the time he was naked one of his friends had stepped between him and the water, shaking his head. Pitter Visser screamed then, and spun away from the black lake, ready to fight Lubbert of Sneek, naked or not. But the man was gone, the post where he had tied his horse at the end of the pier barely visible through the spreading night, as if the lake had risen from its bed to cover the earth with its bitter, unrelenting darkness. When Pitter was absent from the tavern, which was more and more in the days and weeks and years to follow, the men who had stood with them on the dock whispered that the handsome stranger's failure to claim his double-groot before quitting their company was further proof that the devil himself had come to Aalsmeer.

II.

It was still far too early in the year for anyone to be on this stretch of strand, but Jolanda nevertheless put the better part of a league between herself and the trail that led through the dunes before undressing and walking into the surf. Partly it was to get her heat up before entering the brutally cold water, and partly it was to avoid getting her tunic stolen by one of her shitbird brothers or the village fisherboys—if one of them were to be sent after her, or shirk his responsibilities as she had, he could appear atop the dunes and sprint to her wad of hemp cloth before she could gain the shore. Out here, though, she would see anyone walking the beach long before he arrived.

She slapped her lower arms with opposite hands, her indigo fingers leaving ivory stripes on the violet skin, and then the sea was washing over her pale feet. Breath-stealer, flesh-scalder. A cold neuking day, but she always preferred the cold to the hot— even winter nights in the crowded hut were too much like sleeping inside a panting mouth, the warmer waters of Snail Bay too much like bathing in fresh blood.

Jolanda turned and ran from the sea then, the skin of her feet breaking shells instead of the reverse, her breath returning and burning as she charged up the dune. Her run quickly degenerated into a back-sliding climb, and then she spun again, running back down, sand sticking to her sweaty body, settling in her short black hair. The water shone before her, the afternoon sun beckoning her onward. If she fell there, the shells would be merciless, but she had not taken a tumble in the sand for some time, and then she was past the tide-cast ribbon of pink and gray and white shells and was back in the surf, the water splashing and slowing her, a chill cousin to the snatching sand of the dune. Then she did fall, half on purpose, and the shock of the icy sea struck her dead for several moments, the girl forcing herself to stay pinned to the floor of the shallows as the waves pushed and pulled at her, coaxing her upward with the promise of an honest gasp of air. Down she stayed, then whipped herself up with a cry, on her knees in the sand, the breakers crashing over her chest and shoulders, the salt stinging the countless cuts and abrasions she suffered from smashing snail shells all the days of her memory.

More than anything, she wanted to dash from the sea, to pull her tunic over her wet body and run home, to lie down amidst the purple pots until she was smoked like a herring. Instead she clumsily fought the sea and herself and gained her feet, the wind burning her slick skin almost, but not quite, worse than the waves had, and she faced not the dunes but open water. Meeting the hard eye of the North Sea made her feel like Griet from the tales her brother Pieter had told her, Mad Griet, the housewife who harrowed hell itself, afraid of nothing, ready to wrestle the devil and tie him to a pillow if he gave her trouble. That was how Jolanda would always be, she told herself, fierce enough to face hell itself, and so a chilly day at the beach presented no substantial challenge.

In she went again, keeping her head underwater as much as she dared, the inevitable discomfort of her teeth chattering as much a deterrent to surfacing as the frigid water ought to have been to entering it in the first place. Soon she lost the bottom, and knowing full well how foolhardy it would be to swim on, she dove again and kicked her legs and shoved apart the endless curtain of water over and over again, deeper and farther. At last she came up spluttering, the odor of burning shellfish that had dyed her nostrils with its permanent stink as surely as the purple had dyed her arms now forgotten, her shitbird siblings and father forgotten, everything lost in the rush to breathe after being crushed so tightly by the ocean.

Jolanda did not notice the rider until much later, when she was swimming back in. Her skin was wrinkled and deadened, her heart pounding even when she floated languidly on the surface, and when she finally saw him she paused, much as her frigid body wailed at her to keep swimming and quit the sea as soon as possible. She treaded water, wondering if the rider could see her amidst the waves, and then his arm came up in salute, a small brown flag flapping in the sea breeze. Her tunic. Jolanda cursed.

The horse did not move, but the rider dismounted, walking toward the water and calling to her. She could not hear what he was saying and swam closer, knowing her best hope would be if he came into the water after her—she could outswim anyone, and if she happened to be exhausted at the moment, then no matter, for the cold would cripple him worse than weariness hobbled her. Reassured, Jolanda swam to shore.

She stopped when she was able to set both feet on the sand, the relief it gave her beleaguered arms and legs nearly carnal, like fingernails on a long-neglected back. The waves necessitated that she occasionally kick up and float, but she had no intention of coming any closer until she determined who he was—for he was definitely a man, she saw that now—and what he wanted. Part of her supposed she already knew, that it would be what the neighboring fisherboys were always pestering her for, but she told that part to hush.

"You're all right, then!" The man had thick umber hair and a handsome smile, and he stood just beyond the reach of the waves, holding her tunic in one hand.

"Yeah!" Jolanda shouted back, wondering how best to get him in the water so she could steal his horse. She had never ridden a horse before, but had once goaded the man-child Luther into mounting a peddler's carthorse outside the tavern to fine result, and if the idiot could ride a horse, then so could she. She squinted at the man, trying to determine if she knew him or not—the older men of the village all looked the same to her, which was to say they all looked like sand-caked arseholes.

The stranger did not respond other than to stare out at her, and the longer they looked at each other, the more certain she was she had never seen him before. His high hat and clothes were obviously well worn, but none the poorer for it, with the garnet hue of his padded doublet and the fur trim on his cloak implying he might be a nobleman of some standing. But then, she had never seen a nobleman of any standing at all, and so couldn't say for sure. He didn't look like a sand-caked arsehole, in any event.

"How long have you been out there?" he finally called, cupping his hand into the sunset that wreathed Jolanda's head.

"Long enough," she answered, her teeth chattering worse than ever now that she was close to stationary, wave after frigid wave lapping over her. When he did not respond to that, she sighed and swam a little closer to shore, fatigue truly beginning to set in, and she raised her voice even louder. "My father come out. He just run back to start the fish. He'll be back soon. My brothers too, surely."

"No." The handsome stranger shook his head. "You're alone. No other tracks. The beach is always honest."

Jolanda cursed herself for a fool, and swam even closer so that she could fully rest her legs and still flash him some tit. It had worked well enough to lure in any fisherboys whose belt pouches she had a mind to rifle, but the stranger stayed where he was. This presented a rather sizable problem—if he didn't enter the water, she couldn't very well give him the slip and beat him to the shore. She glanced down to make sure her oceanic bodice was still giving up glimpses of her nipples between the waves, and there they were, dark as wet sand and jutting out hard as shells, given the cold neuking circumstances, but still no move from the stranger.

Then, success. As his hand fell to his waist, she considered whether she would risk riding his horse back to her hut to retrieve what food and supplies she could steal, or take the safer path and immediately ride north, sell the beast somewhere along the way, and with that fortune start a new life somewhere far from hair-pulling brothers and switch-happy father. Then she saw he was not loosening his cod-piece but drawing a dagger, and Jolanda chose to take a deep breath rather than uttering the curse that pushed at her tongue.

She dove and swam south, staying down as long as she could. She kept close enough to the shallows to give her legs the odd respite, but stayed underwater as much as she could bear. She only looked to shore after she had dived, quick-surfaced, and dived again over fifty times, which was as high as she had ever needed to count. The line of dunes were as familiar and distinct to her as her brothers, and she saw she was making good progress to the trail despite her exhaustion.

She also saw the silhouette of the rider pacing her along the beach. She dived deeper, swam harder, surfaced briefer, but always he was there. The sun had nearly gone under when at last she recognized the gap in the dunes where the trail ran to her home, and she stopped fighting the sea, letting it hold her steady in its half-tender, half-cruel embrace. The rider waited between her and those dunes, as if neither she nor he had moved a jot from their original positions.

He turned and looked at the trail, then dismounted and approached the water's edge. Jolanda sunk deeper until only her eyes and nose bobbed above the water, but he looked directly at her, and while he still held her tunic in one hand, he also gripped that long dagger in the other, its edge catching the last light of day and burning like a brand. Jolanda knew from the many drub-bings she and the fisherboys had exchanged by the trailhead that no screams would reach her hut, but before she could settle on another strategy, the man's arm cocked back and the knife was spinning high into the air, a twinkling pinwheel that flew to her left and then past her, disappearing into a wave without a splash.

She didn't look back to see his reaction at having missed her, and so pathetically—she knew that she already stood little enough chance of finding the weapon without averting her eyes from the spot where it had sunk. She had only swum a short distance before a part of her protested at the impossibility of finding the knife, of swimming back into the colder, deeper water when she was so close to home and might break from the sea, evade the man, and gain the trail. At this point, however, he owed her at least a knife for her trouble, if not a horse as well, and she would need the one to take the other. And so she swung her arms harder, kicked fiercer, staying to the surface so as not to lose sight of where the dagger had fallen, an ever-shifting patch of sea like any other save that she had put it at thirty strokes away, and now she was but ten.

The tide was coming in, pulling the bottom even farther away, and the sun was only poking over the edge of the waves. Jolanda dove. She was winded and barely brushed the sand before she had to surface. Resisting the push of the jostling waves took what little strength she had, but she dived again, her leanness carrying her down. Even with eyes hardened against the brine she saw little, the sun too low, the bottom too deep, and as the tide shoved her backward, she ran her hands over the rippled sand, a blind woman seeking out a single loose thread in an endless quilt. She came up gasping, dry-heaved twice, gulped the air, then went down again.

And again.

And again.

Lights were coming to her, bright sparks inside her skull, and still she dove, her fingers dredging through the sand. Her hands were too numb to even recognize that they had found the knife until the salt intruded into her sliced right palm. She came up bloody-handed and howling. And dove again, brushing the bottom slowly, carefully, and then, finally, wrapped the fingers of her good left hand around the hilt, a smile not even the dwellers of that deep could see hidden behind her thin lips.

III.

The girl was only a few paces out when Jan found her again, the sneaky bitch having escaped into the liquid shadows after diving for his knife. She was crawling more than swimming, the breakers barely cresting her back as she dragged herself from the sea like some beast of legend. He walked toward her, and she must have realized she was spotted, for she flung herself to her feet and dashed out of the water, charging him with his own dagger.

Jan felt his stomach lurch at the sight, marveling that she could even stand, and then she couldn't, her legs giving out and sending her sprawling in the shells. She gave a cry, and then commenced vomiting with such vigor that Jan half-expected her organs to appear in the frothy stew. She kicked her arms and legs, drowning on dry land as she retched uncontrollably.

When she stopped heaving, Jan approached her, the girl rolling onto her back and revealing herself to be older than he would have imagined from the size of her tunic, perhaps fifteen or sixteen. Her stomach and small breasts were striped red from the shells, and as he appraised her, the deeper cuts began to weep. Oddly, from the elbows down, her arms were almost as dark as the rest of her was pallid, and he saw that the sand coating her right hand was sloughing off in small red clumps. In her left fist his dagger jutted out, black as burnt sugar in the gloaming.

"Get!" the girl managed, brandishing the knife, her accent thick but certainly no poorer than those of the people of Aalsmeer, or worse yet, the Frisians. She would do.

"Are you mad?" Jan asked pleasantly. "You could have drowned."

He tossed the sandy tunic onto her and turned around, his practiced nonchalance belying the ear he cocked for the sound of feet pounding beach behind him. Only the rumor of sand dancing in the breeze. She wasn't moving.

Mounting his horse, Jan looked back at the girl. She stayed where he had left her, the tunic draped over her like the victim of some worse crime, her plain face staring at him with a look of stupid confusion. Jan had hoped it would be a boy.

The trail wound through the sandy hills and ridges, and though he saw the lights of a village ahead, he stopped at the first hut he came to, a rather large, sand-blasted hovel set back in the blackthorn that coated the dunes. The bouquet of rotten shellfish, charred bone, and old piss permeated the place, and there were several rusty cauldrons set in the sand between him and the hut. Jan nodded, remembering how stained the girl's arms were. This would be easier than he had thought.

It wasn't, as it turned out. They slunk from the shadows of the sloe, half a dozen lads between the ages of ten and twenty, all wearing the dull, tongue-lolling expressions of sleepy wolfhounds, their arms dark with dye, their eyes dark with suspicion. He would have taken any one of them over the girl, but she was the swimmer and so there was nothing for it.

"Is your father here?" Jan asked them, but none spoke, and the tallest of them began to stroke the nose of the stranger's horse. Jan reflected on how much easier certain things had been when he rode with Sander. Then sand-warped wood screamed in its frame and a man stood silhouetted in the doorway of the hut, a fire blazing behind him, and Jan dismounted with a sigh.

Inside, the handsome stranger sat on one side of the fire and the father sat on the other, his six sons fanning out around him. It was silent, other than the popping fire, and hard to see through the haze of smoke—judging by the greasy violet stains surrounding the central firepit, the cauldrons weren't always used outside. The shellfish they apparently used to manufacture the dye were kept in damp sacks that insulted the single room like sandbags protecting an island from flood, and the odor of marine decay was much stronger inside than it had been on the trail. One of the boys whispered in his father's ear, and the man nodded.

"Whadja say your name is?" said the father.

"Lubbert," said Jan. "And yours?"

"A Frieslander?" The man scowled. "You a herring-fucker, Lob?"

"No," said Jan amiably. "But I've been known to lay the occasional eel."

"Eh?"

"Only fish long enough," said Jan, demonstrating with his fist. Several of the boys brayed at this, but the father remained unimpressed. He had heard dirtier.

"Verf," said the father. "You call me Verf. You said business. What business, stiffhead?"

"A proposition," said Jan. "I'm traveling back to Sneek, to my family and business. I'm a cloth-seller. I need a servant to help my wife with our new son, but, riding by, I thought—may I drink?"

"If you have enough for me," said Verf.

"Certainly," said Jan, taking a gourd of brandywine from the satchel he had brought inside. He wouldn't have left his saddle untended in these parts if he could help it, but so things went. Taking a pull, he stood, hunched, and moved around the fire, bumping his head on the low ceiling and catching a lungful of wood smoke. He coughed. A boy snickered. He sat back down.

"Ugh," said Verf, grimacing on the drink, but swallowing anyway. "It's spoilt."

"It's supposed to be sweet," Jan explained, which got an even deeper frown from Verf. The man passed it to his eldest son, and away it went into the shadows. "As I said, I'm a cloth-seller—"

"Lookin for a slave," said Verf.

"Looking for someone to help with my wife, yes. I would pay them, of course—"

"Apprentice them," said Verf, and again Jan palpably missed Sander's scowling countenance. People hadn't interrupted him so much when Sander was around.

"I have sons for that," said Jan. "And obviously can't have a tyro who's helping my wife. Can't have a man helping her at all, yes?"

"No," said Verf.

"Exactly," said Jan, eager to get it all out before the girl came home. *If* the girl came home—he hadn't looked to see how bad the cut in her hand was. "I need a young woman who can—"

"No," said Verf again. "They look like girls?"

One of the boys got into a crouch, the brandy gourd in one black hand. The kid actually *growled* at Jan, and he had the sudden, intense urge to murder every one of them and burn their hut to the ground. Rubbing his watery eyes, Jan pressed ahead.

"I saw your daughter on the beach. Swimming. Just the age to help my wife, and—"

"Saw her?" Through the smoke Verf's face looked as purple as his fingers. "Wager you fuckin did."

More of the sons were rising in the miasma, and Jan bit the inside of his cheek. Not good at all. "Listen," he said, "I saw her arms and knew her for a purple-maker. So I came to inquire after hiring her—I can find a servant anywhere, but one who can help with the dyeing of my linen is something—"

"You sure you don't aim to have her dye somethin else?" Verf breathed, his sons now edging around the fire like crabs moving in on a beached mackerel.

"Dyeing some—" Jan began.

"Like the front've your breeches with her fuckin maidenhead?" said Verf, and then, as if concerned he had spoken over his guest's head, elaborated, "Her fuckin cunt blood?"

The revulsion on Jan's face doubtless helped his cause as he spit into the fire and said, "Christ's cross, no! If I wanted that, I'd take it on the strand and not come knocking, don't you think?"

The eldest two boys were now on either side of him, and Jan saw they held shell-hammers aloft, ready to crack his kernel—he wondered briefly if dye could be made from human remains, but then Verf called them off.

"Back, boys," said the father heavily, as if it pained him not to have his guest murdered. "Want Jolanda to tend your wife and help you in the dyein, eh?"

"Yes," said Jan, trying not to reveal his relief as the sons retreated back to their side of the hut.

"No," said Verf, but then another of the boys cupped hand to ear and whispered to his father, who nodded and amended himself. "How much?"

Jan dumped his purse of fake groots on the floor of the hut. He had no concerns over Verf recognizing the money as counterfeit— the cross-stamped coins were convincing enough that the dye-maker might circulate the lot of them without anyone being the wiser. They were thus just as valuable as genuine currency, and after Jan eyed Verf and confirmed from his host's expression that the girl was as good as his, he returned the bulk of the coins to the pouch, leaving only three on the floor. Jan had no idea how much dye-makers brought in, but if the state of their home told him anything, they didn't earn much. Unexpected, that, Jan mused; considering how infrequently he saw purple clothing, he'd have thought they would turn a pretty pfennig for—

The door screeched and the girl, Jolanda, stood framed against the night, her left side hidden behind the doorframe, her hair jutting out like a hedgepig's quills. She must have fallen several times along the trail, for thick scabs of sand clung to her face and arm and leg and tunic and bound hand, and she stared at Jan, motionless, eyes shining. She would have seen his horse, but came in anyway, he reflected, and again he took a chance on her not stabbing him in the back. Turning back to Verf, Jan saw that the dye-maker wore an inscrutable expression as he watched his silent daughter—sad or wrathful, bored or amused, who could tell on that driftwood-twisted face?

"I—" Jan started, but was cut off by Verf.

"We ain't heatin the dunes, chit. Shut it and meet Lob."

"Lubbert," said Jan, but no one cared.

Jan heard her drop the knife in the sand before her sandy left hand slid into the light, and then she closed the door behind her. Her already too-high tunic was shorter than when he had returned it to her, the edge ragged from where she had cut it. If her father noticed, he did not say, nor did he comment on the binding that had already soaked crimson on her right hand. Instead Verf told her to get her arse to cooking for them and their new friend, Frieslander though he may be, and turned back to the handsome stranger. She made a lewd gesture as soon as she was behind her father, and Jan was unsure if it was directed at him, Verf, or all concerned, and then she disappeared into the thicket of siblings filling that side of the hut.

"Three groots hardly seems—" Verf started, but then the girl gave a furious shout, one of her brothers presumably snickering something of import to her.

"Sell me like a whore to that arsehole?!" The girl reared up before her father, the boys parting like some mythical Purple Sea around her. "*Sell* me?! To *him*?! You know what he did to me, on the goddamn beach?"

Jan felt a sudden surge of nausea, like a ghost had reached its spectral hand into his stomach and set to rooting around in his guts. The ghost of avoiding an ass-beating at the hands of her brothers, Jan supposed, a possibility now dead as young Wob Visser of Aalsmeer. He didn't move, however, recalling one of Sander's provincial expressions about the difference between beating a man within an ell of his life and out of it altogether being a matter of how much the blighter fought back.

"What he did." Verf nodded, the question not one at all, his eyes now focused on the dripping bandage wrapped around her hand. "He did that."

The boys were rising, not unlike the heat in the room, but Jan stayed where he was, trying to find the girl's eyes through the smoke. When he did, he could not read them. Her face looked almost beatific, and he supposed they both knew the game had changed and that now she stood between him and a safe shore. This had not been a very good idea, after all, Jan reflected, but even as he saw shell-hammers glinting in the light on either side of him, he found no room for regret. He never did.

"Nah," said the girl, shaking her head. She was still watching Jan instead of her father. "Cut it on a shell. But seeing him gave me a fright—why I fell. Suppose it ain't fully his fault. Suppose."

"Jolanda," Verf said sharply, "I've told you—"

"The devil it matters!" she shouted in her father's face, the shift from calm to furious even more startling to Jan than her lying on his behalf. "You selling me to that poncey poot, eh? Three goddamn groot—"

Verf slapped her in the face. One of her brothers sniggered. She didn't back down, and for a moment Jan expected her to leap on her father, possibly bite him.

"We haven't fixed a price yet," said Verf, and she nodded, gnawing her lip. Then she spun away and with a great deal of cursing set to packing her things. Turning to one of the thuggish lads still looming over Jan, Verf said, "Make sure she only takes a shift beyond what she's got on. And a blanket, she can have *one* blanket."

The haggling that came next was pitiable, and Jan would have been ashamed of himself if he were the sort of man who ever felt such emotions, but he wasn't and so he didn't. Four false groots later, he had an indentured servant named Jolanda, though the sealing of the deal was not without its odd wrinkle—the girl got into a fistfight with the brother overseeing her packing, and in addition to catching a black eye, the young man would have fallen into the fire if his father hadn't snatched him from the brink. After saving his son Verf waded into the row, which by this point involved most of the siblings, and Jan took the opportunity to go outside.

The wind whipped sand into his eyes as soon as he opened the door, and he banged his knee on one of the piss-and-char-stinking cauldrons in the dark, but it was nevertheless a marked improvement. Oh, to see the house burn, and to hear the whole miserable family scream—but the fewer bodies the better, an expression he had tried to bang into Sander's pate. His anger flitted up and died out like the embers leaving the hut's smokehole, and then the door squealed a final time. Verf booted his daughter down the stoop, blood dribbling from her nose and shining between her teeth as she landed in a crouch, sneering up at Jan. He was genuinely taken aback.

"I'd put a leash 'round her neck," said Verf by way of good-bye to his daughter. "She runs off, it's your fault, herring-fucker."

The door shut, leaving them alone with the moon and the sand and the twisted sloe girding the trail. He waited for her to spring on him, but instead she exhaled a long breath and touched her bloody hand to her bloody nose. That was that, then.

"Don't forget your knife," Jan told Jolanda, and she pawed around in the sand where she had ditched it beside the door. He walked on to where his horse was tethered among the black-thorn, his back exposed, his gait steady, the night swallowing him like it takes all those who seek it. Finding the knife, she followed him.

IV.

A dream come true, to be bound in blackness, to be constricted at every joint, to have the air turn to something thicker, heavier, hotter. To be noose-drowned, once and for all. Except drowning, really drowning, was altogether different from hanging, and from the pressure on his clouded skull and the scum slithering across his open, blind eyes, Sander realized he wasn't on the end of a rope. He was underwater.

Canal. Drowning. Arms and legs wrapped in chains.

No, not chains. Clothes caught on something, trapping him down in the filth. Too dark to see.

Canal. Drowning.

Total bullshit. Not like this. Not without rope.

Sander fought his own garments, tearing through the membrane of his ancient tunic. Still snared, somewhere lower. Wriggling out of the tacky sheaths of his breeches, or trying to, his boots complicating the attempt. Really fucking dying down here, only a few moments from passing out again, and for good this time. One leg free and bootless, but the other held at the ankle. All his bones shrieking under his skin, belly feeling like he'd gobbled a plate of hot coals, dead fingers fumbling over dead flesh to get at the boot mooring him to the canal floor like a barnacle's root.

The worn-out leather boot felt like jagged stone, cutting his fingertips as he blindly groped around for the buckle, the slimy webbing of his ruined clothes tickling his face as they floated away while he—

Release! Though, yeah, there was no way of knowing if his

foot had come free or if he'd gone and died on himself. Erring on the side of life, he wheeled his arms and legs, but there was fuck all means of telling which way was up in the black water. Funniest joke of all, to free himself from the bottom but drown for want of a top. Funny.

In darkness that was absolute on both sides of the water, Sander surfaced with a spume, which almost immediately became a significantly thicker sort of discharge. It is no easy thing to tread water and vomit simultaneously, but Sander had pulled the trick before and did so again now. The feat would likely have been impossible if the elbow he had pulled in the hanging hadn't somehow righted itself during his panic-propelled thrashing at the bottom of the canal, or perhaps he had simply overestimated the injury when it had occured; Sander wasn't the sort to question his luck in the best of times, let alone when the devil was clearly still kicking his balls. He couldn't see shit, which was a problem, and he had no idea how long he had been down or where he might have come up, but as another eruption yanked his spewing face beneath the oily water, he tried to concern himself only with the present—it was black as sin, he was still in the canal, and he was puking his guts up like it was Ash Wednesday after a Shrovetide bender.

When his retching trailed off, the coughing began, but finally that passed, too, and Sander took stock of things—first and foremost, he felt like he was dead, which, to date, had always meant he wasn't. Second, the citizens of Sneek couldn't be close or they would have heard his ruckus and nabbed him. Third, where the fuck was he, anyway?

Sander awkwardly swam in the direction he was already facing, trying to stifle the anxiety that any reasonable swimmer might suffer at finding himself alone in black water of unknown depth and distance to shore. There were no stars above him, or anything else for that matter, which was supremely goddamn creepy. He told himself he had floated downstream and gone under a building. That didn't explain how such a thing could come to pass, unless the Frisians were so goddamn stupid they built their towns over water instead of channeling canals through them, but then with Frisians he supposed anything was possible. Better that than his having somehow gone blind, which was too dreadful a thought to entertain.

The black, aquatic experience was unpleasantly nostalgic for Sander, reminding him keenly of the well his father had tossed him in whenever the old man had caught his son sucking cock or stealing coins. The cocks invariably belonged to the other boys in the village, whereas the coin always came from whatever ineffectual hiding place Sander's drunk begetter had settled on that particular day. Regardless of the crime, down into the well went Sander, and down slapped the lid over its mouth, blotting out the world above. At least the well had been full of water; the short freefall into the dark pool was the only part of the ordeal he remembered with fondness, and that would have been far less pleasant had it been followed by a dry landing.

After all the long days and nights spent treading water in perfect darkness with only slimy leaves in the autumn and tadpoles in the spring to keep him company, Sander had done his best to avoid similar situations. And, it must be said, up until this point he had enjoyed some success in that regard. If ever there was a hell built especially for him, he knew it would be just this: cold water, no light, and, worse than the well, no walls to cling to until his fingernails gave out.

Compounding matters, the demon it had taken Sander years of well-paddling to vanquish had evidently regenerated itself, growing strong again in his absence from black water—the unavoidable, obvious fear of what might be underneath him in all that darkness, watching. Sander always supposed his serenity in even the hairiest of hairy fucking situations he owed to his father and that watery pit—nothing was worse than not knowing what was beneath you.

The strategies he had honed as a young man to keep those

thoughts at bay had deserted him, or perhaps simply fallen into disrepair, and try as he might, he couldn't stop worrying. The farther he swam, the more he wondered if he wouldn't have been better off being hanged, and with that thought came the dreadful realization that this could have been their plan all along, staging an easily escapable execution only to drive him here, into whatever abyss they had prepared. He kicked harder, trying to get angry about it all instead of disheartened, and, as if by Providence, the canal became warmer, a sure sign he was approaching either shallow water or the wrong side of a latrine. Which wouldn't be the worst place Sander had crawled from, if it came to that.

Almost safe now, Sander told himself. He *must* be under a building, surely, or the streets of Sneek, somehow. Where else could he be, to not have a hint of moonlight or starshine or—

His hand bumped something solid and he recoiled with a shudder, finding the unseen object far too long, yielding, and slippery for his liking. Then he smelled it, a pungent stench like frogs and fucksweat. Sander got his legs under him to swim back the other way—none of whatever the fuck *that* was, thank you kindly—when his feet brushed the mucky bottom, arresting his flight. Letting his weight settle, the squelching of canal filth between his toes made him wish he hadn't shed his boots before coming to whatever midnight shore he now gained. He was naked and blind, and there was something awful in the dark with him—any two of those in tandem would be bad enough; all three was simply depressing.

Extending his fingers with the trepidation of a man seeking to pluck a golden ring from its unlikely position around the tooth of a dog of unproven disposition, Sander prodded the bobbing object. He felt a puckered rind give beneath his overgrown fingernails. Sliding his hand down what he was hoping was a soaked-to-softness tree branch, he located what could only be a clenched fist. He confirmed this by running his fingers back up the length of the arm to a shoulder, and gave it a push.

A corpse was nothing to worry about, and Sander relaxed as it rocked in the water. Then the water exploded all around the body, and something small bit Sander on the wrist. It held fast, whatever it was, scratching bone, gnawing flesh. He clumsily took a step back and tried to snatch it off but slipped in the muck and flailed about. He found his balance, the water churning under his woolly chin, and another bite struck him, this time a sharp, gravelly pressure closing over the thumb of his free left hand.

Sander gave a hollow little scream, hoisting his right arm from the water and whipping himself in the face with the serpentine horror that had attached itself to his wrist. He made his left hand into the exact sort of fist you should never make if you value your thumbs, with that digit clenched to the palm by the fingers, and bore down on the greasy, mouth-tipped cable coiling around his hand and gnawing his thumb. He felt alien skin and bone give beneath his pressure, his thumb burning worse than ever as he crushed its attacker. The ropy creatures seemed thin enough, and so he brought his right arm to his mouth and bit the one latched to his wrist, which his mind was now calling *eel*, even if the rest of him was not of a mood to hear whatever it was his mind had to say at the moment. The thing was slimy and salty and his teeth went clean through it, a bitter, burning blood flooding his mouth as the length of it fell back into the water. He spit frantically, the numbing liquid convincing his mouth what his mind already knew, for every Low Country boy is taught that eel blood is pure poison.

The unseen surface of the water was roiling all around him, and he felt them butting their heads against his chest and legs, struggling to find a grip with their small mouths. He turbulently abandoned the bottom and made a swim for it. There were several terrible moments when Sander realized he had no idea if he was swimming in the direction of the shore that might not even exist or back the way he had come. Then his palm slapped down into mud and the bottom rose up to slide against his chest. Salvation, but before he could slither onto dry land, an eel nosed against his pouch, coiling its length around his very balls.

Dragging himself out of the water, Sander gave little strangled noises somewhere between barks and sobs as he snatched the monster from his privates and mashed it in his fingers. He was yanking the other eels off him then, a dozen of the snake-fish clinging to his skin and hair with their curved jaws. Spray was still reaching him from the agitated water and he scooted backward in the muck, shivering and slapping himself down to see if he had missed any of the creatures. He had never heard of eels biting much of anyone, say naught of being so fucking vicious about it, but he supposed he had ired a swarm or nest or whatever the fuck you called it. As his heart calmed, he felt around in the muck to retrieve any he hadn't thrown back into the water in his rush to be rid of them; he only found four, and they were small ones at that, but if he could drain their nasty blood, a free dinner was nothing to pass up.

"Grue ruin ger drinner," a voice said far too goddamn close for Sander's comfort. It was a sticky, rattling sort of voice, the sound like a farmer trying to get a wagon wheel free of a muddy pothole.

"Get the fuck away from me," Sander whispered, his tone hard for its softness. He rolled up onto the balls of his feet and twisted around to face the voice in the blackness. Glory's End was at the bottom of the goddamn canal, but the eel bites, while stinging like the devil's own kisses, had nowhere near incapacitated the arms and legs of a man who had recently killed a lippy Frisian barkeep using only his forehead and a running start.

"All grite," said the voice, and a flopping wet sound punctuated the retreat. "Shrudn't ruin tit, ish all."

"Who're you?" Sander wondered what sick fucking jerk-off hid under buildings, tactfully forgetting the many occasions where he had been obliged to do the same. "Where am I?"

"Bell-djrin." It was more of a croak than anything else, come to think it. "Arm Bell-djrin. Grue Bell-djrin."

"*Belgium?* No, *Belgian*? Your name's Belgian? Or we're *in* Belgian? What the fuck does it mean, Belgian? Where. Am. I?"

"Yarsh!" said the voice. "Bell-djrins in Bell-jic-an!"

"Listen here, Belgian, we're under Sneek, yeah?"

"Yarsh, sneak. Sneak undrer Bell-jic-an."

"Fuck. Me." Sander gritted his teeth. Whatever passed for speech with this Belgian made Frisian seem like a coherent, lyrical language. Even if Belgian wasn't a stiffhead working for whoever the mastermind was that had been hiring men to watch Sander and set him up and try to kill him all those times and everything else, well, even then this cunt was taxing Sander's patience.

"Shrow mush," said Belgian. "To trell, to shrow, shrow—"

"Light," said Sander. "Windows, a trapdoor, a goddamn spark on a godloved flinty—light. Understand, Belgian?"

"Grite, grite," Belgian said. "Un momen."

There was the sound of metal scraping on glass, and a faint glow began to emerge in the darkness, a hovering marshlight that blinded Sander as it grew brighter and brighter. He turned away, shielding his eyes with his palm, and as the shadows were shoved back across the softly lapping water, he saw there were dozens of corpses floating before him, windblown leaves on the surface of a well. Beyond the dead men, the far wall of whatever cavern or tunnel he was in rose up into deeper blackness. His eyes were streaming and he rubbed them hard, too hard, milling his muddy palms into the sockets. What in the name of the devil's favorite whore was going on?

There was another flopping noise in the mud behind Sander and, taking a breath, he clenched his fists and turned to Belgian. His host held up the lantern, which, try to puzzle *that* out, looked to be a small glass jug filled with glowing liquid and writhing eels. It was blinding to look at straight on, but the man's webbed fingers partially blocked out the light, and besides, Sander's attention was focused far more on Belgian than on his mysterious eel lamp. Belgian was naked, and rather knobby and bent-looking, but that wasn't what captured Sander's attention—it was Belgian's face.

The man was all chin, the wrinkly, mustard-colored prominence jutting straight out past the rest of his features, which fell progressively farther back as they went up, like a face set in the side of a triangle. Sander immediately realized the word *man* was out of order given the circumstances. Lips that looked like overcooked sausages bursting from their skins stretched around to where Belgian's ears should have been but weren't, and then it smiled. This revealed a dozen twig-thin teeth seemingly placed at random in the nightmare maw, with two fangs the width of Sander's thumbs at the forefront. Above its horrid mouth were two little black slits, and just below where the lumpy forehead arrested the backward slide of its face were a pair of bulbous eyes. They looked like cracked hard-boiled eggs webbed in pond scum.

It took him a moment, but Sander realized with deepening horror that he was looking at whatever it was he'd always supposed was under him in the well. It was even worse than he'd imagined.

"Grite!" said Belgian, holding up a long, crooked piece of serrated bone or shell in one hand and waving the lamp with the other. "All grite?"

It was most certainly not. Sander was far faster than the demon, and before Belgian could use the weapon, Sander had closed the distance and sent his right fist into that giant goddamn chin. The horrid thing started to shriek even before Sander had beaten it to the ground, and as he punched it again and again in the face and throat, he heard its call returned from the darkness. Even with his light-burned eyes watering to the point of blindness Sander could not deny the monstrousness of his foe, the sharp bones too close to the surface of Belgian's cold, clammy skin. He, no, *it*, had gone down hard in the mud, Sander riding it all the way, intending to sit on its chest, pin its arms with his knees, and pound its face until it stopped moving... But like a lazing souse dunked in a rain trough, Belgian suddenly began to thrash and fight back.

The thing was fucking stronger than it looked, and fast, and

its backward-jointed, froglike legs were evidently suited to propelling itself out of the mud; before he could stop the tables from
turning, Sander was the one on his back in the muck, Belgian
chirping and spitting atop him. It reared back, its jagged weapon
held in both hands, and there came a desperate moment where it
paused, blathering unintelligibly at him. Sander used that moment
to gamble on monsters having genitals.

Aided by the slick mud, Sander jerked his lower body toward
his chest, his knees popping out from under the squat Belgian,
and then he sent both feet hammering into the shadowy gap
between its half-folded legs. A ridge of bone or spine caught
between the toes of his right foot, cutting deep, but his left connected with something dangly and soft. Belgian gave a strangled
gasp and collapsed in the mud, dropping the bone knife. The
weapon was in Sander's hand before he was even on his feet, and
he would have ended the monster right there if he hadn't put his
weight on his gashed foot. Sander toppled back in the mud beside
Belgian, cursing along with the wet noises his incapacitated
opponent was making.

Sander rose again, more carefully this time, and, favoring his
good leg, leaned over the crying demon and cut its throat. The
handle of the knife-thing was flat bone, and slippery for it, and
the serrated teeth of the blade caught on something halfway
across, but it did the job, and monster or no, Belgian evidently
wasn't shrugging off a sliced gullet. It made sloppy hiccupping
noises as it bled out, and Sander realized the light was dying,
too—in the struggle the luminous jug-lamp had fallen and tipped
over in the muck. The glowing liquid faded as it mixed with the
filth, the luminescent elvers leaving shiny trails on the shore as
they abandoned the vessel and squirmed back into the water.

Before the light dissipated, Sander saw that in addition to the
very wrong legs and head Belgian had a stumpy, finned tail, the
sight of which made Sander want to throw up all over again.
This was what had been in the well, this was what had harried

him all his life, the villain orchestrating the whole let's-get-Sander scheme that just about every cunt he'd ever met was somehow in on, from his father all the way down to the judges of Sneek, this was it: Belgian.

Probably. Sander knew he wasn't thinking straight, and time would learn him if this was indeed his hereto-unidentified nemesis or just some godforsaken monster or demon looking to do him in, but for now he had to find his way out.

Tearing himself away from the bested fiend, he saw a small table fashioned of rock or coral, its surface cluttered with strange bone instruments. Before he could give the gear a proper going over, something large splashed behind him, and he wheeled around. Squinting into the quickly deepening darkness, Sander saw that rather than a bank proper he had come ashore on a tiny island of muck, black water stretching in all directions, water that winked and blinked and shone with countless stars.

Eyes, he realized as the light failed entirely, not stars—eyes.

The darkness took Sander, as it takes us all, whether we like it or not. He settled into a crouch, planting the heel of his wounded foot as best he could as they squawked and splashed at each other, at him. He may be in hell, but at least he knew where he was, and when you're at the bottom you know there's nothing beneath you.

"Right, then, you Belgian plaguebitches," Sander called into the busy darkness. "Let's fucking do this!"

V.

The day after Jan bought Jolanda, the girl kicked him in the balls and stole his horse. It was not the sort of blow that one can easily shake off; she knew her business well and connected with the tip of her foot, her toes curled slightly back, rather than the kind of amateur ball-kicking where the top of the foot hits the scrotum, spoiling the thrust of the attack. She had bided her time, not attempting her assault when his codpiece was merely unhinged for a piss but instead waiting until their second night together, when the armament was entirely down to facilitate his dropping a deuce.

She must have been watching him, which was downright foul, but at least affirmed her dedication to a task, once she had set her mind to it. He was still squatting when she ambushed him out of the blackthorn, and before he could straighten up she'd taken the fatal step forward that set her foot and grounded her for the kick. It was one of the worst assaults he had ever suffered. At least he didn't land in his shit when his mind decided that he didn't really need to be conscious of the sensation in his loins.

He wasn't out long, but even after he returned to his senses, he couldn't stand, his legs shaking uncontrollably, and he had to lie very still for quite some time, teetering on nausea's edge. Finally he was able to squirm around and stretch his legs out, confirming that, yes, indeed, his balls were in an incredible amount of pain, and on top of that she had stolen both his purse and his sword from his belt. By the time he had gotten back into his hose—and unhooked the codpiece, which was now uncomfortably tight—he was in a black mood.

The whole point of going so far away to relieve himself was to give her ample time to steal the horse, whereupon he would catch her again, straighten her out, and they would establish the pecking order once and for all. The only real surprise was that she hadn't tried the trick the night before, when they had slept for a few hours on the beach after leaving her father's house. Well, that and the whole ball-kicking, which was wholly unwarranted, and showed a cruel streak in young Jolanda that Jan found distressing.

Limping out of the sloe, he saw that while she had taken his camping pack, his blankets and rucksack remained. This only relieved him until he caught the vinegary whiff of piss emanating from them. With a sigh, he rooted through the wet pack until he found a small length of iron, the bar perhaps two fingers wide and half an ell long. He knew from experience that hurling it into a running person's back or legs had a way of flooring the runner without the risk a knife brought to things. Leaving the rest of his gear, he followed the tracks back the way they had come from the bole in the dunes, the setting sun in his eyes.

Mackerel, his horse, was exactly where Jan expected he would be—munching the patch of marram grass they had passed at the edge of the dunes. He hadn't fed the stallion precisely to ensure that Mackerel's stubbornness was even further exacerbated, and wasn't surprised that an equine-ignorant child hadn't been able to move him once he locked his head down and set to eating. What did surprise Jan was that instead of a young woman's footprints leading off he found the young woman herself, sitting halfway up a dune, watching man and horse. His sword was unsheathed and buried in the sand beside her, which restored a good deal of the animosity Jan had lost upon seeing he wouldn't have to spend all night chasing her after all.

"You're hurting the blade, doing that," he called, the metal bar in his right hand tucked back behind his forearm.

"What you want, stiffhead?" Jolanda answered, not moving. She was clever, sure enough—she had climbed the dune and then strafed over to where it was even steeper, meaning he would exhaust himself before he reached her if he made a charge.

"With you?" said Jan.

"What else I care about?"

"You're going to help me with something."

"Tell me what, then," Jolanda said, standing up. "Could've cleaned you while you were crying in your turds back there, so fess up what you want—could've killed you shell-dead and taken it all, aye? Still can, you lip me."

"Come down here so we don't have to shout," said Jan, which earned him a laugh. "All right then, stay up there. What I want is a good swimmer to retrieve something for me. I know where it is, but it's at the bottom of a lake and I can't swim. You come with me and I'll feed you, see that you're taken care of, and if you dive down and bring it up for me, I'll give you a hefty reward, as well as your freedom. Fair?"

"Freedom I got, and this purse of yours seems a hefty reward already," said Jolanda, and Jan hoped his disgust wasn't writ as plainly across his face as it was his heart. He had bought the little bitch instead of trying to kidnap her from the beach on the hope that she would relent to his authority that much easier, but apparently her father was correct—a collar and leash might be the sounder plan. Still, from her current vantage it couldn't hurt to try scratching her behind her ears a little more, and Jan sighed.

"The coins aren't real," he said. "Counterfeit. And rest assured that my offer is limited by my patience—if you don't do as I say, you'll find the only metal of worth is buried in your heart. I'm prepared to let this whole incident go with only the mildest of repercussions if you come back down here and give me your oath to not try this kind of shit again, and then we can make supper."

"Big talk for a stiffhead with a sore sack!"

"Jolanda," said Jan evenly. "I am a man of means, and you're a girl with nothing but what you have stolen from me. Even if you were to evade me tonight and sneak away into the dunes, where would you go? I would be back here with men and dogs in short order, and on horses we would find you, and then we would kill you. If you inconvenience me by forcing such a route, then I will do everything in my power to make your death as—"

"Aye, I get you," said Jolanda. "Big man, big man. But if I don't, that's me in your service, not a slave, and when I get your thing I'm free to go, and with some coin?"

"Yes," said Jan, very tired with the whole affair.

"That's us sorted," said Jolanda, yanking his sword out of the sand. He noticed she wasn't straining to hold it aloft. "I wanna learn how to use one of these. You show me that, we're good."

"Why?"

"So next time I need to sort some neuking ponce, I'll just poke his bacon 'stead of kicking his eggs."

It was a sound point, and Jan nodded. Jolanda began sliding down the dune, but stopped halfway, cocking her head in Jan's direction. He wondered if she would ask, and she did.

"What's that *mildest repercussion* you said?" The sunset made the sword in her purple hand glow a deep red.

"You kicked me awfully hard," said Jan with a smile. "So I'm going to break your fat nose, and then we shall be, as you say, sorted."

"Break my nose?" Jolanda smiled back. "Would've been smart for you to leave that part out till I was down there with you, wouldn't it?"

"I won't lie to you, Jolanda," said Jan, twirling the bar he had cupped in his hand and tossing it into the weeds next to Mackerel's lowered head. "I won't lie to you, I won't rape you, and if you do right by me, you can expect fair treatment. That's better terms than you'll ever hear, and a busted hook as payment for bashing in my privates seems a light price compared to what most would charge."

"And I just take it?"

"I'm not stupid, nor do I suppose you are. You come here and try to give me another kick, and if you land it, that's a lesson hard earned for me, and if I make good on my promise, where your—"

But Jolanda was already barreling down the dune again, dropping the sword as she came. She was favoring her right foot, and he wondered if she had broken a toe on his groin. He hoped so. Then she was in the air, leaping the last few ells to land on top of him, and Jan sidestepped her, shooting out a fist as he did.

The blow caught her in the stomach and her pounce degenerated into a plummet, the girl landing on her face and gasping for air in the sand. Although it brought a queasy pinch to his crotch and a wince to his face, Jan gave her a sharp kick in the exposed armpit, rolling her over. Before she could move, he dropped down onto her chest, knees-first. Her eyes bulged, and from where he half-sat atop her, Jan considered the angle. Then he cocked her chin with one hand, nodded, and punched her flat across the face, snapping her nose—if he had hit her dead-on, he might have driven it into her brain, and that wouldn't do at all, not after what he had gone through on her behalf.

The cracking of cartilage brought some movement back to the girl, and she spit blood on him as he darted out his hand again and snatched her broken nose. It took several sharp twists to get it set, and she didn't make things easier, writhing underneath him like a landed shark. Finally her nose was straight as it was liable to be and both his hands were covered in sticky blood the color of the sea at his back, and he released her. She didn't crawl so much as slither partway up the dune she had attacked him from, her noises not quite the sobbing he expected. No, he realized as he fished his sword out of the sand and retrieved his throwing bar from the weeds, she was cackling, clutching her face in her hands and honking with laughter, threads of viscous blood dangling from between her fingers.

"I'll set to cooking supper," Jan told her as he took Mackerel's reins. "When you're ready, I'll take a look at your hand, see that cut from yesterday doesn't need tending."

Leading his horse back to the bole in the dunes, her deranged laughter at his back, Jan reflected that things could have gone far worse.

VI.

The light was blinding on both sides of the water, and then Sander realized he wasn't bobbing in water anymore at all; it was his eyelids flickering, the sun driving nails of burning fire into his brain. Someone was pushing on his stomach, and he punched the Belgian, which sent the fucker rolling down the bank. He tried to sit up and vomited again, remembering with a start that this had happened several times already, and recently, save for the punching of the ... fisherman?

The man was kneeling on the bank, clutching the ear Sander had struck. A small boat was dragged up on the grassy break in the reeds beside him. There was a net in the boat, and a length of willow with a line wound around it, and two oars—not a Belgian, then, but, yeah, a fisherman.

Belgian? What? Where? The details were already sinking back down in the murk of his headache-echoing skull, and wiping his mouth and peering around, Sander saw only the narrow river slicing through teeth-achingly green pastureland. No Sneek, or Under-Sneek or wherever, and, most thankfully, no slimy monsters. They had come out of the dark for him, and he had fought them all, the bone knife sticking in the first and leaving him empty-handed, hard knuckles hitting harder skin, the chirping Belgians mobbing him, driving him down into the muck, burying him alive, until—

"You're welcome, then," said the fisherman, scowling at Sander.

"Yeah," said Sander. "Where's Sneek?"

"Sneek?"

"Yeah, fucking Sneek," said Sander, mildly less annoyed to realize the man was speaking proper Dutch instead of Stiffhead. "This river comes from there, yeah?"

"Dunno," said the fisherman. "Maybe? Sure."

"Heh." Sander chuckled. "All right, then. Fucking stiffheads."

"Frisians put you in there? I seen you floating in the rushes an—"

"Who the fuck else?" said Sander. "Think I jumped in?"

"I don't—"

"Think they tried to hang me?" said Sander, his tone suddenly severe. The fisherman glanced at his boat, perhaps regretting his good deed. "Think they tried to do me in on account of my not fitting into their little fucking schemes, that what you think?"

"I don't know," said the fisherman, slowly standing up. "I—"

"No, you fucking don't," said Sander. "So don't look at me like that, you value your billy-goat eyes, you—where the fuck are you going?!"

The fisherman didn't answer, darting to his boat and shoving off into the water. He hopped in without a backward glance, and Sander scrambled up, wondering just what the fuck this so-called fisherman knew, if maybe he had been the one to tow Sander all the way out here in the sunshine, and if he really thought he could get away with the river so languid. But then Sander put his weight on his injured foot and toppled back over.

He lay cursing in the grass, grabbing his ankle and pulling his leg up to inspect the stinging sole. The cut wasn't deep, but it hurt like God's disfavor, the wound starting between his big toe and its neighbor and stretching a finger's length down. That gave him pause, and by the time he'd remembered the fisherman, the plaguebitch had already nicked off down the river. A perfect time to assess the situation.

Tunic and breeches? Gone. Boots? Gone. Glory's End? Gone gone gone, gone as the devil's graces. At least it was warm, the sun feeling right nice on his pruned skin—that was something. That, and the only real bits of him that hurt, aside from his pounding head, was his foot and the odd eel bite, so again, groots in his favor. And assuming the fisherman wasn't lying, Sneek was a long way off, meaning the river had taken him far from lynch mobs and Belgians. Again, something. He was famished and needed clothes, but these were minor dilemmas in the overall scheme, and would be righted whenever he found whatever house or village the fisherman had run back to. So yeah, not so bad a state of things, as it went.

Being careful to step using only the heel of his right foot, Sander began hobbling downstream along the reed-skirted river. It was the direction the fisherman had gone, and if the current had delivered Sander from Sneek, then this was doubly the right direction to travel. As he walked he reflected on the state of the day and reckoned he must be far south indeed, given the warmth and greenness of the fields, which were all gray and dead in Friesland. It was one of life's sweet wonders, to stroll naked on such an unseasonably warm day, the breeze drying your hair, the sun roasting your bottom, wildflowers tickling your toes even as their fragrance reached your nose…Then Sander paused, the water gurgling, the birds singing, and stared incredulously at the grassy meadowland that stretched to a border of darker green and brown, where a forest ran parallel to the river. Not good.

Sander resumed walking, limping along even quicker than before, as if he could somehow put distance between himself and the unsettling realization he had come to. Losing a few days for Sander was like losing an hour to daydreaming for anyone else, hardly the sort of thing to read too much into, but this was something else entirely, and boded exceptionally poorly. The farther he walked and the harder he tried to not think about the crocuses and cranesbills he stomped underfoot the more sense it made, in a very tragic sort of way. He came to a willow leaning over the bank, its leaves full and long, and gave a little groan to see young sparrows wheeling though the branches. It was autumn, late autumn, saints knew, it was probably winter, and they had tried to hang him, and now, immediately after all that, here was some, some *tree*, flaunting its leaves, encouraging these stupid birds to wheel around and chirp as if *that* were acceptable, as if it were spring, *late* spring, as if snow wasn't imminent, as if...

Sander sat down in the shade, the spongy loam itching his ass as he dangled his feet in the water. It was shockingly cold, which meant he wasn't dreaming. If that other place, the dark with all the Belgians, if that was hell, and he had bested the demons and escaped, was this heaven? That made some kind of sense. But who was the fucking fisherman, a saint? The Lord God himself? No, that didn't wash... But neither had the Belgians, and they had been real enough.

Hadn't they?

Rubbing his temples, Sander lay back in the scratchy grass, the river hurting his calves with its chillness. What if, he speculated, *what if* he hadn't actually died and gone to hell, what if he'd simply jumped into a canal and floated away, dreaming about Belgians? Good...

But what about his foot? Could have cut it on a rock, a root, anything. Good.

But why the fuck was it early summer—no, late spring, he corrected himself, as if that made a lick of difference, late spring... But still, he couldn't very well have floated downstream, asleep, for half a bloody year. Could he?

Well, no. But he had lost days before. Usually where drink was concerned, but sometimes they just went away on their own and he would awake to find himself in strange places. Often bad places. Once he had come to floating in a well—that had taken some explaining when a farmer finally fished him out, wells in the Low Countries being exceptionally shallow but nevertheless easier to enter than exit. Could he really be sure it had been autumn when he was hanged in Sneek?

Yes.

Well, probably. But what had happened in Sneek?

He remembered a barkeep saying something that had set him off, but the memory wasn't as clear as it should have been for having happened so recently. Whatever it was, the fucker had deserved what he got, though now that Sander was sober and seriously considering it, he couldn't rightly say what had convinced him the man was working for his enemies. Hell, Sander couldn't recall exactly what had made him think he had enemies in the first place, beyond the obvious enemies one makes by virtue of not being a stupid asshole like most people you meet in taverns. He grimaced.

What had happened, Sander surmised, was that he had gone off a little. Not a big deal if it only involved a few days out of sorts, a few fights, some mild convictions that everybody was out to get him…But killing bartenders, being publicly executed, and battling demons down in a giant fucking well were not the sorts of things he wanted to experience, real or dream, for any period of time, to say fuck all of blackouts lasting whole goddamn seasons. He was getting worse.

No, he *had been* worse, but now he was better. He might not know where he was, or even *when* he was, but he was himself, and he wasn't mad. Like a sleeper shaking off a nightmare, Sander kicked his feet in the water and smiled to recall the Belgian fancy he had taken so seriously.

"Ho, friend," came a voice that wasn't as gruff as it probably aspired to be, and Sander sat up slowly, turning to meet the man. Men. Three of them, two leading horses and the third standing behind the others; the third was the fisherman, but Sander didn't recognize the other two. That was probably good, he thought as he got to his feet, there was no reason he *should* recognize them, no way they could know him or he could know them.

"How is it, then?" said Sander, eyeing them more closely. The two with horses had dusty riding gear, and the one who had spoken wore some sort of garish bronze medallion over his linen mantle. They both had swords drawn, and were quizzically staring at the nude man who had come from the river.

"David here says he rescued you from drowning, only to have you attack him," said the man with the medallion. Some kind of rural militia-type, a warden or something, Sander supposed, the sort of cunt who came from the same fields as everyone else but got airs, got all important, got all fancy, taking graaf money to do graaf fucking business, as if the graaf really cared about protecting the men and women who worked the fields so long as he got his cut, as if his bullyboys were anything but that, as if—"I'm talking to you, loon!"

Sander came back to the moment, back to himself, and saw some underfed punk pointing a sword at him in the shadow of the willow. No, not a sword—*her*. The tip of Glory's End winked at Sander even in the shade of late spring, and he answered her whisper with one of his own.

"What the hell you say to me?" the warden demanded, passing the reins of his horse to his companion and stepping closer.

"I said you've got my fucking sword, boy." Sander's grin shone more dangerously than the blade between them. "You give her back now, nobody gets hurt."

The warden stared incredulously at the naked man. He did not hand over the sword. People got hurt.

VII.

On the night the handsome stranger bought her, Jolanda had wondered just what kind of vile shit he intended to do to her. She'd gripped his dagger in her uninjured left hand, but he made no move to take it from her, and not knowing what else to do, she stowed it in the bundled shift and blanket under her arm and let him help her onto the horse. She had often daydreamed of finding a waterhorse and riding it into the waves, never to be seen again save by drowning sailors, but bouncing on an actual equine back through the dunes, Jolanda felt something deep and cold and black as the night sea soak her insides. They left the trail and rode up the beach, back to where she had first seen him, the stars glittering above like the witchfire that sometimes shimmered in the wet sand after a summer wave had broken and fled.

"That's good for tonight," the stranger had said, stopping the horse. They'd traveled farther than Jolanda had ever gone, but the dunes here looked the same as those of her home. He dismounted the horse first, and then helped her down. As he did, she remembered the knife tucked in the cloth in her arms, but it was very late and she was very tired, only the strangeness of the night and the discomfort of the ride and her throbbing hand keeping her awake. Her legs gave out underneath her as he set her down, and she stayed where she lay in the sand, the last thing she saw the silhouette of the Frieslander looming over her.

She was not a dreamer by custom, at least not when she was asleep, but that night Jolanda dreamt of the sea, dreamt she dwelt there the way she had dwelt in the dunes. She and her eldest brother, Pieter, who wasn't a shitbird like the rest and had run away when she was very young, were swimming over the black waves toward some distant, rocky isle. They talked as they swam, as if they were strolling on the beach and not sliding over breakers, and though the sea was dark as the sky, she could see almost as deep below as she could above, and yet was unafraid. She realized they had both changed, and wondered if the man who had bought her was her brother from the sea returned, and so he changed in the dream to the Friesland stranger, but still was Pieter. Only when the dream shifted and they were crouched in the smoky gloom of their father's hut with the purple pots boiling did she realize she was asleep. Still she dreamt on, but when she started awake to a crab pinching a scrap from her bloodied palm she remembered nothing beyond the purple pots.

The crab scuttled into a hole, clutching what she hoped was a scrap of the torn tunic she had bound the wound with and not her skin. She blinked into the hazy dawn, the sand swirling over her like the thinnest silken sheet ruffled by the softest summer wind. She was cold, and she hurt all over, and sand was caked in her eyes and ears and nose and lips and worse places still. She sat up and saw that the stranger was staring out at the ocean, his horse beside him, and Jolanda had the brief but discomfiting notion that they had been conversing just before she awoke.

"I don't know if you caught it, but my name's Lubbert," he said. "Of Sneek."

She didn't say anything, glaring at him.

"If anyone asks, you're my daughter."

She snorted. He gave her some of the horse's oats for breakfast and then they mounted up, riding all day in silence. That night she kicked his balls and stole his horse, and in turn he broke her nose.

Lubbert was an arsehole after all, then, but that was all right—Jolanda had quite a bit of experience where arseholes were concerned, and he wasn't the sandiest of the lot. After she had come back to camp, her face aching, he had sewn up her palm with a needle and spool of white thread he kept in a little velvet-lined sewing box. The box reminded her of her mother's needle case, which her arseling father had sold less than a year after the death of his wife despite Jolanda's protests. It hadn't been as fine a case as Lubbert's, admittedly, but then her mother had been a decent, humble woman, not some show-off poot.

The hurt of his stitching up her hand took Jolanda's mind off her nose, which continued to leak red, runny snot for a few days until that part of her also went silent, and then all that really bothered her was her arse and crotch and legs after spending the better part of each day on Mackerel's back, Lubbert behind her on the saddle proper. His hands never strayed from the reins, and he never removed his codpiece to better rub against her, but even so, riding a horse was pure shit.

One thing about Lubbert was he didn't run his mouth all day, and another was that after breaking her nose he didn't hit her again, which was a pleasant change of pace. Still, she didn't trust him, and if he was half as clever as he seemed, he wouldn't trust her, either. She prodded the lily stitches crossing her mauve hand and smiled at the thought of going home one day, rich beyond dreaming, and flaunting her fortune in front of her brothers, who would still be living together in their father's hut like the nest of shitbirds they were.

The first thing Jolanda realized when they left the coast and began moving inland was that the world is boringly flat, sort of like the sea but with half the character and none of the vitality. They rode inland, and no sooner did they pass the last dunes than Jolanda felt a sudden and unexpected sorrow well up inside her, the dikes of her eyes nearly breeched before she pushed it back down. Scowling at the green pasturelands only occasionally cut by shallow brown canals, Lubbert's inability to swim made a great deal more sense. One of the few things he said to her that first day away from the sea was that nobody out here was foolish enough to make their purple the old way, that he had never before heard of anyone extracting the color from windfall sea-fruit instead of some easier method. She picked harder at the pale thread in her dark palm, and gave a prayer that his balls still hurt.

In one of the larger towns they came to, which was walled and had locks on the river and two-story buildings with gaily painted doors and shutters and red-tiled roofs and all sorts of other things that made Jolanda gawp and smile despite her resolution not to, Lubbert insisted she be fitted for something to conceal her hair. They were already in the sheep-smelling hovel of an old widow when she figured out what he was up to, the silently nodding hag in the doorway giving Jolanda the willies.

"No thank you, *Papa*," Jolanda said with a sneer. "I don't want to cover it."

"I won't have it said my daughter's a slut," said Lubbert, smiling at the puckered biddy. "I'm in need of new hose myself, and while we're here, fit my daughter with everything. A pelisse and bonnet if you can, or just a hood. She'll also need a longer gown, obviously, and underwear."

"I don't need any of that," Jolanda protested.

"You're too old to be rubbing your slit on my horse like a bitch on her heat," said Lubbert. "I shall return shortly."

This horrified Jolanda more than being sold to a stranger by her own flesh and blood, and she had no reply ready as he shoved her past the old woman and closed the door. When she finally let a string of curses fly, the beldam smiled a rot-toothed grin and descended on Jolanda like a witch in the bedtime stories nobody ever told her after Pieter ran away.

Being in a real town—as opposed to the clutch of fish-shacks that passed for a village near her father's house—Jolanda had expected the widow's hut to be clean and bright. Instead it was squalid and dim, humid and cavelike, with a full half of the floor and one entire wall buried in a drift of rags—a witch house if ever there was one. Boringly enough, though, the hag didn't try anything interesting, instead teaching her how to knit leggings for Lubbert from a wheel of greasy, discolored wool. The girl already knew how, having made a dozen pairs for her brothers and father over the years, and the odd set for herself, on the rare occasion when there was enough material left over for her after theirs were done. When real winter came she had been glad for something to gird her legs with as she hunted the frosty dunes for vermin burrows worth digging out to supplement the family diet, but her father hadn't let her bring them with her when he sold her sorry arse.

It soon became apparent that the old woman wasn't going to let Jolanda take away any loose wool and instead planned to outfit the girl from the rag heap, the legging lesson being given solely for future applications. At this discovery Jolanda threw down her needles, declared herself the superior knitter and seamstress in no uncertain terms, and ruled the exercise a waste of everyone's time. The biddy didn't have anything smart to say to *that*, but in retaliation the bitch refused to let her try on any hose, claiming they were only for men.

When the Frieslander came back a short time later, the old woman had already dug through her mountain of oily hand-me-downs and extracted the articles in question. The worst of these was the gown, an enormous serge tunic that the crone hemmed up, though not nearly high enough—it barely came above Jolanda's ankles, and would make the simple act of walking into a chore. Beneath this came the pelisse, which seemed to be a moth-worried cat-fur waistcoat with a ridiculously large bonnet to thread through the gown's neck hole, and beneath *that* a thin linen shift. From the way the woman smiled at her afterward, Jolanda knew she must look like a sweat-wet idiot.

"Beautiful," said Lubbert, inspecting her from the doorway.

"I look like a sweat-wet idiot," said Jolanda, wiping a gown-entombed arm across her boggy brow.

"She says nasty things about you," said the old woman. "Nasty, nasty words. She needs a hiding."

"Thank you," said Lubbert warmly.

"*Thank you,*" Jolanda imitated, pulling a complicated face at the old woman as she mimicked Lubbert's stupid accent.

Outside, Lubbert cuffed her lightly on the bonnet, and she hit him back, which led to a brief but spirited slapping match in the street, wherein they each landed several blows. He was taller and so connected with her face more, but not so hard as he could have, and mostly avoided her aching nose and the head-wrap it had taken her forever to tie down. She was soon giggling despite herself. He offered a truce by way of a cheese he had acquired while she was being fitted, probably to make up for saying that thing about her mussel rubbing on his horse.

Nobody had ever bought her anything before, even if the clothes were horrible and the cheese so salty it made seawater seem sweet. And when she staunchly rejected his offer of a pair of shoes to go with the new attire, he didn't press the issue. Not such an arsehole, then.

They rode on, usually sleeping on the side of the road. The silence of the nighttime fields, beyond the bugs and birds and other noises, put Jolanda very off—to not hear the sea anytime she should listen for it seemed a terribly unnatural and dismal circumstance. Still, the farther they rode and the more Lubbert opened up, telling her jokes and stories and stick-fighting with her when they broke for the day and he let her strip down to her shift, the more she came to appreciate the magnitude of her fortune. He knew more than she thought there was to know, from the name of the village outside her home—Monster, which she had always just called "the village"—to his intimacy with the names of various plants and birds that all looked the same to her.

"It's Frisian, not Frieslander," he said when she asked him if all Frieslanders were as fucking poncey as he was. They were riding, and though she said it expecting a hard pinch or slap upside the head, none came—a disappointment, as she was bored and had an elbow already tensed to fire into his slight potbelly. "Most of them can't afford such fine clothing, if that's your question, and even if they could, it's not practical for hard labor and fishing."

"Frisians," she repeated the word. "Heard you're all child-rapers."

"Rapists," said Lubbert, "and nobody is all anything. As it happens, Frisians claim descent from Friso, a heroic champion of long ago. This Friso served under the god-king Alexander, who was one of the Nine Valiants—the nine greatest men who ever lived, if you believe the scholars. In payment for his homage, Alexander awarded Friso any land he should choose, any property in all the world. Friso decided on Friesland, and true Frisians are his heirs."

"Oh," said Jolanda, trying not to be impressed. "They are?"

"No. That's just what they tell themselves. Friesland is a dank and stormy place, and floods often. Frisians are descended from whatever poor bastards didn't have anywhere else to go. Perhaps it's where criminals were banished from worthier lands. Don't tell a Frisian that, though."

"Aye, that sounds more like stiffheads than old kings and all."

"For that, they're stern people, to live in such a place. The Counts of Holland once tried to seize it from them, but the Frisians fought them to a man, and came out the conquerors. Better dead than a slave, is what the Frisians say. What does that tell you?"

"Better dead than a slave." Jolanda nodded with approval, thinking on the sword Lubbert had promised to buy her once they retrieved his sunken treasure. "Means if someone tries to put you under 'em, you fight to the death, 'cause if you're a slave, they might kill you anyway."

"No," said Lubbert, "it means Frisians are madmen who will lay down their lives to protect a mud puddle, so long as it's *their* mud puddle. And it means if you already have a good thing—all of Holland, say—don't go pissing away your resources trying to snatch up something else just to have it. It's like fighting a dog for a bone when you've already got a joint of lamb on your board."

"Oh," said Jolanda, and they rode on. She could feel herself getting cleverer the longer she was around Lubbert.

They took their time getting to wherever it was they were going, cutting northwest for days only to double around to the south again, winding their way from Holland clear to Guelders and then back through Holland again. As the days turned into weeks, Jolanda grew used to riding a horse, the weight of a sword, and spending long stretches of time around another human being who wasn't constantly trying to beat her, grope her, or both. When they camped near ponds and lakes, she would practice her diving, Lubbert throwing his small iron bar into the center and sending her swimming after it. She always found it, the little bit of muck and waterweeds nowhere near so distracting as saltwater stinging her eyes or waves shoving everything about. The only thing she missed, she thought as she dried out by their fires, were the dunes; the occasional grassy dike crossing the fields was hardly a substitute.

Rotterdam, as she told Lubbert several times in as many hours, was breaking her fucking mind as they walked Mackerel through its cobbled streets. At one point she became so overwhelmed that she had to sit down on a stoop, shuddering, and Lubbert laughed, crouching down and putting his arm around her.

"My first visit to a city I nearly pissed myself," he said with a wink.

Jolanda smiled. He was such a fucking poot it was unbelievable.

The street was thronged with men and women and children and beasts, a market day in late spring, and looking up into eyes the brown of old marram grass on the dunes, a smile warm as the beer he had bought her upon gaining the city gates, she heard the sea for the first time since leaving home. For a moment she considered leaning forward to plant a kiss on his cheek, in imitation of the fisherboys who had sometimes tried that approach after pinning her, only to find themselves with a split lip when she head-butted them. Quick as the thought came, it fled, making her blush and stare down at where the filth of the street broke upon the stoop, a frozen black wave.

"Jo," he said softly, and she felt herself go all stupid to hear him call her that. "Are you all right?"

"I'm sorry I kicked you," she muttered, not really meaning it, but figuring she owed him something for thinking such an idiotic fancy.

"Not another word," said Lubbert, flicking her on the nose. It hurt. "I always give as good as I get, no?"

Jo was back up and they were slapping at each other again, people grumbling around them as they reentered the current of crowded bodies flowing through the city. All day she revisited the illicit thought, and each time she did, it made her feel sick to her stomach. In the afternoon, however, he showed her something that finally took her mind away from stupid daydreams—it was the sea, there at the edge of Rotterdam. Well, almost. The Merwe was so broad here she could pretend the river was her beloved ocean, with the growing harbor to their left and the city curving inland behind it to frame the wide, choppy expanse.

"Almost as good as the sea," she told him, which was high praise indeed.

"Better than," he corrected her, which was heresy to Jo, but given the heretic in question, she was willing to let it slide. "And trust me, Jo, you've not seen anything yet."

They watched gulls diving and dipping over the river for a time, and then returned to the common room of the Young Harbor, an inn on the noisy Marktplein. After he confirmed that the barmaid would mind her, Lubbert paid for a hot supper, beds in the loft, and a few beers for Jo, then departed to see about boarding Mackerel and booking passage to Dordrecht. The nearly empty common room smelled like wet dog and moldy malt, and had a mean draft that felt like heaven after the hot, crowded streets. Jo settled comfortably back into her chair at the corner table where Lubbert had placed her, a warm mug of beer cradled in both hands.

A man came in almost immediately after Lubbert departed, a tall, brawny sort with a sword hanging from each hip. Rather than making for the bar or one of the unoccupied tables, he sat down across from Jo. He had a snarled blond mane that hung limply around his shoulders, a bushy, uneven beard, and bluish-gray eyes that were wild and dark as storm clouds rushing across a sky that had been clear a moment before. He stank like sour beer and sour sweat, his clothes were caked with dirt, and an ugly circular medallion dangled around a thick neck that was striped with old scars and new scabs. Jo tried not to let the goon put her off her stride, but he was big and ugly enough to get her heart paddling a little quicker than usual.

"Hey," said the man. "Who're you, then?"

"Leave her alone," called the barmaid. She was young but nowhere near so young as Jo, and held an empty tankard in her hand with an air of casual menace as she came out from behind the bar. "I won't tell you again, get up!"

The man's face darkened, his jaw setting so hard Jo heard teeth click. Even when Lubbert had broken her nose, Jo hadn't really been frightened, but she was now—something about the stranger smelled wrong, dangerous, and she half-expected him to fly at her or the barmaid. Instead his narrow eyes suddenly widened and he beamed a bright smile in Jo's direction as he bolted to his feet, his chair clattering back as he turned to the barmaid.

"It's all right, *love*," he said placidly. "Just making sure it wasn't lost, little girl like that, place like this."

"Sit somewhere else or get out," said the barmaid, but now that she was closer, Jo could tell the woman was uneasy—her shaking legs were making her stained apron tremble, and she was holding the tankard wrong if she actually meant to bottle this thug. Jo felt her own fear melt into that old fury on the barmaid's behalf, this overgrown bruiser throwing his weight around, acting hard... But then he turned his smile back at Jo, and she went all queasy to see how sharp his eyes were, the wrath in them so at odds with his easy grin, the open palms he raised in her direction.

"See you about, then," he told her, and much as she wanted to meet his glare, Jo found herself staring down at a puddle of beer on the worn table. She hated him in that instant more than she had hated any man, and when she forced herself to look back up, he was gone, the door of the Young Harbor rattling shut behind him. The barmaid gave Jo a pitying frown.

"What a bastard," said the woman, wiping back her sweaty bonnet. "Let's take that beer in the kitchen till your da's back, yeah?"

"Aye," said Jo, giving the door a glance as she rose to follow the barmaid. When Lubbert returned, they would have a talk about her getting a sword sooner rather than later.

VIII.

True dark was still a few prayers off but it was past suppertime when Jan picked his way back toward Marktplein, the earlier traffic diminished to only the occasional beggar or cluster of youths. The narrow stone streets enclosed him warmly, like the walls of a childhood crib, and he shook his head to think of the ugly, broad avenues of the Empire and France, the squat, low buildings of the rural neighborhoods he had traversed to return to his birthright. Holland had its share of deficiencies, to be sure, but he would take it over Brabant or Zeeland or Guelders or anywhere else, and at long last he was in a position to take what was his.

Mackerel fetched a good price—even if Jan had bought the horse instead of stealing it from a Frisian stable the previous winter, he would have likely turned a profit. Then he found a boatman who would take them down the Merwe to Dordrecht in the morning for a far sight less than he had ever paid to cross, as clear as signs came that people had adapted to the city becoming an island. To top it all, the girl had come around, though it had taken even longer than he'd feared and they'd dicked around clear to Guelders before he was confident enough in her favor to institute the next phase of the plan. If she still distrusted him, that doubt was tempered by blind affection and loyalty, as winning a combination in a girl as it was in man or dog. Things could scarce be better if—

An arm burst from a shadowy gap between the houses to his left, and before Jan could cry out, he was snatched by the cloak and spun into the alley. The back of Jan's head cracked against a brick wall, the blow sending sickly tremors all the way down to his toes. Instead of pawing at Jan's waist for his purse thongs, meaning theft, or covering Jan's mouth, meaning murder, the assailant's hand went to Jan's throat. Jan blinked away the tears that being smashed into the building had summoned, but before he could even make out the man's face, he knew him by the gently squeezing fingers and relaxed.

"Fucking cockstand," said Sander, but he was smiling.

"Good to see you, too," said Jan, his own hand going to the other man's throat. Sander let him go even as Jan began to choke the bigger man, who gave a happy sigh that turned to a rasp as his windpipe was compressed. "How in God's graces did you get out? They said you died after I slipped you the sword."

"Clughhh," said Sander, and Jan gave him a final squeeze before letting go. Sander looked good for a dead man and damn good for having spent half a year looking after himself, but by any other standards he looked truly abominable. He beamed at Jan, tears leaking down into his beard as he recovered from the light throttle.

"Went into a canal," said Sander, and paused. Jan waited, his old partner giving him one of those calculating stares that so discomforted people, and finally shrugged. "Blacked out. Woke up a month or so back, up in Holland proper."

"That right?" said Jan, looking with a more critical eye at the hanged man. Even for Sander that was a bit much, and from the man's somewhat anxious expression he evidently knew it. Still, he was clearly looking for reassurance, and Jan fed it to him. "Well, I've heard plenty of men who've been walloped in the skull have trouble remembering things from time to time, and that crown of yours has been a regular bung long as I've known you."

"Yeah," said Sander, though he didn't seem convinced.

"Have you blacked out much since?"

"No," the big man said, brightening. "Not once."

"Well, that's it, then," said Jan. "I wouldn't question it further. The important thing is you're all right, I'm all right, and here we are, with fortune closer than it's ever been. I've even found us a swimmer, so you won't have to worry about that end of things, after all—I know you had your reservations about diving yourself, so I've settled that for you. All that's left is to pick it up."

"Thought you'd maybe took up pimping again," said Sander, and there was an edge to his voice that Jan recognized of old. Good as it was to see him again, the last thing Jan needed was Sander complicating things with his jealousy . . . But there were easy enough methods of assuaging that, and agreeable methods they were.

"How long have you been watching us, then?" Jan hoped his annoyance came through.

"Heh. Just the day," said Sander, what passed for a sheepish expression crossing his wolfish face. "Was over in Dordt for a week, stayed with Poorter. He said you'd be back 'fore the summer heat, but thought I'd meet you halfway. And here you are."

"Here I am. Here we are. Do you need a drink?"

"Do fish get wet when they fuck?"

"I expect they do," said Jan, and he felt something sharp and hard pass through his chest, a shock of relief that his faithful Sander had again cheated death and returned to him. He stepped forward, Sander standing his ground, and they kissed in the shadow of the alley, Jan delighting in the awkward shyness his partner had not shed even after all this time. Jan worked his fingers into Sander's tangled hair, getting close to the scalp before making a fist and tugging, his other hand back at the man's neck until Sander's kiss became a dry gasp, and then they reluctantly parted.

"Got a room at that place?" Sander panted.

"Just a common loft, and I've already paid for it," said Jan. "But I wager we could find somewhere more private in this grand old sprawl, eh?"

They walked along the new dike away from the heart of the city until they reached the half-built storehouse Sander was camping in whenever the builders left for the day. There they urgently fucked in the dirt, Jan being far gentler with Sander than he would have had they something more substantial than spit to facilitate affairs. As it stood—ho ho—Jan could barely get more than his point in, and didn't push things lest he have a mess on his hands without a washrag at the ready. Afterward they leaned against the stone wall, sweaty and sated as they were liable to get without the benefit of a bed, cod oil, and a length of rope longer than the medallion cord Sander had snapped with an errant buck when Jan had pressed too deep.

Walking back to the Young Harbor took a bit longer than leaving the city center had, the men holding hands until the after-supper drinking traffic picked up. Jan had gone over things with Sander again, but even still he could tell his partner had reservations about working with the girl. Lord knew how much worse it would have been if he had found a boy to do the swimming instead. At least Sander had promised to stick to the Lubbert-of-Sneek story around her, which would be something, assuming it lasted.

The barmaid gave them a strange look when they sauntered into the bustling Young Harbor, and looked positively concerned when Jan paid for Sander to sleep in the loft as well. She took the coin without a word, however, and fetched Jolanda from the kitchen. The girl was drunk, possibly very drunk, and blathering something to the barmaid, but when she saw Sander, her crooked posture straightened out and she balled her hands into fists.

"Daughter, this is my brother Sander," said Jan. "Your uncle."

She blinked foolishly at Sander, her face contorted as if she were being introduced to a talking eel and wasn't sure if she should hurl it to the ground and stomp on it or curtsy.

"We met earlier, didn't we, missy?" said Sander, setting Jan's teeth on edge. The bastard hadn't said anything about—

"Think you're fucking hard?" demanded Jolanda, glaring from Sander to Jan. "This cunt acted hard. Tried to scare me."

"Don't talk that way to your uncle," said Jan, hoping to pacify them both with his charm. "He has an odd sense of humor, that's all."

The girl looked warily at Jan, but Sander was evidently in a good mood and didn't exacerbate things—a welcome surprise. Instead the large man silently extended his palm to Jolanda, who eyed it suspiciously but made no move to take it.

"Fine then," said Sander, yanking his hand back and scratching his beard. "Time comes, don't forget was you decided to be the bitch first."

"I'm going to fuck you up," said Jolanda, whatever she had been drinking giving her voice an evenness the rest of her lacked; she was vibrating, like Jan's father at the start of one of his fits. "Hear me, big man? Ask your fucking *brother* what happens to arseholes who give me trouble."

Sander adopted a silly lilt and bobbled his head and shoulders around as he smiled at Jan and asked, "*What happens to arseholes who give her trouble?*"

"She kicks them in the balls," said Jan.

Which is precisely what she did.

IX.

Sander hated to admit it, but the little fucking bitch had some serious grit. They had gotten into it at the tavern after she'd bruised his pouch, his usual disinclination to punch children overlooked given the nut-aching circumstances. If Jan hadn't gotten him into a headlock and choked him unconscious, Sander might have seriously hurt the girl in his rage—short indeed was the list of individuals he would let live after such an offense. He returned to consciousness on the street, the trio having been ejected, forfeiting the coin Jan had already paid to stay in the loft.

The girl extended her hand to Sander where he lay in the alley, flashing him a loose-toothed smile as she said in a gruff voice, *"Time comes, don't forget was you decided to bitch,* Uncle."

It took Sander a moment to realize she was making fun of him, but when he did he returned her smile and took her hand. Just as he tensed to jerk her to the ground, though, the moon crawled out from under its cloud and shone on her puffy, dripping lower lip and fast-swelling cheek. Seeing that the damage was respectable enough already, he settled for viciously crushing her hand in his. Her face twisted in pain but she didn't try to pull away, instead vainly trying to squeeze back as he mashed her fingers together.

"Enough of that," said Jan. "You two get into it again, I'll make you both regret it."

Sander's "Fucking doubt that" overlapped Jolanda's "Fuck off," and this time the smile he offered the girl as he got to his feet was more sincere. This only seemed to piss her off more, but that was the way with stupid fucking kids, he supposed, bust them in the face and they think you're all right, but try to be nice and they give you the rude lip. What was Jan thinking, bringing children onboard...

The next morning Sander's head hurt like a right bastard, and even in the best of circumstances the float down to Dordt made him cross as Black Pete's fingers when the devil made a promise. Going along the Merwe was fine, as the river was wider and deeper but otherwise not too much different, but near about when Papendrecht came into sight, you could also see—

"Christ's crown!" said the girl, which was a pretty good curse, one Sander had every intention of stealing. He lolled his head back and stared up at the sail above him rather than deigning to acknowledge the stupid fucking meer. Of course the half-titted halfwit would piss herself over the world's biggest mud puddle, she was just a kid.

"I told you," Jan said, making Sander wonder just what it was the old rooster had coughed up in her ear. "*Much* better than the sea. The water's sweet, or sweet enough, and the tides aren't too stern at all. Wait till you see it on a sunny day, it's like a lake of brandy."

"I didn't know," she said, and stealing a glance, Sander saw her staring out from the prow at the great gray plain of water.

"Well, it wasn't here a year and a half ago," Jan said from where he sat behind her. "This was just where the Merwe met another river, and you could cut back around to Zeeland or go clear down to France and bring back all the wine your hulk could carry. But then a flood came along on Saint Elizabeth Eve, and found the place so appealing it decided to stay. Now Dordrecht's got a lovely inland ocean to keep her safe from marauders."

"It beautiful," she said with a sigh. Sander wanted to throw her in, see how pretty she found it once she'd bobbed into a bloated corpse or three.

Ought to throw Jan in, too, telling her such fairy stories about the dreadful, haunted swamp-sea this place had become since the flood. Everything south and everything west and maybe everything under them had been the Groote Waard, and such beautiful sward it was, pastureland and cropland and village land, and yeah, all right, some swampland right around the walls, too, sure. But mostly it had been green and gorgeous, and now it was all bleak, dirty water that sometimes revealed a ragged roof or a bony treetop lurking just beneath the surface like an old log in a creek.

And all for what? A little coin was the answer, was always the answer, no matter the question. Sander had heard that the reason the flood got all the way up here from the sea was that greedy fucking graafs had been aiming to finance their private wars on the cheap, and so ordered their peat-cutters to dig out the backsides of all the dikes. First big storm to come along pushed the waters right through the weakened barriers and up the rivers, drowning thousands upon thousands of honest folk what didn't have nothing to do with peat-cutters or graafs, Hooks or Cods, and turning the whole place into a great festering lake. Oh, what Sander would give to lay his palms on the plaguebitches responsible, graafs and peat-cutters alike...

The vessel slid onward. Jan settled back against the gunwale and dozed contentedly, Jolanda stared all around in amazement, the boatmen fidgeted with the rigging, and Sander blew his nose into his sleeve. It looked like he had dipped his cuff into egg yolk.

As they progressed across the meer, a light drizzle began to fall, which cheered Sander somewhat—now at least Jan wouldn't be able to dream through the passage. Sander's cloak had long since lost any grease or oil its original owner may have waterproofed it with, but he didn't mind being wet so long as he wasn't also cold, and it had been a balmy if lead-tinted morning. The girl gasped, and Sander saw Dordt rearing up before them like some great shipwreck in the flood. Despite himself the sight of the city kicked Sander in the balls of his heart, was how he would describe it, a queasy, painful sort of feeling, and here he had only been gone from the place a week.

Before the dikes had broken, Sander had considered settling

somewhere in the vicinity when his wandering days were over—not close enough to his hometown to chance being recognized, of course, but *someplace* out in the Groote Waard. Get some fucking sheep, maybe, like he and his da had done. Only, yeah, with some tidy lad to share the life with instead of that old bastard, devil burn his bones. Here Sander was, back again, only the hut where he'd dropped out his ma was gone and the fields were gone and the whole fucking village where he had grown up was gone, and all memory of his asshole father, too, gone like his left eyetooth—so it wasn't all bad. Looking at Jan, who had sat up and wiped the sand from his eyes, he knew the fancy bastard never would have settled for some sheep and a hovel even if Sander had risked settling down in the region, so maybe it didn't matter that the flood had taken it all. Living in the city itself surely wasn't such a step down, as stairways went.

They'd done a decent job building things up to accommodate the raised waterline, and the city walls were the city walls were the city walls, but now the great gray ring of Dordrecht was an island of stone and not a river town in the midst of bustling farmland, with huts and barns pushing up to the marshy edges of the place. Dordt was alone now, a great tombstone for the people of the sea-taken Groote Waard, and there was not a building in the city that didn't have a watermark somewhere along its flank from where the flood had pushed in before admitting defeat and retreating back to its newly conquered realm outside the walls. Fucking place still stank like bog rot a year and a half on.

Jan was chatting with the boatmen as they maneuvered the vessel along the city wall jutting up out of the river, past the main entrance to the old harbor. Instead of mooring the boat there by the Big Head's Gate, the arch of which was still crowned with scaffolding like a wooden coronet, the boatmen coasted south, passing the new harbor as well. Lousy Rotters meant to put in at the back entrance of the old harbor, Sander realized, and he pulled his hood farther down over his nose, trying not to let himself get worked up.

The only reason anyone coming down from Rotterdam would enter the old harbor the long way 'round was if they had some business with the militiamen in that particular gatehouse…

In the name of Christ and his precious mother, if Sander was that business he'd take every one of these treacherous, ball-washing boatmen to hell with him.

The gate was open at this entrance, and the boatmen steered them out of the current and into the canal that fed into the guts of the city like an architectural cunt. The half-finished tower of the Great Church rose on their left, but sure enough, these false bastards had directed the boat toward the right side of the channel, straight at a small dock just inside the city walls. The dock protruded from the gatehouse, and as Sander rose into a crouch he saw a door set in the building's wall swing open and an ancient militiaman step out onto the dock.

Credit where it was due, whichever of the boatmen had recognized Sander and decided to turn him in had played it cool; Sander hadn't suspected a thing until they'd gone for the back way into the harbor…but it would take a lot more than some old fucker and a couple of boaters to take out Sander Himbrecht, that was—

"You," the militiaman called, pointing directly at Sander. "You there!"

This was it, then. Sander should have known better than to let Jan talk him into returning to Dordrecht. He'd been back twice already since Jan had proposed the plan, and begging fate for a third uneventful trip to the city had been greedy, he'd known that. He wondered if this old bastard on the dock was someone he'd personally pissed off in his youth—must be, to recognize him before the boatmen had even announced their bounty.

"Right, you fucking assholes," Sander muttered, straightening the rest of the way up as the boat bobbed to the dock. "Let's do this."

"Outta the way," one of the boatmen said, stumbling around Sander with a hefty crate in his arms.

"You there," the militiaman repeated, still pointing at Sander. "Give Kees a hand, you churl! Twice as big, and standing 'round 'stead of helping. Ought to be ashamed!"

What?

"I got it, I got it," said the boatman carrying the crate—Kees, presumably. He leaned forward over the bow, and as they came abreast of the miltiaman he clumsily deposited the load on the dock. "As promised, friend."

"Come by after you're settled and help me with a bottle of it," said the militiaman as the boat glided past the dock. "But ditch that lazy lummox first!"

Oh. Excise tax dodgers. Sander was in such a good mood at being proved wrong about the boatmen's reason for using the back channel to the harbor that he waved at the old militiaman instead of leaping onto the dock and working him over for taking such a surly tone. The geriatric gave him the fig, then knelt to retrieve his illicit crate.

They slid easily up the narrow channel, the backs of houses lining their approach like the sorriest fence you ever saw, to where the canal widened into the old harbor proper. There were fewer boats than usual at the slips, but leave it to the fool-headed Rotters to ease on over to the far end of the longest, greenest pier in the place, the quay running abreast of the harbor wall. Sander hopped out of the boat, whereupon he slipped on the slick wharf and almost went back over into the water.

The girl laughed, an ugly, braying noise, and jumped up after him—and slipped as well. She would have bashed her face into the harbor wall if Sander hadn't snatched her arm as she fell, and after comically kicking her legs against the slimy pier for a moment she found some purchase and settled down into a crouch. She looked like a land-reared dog thrust onto a boat.

"Enough playing around," said Jan, stepping carefully up after them and walking down to meet the excisemen at the foot of the quay. "I'll get your entry, Sander."

"Gone up," Sander said, spitting an oyster of phlegm in their direction. "Shameless."

"You pay to go into the city?" said the girl, slowly straightening up.

"More and more every fucking day," said Sander. "'Fore the flood was bad enough, but now they really got you by the short and woolies—already paid to get out here, waste of coin to go back. Fucking sheepheads."

"What?" said the girl, making Sander squint at her—was she really that thick? "What's a sheephead?"

"Me and my da, we did sheep out in the country," said Sander as they walked down the pier, the algae-speckled harbor wall on one side and rundown rowboats bobbing on the other. She took her time to avoid slipping, he took his to stall long enough for the taxmen to piss off back into their taxhouse overlooking the quays—never knew if one of them would recognize him, even if the boaters and militiaman hadn't. "Sometimes had to get a sheep inside the walls, right, if we was planning on selling an old one off. Yeah?"

"Mmm," said the girl watching her feet as she walked. She moved funny, like as not still wobbly-legged as a sea-shaken sheep herself from the passage.

"Out in the ward everyone's got sheep, so mutton don't get you much, but in the city people ain't got room for 'em, so we can turn a better coin. But. Problem—Dordt's run by greedy bastards who'd pimp their mothers if anyone would pay for the old bitches. They start some rumors, baseless ones, about our mutton making people sick. So the watch got instructions not to let us take our sheep in unless we bribe them good and proper, and if we paid that ransom, we'd be worse off than losing one to a wolf. So we'd…" Sander trailed off, seeing the excisemen hadn't pissed off after all, but stood waiting for them with Jan at the top of the quay stairs. "Tell you later."

The taxmen didn't know Sander, thank the devil for a change, just wanted to give him the eye and the lip. After the sheepies went back to their pen, Jan led the way over toward Varkenmarkt. The streets of Dordt were narrower than those of Rotterdam, and the air was thicker, wetter, colder, as if an invisible fog constantly haunted the city. The whole tone of the place had gone down since the flood, riverfolk trying to become islandfolk and doing a day-hire's job of it—poor, in other words, piss poor. Shadowy figures watched them from doorways, as shadowy figures are wont to fucking do.

"What were you saying?" the girl asked Sander. "You never told me what a sheephead is."

"He's a sheephead," said Jan, nodding at Sander. "A sheephead's a person from Dordrecht."

"You ruined my story, you twat!" Sander shouted.

"I doubt that," said Jan.

"Roll your fucking eyes again, Jan, fucking roll 'em!"

"Shut up, *Uncle*," said the girl. "I don't know what he even meant, so shut up and finish the story. And what's a Jan?"

"He's fucking Jan," said Sander, "not Lobby von Frisian or whatever the shit he told you, fucking Jan."

"Is that true?" The girl sounded hurt, and Jan's eyes narrowed, the only sign he was probably peeved.

"I go by a lot of different names, Jo," said Jan. "So many I lose track of them myself."

"That fucking crook seem like he ever lose track of anything to you, Jo?" Sander said with satisfaction. "He was running some game, same as always."

"Jo," said Jan, "it's like this—"

"Just shut up!" She looked like she might cry for some stupid womanly reason, her fists balled up, her cod-belly white face now streaked with red. "Shut up!"

"Thank you for that," Jan said coldly, digging his fingers into Sander's shoulder as the girl sped up, walking in front of them. "What the fuck's gotten into you? You finally lost your wits altogether, you mad bastard?"

"My mistake," said Sander, happy to have traded his anger to

Jan in exchange for the man's calm and unwilling to swap back even if his partner was trotting out the *mad bastard*s and *lost-your-wits*es. "We sheepheads aren't known for being clever, are we?"

Jan released him with a curse, and stormed ahead. He put his hand on the girl's shoulder, but she pulled away from him. Sander smiled to himself and also picked up the pace, coming up along her other flank and resuming his story.

"So anyway, we didn't want to pay some cheat-price to get our sheep into the city. So what do you think we did?"

She was staring straight ahead, her face set, and they passed the cross street they should have taken to get to Poorter's shop. Jan didn't steer them down it, and Sander didn't correct their course. There wasn't any hurry, and it was good to be back on Dordt streets, dour though they were. Seeing what had happened to the place was akin to watching a dog you owned but never particularly liked get beat— you might not care for the dog so much, but it was your fucking dog, and who enjoyed seeing an animal take a hiding?

"We dressed them sheep up like men, with my da's coat and my drawers and this old straw hat we shared, and we'd lift 'em up and walk on either side of 'em, like this." Sander dipped his arm under the front of Jolanda's armpit and wrapped it around her back, and pissy or no Jan did the same, so they hoisted her up and half-carried her, the heels of her bare feet bouncing on the cobbles. She was giggling despite her obvious reluctance as they walked her down the street, Sander smiling over her head at Jan. "So in we'd walk past the militia, the city watch, who back then didn't charge just to come in for local folk but did for our sheep, right. We'd wait until dusk so the gate would still be open, but it'd be dark enough that the sheepy in his pants and coat and hat might look like an old man or drunk or such we was helping along, and in we'd walk right past the stupid fucking watchmen supposed to be eyeing old Himbrecht to make sure he and his son didn't sneak no mutton in without paying the toll.

"Now, one of these militiamen was an old piss-catcher who—

from Tilburg, I mean, a dirty sod from Tilburg, and every time we walked past them watchers with a sheep 'tween us, he'd give us a hard eye from up in his tower, but he never come down. So we been doing this for years, walking the sheep inside, and finally I see him stand up and squint down at us and I think for sure we're nabbed this time, but then he sits back down and I hear him say to his partner up there, *You Dordrecht…you Dordrecht…you—*" Sander fell into a sniggering fit.

"What?" said Jolanda, squirming away from them and dropping back to the cobbles. "What did he say?"

"He said, *You Dordrecht boys look just like sheep when you get old,*" said Sander, and cackled. Jolanda blinked at him.

"That didn't really happen," said the girl, but she wore the expression of one who hoped it had. "You're a lying mussel, just like him."

"The devil take me if I am!" said Sander. "I heard him myself."

"Well, it's not really funny," she said.

"You just don't have a sense of humor," said Sander, crossing his arms.

"And that's why you call people from Dordrecht sheepheads?"

"Yeah," said Sander, disappointed in her reaction.

"So why do you call people from the other place, the burg, why do you call them piss-takers?"

"Piss-catchers," said Jan. "Tilburg's a textile town, and they use urine to bind the dye color, as I'm sure you're aware. So they catch their piss instead of dumping it out."

"Bah!" said Sander. "That's not why!"

"Why, then?" asked the girl.

"It comes back to my gran'da," said Sander. "He was passing through Tilburg one winter and this old wifey let him come in to stay the night since her husband was gone. He was already blind drunk, my gran'da, and so when she had her back turned, he took one of her crocks to make his water in, and—"

"Here we are," said Jan, and to his disappointment Sander saw they had indeed meandered back to the low house where Poorter kept shop, his door another nondescript gray break in the winding wall of buildings. "Stories later, we may be in town for some time if the Muscovite isn't about."

"It probably wasn't funny anyway," said the girl, but when he went to pop her upside the head, Sander saw she was grinning at him.

X.

Part of the reason Poorter Primm loved Dordrecht was that the city, like himself, had once been grand despite its heritage and well respected despite its coarseness, only to fall victim to the sort of luck that would make a toothless beggar lying half-dead in a ditch with a drowned dog for a pillow and a rat waiting to bite his dick every time he passed out shake his head sadly and say, "Tough tit, old man, tough tit." This shared ill fortune made him feel a solidarity with the place beyond mere civic affection, and he had long since resolved to never leave the island if he could help it—if things were this bad within Dordrecht's walls, he couldn't imagine what they were like without. Besides, it was getting better, slowly but surely, and who knew, in another decade or two the city might fully recover from the flood that had sunk Poorter's business into a miserable mire as surely as it had done the same to the Groote Waard.

A knock came at his door, which was intensely frustrating, as Poorter had eaten something evil the night before and had only just unfastened his belt for the fourth time that morning. Wincing at the chamber pot, he closed his eyes and breathed deeply, like an archer trying to steady himself for the shot, and his guts stabbed outward again. The luck of the sheep, all right: live in the shit, get fleeced often, and all to end up as mutton, Poorter thought glumly as he waited for the tempest in his belly to calm before answering the door. The knock came again, but this time he recognized it for what it was—two sharp raps, a pause, and three slow, light ones. The return of the Tieselen bastard banished Poorter's cramps and he hurried to the door, a silent prayer on his lips that the madman who had so recently haunted his house was not attending his master.

He was, Sander giving him a nod from behind Jan, and there was also a moppet on the step behind them. He was about to run the urchin off, but something about her feral looks gave him pause, and then he realized she was with the two men. A memory came unbidden to Poorter of a happier time, when he had opened this door to find none other than the count of Holland himself at his step, along with a trio of visiting French dignitaries whom Count William intended to outfit with the finest—and most expensive—pieces Poorter had on hand. Now the count was dead of dog bite, Dordrecht was an island, Poorter had the trots, and instead of nobility throwing coin at him he had three shifty hoods dirtying his stoop with the obvious aim of an invitation inside and, if his luck was really shit, a prolonged stay on the floor of his kitchen. Poorter's luck was, as usual, ludicrously lousy, and it would be a week before they left for more than a few hours at a time . . . But he didn't know that yet.

"Master Primm," said the bastard with a bow. "How does Providence treat you, old friend?"

"Shortly," said Poorter, "and without the courtesy of pretense that all is somehow not what it most certainly is."

"That's Poorter," Sander said, elbowing the urchin. "He's like that, but not such a bitch as you'd think to look at him."

Poorter offered the psychotic layabout and the child prostitute or whatever she was a winning smile and ushered them all inside. Jan was being his usual charismatic self, complimenting Poorter on his stained bedshirt and cluttered workshop, but Poorter's attention remained on the girl. Both Jan and Sander could be trusted, at least insofar as they were likely to request that he put them up and therefore wouldn't nick something immediately, but Poorter hadn't scrounged the little coin he had to his name by being the sort of fool who would turn his back on an unknown child.

Satisfied she hadn't filched anything from the workshop, Poorter held open the kitchen door and Sander, never one to stand on ceremony when he could sit on his ass, immediately took the nicest chair and would have put his feet up on the second best if Poorter hadn't arched his eyebrows and pointed at the man's mucky boots. Sander pulled them off, clods of filth spattering the woven reed mats covering the stone floor, and handed them to Jan, who had already stripped off his. Poorter noticed that the girl didn't wear shoes, further confirming his suspicions that she was some beggar-child they had picked up for purposes best not inquired after. Unless ... But Poorter dismissed the notion at once, the idea of either of them getting on a woman no more likely than his getting on an otter.

"Arcubalistarius, I have need of your service," said Jan after he had exhausted his empty platitudes and his two companions had set in on the leftovers Poorter had offered them, the same bluish mutton that he blamed for his morning's bellyache.

"Anything, my friend," said Poorter, smiling back. "Provided, of course, that I can provide."

"Specifically, I have need of your floor."

"Indeed," said Poorter, assuaging his irritation by admiring the amount of sour lamb Sander was putting away, the man first sucking the fat from the cobalt-streaked meat, swishing it about in his mouth, and then chewing the flesh itself with a relish that bordered on the obscene. The girl had nibbled a little but put the rest back on the plate they shared, the runny grease leaving the tips of her dirty fingers shiny. Her hands and forearms looked badly bruised, and at the thought of harboring some abused child Poorter felt his indigestion return. "For what duration?"

"That depends entirely on uncontrollable elements," said Jan. "But I'll have an idea soon. I have to run some errands, if you wouldn't mind keeping an eye on these two while I'm out, and then we'll discuss duration over supper. My treat."

"Indeed," said Poorter. "And shall I invite Laurent as well?"

"That shouldn't be necessary," said Jan. "I'll call on him this afternoon."

"Is that wise?"

"Wiser than his calling here, given the circumstances. Where are you keeping my things?"

"Stay here, I won't be a moment," said Poorter, ducking back into his workroom. He was a portly man, and not predisposed to haste, but he hurried between the cluttered tables with both speed and alacrity, eager to get back to the kitchen before his cutlery went missing. He lamented his lack of maid or apprentice for the umpteenth time, but the last pair he'd employed had eloped with one another and a small fortune in his completed crossbows and finer components, including a filigreed lock plate that cost more than he paid the maid in a month. If his guests were to steal the knife he had provided them with, he would be cutting his meat with arrowheads.

Fishing out the satchel Jan had entrusted to him during the bastard's last visit, Poorter returned to the kitchen door, but paused at hearing a quiet exchange between the men:

"Can't anchor me, you plaguebitch!"

"No, but I can beg that you listen to reason. When we're back, you can go out as much as you like, but until then do us both a favor and be patient. I'm sure he has some cards."

"I have a Karnöffel deck," said Poorter, entering the kitchen when it became evident the conversation was over. "And a chess-board. I have much to do today but you two—where's the girl?"

The small kitchen had only the table the men sat at and another, narrower board beside the cooking hearth, and as she was neither at the first nor under the second, she was not in the kitchen. She had either snuck into the workshop after him and crept up into his loft or—the sound of retching came from the tiny closet in which he kept his chamber pot. Relieved, Poorter tossed Jan his pack, and the man began to strip without even loosening the drawstrings on the bag. Sander leered at him as he did, and Poorter wearily went back to the workshop, opening sash and shutter to let in what murky light dripped down with the resumed rain.

Jan went out a short time later, his brightly colored velvet doublet, embroidered shirt, and spotless hose almost blinding compared to the dusky, dusty ensemble he had arrived in, glossy black turnshoes squeaking on the floor of the workshop, a hooded cape pulled over his freshly rinsed hair. The bucket in which he had washed his face and hair shone in the watery afternoon light, the sheen on the surface a greasy mirror to what remained on the plate Sander had cleared of mutton. But then the madman raised the dish and set to licking it, spoiling the dichotomy. The girl was out of the closet but looked far from hale, and the sight of Sander polishing the plate with his tongue brought a fresh grimace to her hollow cheeks. Poorter would have sympathized, had he been the sympathetic type.

The front door closed behind Jan, and Sander immediately stood up, dropping the plate on the table with a clatter. "Right, that's me out. Spot me a groot."

"I will not," said Poorter, bristling at the demand, expected though it was. "And Jan—"

"Is gone out, so that's me, too. Five mites, then? You can afford it, I know you can."

"No."

"Fine." Sander glowered at Poorter. "See you at supper."

"Plate," said Poorter, nodding at the bucket Jan had washed in.

"You heard," Sander told the girl, who responded by giving him the sort of look that would stop a rabbit's heart. Picking it up himself, Sander cocked his arm back as if he were going to strike her with it, but she didn't flinch. Sander snickered, squatting over the bucket and rinsing the dish, and Poorter sighed. It was going to be a long visit.

After the plate was washed, Sander made to leave without the girl, whereupon a debate ensued between the men as the urchin looked back and forth between them with growing disgust. She wouldn't look Poorter in the eye and hadn't said a word since arriving. Sander only relented when Poorter agreed to lend him a few pfennigs in exchange for taking the child with him, the child *he had himself brought into the house.* As Poorter closed the front door behind them, he saw Sander give one of the coins to the girl as they ambled down the street. If there was anything worse in all the world than a born cheat, Poorter didn't know what it was, and he sat down on his bench to do some honest work before the robber crows again descended on his house.

XI.

Jo spent five nights in the house of Primm, nights that were even less comfortable than the days thanks to Jan and Sander banishing her to the dark workshop while they used the kitchen for their private purposes. Jan was, well, Jan as ever, but the company he kept put her out. Poorter was suspicious of eye, large of girth, baffling of mouth, and generally vain and self-important, with a fine powdering of cookie crumbs forever lingering, licelike, in his thin mustache. Unsettling as the rich crossbowman was, Sander was worse. Why a man such as Jan would take the company of Sander was beyond her, for the bully was loutish and often scary, and, unlike Jan, anything but good-natured when she engaged him in a slapfight.

When they'd left Poorter's that first Dordrecht afternoon, Sander had taken her to a cramped, smelly tavern in the shadow of an Augustinian monastery, insisting on buying her an ale and telling her some inane story. When she'd politely mentioned the inanity of said tale, they had gotten into it, and he promptly landed a smack to her ear that left her stunned while he laughed in her face. She lost her temper over it, tears in her eyes as she screamed at him not to hit her so hard. As she railed at him, he began breathing too fast, panting like a sick dog, eyes bulging like a cooked fish, and then he wordlessly stood and led her back to Poorter's house. Supper that night had been miserable, with Jan and Primm talking obliquely about things she didn't understand while Sander scowled mutely into his soup, as if something in the fishy broth personally offended him. He didn't speak to Jo for two days.

That first night, they had all slept together on the floor of the kitchen with Jan between her and the sulky man-child, but the second night Jan gently requested that she sleep in the workroom while he and Sander conducted their business. Sander was in the privy and Primm already retired, and so, with the twin sources of her nervousness removed, Jo chanced engaging Jan—he had held forth quite a bit about Dordrecht and Holland and Duke This and Duchess That and Some Bitch during the long day of sitting in the kitchen, but rare was the occasion where neither of the other men were present.

"Why?" she said, not caring if she sounded petulant.

"Here," said Jan, going to the door and tapping a small black gouge in the wood. It looked like a knothole, but when she inspected the other side of the door, she saw that it was dug out. In poor weather Primm would test his devices inside, and the targets he hung from the door were often insufficient to fully stop the quarrels from such close range. "Though I don't know if you'll like it."

"Eh?" She squinted at him, as though he were already on the other side of the peephole.

"We're lovers," said Jan, lowering his voice despite his seeming nonchalance. "We'd like to fuck, though Sander's the shy type, so he wants you out. Personally, I don't care if you watch, but don't tell him that."

Jo gawked at him, then giggled, than gawked again when she realized he wasn't in jest. She could feel her cheeks flaring hot even as her belly went cold, and she turned to flee into the workshop before Jan saw her cry. It didn't make any kind of sense at all; she didn't even know men really did that to one another outside of insulting allegations, or how. That said, the source of her sudden shame and misery was much closer to her heart than an abstract confusion about the logistics of coupling.

The workshop was dark, Poorter snoring above, and just as a sudden fury boiled up inside her and she spun to slam the door shut behind her, Jan appeared in the doorway, the fingers he had stretched out to the nape of her neck now grazing her throat. She froze, and he followed her into the darkness, his hand pressing in until the crook between thumb and forefinger was tight against her neck. His fingers closed softly, and she gasped as he leaned in, his face in shadow blacker than the bottom of a purple pot, his breath warm as the side of the cauldrons.

"I want you to watch, Jo," he said, breathing on her face, the smell of tart ale and coriandered pike almost seeming sweet. She closed her eyes from the heat. "And don't you be jealous, understand? He's just going to tide me over until you're ready, and then I'll be done with him and it'll be just you and me, all right? But you need to watch, to see if you can please me like he can. It's important."

She would have kicked him, she would have bit him or some-thing, but she found her limbs had grown heavy, and even step-ping back as he moved closer was like trying to swim in a wet tunic. His other hand landed on the top of her thigh, the fingers bunching up her shift, and she felt as if she were a fathom under the sea, her chest pinching, her breath gone, and then his fingers were on bare skin—she had stripped down to her underwear early in the evening, the heat of the cooking hearth driving the layers off her limbs like a butcher skinning a pig after roasting off its hair. She keenly remembered one of the fisherboys getting this close after tackling her in the dunes, remembered ramming him in the nose with her forehead and sending him crying into the blackthorn, but she didn't move this time. Jan's fingers with-drew slightly, the tips grazing her thigh as the shift pooled in his palm and spilled over, and then he was sliding up, between her legs, and she would have begged him to stop if she'd had the breath.

"I'm mad for you, Jo," he murmured, and she realized her dif-ficulty in breathing came in part from his gently throttling fin-gers encircling her neck. He seemed to think this was sexy, but he was way out of order on that—it creeped her out, soured the whole thing. His other hand was hovering so close she could feel its heat through her patch of wiry hair. "*Mad.* But I want a woman, not a girl. So you watch, and think if you want to give me what I want to give you. After we retrieve what I'm looking for, we'll have a talk and see. And then it'll be just you and me from then on. All right?"

Jo heard the privy door open in the kitchen, Sander saying something that was incomprehensible to Jo, coming as it did through a great depth of water or some colder, crueler substance. Jan drifted back out the door, like a rubbing-up rag caught by the wind at the edge of her father's sandy yard, and then he pulled it shut after him, a beam of light stabbing out of the peep-hole to shine upon her heaving chest. It brought her to the surface, that light, and she fell to her knees, her breath coming in sobs, her knees trembling, her stomach roiling like it had after eating Poorter's mutton the morning before. What in all the devils of the sea was wrong with him? With her, that she hadn't broken his face for squeezing her throat the way he had? The rest of it had been all right, but *that* had been downright scary…

When they started to make noises, she fled to the rear of the workshop, crawling under the table and crying herself to sleep. It was almost enough to make her miss her old life, miss the grunting, smacking, farting mass of brothers and father crowded together in the dark, the heat of them clinging to her like a tunic after a swim if she didn't have time to let the air dry her before slipping it back on, and she shivered miserably, pulling her knees to her chest. Summer though it was, she felt a chill unlike any found in the deep, and wondered just what she had fallen into.

The next morning Sander's spirits seemed much improved and, finally breaking his silence toward her, he offered Jo a tug on his breakfast bottle. He wore an almost normal smile and joked about, as though nothing had ever been queer between them after his cuffing her in the tavern that first afternoon. She went along with it, but secretly hoped Jan would get sick of his craziness and run him off right away. It didn't seem likely, however, knowing what she now did.

Jan took her out for a walk, which restored Sander's only just-vanquished grumpiness when he was instructed to stay behind. Jo let Jan show her the churches, and then the mint from whence he'd stolen a plate with which to conterfeit groots, but then she demanded to be taken to the harbor and sent home. He laughed and took her to the new harbor, but of course she had no coin, nor would she ask him for any, and so she just stared bitterly at the moldering quays and the bobbing boats.

"I'm not going to coddle you, Jo," he said lightly from behind her. "Nor will I apologize. What I do is my business, just as what you—"

"I thought you were different from them," she said, dismayed to hear her voice crack at the memory of the fisherboys harassing her, the sometimes-fun, sometimes-not attentions they gave her. He couldn't have known to whom she was referring, but it didn't stop him from answering.

"I'm different from anyone you've ever met, Jo," he told her quietly, the humor gone from his voice, but also the self-assurance that had galled her at first and then won her over with its certainty. He seemed almost melancholy, and she didn't pull away when the hands that had touched her with such purpose the night before settled hesitantly on her shoulders, landing light as young gulls on the sloe branches before they'd learned the cockiness and bravado of their elders. "But then, you're different from anyone I've met, too. You . . . frighten me, Jo."

She laughed at that, hating the ugly goose-honking sound her laugh had become ever since he'd put the crook in her half-healed nose. Turning to him, she saw how serious his brown eyes were under the cowl of the hood he wore despite the break in the rain, and she caught herself. "Don't be daft. What you got to fear from me?"

"You…" He paused, licking his full lips, and then shook his head, a fey smile again playing at his mouth. "You make me doubt things. About myself. Things I took for granted, like preferring fellows to lasses."

"Probably 'cause I look like a boy," she said, averting her eyes and brushing the back of her short-cropped head with a wincing touch, as though she were testing a fresh wound.

"No," he said with that old confidence. "You're a beautiful young woman, and—"

Jo kissed him then, but with her eyes so tightly shut she missed a direct connection and their lips only met at the corner. Before she could fall back in embarrassment or try again, he had seized her around the waist and crushed her to him. Their lips recalibrated and she desperately shoved her tongue into his mouth, their teeth clicking painfully together, and she found his squirming, moist muscle at the ready to play with hers. She thought of the inside of smashed sea snails and her stomach lurched. After a moment, or maybe an eternity, he pulled her away with that same prodding gentleness that filled her with such confusion.

"I want many more of those when we're done with this business," Jan said when he caught his breath, for he seemed as dumb as her for a moment afterward. "But for now you keep on like nothing's changed around Sander, all right?"

She nodded, unable to look at him for a moment, and when she did, he'd somehow conjured up a beautiful blue cloak in his perfect hands. He was holding it out to her, which obviously meant she was to have it, but she couldn't make her weak fingers take it. It hurt her eyes to look at the gift, and then he was moving behind her, wrapping it around her shoulders as he went on talking. For some stupid reason he was still hung on Sander, even though she'd already resolved to do as Jan wished—why couldn't they talk about the cloak instead?

"We need him, and I don't need to tell you he's got a temper. So I keep him happy for a little while longer, and then we'll leave this stinking place, go somewhere new. But for now you'll keep our secret."

It wasn't a question in either of their minds, she figured. Even still, despite his reiterated request that she spy on them Jo fled back under the table that night, disgusted not only by the sight of Jan's cock plunging between Sander's beard-wreathed lips but also by some less definable quality to what they were doing, or how it made her feel. The fourth night they did nothing and allowed her to sleep between them, but she lay awake long after the light went out ruminating on what she had seen and what might lay in store for her, wondering if she could give Jan what he said he needed. She wasn't an idiot, of course, and knew what might come after a sucking off, at least for men and women, but still—knowing what to do and choosing to do it were two very different pots of purple.

Then another tedious day in the kitchen, with Karnöffel becoming impossible when Sander threw down his cards in a huff and refused to play anymore on the grounds that it was an evil game indeed where the Devil trumped the Pope. Jo did not recall such piety when he had been the one to draw the Devil instead of she in previous hands. She finished the hat she'd begun knitting for herself with the small bundle of wool Jan had bought her on their walk back from the new harbor the day before, and although it was a shapeless, rather ugly sort of cap, she was nevertheless pleased with herself. It was sky blue, and matched the cloak he had given her— she could tell Sander was jealous of her new cape, but rather than pleasing her, this somehow made her pity the mad bastard.

That night Jan sent her into the workshop again, and she quietly moved one of Primm's stools to the door with the resolution of watching Jan and Sander through to the bitter end of their business. Jo could not quite make sense of how watching them made her feel, for it seemed equal measures nausea and hunger, pain and pleasure, and she could in no way account for the jealousy she felt toward Sander, considering how wracked he appeared throughout the proceedings. The workroom was too damn hot, in any event, and the stool too damn hard, but watch them she did.

The peephole did not grant her a wide view of the kitchen, for the door was thick, but anytime Sander seemed to be drawing them away from her range of vision, Jan brought the other man up short, insisting they couple there in the middle of the room. Even without the occasional glances Jan cast at the door, she would have suspected his intentions in keeping them thus situated, and every time his eyes flicked in her direction, she felt herself go cold and squirmy, as if she were the one up to mischief.

This night she did not flee when Sander knelt in front of Jan and undid his codpiece, though the site of his engorged, reddish instrument jutting out only to be gobbled by Sander reminded her uncomfortably of the disagreeable mutton she had eaten the first day. Jan groaned softly to have himself consumed by the larger man and, seizing Sander's shaggy locks, thrust himself deeper into his partner's mouth, which caused a spluttering on Sander's part. She expected this to be met with violence or at least reproach from the chronically antagonistic Sander, but his only response was to issue his own muffled groan and drive himself farther toward Jan's crotch, threads of drool catching in his beard as he gagged himself on his lover's cock.

This went on for some time, and Jo began to assume that this was the extent of how men fucked each other, that what her brothers and the fisherboys had alleged about one another was mere filthy invention. Then Jan abruptly removed himself from Sander's mouth, and both shimmied out of their clothes. Sander lay back on the ground, propping himself up on his elbows and spreading his legs. Jan knelt between his partner's knees, a jar he had retrieved from somewhere beyond Jo's sight in one hand as he slowly pulled back Sander's foreskin. Jan then hunched down to kiss the exposed tip of Sander's erection, which was more purple and knobby than his own, and then set to licking his way down to the man's balls.

Jo could scarcely breathe, telling herself how revolting it was even as she pressed her forehead harder against the door, licking sweat from her lips. Jan was tonguing Sander's sack, and then went lower still. At this Jo pulled away from the door, refusing to believe it, remembering the feel of his lips on hers, the taste of that very tongue, and then she was back at the peephole.

One hand tugging vigorously on Sander's cock, Jan straightened up and dipped the fingers of his free hand into the wide clay jar. They emerged glistening, and he ducked back down, now properly taking Sander into his mouth even as those shining fingers vanished between the man's thighs. Jo told herself it wasn't what it looked like, but as if Jan heard her, his shoulder shifted, causing Sander to grunt and buck. Then Jan abruptly released the cock from his mouth, straightening up but remaining on his knees, his hand working between Sander's legs.

Sander was squirming and panting as Jan's wrist canted back and forth like the lock on one of Primm's crossbows. Sander lowed cowishly and drew his knees almost up to his chin, rocking his lower body even farther off the floor to meet Jan's busy fingers. With his free hand, Jan shoved their shed clothes underneath Sander's raised arse, cushioning the man's tailbone as Sander settled back down. Then Jan removed his fingers, making Sander gasp and again rock his arse up in the air, as if the floor scalded him. Jan dunked his hand back into the jar and wiped something greasy on his cock, the oily sheen of it making his organ look like some bloody weapon, and his fingers went back between Sander's legs.

Jan's hand tarried only a moment this time, before going to one of Sander's splayed knees. Holding the big man steady, Jan scooted closer and hunkered down. Sander's eyes were closed, the man muttering some fervent prayer or vicious curse, and Jan turned to the door and offered Jo a wink, which was just...she didn't even know what. Then Jan turned back to the quivering man beneath him and set to his business. Sander's leg mostly obscured the penetration as Jan slowly eased himself forward, two fingers pressing down on the ridge of his cock, but Jo wasn't so thick as to not recognize a buggering when she saw one.

Despite her resolution to stay until the finish, that was enough for her. The unexpected stiffness and accompanying back-twinge as she withdrew from the peephole almost made her cry out, but she caught herself and stayed quiet. After a moment of reflection on what she had seen, a deep sense of shame settled over her like an itchy blanket on a hot night, and she slunk to her bedding. She didn't want to be here, didn't want to have anything to do with these nasty poots. Especially Jan.

Or maybe not? Maybe she wanted him to kiss her like he kissed Sander when they were just setting in? Maybe she wanted...

She wanted to die, or, failing that, to fall into a deep enough slumber that she could convince herself the whole night had all been one of her rare nightmares.

Sleep, however, proved slippery as an eel, escaping between her fingers each time she almost seized it, so the morning found her as unrested as she was uneasy. She stayed on her pallet of rags long after noises began to come from the kitchen, and only when Primm began to stir in his loft, his snores giving way to phlegmy throat-clearings, smackings, and swallows, did Jo rise with a miserable sigh. She went to the kitchen, but as she put her hand on the door, she heard Sander barking at Jan and paused.

"—fuckin kid, Jan! It's not right!"

"Keep your voice down," came the reply that she barely made out, and she pressed her ear to the peephole. "You asked."

"Yeah, but I thought—"

"Quiet. Down." Jan's voice was hard as she'd ever heard it. "Don't. I'm tellin you, if you give me any heed at all, don't."

"I give you heed, Sander, more than any else. But I can't let you ruin this. She—"

"—'s a little fucking girl!"

There was a pause, and she wondered if they were waiting to see if Sander's newest outburst had awoken her. Just as Jan began to speak again, Primm launched into an especially moist snort from above, and she only caught the end of what was said:

"—a woman, and a capable one at that, not some mooncalf or babe, so spare me your moralizing, Sander. After all *you've* gotten into, I'd think you'd be the last one to be a bitch about this. Or are you just jealous I might use your rope on her?"

"Cunt!" Sander shouted, and before Jo could move, the door flew open, cracking her head and sending her sprawling. Sander stared down at her, livid, and pointed a blackish nail in her face. "Stupid little slut! Get to fuck! Out, before I brain you!"

"Not in the house." Primm yawned, his ladder squeaking as he descended. "Please."

"Fat fucking pudding sack!" Sander bellowed. "All you, you, fucking meat-bag pudding sacks!"

And then Sander was wrestling with the front door, throwing back the latch and launching himself into the drizzle, his final curse wafting in with the stink of mildew and offal. Jan stood in the kitchen doorway, watching Jo as she picked herself up. Her scalp was bleeding into her eye, a cracked goose egg. She could tell he was cross, but wasn't sure if it was with her or Sander or both of them.

"Clean yourself up," said Jan, turning back to the kitchen. "We've got a lot to do if we're going to get a move on tomorrow."

Walpurgisnacht 1423

"Belling the Cat"

I.

Jan had put up with just about enough of both Sander and Jolanda's shit, respective and collective, and to make things worse, the Muscovite, Andrei, seemed much more honest than Jan had originally taken him for. One whisper of Andrei's thick foreign accent and Jan had assumed he was at least a thug, if not an outright cutthroat, pimp, or rapist, but the more they talked the less crooked the Muscovite seemed. This could be a serious problem, as Andrei had permanently settled in Dordrecht and therefore the potential for complications grew with each oar-stroke.

Jan had half a mind to stick his sword in all three of them and finish the quest himself, but obviously he wouldn't, preferable though it might seem in the moment. He and Andrei had found Oudeland again together, true, but that was some time ago, and all the meer looked the same to Jan's land-loving eyes, whereas the Muscovite claimed to remember the way. Then Sander and Jolanda each had their uses, annoying though they had proven of late ...

Either one he could have handled easily—the ride to Rotterdam with Jolanda hadn't been bad, and he knew that for all his idiosyncrasies Sander was agreeable enough in isolation, and a solid partner to boot—but put them together and, saints alive, it was like juggling cats, or some similarly onerous task that was liable to leave one bitten, bloody, and annoyed for even thinking such a thing would be feasible in the first place. He ought to just leave them to each other when all was said and done, which was no less than they deserved, given their behavior. Jolanda's jealousy at least made a kind of sense, given that she was a moonstruck little girl, but Sander's behavior was simply bizarre—perhaps he really was losing his mind for good this time.

The girl sat in the front of the large rowboat, the Muscovite's scrawny gray tabby purring in her lap. Behind her, Jan leaned against the piled gear, while behind him Sander and then Andrei manned the twin sets of oars from their respective benches, propelling the craft over the surface of the inland sea. The Muscovite, though shorter than Sander, had the brawn to bear out his claim of having rowed up and down every river on the continent, and across several seas besides, and as fast as they were skating across the water, Jan could tell the man was putting less than his all into his strokes. Sander's oars had slapped more often than they cut at first, but now he had his stride.

"We fly!" Andrei laughed, nodding down at the water. Glancing over the side, Jan saw the shadowy frames of houses just beneath the boat, the thatch of their roofs long since claimed by tide and rot. The sight must have been a common one for boatmen who plied these waters, but the Muscovite clearly still delighted in it. "Like angels, Rutte, like angels!"

"Like crows," Sander grunted. "And his name's Jan."

"Eh? Jan? Not Rutte?"

"That's right, Andrei," Jan said with a sigh, not turning. How many times had he told Sander to use the alias around their foreign accomplice? "Jan."

If discovering that the man he had known as Rutte for over a year was actually called something else bothered Andrei, he gave no indication: "We fly like crows, Jan!"

"Indeed." Jan smiled to himself, imagining the Groote Waard as it had been in his youth, imagining himself lying in the sheep meadows watching the clouds, imagining the sight of a boat cutting through the puffy white sea above. He waved up at himself. He waved down at himself. The vessel glided along the open water, occasionally slicing through a fence of young reeds where a dike crossed the sunken countryside, and Jan felt a deep, cool tranquillity swell in him, just as the deep, cool waters had swelled in under the doors of farmer and graaf alike. He was coming home.

With this thought came another of the rare stabs to his chest, a sensation that only Sander inspired with anything resembling regularity. After all this time, not just from the point of the flood but ever since he had found out as a boy what might be his if only he could find a way to seize it, here he was, and with the means of his salvation at hand. The digging pain in his heart intensified, not from this homecoming, however, but from the sudden and intense concern that all might come for naught—the girl might not be able to find the prize in the dark depths, or the house might have filled with mud, or it might be gone entirely, the old bastard might not have perished in his house but instead tried to flee with everything he had, taking it all with him, only to be washed away, anywhere in the wide drink, gone forever. Gone. What then?

Jan was not a fool. All this had been considered at length, and even if it came to nothing the lawyer, Laurent, seemed optimistic that things should still work out, as had Jan's other secret confederate, a nobleman of no small stature. But then everything that came after this was less important, if Jan were to be honest with himself, everything beyond this flooded land was dreamlike, insubstantial as clouded breath on a winter's morn, and only by taking the physical artifact could he transform—it was a witch's tool, a magic ring, a relic, not something to be faked, as Laurent had suggested. After all, Jan was genuine, so should not his proof be as well?

Or perhaps Sander's superstitious nature was simply rubbing off on Jan. The point was, the ring was down there in the dark, waiting, and he would have it, and then he would be graaf instead of grift, count instead of cunt. Finally.

II.

Sander was trying to cool his stewing anger at Jan, but he might as well have been blowing on the summer sun. He should have expected something along these lines, considering the coldness of the bastard in question, but no matter how adamantly he told himself he should have seen this coming, he still boiled to think of it. That it bothered him as much as it did was not something he focused on for very long at a stretch—such thoughts were too knotty to properly sort out, and of course if he were in Jan's position, things might be different and all, but still, it was a dark fucking play no matter what cards you were holding. Graafs and the like had to be careful, Sander got that, especially fake graafs like Jan, and yeah, you didn't want people talking, spreading rumors, all that, but after all the time and hard work and, yeah, well, call it what it was, love, it felt ruthless as a raven's mercy. It wasn't like Jan was staving in Sander's head, but for some queer reason it felt like his heart had suffered a blow—which was just stupid, since Sander had always been the harder of the two.

Except maybe he wasn't, Sander admitted as he gave his oars an especially healthy jerk. Sander might be more eager to wade into a fight or, sure, yeah, a murder or two, but Jan had a whole different sort of edge to him, maybe the difference between a sword and a fish knife or something, a shaving blade. Whatever. Point was, part of the attraction had always been Jan's willingness to overlook Sander's more violent excesses; angel's honesty, the man had shown no more disgust toward Sander's crimes than he had to the occasional smear of shit on his cock mid-fuck—at worst, a vaguely annoyed sigh, a wipe of a rag, and a resumption of business.

Why, then, the surprise? No, surprise was all right, why then the anger, the, well, the hurt? That didn't make half a whore's lick of sense. Would it have been different if the little mussel had been a lad, some fit little blondie or ginger grinding on Jan? Maybe—or maybe it would have made it worse, devil only knew. Point was, smart tactic or no, Sander would have another wee word with Jan when the girl wasn't about, and on that wager a betting man might turn a healthy profit on even short odds.

Then there was this dogdick in front of him, this squinty little ball-washer who had been trying to fuck with Sander ever since they set out. As if reading his thoughts, the Muscovite brought his oars back too fast and spattered Sander's face with meer water, further fermenting his sour mood. He *was* fucking with him, the prick.

"You fucking with me, you prick?" demanded Sander, setting his shoulders and dragging the oars through the meer as hard as he could, splashing them both as he ripped them up at the end of the stroke.

"I would not with you, my strashniy droog, not even for money." The Muscovite smiled over his shoulder, his teeth yellow as old butter. This was accompanied by another spritz from his oars as they came back.

"Keep it up," Sander snarled. He considered throwing the man overboard. With his back to Sander, he'd never see it coming. "Keep it up and see, ball-washer. Highest tree catches the most wind."

"Velik telom, da mal delom," the Muscovite sang, his voice rolling across the watery plain, his eyes closed as he rapturously belted out his stupid-sounding ballad. "Velik telooooooom, da mal delooooooom!"

Sander felt a brief but strong urge to stand and beat the man to death with his bare hands, but he knew from experience that brawling in boats invariably led to his going in the water, and after the whole falling-into-a-canal-and-waking-up-in-hell business he was especially wary of going overboard. Let the prick sing—he'd be warbling another tune when Glory's End was buried up his ass. Besides, it was bad luck to attack a man on his own ship, rublehead or no.

"Is that it?" Jan called over his shoulder to the rowers, and Andrei ended his song as abruptly as it had begun.

"Da, good eye, Rutte!"

"Jan," Sander barked. "Jan!"

"Doesn't make his eye bad, zhopa."

"San. Dur," said Sander. "Sander. Call me more of that noise and see."

"I see good enough, Sander, I do!" said the Muscovite, still half-turned on his bench, a smile forever lingering at his lips like herring grease after a summer dinner. "But do you?"

Sander saw, all right, he saw just fine. He and Jan had talked it over the night before and both agreed the boatman couldn't be trusted, although Jan had it all backward—he thought the shifty emigrant was too straight, whereas Sander could see that the Muskie was as crooked as a pig's tail. After working with Jan to locate their destination shortly after the flood, and now the Hollander's return with two assistants and three bulging satchels, the foreigner was bound to suspect a treasure hunt. That he had not said as much upfront and demanded a cut there in the tavern where they had discussed the terms implied he meant to cheat them out of the lot, like as the devil doing sin.

Everyone had heard stories about breaker crews hiding in the massive meer the Groote Waard had become, some of the pirates simple opportunists salvaging what they could from the towns the tide gave up, others the former villagers themselves without means of subsistence beyond banditry now that the lands and livestock they had worked were gone—if the landowning graafs and hertogs were desperate, pity then their farmers and shepherds. Assuming Andrei spent as much time on the meer as he claimed, then he would be working with or for some crew or another or he would have lost his boat and likely his life long before—there being fuck all in the way of taxable worth out here, neither graaf nor city was inclined to waste a groot patrolling the waters for brigands. If the Muscovite colluded with some breakers to rob Jan and company, then the only question was whether he would have given his confederates the probable location of the treasure itself or, as Sander suspected, arranged an ambush spot somewhere on the way back to Dordt.

Point was, the plaguebitch may have fooled Jan, but he wasn't fitting Sander with no woolen blinders—whoever heard of an honest Muscovite? Obviously the villain intended a robbery.

Sander dearly hoped so, yes he did.

A low mist had come up, clinging over the surface like a cold stew's skin, and twisting around for a look, Sander saw tendrils of it catching in thin dead branches jutting out of the meer. The limbs—twigs, really—extended in a field for at least fifty paces, or swimmer's strokes, or whatever, and beyond them the haze thickened. The bottom of the boat scratched over something, which brought an unhappy surge in Sander's belly.

"Careful, now, careful," said Andrei, slowing the boat with his oars and then pulling them in as far as the rowlocks allowed. He clicked his teeth as Sander did the same. With the oars, that was—clicking your teeth at someone like you were addressing a horse or a dog was a good way to get your ugly head split, in Sander's estimation. This would be a fine place to do it, too; endless gray water, gray little sprays of wood rising from it, gray drifts of mist hanging, boxing them in, and a gray sky above . . . Place could do with a splash of color, red or otherwise.

The fingers of willow that remained above the surface had long since relented to the water's intrusion, and rather than snapping, they bent away from the boat, rubbery as the arms of squid. Looking over the side, Sander could make out a tangled maze of murky limbs leading down into darkness. The sight of the arboreal reef brought him a sudden and acute dizziness, and he closed his eyes, trying to find his suddenly cagey breath. It had been easy to forget where they were when he was intent on the rowing, or daydreaming about Jan's cock, or daydreaming about kicking Jan *in* the cock for his cruel, selfish attitude, but now, with a willow wood underneath them instead of the other way around, Sander found himself unable to avoid the grim truth—his whole life up until he'd had to quickly quit the place a few years ago was beneath them, waterlogged and dead as a drowned hound, and they were floating above it all like . . . what'd the Muskie say? Like angels.

Or ghosts.

It was a chill fucking thought, and Sander tried to turn his mind from it by opening his eyes and focusing on the task of hating the Muscovite, who had stood and used a long quant to guide them over the forest, pushing off of the sunken limbs with his pole. Besides, Sander's village might have been just *like* the prosaically named Oudeland, but it wasn't as if they were actually above his birthplace . . .

"There," said Jan, not even trying to hide his eagerness as he pointed to a low thicket of rushes a short distance off. "Look, the water's down from last time!"

"Good to fish here," said Andrei, setting his pole back in the boat and resuming his seat at the oars as they drifted out of the treetops. "You can see them, lots and lots."

"Is that a house?" the girl asked from the front of the boat. She had barely spoken above a whisper, but it was so quiet here that Sander heard her perfectly. Following her gaze, he saw a thin ridge rising a thumb's length from the water, and, as they left the willows behind and came abreast of it, Sander saw it was indeed the top of a sunken building's wall. His hand strayed to the medallion at his neck, the one Jan had tried in vain to convince him to discard instead of threading on a new cord, and brought it to his quivering lips. The crude figure on the bronze disc was a saint, Sander had decided, which particular saint it was varying on the circumstance. Right now she was Saint Walpurga, for obvious reasons. This place gave him the creeps, his mind unsure if the decomposing visage of his father, a bone-wielding Belgian, or both were lurking inside the flooded house beside the boat.

"You've been out here since, then?" said Jan, looking intently at the Muscovite. "Do a lot of fishers work these towns?"

"Nay, Hollanders are scared. No, not scared. They are... suevernyĭ?" Andrei examined the mist sliding around them and found what he was looking for there between the water and the vapors. "Superstitious. They are superstitious, do not fish here. They say, *V tihom omute cherty vodyatsya*."

"Fucking doubt they say *that*," said Sander.

"Hard to translate. In deep water is... Nay, in quiet... In not-moving river... hmmm."

"Still waters run deep, yeah, I've heard that," said Sander. The expression had never made much sense to him.

"Still! Yes, *still* water," said the Muskie. "Thank you, Sander. They say, in deep, still water of a river, there lives the demons. Yes."

"Ah," said Jan. "But you're not superstitious."

"Nay. My nets bring in some bones of people who go in flood, some bones with meat on them yet, da, but no demons. No ghosts. Just bones."

"Bones with meat on 'em," Sander said quietly, making no move to resume rowing himself. What the Muscovite said about demons in the river was even more puzzling than the proverb about still waters running deep, and a good bit more unsettling, too.

"Some," Andrei shrugged as he dipped his oars again. "Some not. Some just teeth, just bones. Busy fish. Fat fish."

"And you sell them, the fish you catch out here?" It took a lot to give Sander pause, but this sufficed. The Muscovite was an even dirtier prick than he'd suspected.

"Fat fish," said Andrei, making a slurping noise. "Carp and bream and eels eels eels, nets full of eels."

"Eels," said Sander to himself, wondering how this could get any worse.

"Ah," said Jan. "There's the graveyard, past the church spire. Moor us against that crypt."

That was how it got worse, then. How in the mercy of all the martyrs was there a graveyard out here? Total bullshit. If there was anything worse than a cold, dark body of water it was a graveyard, and a graveyard in the middle of a cold, dark body of water was a possibility so hideous it had never before crossed Sander's mind. He'd not set foot in a churchyard before, but then he'd never kissed a jellyfish, either, and still knew that was a bad idea. No whistling, no winking, no cursing, no visions of cock, no visions of violence, nothing to attract notice, just quiet, peaceful thoughts. A light veneration of the saints, maybe.

"How's it above water?" the girl asked, and Sander hated that she'd pointed out something even less natural about the place—instead of being safely tucked under a wet mantle at the bottom of the meer, a few slabs broke the surface, fencing the breaks of young rushes into uneven rows, and the boxy top of a crypt reared before them, all mossy and horrible.

"Early on, a Tieselen graaf wanted a lake to fish here in Oudeland," said Jan. "So he dug one. He planned to burn off the peat and catch the salt, as was common wisdom even in those benighted days, but Oudeland also had the priory, the land split between church and graaf. The priest insisted a part of the cleared earth be used to build up a proper churchyard, for one could not dig a man's depth without drawing up water, and the old churchman feared to have his bones resting in wet mud instead of dry earth. So between the church and the graaf's house a hill was erected, and to ensure it was high enough above the waterline, they simply built it over the old potters' mound."

"Aha!" Andrei chuckled. "Is the way here, there, all places—poor man on bottom, rich man on top."

"Precisely," said Jan. "The poor were added to the sides of the hill, so it grew ever outward, the priests went halfway up the slope, and the lords with their stones went atop it."

"Ought to keep 'em inside the church like a proper place," grumbled Sander, squinting into the depths. The water looked darker here.

"But then we'd have nowhere to sit," said Jan. "Steady now, steady."

The boat bobbed between two stones, green rushes scratching the sides of the boat, and Sander realized the blackness beneath him was likely gravedirt instead of impenetrable depth. Small consolation. Then, as he looked, a dark shape nearly as long as the boat appeared through the shallows, coasting under the boat. The vessel rocked as something brushed its bottom.

"Devil's dick!" Sander leapt to his feet, yanking the oar from its rowlock and brandishing it overhead. "Was that?!"

"Sturgeon," said Andrei. "Sit down so I can pole us."

"Sturgeon." Sander panted the word, glaring between the stones. "Sturgeon get that big?"

"Bigger," said Jan, leaning over to grab the edge of the crypt. Bastard hadn't seen it, Sander knew, but he couldn't quite find the words to call Jan out. Sander resumed his seat, but something about the Muscovite's manner recaptured his attention. The boatman was up again with the quant in hand, but rather than focusing on mooring the boat, he was staring at the front of the craft, at the back of Jan's head. No, not Jan—the girl. And he was smiling a dirty fucking smile, the sort of smile Sander himself had worn when they'd put the noose around his neck back in that shitty Frisian town.

A sudden disgust tugged at his guts like a swallowed fishhook— the things men did to half-grown kids made him want to murder the world. The reason that wench back at the Rotter inn had gotten all lippy with him when he'd first introduced himself to Jo, after all, was nutsacks like this Muscovite here, fantasizing about screwing the poor slut before she'd even grown a proper pair of tits. Sander was sucking cock by her age, admitted, but boys grew up quicker than girls, didn't they, and even an eager lad like he'd been hadn't let anyone up his backside until he was way older than her. Probably, it was impossible to tell how old a girl was at a glance.

Why the fuck should it concern him what this rublehead wanted to do to her, anyway? What Jan intended come full circle, that's why. Little slut being doted on and given kittens to cuddle and treated like a countess instead of a piece of cunt, oblivious to what men saw when they looked at her, just...just dark, was what it was. Dark.

Unless she wasn't oblivious. Unless it wasn't so dark. Unless Sander was the oblivious one. Wouldn't be the first instance, he allowed, wouldn't be the first at all. Sudden as a strike at a fishing line, Sander realized all three of these plaguebitches could be working together to murder him, not just to cheat him out of what he'd worked so hard to secure, but straight up bloody murder in the fucking fens.

This thought, rather than being immediately spit out like a fleck of bone, was cradled like a jewel of good fat in his jowl, savored and worried and cherished, and the more he played with the thought, the more sense it made. This did not upset him, but instead brought on a certain equanimity that carried an almost metallic taste to it. His palm left the locked oar and brushed the pommel of Glory's End, bringing a shiver of raw pleasure to both him and her, as if he'd pulled back his foreskin and brushed a feather over it. Come on, then, you ball-lavering dogdicks, come on and see if—

"See, Sander?" The Muscovite breathed behind him. "You see?"

"Eh?" Sander blinked, glancing up to see the Muscovite still staring ahead with that lewd smirk on his face despite Jo's having climbed from the boat onto the crypt beside them. If he wasn't spying on her...

"He is there, yes? Ahead, beside krest? Beside cross?"

What? Sander followed the man's gaze and saw the huge silhouette of the sturgeon, or perhaps another overfed fish, lying in the shadow of a grave marker. The fish was so large its smooth brown head broke the surface, giving the impression it was watching them. Then, as if his eyes had piked the monster, it churned the muddy shallows and was gone, leaving Sander shivering. Somehow, the Muscovite eye-fucking a giant fish was even more obscene than if he'd actually been sizing up the girl.

"Sander," said Jan from just above him. "Come on up, lad."

Sander frowned at his lover, Jan squatting atop the slimy, black stone of the crypt. There would be room enough for the four of them atop it, he saw, and the thought restored his faith in Jan, at least a little. Come what may, Jan wouldn't sell him out for a fish-hungry foreigner or a mouthy sprat. He reminded himself how fervently he'd believed the flood itself had been some attempt on his life, personally, by enemies unknown, and how Jan had helped break him of that, what was the word, *conceit*. A niggling part of him protested that of course Jan would seek to disavow him of the truth, but Sander pushed it down, just as he always did. Jan might be working for them, granted, but if he was, Sander was certain the man did so in ignorance.

Reasonably certain.

Anyway, onto the crypt, the Muscovite giving him a leg-up. The girl was already up and had her back to them, staring down at the wide smear of mud and rushes that pushed up to the edge of the crypt on the opposite side, and Sander had the impulse to shove her in, tell her to swim the fuck back to the sea if she was so keen on getting wet. There was a bit of ebony mold or muck under boot, making the narrow slab dangerously slick, and without turning, Sander decided, "Muskie stays in the boat. Not enough room."

"Sander—" Jan began, but Andrei waved it off.

"Is good with me. I like the island that floats to the one that does not."

Sander hated the man for his acumen, and kicked a clod of

filth into the boat. The Muscovite's eyes narrowed at this and he muttered something in his ugly fucking tongue. Sander winked at him.

"This is it," said Jan. "Still up for it, Jo?"

The girl looked over her shoulder, and Sander smiled to see some of the iron had gone out of her. She looked scared. Then she nodded, once, but firmly, and Sander sighed. Stupid little slut.

"I can...I'll...You want me to swim here? Bring something up?"

Idiot.

"That's right," said Jan cheerfully. "But let's get settled first, have a bite and a drink."

The Muscovite maneuvered his boat around the crypt to the wee mudbar on the far side of it and beached the craft in the filth, though it was obvious the ground was far from solid. There the man set to checking his net and then whetting the tip of his gaff hook, his cat sitting on the prow inspecting the muddy flat with the displeased air of a graaf surveying a frost-burned field. Jan and the girl had used an oar to scrape most of the muck off the crypt roof and sat with their legs crossed, sharing a loaf of rye and a cheese wheel. Sander was done with sitting after that interminable float, however, and paced as best he could—three steps down, two across, three back up, and then over and down again, the two assholes sitting in the middle of his circuit giving him dirty looks that he studiously ignored.

This was it, then. Oudeland. Jan's birth home. Sander contemplated the stubble of reeds and boils of stone, the crumbling church spire over there across a stretch of open water, the spindly treetop behind them with what looked to be a ram's skull caught in the branches, the few silhouettes of sunken buildings on the edge of his vision, the leagues and leagues of *nothing* vanishing into the mist. Hell, he thought, was water. He wondered at it, all this flood where earth had been, all this quiet where so much noise had risen. Well, not exactly here; the graveyard had probably been pretty solemn and all, and his stomach flopped anew at the thought of his precise location. He imagined the corpse beneath them crouched in the corner of his tomb, skull pressed to the ceiling, eavesdropping on the thieves upon his roof.

Dreadful thought.

But then they all were, these days.

III.

Margareta, the cat Jo had held for most of the journey, eventually dared the mud to join them on the crypt, skipping over the quaggy island and springing onto the roof. Her legs were muddied almost to her belly and she immediately set to cleaning herself on the edge of the stone. Jo worried that Sander might give her a kick, for he seemed like that kind of a man. Her father would have, surely, or one of her brothers. Instead, he finally ceased his strutting and crouched down, rubbing the puss's bobbing head with the back of his fist. Crazy neuker.

"There," said Jan, pointing with the nearly empty jug of flat beer. At first she couldn't see anything beyond the moored boat where Andrei napped, for the mist had thickened while they ate, but then she made out a patch of shadow in the miasma. A short distance from their roost the little isles of muck and reed that spotted the graveyard gave way to deeper, unbroken water, but a ways out another stand of rushes protruded from the meer. Squint as she did, she could see nothing but the small thicket of dark stalks.

"The reeds, then?" she asked, and trying to kindle herself for the chill of the swim, got herself properly annoyed. "Why aren't we moored there, then? Like seeing me shiver?"

"That's it, all right," Jan said. "Means the roof hasn't caved, at least not completely. We'll take the boat over when we're ready, but it's too chancy to beach on it while we sit around—last thing we want is to knock some bricks loose."

"It's past time you told me what *it* is, *Lob*," she said. "Can't well find your shit if you don't tell me the shape of it."

"His fucking da's house, is what it is," said Sander. He'd swooped up the cat and held her under one arm, gesturing with the docile animal as he spoke. "Flooded as the rest, so he wants you to swim in there and get his ring."

Jan nodded genially, which only irritated Jo more.

"There anything you'll tell me, instead of my hearing it from him?" she demanded. "Swear that cuntbitch is more honest than you, and that's saying something indeed."

"Slander me at your peril, slut," said Sander, pointing the cat at her. "Eager enough to use the words I taught you, even if you're wrong about the how of it. *Cuntbitch* is only something you call women."

"Didn't teach me that, nor nothing," said Jo. "My papa called me such more often than my name, and woman or would-be, I'll call you whatever I see fit, shitbird."

"Explain yourself, whore, or taste my fucking heel," said Sander.

"I mean honest folk don't tell them tales you're always on about, all them myths and ghost stories and horseshit—"

"Explain the *would-be woman* shit you said, I mean. And anything I tell you is true as apples are green—even a stupid little kid like you'll know that lying in a graveyard's not even possible, why they hold councils and such in—"

"I'm in love with you, Uncle Sander, and think you're a handsome fellow with all kinds of clever about you," said Jo, her eyes closed and her gaunt cheeks puffed out in a smile. "I'm also the countess of fucking Burgundy."

"Goddamn cuntbitch!" Sander shouted. "Bringing all kinds of ruin on yourself, saying such things in a churchyard! I didn't mean it wasn't possible, I meant it wasn't possible without damning yourself, sure as spitting on a church door!"

"Yeah, 'cause that's what you said, Uncle." Jo rolled her eyes as the man seethed, and she again worried for the safety of the cat he held.

"In any event," Jan said easily, "it's time to go in. I don't wish to be out here any longer than necessary."

"Spill your fucking guts already, you lying piece of gooseshit," said Jo angrily. "He might not shut his goddamn mouth, but I'll take that to your never unhinging yours."

"The less you know—" said Jan, but Sander jumped in, clearly eager for a last word or twenty.

"Tell the wee cuntcrease, already!" Sander's spittle rained down on them. "You're going in there to get his da's ring so he can pretend he ain't a bastard, so he can pass himself off as something fine and dandy in Dordt and elsewheres. You get the ring, he gets himself graafed, and that's the whole fucking truth from an honest man to a stupid goddamn slut without the sense to use words for what they do. You know what's good for you, you'll swim off with it yourself and cheat the cheater of his loot!"

"That's quite enough, I think," said Jan in the sharp, clipped tone he adopted when he was annoyed.

"I don't know what he said," Jo replied, looking back and forth between them. "What's going on? You're a...what?"

"Better you—"

"No!" Jo stood. "You explain it, *Jan*, or I don't swim. Your choice."

"Remember this," said Jan, but he was looking at Sander. "It's like Sander said. My father was graaf of Oudeland. He fucked my mother, the widow of a local miller. She bore me, and as his wife gave him nothing but daughters, he took an interest in me— tried to play it off, of course, as something other than what it was, but when I grew older my mother told me the truth of it, and when I confronted him, he admitted to being my sire."

"So you really are a rich man," said Jo in wonder. "I'd started thinking you were lying about that, too."

"Not yet," said Jan stiffly. "He was a strange man, I realize now, or I should never have discovered what I did; he never would have done the things he did. He was...touched, my father. Wracked by demons, fight them though he did, and I wonder if that had something to do with it."

"Demons," whispered Sander, his eyes widening as he dropped the cat. She threaded her way around Jo's legs as Jan finally stood as well. It cheered Jo to see that Sander seemed surprised by this admission, but the seriousness of Jan's expression unsettled her. Unlike Sander, who saw spirits in every moonbeam and portent in every bird cry, Jan had never spoken of such things, and it troubled her greatly that he did so here, in a flooded graveyard she would soon be diving into. A strong regret for pushing the issue warred with a gloating pleasure at having finally got him to open up.

"So they say. He had fits where he would lose himself. The priest claimed it was possession, but he was the sort of churchman to look for such things. Often my father would catch a whiff of something strange, something otherworldly, and then he would fall and thrash, sometimes frothing at the mouth. I saw an old dog run over by a cartwheel once, and he looked just like it, shaking and spitting and such. But he always recovered from them, and they were not a common occurrence."

Jo and Sander exchanged worried glances, and she picked up the cat, holding it to her chest. The mist seemed ever thicker, despite a chill breeze that had picked up across the meer. Jan looked out to the rushes where the graaf's house presumably lay buried.

"He did not think highly of women, even his daughters. He wanted a son more than anything, and I was as close as he seemed liable to have, for his wife was getting on in years, and when she did manage to provide him a child, it was invariably a girl, even the stillbirths. So he had me from a young age as a servant, to keep me about, to watch me, and wherever he went, riding or fishing or hunting or even to the cities on business, he had me with him. He was a Hook through and through, and lectured me on politics as well as training me for combat. He also educated me, though I didn't know the queerness of it at the time, for letters.

"He had a plan, you understand—I was a bastard and would receive nothing, much as he might wish it, but if I were a legitimate nephew, then I could inherit his estate instead of whoever married his daughters. It happened that he had a younger brother, who had gone abroad to seek his fortune. This brother had died not long after leaving home, but my father, long-sighted man that he was, concealed this information from all—my mother had birthed me by this time, whereas his wife had only borne him girls, and even then, all those years ago, he plotted to break the world for me. Strange."

There was a look to Jan that Jo had never seen before, an almost doleful grimace. Perhaps this was how he looked when he told the truth. The cat squirmed and Jo let her drop back down.

"I fought for him when war flared up with Brabant, and even went to court with him, and he put everything in place for my ascension following his death. A lawyer in Dordrecht was given the various correspondences between himself and his long-dead brother, letters that he wrote one side of and I the other—if you are familiar with letters you can often spy a difference between one man's style and another's, hence the wisdom in our strategy. These missives were detailed enough to leave no room for doubt as to the legitimacy of the fictitious nephew I would become, but vague enough to avoid falling apart under scrutiny—a younger brother finding fortune, property, and a wife of minor nobility in the wilds of the East is not so unheard of, neither then nor now. The letters I wrote in the name of my deceased uncle made much mention of a son named Jan, a nephew to my father, and how the boy should visit soon, very soon.

"The final touch would be his brother's ring, which bore the Tieselen seal—my family's crest. My father received it with the news of its bearer's death when I was still in swaddling rags—he kept this ring behind a loose hearthstone in his bedchambers, though he showed me its hiding place so I could retrieve it following his death. Then I could escape Oudeland and journey to the lawyer in Dordrecht, who would assist with the rest—I would become Graaf Tieselen of Oudeland."

"And everyone hereabouts wouldn't know you for the servant you was?" said Jo. It seemed an obvious question to her, but Sander stared at her agape, as if she had hit on some unexpected snarl that not even Jan had considered.

"Of course they would," said Jan. "Which was why I was to give myself time to grow a beard before coming forward, and even then be sure to take my father's city house in Dordrecht instead of the family seat in Oudeland. As I said, my father had a long vision, and early on had inserted himself into Dordrecht, though his peers scoffed at his dirtying his hands in what they called peasant business. Which is the only reason we're out here—becoming graaf of flooded fields would do me no good at all, but unlike most of these shortsighted Groote Waard nobles, now property-and-pfennigiless from the flood, I've got a fortune tied up in a Dordt-based wine importation business. It's fallen to my father's wife's family, but if a direct male heir were to emerge now…"

"So the flood came, and cheated you of your rightful place, aye?" asked Jo. It seemed like one of the tales her brother Pieter had told her as they worked Snail Bay so long ago.

"No," said Jan with a twisted smile. "Something worse arrived. That sow of his finally bore him a son, and that was that. He had me kicked out of the house, lest I try to murder the boy. To his credit, though, he gave me a small purse of money. To find my way, he said."

"Would've ratted him out to any that'd listen," said Sander bitterly, and it again occurred to Jo that he might not have heard the entirety of this story before, either. "Would've found a way to fix 'em."

"Even still, he did me better than yours did you, to hear your tales," said Jan, though there was no sting to his voice, only a sort of grim humor. "And who would listen? The word of a bastard is just that. I left Oudeland and went directly to the lawyer who held the fictitious correspondence. I paid him every coin my father had given me to keep those letters safe, even if my father instructed him to burn them, which, it turns out, he did."

"Burned them?" asked Sander. "Then how—"

"No, no," said Jan. "My father ordered him to destroy the letters shortly after my visit, apparently, but Laurent, the lawyer, was honest to his bribe—he told my father they were burned, but kept them safe for me. And here we are."

Jo's chest pounded as she looked at him, the clement brown eyes that matched the hair framing his handsome face, and she decided that even if she were to die in the attempt, she would bring him his ring. Such a strange creature was he, scarcely human, but she realized they were not so different, him and her—he had been hurt by his family, just as she had been done wrong by hers. And he was of noble birth, bastard or no, which explained his aloofness, his airs. Yet for all that, he had a softness, she saw that now, and if he kept it locked up, safe from harm, who could blame him?

Not her, certainly. She stepped closer and gave him a kiss on the cheek, a sudden sorrow coming upon her like a jellyfish carried by a wave. She imagined she would start her moons soon, all these strong, inexplicable pushes of emotion.

"Quit swooning over His Highness and get your scrawny ass in the water," Sander snapped, and she supposed she had made him jealous with her kiss. Good. Meeting Jan's eyes, she blushed.

"Here," said Jan, snapping a rush from beside the crypt and squatting down. He set to sketching the outline of a square, scratching it into the harder muck they had not been able to completely kick from the crypt. He then made a smaller square inside the first, the two figures sharing their bottom lines. "This is the hearth. It's set against the wall of the bedchamber, the back wall. There's only a single fireplace in the room, so you should find it well enough. The loose stone the ring's under is here, on the base at the left side. The stone is free of mortar, unlike the rest."

"Easy," said Jo, but then a thought came to her. "So why haven't you swum down yourself to fetch it?"

"I tried," he said, and Jo thought he might have bristled a bit, like a flexing hedgehog. "When we came out here, Andrei and I. It was too deep, though, too dark. And, Andrei said, too fresh after the flood—silt was stirred up, it was like swimming through a sand dune. I didn't want to give up, however, and almost drowned myself in the process."

"Hard to imagine you being foolish like that," said Jo quietly, shyly. He returned her smile and ignored Sander's snort.

"Well, I was. The water was higher, then, and covered the roof, so I had to swim down and go through a window. The shutters were locked from within, from before the flood, and hadn't rotted enough to come loose, so I had to enter one that was unlatched on the ground floor. The bedchamber is on the second. It was black as old blood down there, and I got turned around in the dark, couldn't find my way out until it was almost too late."

"So now you want me to go down there, blind and all, and get inside and feel around for it?" She hadn't meant for it to sound so hard coming out, and worried he would think her frightened. Which she was, maybe.

"Yes," said Jan, as if it were really that simple. But then, she supposed that for him it was, and so it would be for her. Having shrewdly forgotten her uncomfortable pelisse at Primm's and keeping her wonderful blue cloak folded neatly in her satchel rather than risk dirtying it, she was able to pull off her gown in one easy motion, leaving her naked save for her thin shift. The sensation of fresh air on liberated skin distracting her from her time and place and trial, she looked at the somber meer with new eyes. Dark though it was, and sinister, at least if she were to die here, she would die wet.

"Let's do it, then," she said, suddenly eager to prove herself, to bring up Jan's fortune in half the time it had taken him to try and fail. Neither this meer nor that bastard of river and ocean they had crossed from Rotterdam to Dordrecht had called to her the way her sea always had, the surface here too calm, the water here too sweet, but he had chosen her for this and she wouldn't disappoint. Sander had gone quiet, as had Jan, and looking between them, she supposed she had startled them both with her eagerness. "Why I'm here, aye? Let's have me do my purpose and go back to being a worthless cuntwhore, eh, Uncle?"

"Cuntbitch," Sander corrected, but he looked…she wasn't sure what, almost scared? Sickened? No matter—she pulled her shift over her head, hoping it would make him uncomfortable rather than interested. It seemed to have the intended effect; he turned away, whatever stupid expression he was wearing deepening in its displeasure.

Then a hand was on her bare arse and she jumped, her heart and her guts oozing happily together, the calluses of Jan's fingers scratching her as he cupped the cheek and gave it a light squeeze. Then he was past her, before Sander could notice, she knew. Someone else evidently had, however, the furious-sounding Muscovite shouting from his boat:

"I did not agree to be party in such obscenity, Hollander! Unhand devushka, or I shall abandon you here!"

Mortified and unsure what else to do, Jo spun around and jumped into the water.

She knew better than to dive, considering how shallow the meer was directly around the crypt. Even without a visible mudflat on the side from which she launched, her feet sank in filth almost immediately after hitting the water. She went in near to her waist, the warmth of it making her gasp, and she wriggled out of the mud with the vigor of a nested crab escaping a burning piece of driftwood. The water barely covered her as she slid along the muddy shallows, blackness clouding around her as she frantically strove for deeper water, desperate to escape the cackling laughter of Sander and the angry yelling of the Muscovite. Then she had it, kicking off a stone marker to her side and propelling herself down and under, twisting around and rubbing the tenacious smears of filth from her legs before resurfacing with a gasp.

At first she couldn't see the men, open water steaming before her, and she idled there, letting her embarrassment flow out with the piss she'd been holding all morning. Let the Muscovite chide Jan for his blatant groping, then—the pervert deserved it, touching her up out in the open like that. She certainly didn't want Andrei thinking she'd consent to such behavior; what with his cat, his obvious love for the water, and his constant harassment of Sander, she had warmed to the boatman at once, despite his foreign nature, and she would hate for him to think she was the sort of girl that would let any fellow, even her beloved, paw her naked arse in front of other men. She'd have a word with Jan about his forwardness when all was said and done...

Cocking her ear, it sounded like Sander's sadistic laughter and Andrei's chivalrous outburst had coalesced into a general hallooing after her, and so she swam leisurely toward their voices, keeping to the deeper water and circling the marsh of stone and rush. There they were, all three back in the boat and edging out past the last gravestone. Jan waved from the prow and pointed dead ahead, and she felt the old coals begin to glow as she swam unfettered of muck and shallow, racing a boat rowed by two stout men and quickly taking the lead. She realized they were holding back, which irritated her immensely, but before she could call them on it, she saw the stand of reeds jutting up before her and stopped paddling, bringing her legs underneath her to tread in place while she inspected the floating thicket.

The mist looped around the stalks the way the cat had around her legs, and suddenly the water felt unpleasantly cool instead of cloyingly warm, the gravedirt—for that was what it was, after all—that had caught in her hair bringing a faint earthiness to her nostrils that she had never found in the sea. She must be careful here, she knew, far more careful than she had been before—Jan had told her there were no sharks nor jellyfish here, but as she treaded floodwater she wondered if he could be sure, here where the abyss had called without invitation and then elected to stay.

"And how is the water, my fine bream?" Jan called as Sander and Andrei set their oars and brought the boat to a rocking halt. There was no more current or pull here than there had been in the canals and ponds she had practiced in, and the boat sat in the calm water as if beached on a sandbar.

"Too warm," she said, willing it to be so again. "And it smells."

"Then you had best be quick about your business, yes?"

"Fucking prick," she said. "Stone in the bottom of a her, a what, a hearth, on the upstairs?"

"Yes, at the front of it, on the left. The hearth protrudes from the wall, so feel along the wainscoting until you find a ridge of rougher stones. From there it should dip well in, where the fire goes. I'd hoped to try and go down a chimney but they were both clogged up when I came through, and I can't imagine the situation's improved in the year since. But hopefully the roof will give, and if not Sander's going to help you with a window."

"The devil I will." Jo could hear Sander but couldn't see him from her low vantage, only Jan leaning out over the nose of the looming vessel.

"We've been over this, Sander," said Jan, his lips now straining against his teeth. "And you agreed—"

"You didn't say nothing about swimming in no graveyard."

"The graveyard's back there, not—"

"Not for the love of God, so that leaves the odds of me doing it for the love of you awfully fucking short. Get in yourself, Graaf!"

"Fine," said Jan, casting a dirty look over his shoulder. "Grown man scared of his own shadow. Pathetic."

"But dry," came the response, followed by a chuckle from the Muscovite.

"Bring us closer to the roof, then," said Jan, and following some muttered word from behind him, added, "Just give it one stroke and that'll be that. Jo, climb up on the roof there and see if there's any holes leading in."

She paddled closer to the island, and felt gooseflesh spread all over her back as the change in angle granted her a peek at what lay below. Instead of shallows giving way to land, there was indeed a house suspended in the water, its wall rising straight out of the dim depths. Squinting into the murk, she saw it was a right grand manor at that, with two rows of shuttered windows striping the brick wall and the blur of a wide door at its base, only instead of tile and chimney, or even straw and smokehole, there was a cap of mud and rushes topping the building. It was the most wonderful thing she had ever seen, yet also the spookiest—she half-expected one of the windows to spring open at the push of an occupant, so pristine did the sunken building appear. As she drew nearer, however, she better made out the details of decay and erosion writ on door and wall, shutter and stoop, and its proximity to the flooded graveyard made her wonder what sort of host might dwell there.

Stupid fucking neuker Sander, putting such thoughts in her. Fish and eels were the only tenants in that dark keep, nothing more. As she reached the marshy roof, the house fell from her sight as neatly as if it had been swept away by the flood. Planting her hands in the mud to pull herself out of the water, she found the muck yielded to a hardness beneath, like stepping on a rotten fish at the shore and feeling bone beneath the putrescence. She heard Sander whistle as she hauled herself up, and as she got to her feet she took a handful of mud with her, tightening her fist to pack it as best she could.

Jo twirled and fired. To her horror, the missile whizzed past

Sander and struck the Muscovite in the back of the neck. He barked, and would have lost his oars if they weren't secure in their locks as he threw up his hands in delayed defense. Everything went quiet, with no marsh bird or fish jump to break the hallowed silence, and then Sander howled with laughter, giving Andrei a vicious slap to the back as he winked at Jo.

"Sorry!" Jo cried. "Shit, Andrei, I'm sorry, really!"

The Muscovite had stood, his hands curled into tight fists, but, perhaps realizing it was Jo and not Sander who had hit him, his wrath seemingly left him. He unballed his hands, stretching the fingers.

"Dermo," said Andrei, wiping the mud from his nape. "You are a good aim, devushka."

"I was trying to hit the plaguebitch in front've you," she said. "I swear!"

"Lucky you didn't," said Sander.

"Enough of that," said Jan, but Jo thought his eyes seemed alight with shared mischief. "How firm does it feel?"

She hopped demonstratively, sinking almost to her ankles before the slate or whatever it was stopped her.

"Right, grab the nose and hold her steady," said Jan, and with her help they got the prow of the boat well enough stuck against the lip of the roof. Then Jan slowly extended a foot, and, cautious as a cat examining its reflection in a puddle, patted the ground with his boot several good times before stepping down. The smile on his face as he relaxed and peered around was so genuine, so open, and so, well, *happy*, that it brought the same squirmy feeling to Jo that spying on him and Sander had several nights before. That was just weird, was what it was.

"Shit, Jo, look out!" Sander called. "Something bit you!"

"Huh?" She reflexively high-stepped it backward, trying to see what was around her ankles.

"Here and here," said Sander, touching his chest. "Gnat or mosquito, I'd say—nothing bigger than that."

"What?" She dug her chin into her chest to get a look, and then she got it. The sight of her pebbly nipples jutting from her chest brought a keen and cruel reminder of how exposed she was. She turned her back on the boat and the braying arsehole, Sander clearly not above laughing at his own joke. She would have found her rage and fought him then, surely she would have, but then Jan shouted triumphantly and waved her over to where he stood amongst the reeds on the little island they shared. Following his finger, she saw a small pool of water in the muck, and as he leaned forward beside it, pressing down with one foot, the puddle bubbled a little.

"Ax," he said, and returned to the boat while she squatted down beside the pool, telling herself it was to have a better look and not to shield herself from Sander's further jeering inspection. Reaching into the hat-brim-wide puddle, she could not find its bottom, and dropped to her knees as she stretched farther and farther down until she was up to her elbow in the water. It was colder than the rest of the meer, and darker. Sitting back up, she brushed something sharp on the edge of the hole, an angry red stripe rising on her forearm as Jan returned with an ax.

Neither Sander nor Andrei set foot on the roof, the men content to sit on their rowing boards and share a bottle the Muscovite had produced while Jan expanded the hole with his ax. In addition to all the splashing and squelching, the ax occasionally made clattering and crunching noises, after which he would pause and have her reach in to dislodge whatever scrap of wood or tile he had hacked loose. He had removed his old doublet, the fancy clothes he had worn in Dordrecht left in the care of Primm, and when this did not seem to speed up the work sufficiently, he hoisted his shirt over his head. Jo admired the fine hair on his chest, wondering how soft it must feel, but this only reminded her of how naked she was. If she had known how long it was going to take, she would have put her shift back on, at least. Jan finally stepped back and nodded down.

"See if you can get in, then," he said, and though the pool

looked little bigger than it had when they'd started, the small heap of rotten wood and broken ceramic encouraged her. She sat down in the muck and scooted forward, leading with her legs. Her feet found where the hole opened up, and as she slid into position, Jan came around on the other side of the pool and took her hands, helping steady her. "Ready?"

Of course she wasn't, and couldn't even muster a lie, but he tugged her forward all the same. Her bottom cleared the edge of the roof just as he released her. With nothing to hold her aloft, she fell into blackness, one elbow cracking smartly against a tile and her back scraping on the rim as she went. The water was much murkier here, much colder and much darker, and she surfaced with a cry, Jan standing over her, impossibly tall.

"Just like on the beach," he said, so quiet she could barely hear him. "This is you, Jo. How I'll always think of you, just like here."

"Cunting cold!" she gasped.

"This will be the attic," said Jan. "Your first trial is getting down from there, into the house proper. There are a few trapdoors, so find one of those and pull it up, and then you'll be able to find the bedroom."

As he spoke, another face appeared between the rushes—Sander. He had lost whatever humor mocking her had given him, the same sort of mean expression on his ugly face that her father had worn on many a return from selling purple. He had a coil of rope in his hand that he thrust at Jan like an accusation.

"Tie this around her."

"What?" That Jan was likewise perplexed by this heartened Jo; Jan making her feel stupid was one thing, but Sander making her feel thick was in no way acceptable.

"If she drowns," said Sander, looking down at her as he did. "We'll be able to reel her back in."

"She won't," said Jan with a confidence Jo wished she shared.

"Look, she drowns, we'll bury her back in the mud of that churchyard. Least we can do for her after all she's done, a Christian burial. I don't care to think what'd happen to a soul that was left to float out here instead of put properly in the ground."

Jo didn't, either, and went under at this, spinning down into the frigid ink for what should have been an eternity but instead only lasted a moment before she jabbed her toes through muck and into something hard, painfully jamming them. Pushing the rest of her air out to help her settle on the bottom, she peered all around but had stirred up too much silt to get a proper bearing on where she was. Beyond freezing her bits off in a flooded house on account of a shady man she fancied, of course. Now that she was down, however, she saw that it wasn't so dark, after all—the hole let in enough light that the task would be easy once the bottom settled. Squinting through the gloom, she saw a patch of deeper blackness just beside her, and kicking above it, she saw that it was a narrow crack in the attic floor.

Reaching down and feeling a beam as soft as young cheese beneath her fingernails, Jo pulled herself down through the crevice and found herself in a twilit room, the moldering shades of furniture floating beside her. It was at once beautiful and horrible, like smashing the snails to get at their brilliant guts, and she let herself sink all the way to the bottom, the little light that wound its way down through the stacked holes above casting a gray pallor. Forcing herself to be still and staying down long after she wanted to come up, at last she kicked off the floor and swam for the attic, and from there to the surface—the bottom of the room had a strange feel to it, nowhere near so muddy as above but with plenty of its own gritty sediment.

"—fucking mouth's to blame, so…" Jan trailed off, and she saw Sander's face was the same bright red that his cock had been after Jan had given it a suck. She immediately hated having drawn the parallel and turned back to Jan. He smiled his familiar warm smile, and she cursed herself for having ever doubted him. He never smiled that way at Sander. "How is it down there, then?"

"Simple," she said, surprised to find her teeth chattering. "Going to be easy."

"Good! Wish I could have used the roof last time, as I said— had I known how straightforward it would be to get in this time, I would have come alone and never bothered finding you."

"Oh," said Jo, but ever careful with her heart, Jan added, "But I'm glad I did."

"You're the worst ball-washer of them all," said Sander, not with anger, but something like sadness to his voice. "I might be a killer, yeah, sure, but you...you're wrong inside, love, you're truly fucking twisted. A pig's dick."

"Give us a moment, Jo," said Jan, his eyes never leaving hers. "And for God's sake, be sure to come up often for air; there's no need to push yourself when this hole's right here."

Then she was back down, something awful as the rich man's mutton twisting in her stomach. Part of her delighted to see Sander resigning himself to this, to know that it was all out there and Jan was taking care of it and there was a reason why Sander had always been so nasty to her, to know it was something as simple as jealousy. Still, it was a lousy time for it all to float up, with her down here recapturing Jan's glory and Sander not having any place to run off to with his broken heart. She wondered what it would be like to be trapped out here in the swamp-sea knowing Jan was going to quit her when they got back to Dordrecht and settle down with Sander...but then that was hardly her fault. It wasn't like she'd stolen Jan away, and even if she had, well, Sander wasn't right in the head, and a total fucking arsehole besides.

In her reverie she almost clipped her tits on the attic hole, but caught herself and flitted down into the room she had found, dodging lumpy, indiscernible obstructions and coming almost at once to a wall. It was alternately slimy and rough, and, orienting herself as best she could, she set to moving along the brick, feeling for the fireplace. This was going to be easy.

IV.

Once Jo got the knack of passing through the attic and reaching the bottom of the room beneath it without stirring up all the filth, her exploration went quickly indeed. She determined on her third dive that there definitely wasn't a fireplace in the chamber, but she waited until surfacing from her sixth to tell Jan that. Part of it was reluctance to pass through the black doorway that led to the rest of the house, but part of it was also curiosity about this first room—now that her eyes had adjusted to the murk, she could properly explore. A chair had worn down most of its back scraping against the ceiling, and other, less identifiable scraps of wood drifted around her as she idly investigated the chamber— one hillock on the floor revealed itself to be the remains of a bed, and another a heap of mud-infused cloth that disintegrated between her fingers when she prodded it. It should have been great fun, but the dark rectangle of the room's only doorway seemed to watch her like an unblinking eye, and if she had her back to it for more than a few moments, she felt a stupid panic rise in her that would respond to neither wisdom nor begging, only a glance over her shoulder to verify that nothing terrible was lurking there.

"No fireplace," she finally panted, bracing her elbows on the muddy rooftop to give herself a rest before further exploration.

"Of course not," said Jan. Sander had buggered off somewhere, and good riddance. "You're in the middle of the house, one of the daughters' rooms. His will be at the end of the hall, that way."

Following his finger, Jo scowled. "If you knew it weren't his place, why'd you let me poke 'round so long? And why not dig through over there, in his room?"

"Just getting you used to the task," said Jan, offering her the coil of rope. "Clearing a new hole might cave in the whole roof, and besides, you'd still need to find a way out of the attic—this one will do just fine."

"You really think I'm going to drown?" she asked, not taking the rope. "I won't tie it on, Jan—I'm coming back up, and with your ring."

"Do or don't tie it, but take it with you, and unspool it as you go—it's to find your way back if you get turned 'round in the dark. Here," he said, picking up the ax and burying its head in the muck beside her, causing the lip of wood she rested on to vibrate. Tugging the haft, and confirming it was well embedded, he tied the end of the rope around it and dropped the rest of the coil into the water beside her. "Sensible, yes? It will be darker in the rest of the house."

"All right," she said, suddenly aware that she hadn't checked the doorway in several minutes and from her current vantage couldn't see shit. There could be a whole mob of the river demons Andrei had been talking about gathering beneath her, waiting to pull her down and—

"Are you?" She blinked at his question, then nodded quickly. "Right, then, back down. Remember, it's the end of the hall, that way."

In the short span it took her to reach the doorway she was utterly mixed up and had no idea which direction he had indicated, but that was all right. She was in no hurry, the stupid rope being a right pain in the arse to uncoil as she swam, and fish had balls if the water on the other side of the doorway wasn't even colder and darker. She was dimly aware that a tunnel stretched in either direction, but beyond that could make out nothing. Total bullshit, as Sander would say. She set off down the hall, paddling slowly to feed the rope out evenly, and in only a few strokes the duskiness of the first room was replaced with impenetrable blackness. Her lungs began to burn as she slowly advanced, but she still hadn't bumped into the end of the passage. Pivoting in the water, she dropped the coil and went back the way she'd come—it was much easier to return, for a weak light spilled out of the doorway, and besides, Jo always swam faster with dark water at her back.

She stayed at the hole with Jan for a few dozen breaths, and when her breathing was again easy, she went back down to the corridor, feeling along the rope until she found the coil and scooped it up. Goddamn rope. She didn't realize she had entered another room until she made out a faint line of light to her left, and swimming for it, she discovered the springy wood of closed shutters. She tried to push them open but they wouldn't give, and when she tried pulling, the slat she gripped came off in her hand, letting another meager slash of twilight enter the room. Then she needed air again, but before she went, she wedged what remained of the coil into the gap she had made in the shutters. Swimming back down the hall, she realized from the stabbing in her chest that she had taken too long—she had to be careful about that down here, where it wasn't as simple as kicking up to break the surface.

This time Jan wasn't at the hole. Air, and then back down. She swam much quicker now that she didn't have the rope to fuck about with, and promptly bashed her shoulder into the doorframe at the end of the hall. She felt the bubbles of her mute cry tickle her cheek as she floated in place, clutching herself in the darkness, and then she pushed the soreness away and propelled herself into the room. It was still black, the smear of light the broken shutter slat admitted only making the rest of the room darker for it. She had a thought, and yanked at another slat until it came away. Then it was back along the passage to the hole, her entire left side throbbing from where she had rammed her shoulder.

Jan still wasn't back, and she spent the next three dives working at the window shutters until she had torn open a big enough gap to squeeze through. Then she spent another breath making it even wider, just in case. With the exception of a patch of silt-strained half-light around the window, the room was still dark as a moonless night, but instead of returning to the hall Jo squirmed through the window, out into the meer. She surfaced with a whoop beside the roof-island.

"Dermo!" Andrei cried, and she saw he and Sander stood in the boat that now floated halfway between the graveyard and the house. Sander held a long pole and Andrei a net, and peering harder at them, she realized they were poised to launch their implements at her.

"Get yourself spitted, you stupid slut!" shouted Sander.

"What are you doing?" she called, splashing around and grabbing a handful of rushes to moor herself. On this end of the house the marshy roof sloped down into the water rather than abruptly dropping off, and she hauled herself backward up the muddy incline, feet still dangling in the water.

"That sturgeon's around here," said Jan from over her shoulder, and she saw him gingerly picking his way toward her over the muddy flat. "They went out to try to catch him."

"Sturgeon big?" She eyed Sander's pike. They'd been talking about the fish that bumped the boat when they first came to the cemetery, but she hadn't seen it herself.

"Bigger than you," Jan said but, seeing her expression, added, "they're not like sharks or anything, they're bottom dwellers."

"Not sturgeon!" Andrei called excitedly. "Catfish! Saw his hairs, big, big catfish!"

"What's that?" Jan shouted back. "Catfish?"

Jo pulled her feet out of the water in what she hoped was a casual fashion.

"Rivers back home, have big fish with hairs. No, not hairs— *mustaches*. Big fish with mustaches."

"If you're fucking with me…" she heard Sander grumble from the boat, his head still directed down at the water.

"What do they eat?" Jo called.

"Muddy stuff," answered the Muscovite. "Worms, bugs, river shit."

"Bottom dwellers," said Jan knowingly. "I was worried you'd get turned around down there, but this is it. See?"

He scraped the moss from a small hillock she had scarcely noticed beside her and revealed black brick underneath the boggy vegetation. A pile of brick meant exactly fuck-all to her, other than—oh. A chimney. And a chimney meant a fireplace. Then his hand was warm on the back of her neck, the damp knuckles kneading her the way she'd kneaded dough on the rare occasions her father brought home flour. She wondered if Jan would have her make bread for him or if they'd have a servant for that, if they'd live in a house half as big as this one. A stupid thing to think, but she closed her eyes and thought it all the same, enjoying the feel of his fingers on her. She'd grown up so much in so little time.

"Bring it up, then," he said, nearly panting the words. She looked at him and saw he had a knife in his hand. Her heart quickened, imagining how it would feel if he were to jab her in the back with it—probably no worse than being fucked up the arse, as seemed to be his preference. She'd tried to get a finger back there after watching him go at it with Sander and the result had been less than delightful—it wasn't the first time she'd been given cause to think her darling might be every bit as gnarled inside as her, just in different ways. "This ought to help get the stone out, but don't lose it."

It was the same thick, dull sort of blade she had used to pry open flat oysters for her father. Before she could look up from the knife, he had pecked her on the cheek, then stood upright, popping his knuckles. She pushed herself off the edge of the roof and sank quickly, before she could hear any taunts from the boat.

What a life she was having, she thought as the cool tenebrosity thickened around her; it was like sinking into an old soup. There was the window, but just before she ducked inside it, a light shadow at the end of the wall caught her eye amidst all those deeper ones. She paused, trying to make out the blurry silhouette, and then it coalesced, like a shell taking shape as a wave washed it clean. It was a huge fish rounding the corner of the house, and she felt a moment of profound, ancient fear at it, for in the sea few things that large are good to meet without the bottom of a boat between you. Then she remembered that it must be the sturgeon or catfish or what, and that it meant her no harm. She momentarily thought to surface and tell Sander and Andrei, but then remembered what a cuntbitch Sander was. She waved at the fish, which was indeed as big as her, then pulled herself through the window.

Feeling her way along the wall, she found the uneven stones of the fireplace almost at once and clutched them tight, pulling herself down to the bottom. There was a thick film covering the floorboards and the base of the hearth, the layer of slime making it difficult to tell where one stone ended and another began, but before she had even exhaled, she felt one wiggle a little as she pressed on it, like a loose tooth. The stone was maybe a hand's width up from the floor, and poking around with the tip of the knife, she finally found the seam and slid the blade into place. She began to rock it free when it occurred to her she must go slow, lest the ring fall out with the hearthstone—blind and deaf as she was, she would neither see it drop nor hear it clink on the ground, and so taking her time to loose the stone seemed wise.

Leaving the knife embedded, she swam back to the hole, but just before she slipped through the window, it seemed to wink at her. The shadow of the boat falling across it, she thought, but hesitated at the opening, hands on the soft sill, legs floating ceiling-ward behind her, eyes squinting into the gray water. Nothing but the meer.

Digging her nails into the wood to pull herself out of the

house, she felt a draft billow through the window, and again she paused, the breeze of cooler water giving her chills. That was just queer, but, as it shook out, not as queer as what happened next: a massive horror reared up before the window, conjuring another string of bubbles from her mouth as she pushed back from the sill, limbs flailing in the thick gloom. In the act of revealing itself it blotted out the light, but before it was swallowed by its own shadow she made out a bulging eye as big as her fist, and a mouth as wide as she was, edged by waving, fleshy fronds. It seemed to be snuffling at the window like a dog after a turd, and bottom dweller or no, Jo launched herself out of the room and down the black hallway, chest aflame, coming up with a cough at the original hole in the middle of the island.

"I'm over here!" she cried as she tried to scramble out of the water, but her bruising shoulder and shaking fingers thwarted her attempts and she slipped back down, splashing about in the narrow opening. "Jan!"

He came dancing over the mud, always watching his feet, and then he had her and hoisted her up, scratching her thigh this time on the lip of the hole. Rather than holding her, as she keenly hoped he would, he set her down in the mud and squatted down beside her. She tried to touch his arm and he pulled back a little, looking at her curiously. She supposed he was trying to keep his clothes dry, the goddamn son of a bitch.

"Fucking arsehole!"

"What? What's happened?"

"That fish," she said, pulling her knees up to her chest. Now she felt silly, and tried to laugh it off despite the fear still thundering through her sore limbs. "That fucking cow of a fish wouldn't let me out the window."

"Ah, I thought I saw him." He didn't turn enough to keep her ear from ringing as he shouted, "Oi, Sander! He's over there! Where Jo came up before!"

"I found it," she said, panting, but seeing the excitement on his face, hastened to add, "the stone, like. Got the knife in the crack, but wanted to be full of air when I worked it out."

"Clever," he said appreciatively, then bellowed again, "over there, I said! Quick now!"

"I'll be getting it for you, then," she said, getting up and eyeing the hole with something less than eagerness. She looked hopefully to Jan, wondering if he would steal a kiss or maybe cop another feel now that they were somewhat shielded by the reeds, but his eyes were on the boat drifting back toward the roof.

"Use this one until they've got the beggar or run him off," said Jan. "And do be—"

But she didn't hear what she should be, for she jumped back into the room, this time neatly clearing the edges of both roof and attic hole, then shooting off down the hall. In a breath's time she would be back up with the ring, she promised herself, and then she'd have a kiss or cast his treasure back into the deep. She stopped stroking as the pale gloom of the bedchamber appeared through the darkness and she let herself drift, arms extended to feel before her and thus avoid bashing into the wall or doorway again.

Just as she did, her right hand connected with something hard, and though it stung her palm a bit, she smiled at the sensibility that had spared her another battered shoulder or elbow. Whatever it was gave under her momentum, and to her surprise more wan light broke from the side of the hall. She dipped around to inspect the new window, only to realize she had inadvertently shoved ajar a door leading off of the hallway. She leaned against the dark wood, churning the water with her legs to propel herself, and rather than swinging open, it simply fell forward, taking part of the disintegrating frame with it. The light on the other side was dim, but compared to the murk of the initial room and the near blackness of the bedchamber it was positively brilliant.

The door she had knocked loose fell with the strange slowness that water imbues things that ought to tumble quickly, finally landing on a staircase leading to the ground floor. As she watched, it slid down the steps and bumped to a stop where the stair met the far wall. Swimming down after it, she saw that while the stair followed the wall of the house on her left, to the right it was open, with only a skeletal banister fencing her off from what had to be the kitchen—that flanged lump in one corner must be a hearth like the one in Primm's shop, only much larger, and there was a long table that shone white as bone when the rest of the place was all browns, grays, and blackish-blues. This room must be as wide as the whole house, for open windows on either end of the kitchen let in moon-pale illumination.

Then Jo saw the cook, and raced the bubbles of her yelp back up the stairs, cursing herself for not just retrieving the ring and getting out of this doomed place. The woman, for somehow she was sure it had been a woman, was crumpled in a corner, an edge of rusty shadow in one wasted hand, a bowl of black lumps before her, and a barrel to her side. Just a pile of old bones, aye, but Jo had only seen a few corpses in her day and none of them were happy memories—her fever-wasted mother when Jo was but a child, the tide-bloated and eel-gnawed fisherboy Aernt washed ashore after a storm, and, well, that was all up until this anonymous dead person. There had been nothing there but a black shape wreathed in tendrils of corruption that swayed like the eelgrass that grew in the shallows of Snail Bay, but now that she was at the surface Jo was sure she had seen a smiling skull, empty eyes watching her.

Shit.

"What is it?" said Jan as she spluttered on the edge of the hole.

"What?" she gasped. "What?"

"Was it the fish?"

"What? No, no," Jo shook her head, clinging to the roof and forcing herself to stay in the water—if she got out now, she'd never go back in. This stupid goddamn house… "Some old bones is all, gave me a fright."

"In his room?" Jan asked quietly, something strange to his expression. "He…"

"Nay, in the, I guess the kitchen? Down the stairs, next to the room?"

"Why did you go down there?" he asked, and though his tone was easy as ever, she felt a surge of guilt at disappointing him.

"I got…the door, it fell. I got turned 'round, was all. Saw someone down there."

"Probably just your eye fooling you, Jo, nobody—"

"I saw her! I'm not like Sander, I see what I see and know it when I do, God's wounds. Now I'm to get your ring, and leave her where I seen her."

Down she went before he could doubt her further, and she forced herself to enter the black passage just as quickly as she had before discovering what lay beneath it. It was much easier to navigate now with the stairwell letting in a little light, and she kept her eyes straight ahead as she kicked past it and entered the bedchamber. It was still like the bottom of a well in here, with the window and now the doorway letting in halos that did fuck-all for her against the rear wall where the fireplace lay. Crossing the room, she became tangled in wet webbing that almost made her die of terror before realizing in the doorway's trickle of light that she was caught up in old blankets drifting over the large, decaying bed. Freeing herself, she kicked into the deeper dark, resolving to get the ring this time or drown down here.

When she couldn't get the stone loose, she considered the window, but lest the fish still be lurking, she went back down the hall and up through the hole. Jan didn't say anything and neither did she, and then she was back at the hearth.

Come on, cuntbitch, she thought, and then she had it, pulling the knife out and letting it sink to the bottom as she got one hand around the small stone and basketed the fingers of her other beneath it. The block came easily but still she took it slow, and then it was free. Nothing dropped into her palm, and still clutching the little hearthstone in her other hand, she gingerly slid her fingers into the gap.

There was something there, something softer than a ring, and larger. Dropping the stone, she now cupped that hand beneath the recess as she withdrew the thin, square object tucked back in there. It felt like lean leather, but squeezing it all over, she detected no hardness in its center, no circle of metal to make her grin in the dark. When it was out and again nothing dropped into her hand, she shoved her fingers back into the gap, desperately now, but nothing met her touch but smooth rock. Christ's crown...

Pinching the square tightly in one hand, she slowly patted the slick floor in front of her, her heartbeat picking up like a fast-building squall. It had to be here, it had to be. Before she real-ized it, bright flashes of light were popping all around her, and then she was drowning. There was no time to use the hall, and she clumsily made for the gap in the window. Tearing herself through it, swimming up, up, up, with the soft square crushed in one fist, her head and chest angrily pulsing, she surfaced with a gasp that was even more painful than the choking had been. Her stomach shuddered as she slammed herself against the muddy bank of the roof, pulling herself up even as the tears came and the sobs cheated her of the air she had freely won.

Jan was by her side, then, cooing to her, but all she could hear was the pounding of her heart, the crashing of the sea inside her skull. Miserably, she offered him her closed fist and, a look of rapture on his face, he took it in both hands. She sobbed louder, and he tried to pry her fingers apart, but she wouldn't give it up, wouldn't let him see that she had failed him, wouldn't—

"Jo," he murmured, and she let him have it, falling away as he felt it, took it, his delight turning to confusion, and she had half a mind to drown herself. The best she could manage was to fall back in the muck, panting and weeping as he examined the square. He unfolded it carefully, and nothing fell out of it because nothing had ever been inside it.

"Shit," he said quietly, sweetly, as if the rectangle of vellum were a small, frightened animal he was trying to calm. He flipped it away and it landed beside Jo. Something had been written on it, once, but even an illiterate of her caliber surmised that the smear of old ink was illegible. He stared down at the mud, his face as unreadable as the vellum.

"It wasn't there," she finally croaked when she was able to sit up and speak without fear of vomiting. "I swear. I looked. I felt. I was so careful, Jan!"

"You got it!" Sander called from the boat. Jo saw that he and Andrei were floating nearby, pike and net held lazily underarm as they watched the pathetic sight on the shore. Jo hated Sander so much she could taste it, a burning bile in the back of her throat.

"No, it's a letter," said Jan. He was still looking at the mud between his boots, his voice too low to be addressing anyone but himself. "To me. From my father. He must have thought I'd come back, sneak in, and try to steal it. So he left me that, to taunt me. Or maybe apologize. Something."

"What?!" shouted Sander, much louder than he needed to. Probably to make a point or something. Jan ignored him.

"How do you know?" she asked, staring at the ruined sheaf.

"Because I'm not a complete cretin," he said tiredly, as though he had been the one to near-drown himself down there. "What else could it be?"

"Oh," she rubbed her wrinkly hands together, trying to bring the feeling back to them. At least she was done with—

"Back down," he said, a faint smile drifting up the creases of his face like smoke looking for a chink in a ceiling. "If there's someone in the kitchen, who knows. Maybe."

"What? What am I—"

"You go back down and search the body. His hands. The floor around him. There's no way of telling where he hid his brother's ring, but he rarely took his own off."

"She hasn't got it, then," Sander told the Muscovite, no doubt straining his voice to ensure Jo heard him. The shitbird. "We'll land this fish 'fore she brings it up!"

Jo ignored him, trying to hook Jan's eyes on hers. "It's not him. The kitchen, it's a woman."

"And how do you know that?" said Jan, finally meeting her gaze and spooking hers in the process. "No, it doesn't matter. Search him, her, it, just go. And if it isn't him, search every other room to see if he's down there."

"It's too dark," she said. "How am I to see?"

"You saw the one in the kitchen well enough." He smiled coldly, not attempting to blunt the sharpness of his tone. "And you found the hearth, so if he's here, I trust you'll find him. Now, go."

So go she went, goddamn his eyes, diving right off the roof without a care for whether the fish was still down there or if Sander speared her or she drowned for real this time. The plunge carried her past the second-story window, deeper into the meer, and then she curled through an open kitchen window and almost rammed into the seated corpse. She kicked backward, stirring up the muck that covered the old stone floor. Her toes cut through the thick sludge as she righted herself, floating in front of the woman, for woman she had to be—she was all black and bone, and her clothes had dissolved to mist-thin shreds, but what man had ever sat so hunched and miserable, had found himself so busy with work he could not quit it even to avoid his death? It was strange and terrible to see her thus frozen, as if the house had filled in an instant but the weight of her responsibility had kept her stuck to the floor down these many cold days and colder nights.

How *had* this come to pass, she wondered, what sort of flood took this poor bitch so unawares that she didn't even drop her peeling knife, and yet hadn't cast her about in its torrent? She should have been dashed against the walls, blown out the window, tangled in the banister, not left to sit quietly in her corner. It was a queer thing, and made Jo icy and ill to think of it.

Quickly then, woman or no, Jo went for the hands, squinting for a gleam of color, and when that failed, extending her own fingers to stroke the blurry digits that lay arrested before her, bones woven together around the rusty knife like a sparrow's nest upon a blackthorn branch. Nothing but pale twigs that felt softer than they should have, and with a sandiness to them that made Jo recoil as if her hand had been stung by a switch.

That was that, then, but as she turned back to the window she had swum through, something shiny snared her attention. It was a golden bar above her, where the hazy wall opposite the stair met the distant ceiling, and though her chest was beginning to tighten, she swam quickly to it. Another door, she realized, but there was light on the other side of it, not the dismal gloom of this sunken place but real, blazing light, and she let her fingers pass through the crack of brilliance shining through. The light seemed to skip over her fingertips and she smiled in the dimness. She must be drowning again, but before she fled for the surface she wedged her fingernails into the spongy seam, hooking the top of the door and kicking backward off the wall.

The door didn't budge, but a splinter drove up into the bed of her pinky nail, and her gasp turned into a painful choking as a dark ribbon began to unspool from her fingertip, winding around her in the water. Shit, she really was fucking drowning. Fighting the jagged ache in her stomach and chest and the stinging in her finger and the ever-thickening water, she made for the window. A familiar, bulky silhouette passed before it, but she kicked ever harder, having more important things to worry about than some goddamn mud-munching fish.

Just as she passed through the portal, however, there was a burst of light from behind her, and even as she was planting her foot against the sill and launching herself up, up, up, she clearly saw her shadow cast out upon the muddy floor of the meer. The door had opened, she knew, and as soon as she had another breath she would see what lay beyond it, in the light.

V.

Jolanda had been down too long, and Jan sighed with frustration. He had as good as held her under himself, letting her dive again after she had surfaced with a bloody finger and a wild, dangerous smile that looked far too much like those Sander wore. Jan had initially protested her going back in so soon, before she had even caught her breath, but she had told him she was sure that the ring was at hand, and so he had let her go.

Now she was bobbing against a ceiling, mouth frozen open, bulging eyes staring at nothing. Or maybe she had tried to force her way through a new window and become stuck in a gap between slats, fingernails peeled back from clawing at the wood, knees black from banging at the frame. What a horrible way to die.

Only now did it occur to Jan that he hadn't reminded her to retrieve the rope and play it out as she had before, and he gave another long sigh as he took off the shirt he had only recently put back on after hewing open the roof. First would be to find the window she used to enter and exit the bedchamber, which would take him to the rope, and then he would use it as she should have as he went from room to room and—

She gasped, the splash of her surfacing somehow waiting for her to take in the air she must so desperately have needed before crashing all about her. She was close enough that he could have jumped out and landed on her, had he been of a mind. Her back was to him, and her whirling arms immediately began to carry her away from the roof, toward the graveyard. The boat was right there beside her, but she seemed blind to it, deaf to Sander's laughter as she passed the vessel, and then the big man's cackling lurched into a shout as the boat pitched to the side. Sander fell into the bed of the violently rocking craft, and the Muscovite, who deftly kept his feet, gave a cry as he launched a spear. Jan realized what must be happening even as he backed up enough to get a good leap. That goddamn fish wasn't such a bottom dweller after all, and as Jan jumped for the boat, he saw its black shadow in front of the vessel, cutting along after the girl. The behemoth was longer than Sander was tall.

Jan fell short of the boat and plunged into the water, but as soon as he broke the surface, Sander snatched the bare-chested man by the wrist and hoisted him up. It was like riding a pendulum, the boat nearly tipping every few seconds as it dipped from side to side, and then Jan was dropped into the bed of the boat and Sander fell atop him. Jan lay perfectly still lest they capsize, and Sander loomed above him, a look that was somewhere between pleasure and fury on his bearded face. As they pitched from side to side without sign of slowing, Jan felt with sudden, dreadful certainty that something was very wrong with Sander, that this was not the man he had shared so much with over the years—it was as if Sander were smoother, cleaner, clearer of eye even here in the midst of justifiable panic, and Jan's heart jumped in his chest. This wasn't Sander—this was a stranger.

"They fuckin sent it!" Sander hissed. "Some kind of hell fish, sent up to thwart us!"

Jan relaxed at this. Same old Sander. "Off me, but careful about it! Get us after it, man!"

Sander slithered backward and was on one of the benches before Jan had even sat up, the Muscovite so excited he had lapsed into his native tongue, babbling and pointing as he dropped onto the other rowing bench. The boat had been facing the roof, but together they brought it around fast, and then the vessel leapt forward like an otter after a bream. There was Jo, halfway to the rush-guarded border of the cemetery shallows, but where—

—The fish was following her but was closer to the boat than the girl, and Jan supposed his own fall into the water must have caused it to double back and investigate before resuming the chase.

"You said it ate mud and worms and shit!" Jan snarled, squinting to get a better look at the fish. It was a true monster, all right. "What's it doing after her, then?"

"Sometimes the big ones have rats in the belly," Andrei said, panting. It was hard to tell from his tone if he was gleeful or horrified. Jan dared not take his eyes off the fish and the girl. "Da, they push the mud for dinner, but big ones also have rats. Ducks, even."

"She look like a ball-washing bird to you!?" Sander shouted. *He* was decidedly gleeful.

"Pushing mud for dinner in, in … graven yard? Da, pushing mud for dinner in graven yard, he finds more than worms. He finds dead men! Maybe he has grown a taste for us after this dinner, da?"

The fish was right on top of her—she was an instant away from being bit. Shaking the water from his hair and eyes, Jan looked behind him for a pike but saw something better—the Muscovite's cat was just behind him, taking advantage of the chaos to creep forward and steal from the small net Andrei had been casting before the Leviathan arose. The net had trapped a few bream that now flopped about, the tabby cautiously slapping at one as though the fish were hot and might burn her paw. Jan had her by the scruff in an instant and, ignoring the claws kicking at his forearm, he spun around and hurled her.

The cat tumbled through the air, a horrible mewling instantly drowned out by the Muscovite's frantic cry, and then she slapped into the water. The fish had gotten too far ahead for Jan to see whether it took the bait or continued after the girl, but Jolanda was still above water, which—

—Jan was on the floor of the boat, blood burning his eyes. If he hadn't been squatting when he'd thrown the cat, he would have gone in, maybe drowned, but instead he'd simply slumped down. He had pissed himself, he realized, his legs wetter and warmer and—

—Christ's wounds. Sander had nearly decapitated Andrei, the fallen Muscovite's twitching body taking up the bulk of the craft between Jan and the rowers' bench, where the mad bastard had resumed his seat. Sander worked his oars furiously, his face nearly as red as the blood soaking Jan and everything else in the bottom of the boat as he braced himself and strained his arms. They had slowed, reeling drunkenly over the meer instead of sliding neatly across it, but they were still moving forward. Only a few dark cables and a palm's worth of skin connected Andrei's shoulders to the head that lay heavily on Jan's foot. He kicked it off, trying to sit up straighter, but then the boat careened to the side, burning wet garbage forcing its way up and out of his throat, the hot sick bringing with it the worst headache of his life. Still, he was better off than the man he was puking on.

"Get the fuck up," Sander groaned, his tone the same as when he was being speared on Jan's cock. "Couldn't've done much. Weak cunt."

"Ugh," said Jan. He spit, only to have the slimy rope swing back under his jaw and stick in his chest hair.

"Fuckin rublehead. Lost it. Oar. Dropped you with it. I dropped him."

"Jolanda," Jan managed, bracing an arm on the side of the boat and pulling himself farther upright. "She—"

—Screamed, somewhere close. It might have been his name. Jan squinted into the returned mist, the tombstones and rushes waiting just ahead to greet them. Sander grimaced as the oars dragged through the water as though it was honey, pudding, old blood, his breath wheezing, his hands bloody, and Jan picked up the sticky red sword Sander had dropped beside the dead Muscovite. Fucking bottom dwellers.

VI.

The rushes cut her arms, but Jo didn't feel them as she squirmed through the muck of the graveyard, trying with all her might to keep from retching. Breathing was like drinking boiling dye, the heat of each inhalation striking her like a father's fist to the belly, but to give in now, to let it all spill out here, that would be worse than never having found it, worse than never making it to dry land, to safety. Except it wasn't dry, and as something whipped her calf hard enough to draw her notice along with a stripe of blood, she realized she wasn't safe.

What she had hoped was an island in the cemetery was nothing more than a small patch of mud and reeds that barely broke the surface, and that fucking fish had followed her up onto it, beaching itself in the mire and wriggling forward in monstrous parody of how she had gained the marshy prominence. The meaty whisker that had struck her leg protruded just above its yawning, fat-lipped mouth, and seeing it in the light of day, she wondered how she had evaded it as long as she did, the size of the thing unbelievable. She kicked its lip, pushing herself forward in the mud as it eagerly squirmed after her, cutting itself a channel in the muck as Jo slid back into deeper water, the bar of sediment crossed as quickly as it had been gained.

The mud she'd acquired bled off her, clouding the water as she swam, but before the swirling brown sludge obscured the bottom, she saw there were stones beneath her, and then more of them were rising up beside her. These were just little markers, smaller than she was. Nothing to afford sanctuary, nothing to buy her even a moment to catch her breath. A great splashing came from behind and she knew it had freed itself from the mud-flat, that it was back in the water proper, that it was moments away from having her in its belly. She swam harder, too hard, blind from tears and mud and exhaustion, not even trying to breathe anymore as she hauled herself through sludge and water with equal ferocity.

Then her forearm smashed into stone, the pain of it forcing a gasp, and she floundered as the fire in her lungs was smothered out by the splinters of ice shivering their way through her arm. She would have gone under if there had been anywhere to go, but she had nearly beached herself again, the water barely up to her waist. Filth running down her cheeks, she looked back toward the monster and there it was, barreling down a canal between the stones and rushes, its whipping barbels churning the surface before it. The crypt, she realized, her numb mind finally absorbing where she was; she had swum into the side of the crypt. Its roof was right there, close enough to touch, but as she deliriously reached up to grasp it, the bog seemed to pull her back down—as soon as she had set her feet on the bottom, the mud had begun to swallow her.

The fish hit her, and hard, water splashing, those sharp whiskers scraping her raised arm, her bare breast, her side; it fucking had her, the weight of it knocking her back. She gave up, falling against the crypt with a final desperate cry. It had her.

Except it didn't. Jan had jumped between them, she saw, jumped into the water to save her. It had been him half-landing on her, not the fish, but even as she saw him, the monster struck. Jan's body was suddenly thrashing between her and the fish, the brown water flaring red all around them, and she sank farther into the mud, gibbering at the sight of her beloved taken by a seabeast out of legend or nightmare.

And take him it did, the catfish suddenly twisting away and shoving itself back into deeper water, a broken arm ending in a limp-wristed hand cutting the surface like a pennant before the fish dove and vanished, taking him down into the dark.

Jo let the swamp pull her down after him, the water lapping at her throat, and she sobbed, choking on the air as if it were smoke, as if it were brine. Then something else was on her, something crawling through her hair and over her shoulder, and she retreated deeper into the muck, unwilling to let it have her, not ready to—

"—fuck's wrong with you, get up 'fore it comes back," said Sander, his fingers like hooks digging into her armpit. It was not the sight of him hanging his upper body off the crypt to pull her up that brought her around, however—it was the figure holding Sander's belt to keep the bigger man from falling in. Jo's cries turned into ragged laughter to see Jan standing above her, his legs bloodied from his encounter with the fish but seemingly intact, whole, safe. Alive. She gave herself to Sander then—much as she wanted to use him as a scaffolding and scramble up to Jan, she was too fucking tuckered.

Jan helped Sander squirm back onto the roof with Jo in his arms, and there they lay for a time, Sander and Jo panting side by side as Jan stood over them, grinning. Sander was soaked in blood as well, and she wondered how they had conquered the fish after it dove with Jan, but she was still having trouble breathing, so the questions would wait. Besides, she had something to say first.

"Got it," she finally managed, and as she did, Jan sank down beside her, settling on his knees and drawing her up, holding her against his stomach. Sander scrambled away from them, his satisfied expression shriveling and darkening like old sea grass tossed onto coals. Jan's bare belly was warm against Jo's cheek, and she let the tears come faster as he took her hands in his. "Got it."

He was feeling her fingers, she realized, which was a disappointment, albeit an understandable one. She smiled to herself, nuzzling the nest of hair on his stomach. He would be so proud of her. His voice broke as he said, "You dropped it, Jo."

"No," she said, unable to keep the smirk off her face as she raised her head to meet his gaze. "I haven't. Just have to wait a day or two."

"What?" He almost looked angry. "What are you—"

Jo swallowed loudly, and pulling a hand away from him, touched it to her stomach as she curled up tighter against him, the stone beneath her no longer so sharp, no longer so cold. Her other arm began to sing its agony again, but she ignored it, closing her eyes and pressing herself harder and harder against him, trying to sink into his very guts as he murmured, "Clever. So clever. You swallowed it when you saw the fish?"

"Aye. It came in a window…" she said, refusing to remember what came before it, refusing to see what had so transfixed her down there. She had thought she was drowning, and dreaming as she went, but here she was, and so the long yellow table, the dead people sitting at it, the eels, all that—

—She bit down as something pushed into her mouth, trying to wriggle into her belly, a fucking eel, it—

—Jan slapped her across the cheek and she relaxed her jaw, easing her teeth off his fingers as she looked up at him, confused, afraid. He smiled, working the digits farther back, making her gag. "We can't wait, Jo. We can't. Now, don't you bite, you be a good girl and—"

—She gagged again, her eyes watering, trying so hard not to bite him as he worked the back of her throat over and over again, Sander saying something, Jan saying something back, and then she was sick all over him, trying to stop herself and trying to give in all at once. His fingers were out and he let her squirm away from him. She was crying then, not for relief that he was alive, that they were alive, but crying at her own folly, mooning over the first man who seemed to take an interest. The only interest he'd ever had was in his stupid ring, the ring she had taken from a dead man's hand. Christ's crown, she'd taken it off a putrid finger and gobbled it up like a sloe berry, and the thought made her gag again, but nothing more came up.

"Ha!" Jan cried. "Ha!"

Wiping a cold, wet wrist over her eyes, she saw Jan hold up the small band. Threads of clear nastiness dangled from it, but he seemed not to notice, trying it first on one finger and then on another until settling on the middle digit of his left hand. The gold sparkled, and she realized the sun must be shining somewhere out there beyond the mist, marveling that it was not midnight, not black as the deep up here. It had seemed an eternity since they arrived, since she had first dived down, but looking at the puddle of puke forming a moat around Jan's knees, she saw that the dinner they'd shared on this same crypt had hardly begun to break down.

Jan rose, webs of vomit and gore strung through the patch of hair on his belly, trousers soaked through with blood and bile, and Jo looked away from him, ashamed of herself. Sander stood with his back to her at the edge of the crypt, and she heard Jan drop down into the boat. Andrei was nowhere to be seen, and she realized who had flopped down into the water between her and the fish. That poor, wonderful Muscovite, sacrificing himself to save a girl he didn't even really know, while Jan and Sander sat back and watched him do it...

She shuddered, suddenly very cold, suddenly missing the purple pots, her shitbird brothers, the clumsy attentions of the fisherboys whose deceptions were plain as their attempts to look older by growing weak little sand-beards. Sander's shoulders tightened, as though wincing from her gaze, and he turned to her. Their eyes met, and she saw a strange sorrow in them, a misery she never would have thought him capable of, and a tight fear pierced her heart. No, not that, he wouldn't—

"Jo," said Jan, the boat creaking, but still she wouldn't turn to him. She focused on finding any shred of strength that she hadn't left in the water, sitting up and wiping the spew off her bare chest. She was more aware of her nakedness than she'd ever been, and just wanted to get to her wadded shift and gown that still lay near at hand, the fabric soaked through with meer drippings; she just wanted to put it on and cover herself and be somewhere warm, and she would never tell, she would never speak a word of what she had seen here, what she had heard, what she had done.

No. She was just tired, was all, she was tired and had worked herself into a frenzy, what with that great big fucking fish, and then Andrei dying to save her, and now that it was over she wasn't thinking clear. It was like when she had near-drowned the night she'd met Jan, and had to haul herself to her feet and trudge home in the dark, her hand bleeding out, too intent on getting home to think of what she'd do when she got there, where she'd plant that knife of his she held in her quivering hand. Get up, she thought, trying to will her sore frame into motion, just get up and get dressed and everything will be better, everything will—

—Hurt exploded in her left cheek like a knot popping in a fire, and then the right side of her face blasted away that pain with an even harder blow, her whole head engulfed in fire. She tried to jerk away from it, from the too-hard crypt she had collapsed against, facefirst, but as she did, everything swam, and the world tilted, and she found herself sinking beneath a shimmering wave.

Her head was lifted, tender fingers on her neck, but the pain this brought pushed her deeper into the water, down into the muck at the bottom, and she wondered if she had ever found the ring, if she had ever seen that macabre, impossible sight at the sunken dining table, or if she were drowning in the blackness, dreams taking her as the world left her. Then she heard his voice, drifting down, and she kicked up, floating higher and higher. She blinked away the tears, trying to see, trying to breathe, beholding Jan reaching down through the sheen to save her, to lift her out of the water, but something had pinned her just under the surface, crushing down her arms, her chest, her throat.

No. No, no, no. Jan was sitting atop her chest with his knees on her arms, and he had coiled a cord around her neck, perhaps the rope she had used to plot the black hallway of the flooded manor. It tugged her in opposite directions, the cord, a pinching heat on either side of her throat as he pulled harder, and she realized the pain in her chest wasn't just from his tailbone crushing her tits.

She was drowning up here, and too late she fought him, fought him as fierce as she could, but she was trapped, and there was no voice to speak with, to threaten or beg. He had taken even that, and as his arms spread farther, snow began to fall around them, ever-widening flakes rising up from the mist. Sander was standing over her, his voice a garble, brilliant white powder erasing his features, and then Jan's, and then, finally, her own. The light took her, as it takes all who seek it.

VII.

"Why?!" Sander was shouting in Jan's face. "Why's she got to, why?!"

"Because you had to make sure she knew what we were doing," said Jan, relaxing the rope from around the girl's neck. Her skin was raw beneath it, and he pulled the cord loose with his finger. She managed a wheezing gasp, but her eyes remained blank and dull, staring at whatever it was people saw when they were down that far. "Because you—"

"Fucking liar," said Sander, his hands opening and closing in nervous clenches as he stalked back and forth, the narrowness of the crypt reducing his histrionic posturing to a quick step one way and then a quick step back the other. "In Dordt you said, you said you'd do it, and she didn't know then, you were always going to—"

"But I might have changed my mind," said Jan, never taking his attention off the girl. She looked dead already, but he could hear the life returning to her in reedy breaths and he didn't want to be distracted if she woke up. "You've ensured I can't, not now. She knows who I am and what we're doing. So she dies. You had a point before, about her not knowing any better, so maybe we could have just turned her loose somewhere. Not now."

"She's a fucking kid! Just, just let her go, leave her out here, nobody will come and—"

"That would be crueler," said Jan. "Much. And who knows, maybe she'd swim all the way back to Holland, and then what? What in God's name had gotten into you, Sander? When did you turn into such a bitch?"

"Just do it, then!" It was more of a scream than a shout. Did she remind him of someone? A sister he'd never mentioned? A daughter? No, Sander was gay as a goose, and a sister seemed unlikely—maybe she looked like a boy he'd known, what with her short hair and blunt features. Then Sander's voice dropped, became the deadly serious hiss he adopted when *They* were playing into his fears, the nameless, faceless conspiracy that was always plucking away at the hem of his reason. "Why aren't you doing it, why the fuck are you playing with her if—"

"Get back in the goddamn boat," said Jan quietly, finally looking up from the girl and retightening the rope as he did. She didn't wake up, but her body began to shudder as he cut off her air again. "I didn't want her shitting herself while we were talking, is the reason, but we are *done* fucking talking about this."

"Fine," said Sander raising his palms and backing away. He almost toppled backward into the water before catching himself. Jan smiled at this, turning back to the girl. Her face was going as purple as the hands jutting out from under his knees, blankly slapping the stone as she died. Of all the complications, he never would have predicted Sander going soft. A fortnight from now they would be lying together in a comfortable bed and the big bitch would roll over and mutter an apology to the wall—for all his hardness, Sander was never able to look Jan in the eye when he said he was sorry—but in the meantime, let him sulk.

The boat rocked in the water behind Jan as the madman fled as far as he was able. Jan's eyes shifted from the girl to the ring she had found him, the gold band encircling his finger just as it was always destined to, just as the cord was always destined to encircle Jolanda's throat. It was a kinder end than the miserable life of a dye-maker's daughter, and in their merry time together he had shown her more happiness than she had ever known, would ever *have* known. It was a kindness, and he eagerly gave it to her, Graaf Tieselen of Oudeland pulling the rope tight as the spark went out of her blind, distended eyes.

VIII.

Jolanda stood on the beach, sand slicing between her toes, and peered into the maelstrom. It was all around her, the snow gone and replaced with swirling thunderheads, and she wondered how she knew it was a beach, for it was black, black as anything she had ever seen, with no star nor moon nor scrap of coal beneath the purple pots to shine in that night, in that gale, and the wind howled and the rain whipped, cutting her cheeks with its edge. Her head felt like a sloshing, boiling kettle of dye, splashing out onto the sand, scalding her neck and tits, and she realized she was going to be sick, that she was going to puke, but not from her mouth, not from her stomach, but from her very skull, and she felt a sudden and deep fear fill her. Not for the storm around her, nor the tempest within her, but for something else—the realization that she was not on a beach, not in a maelstrom, not anywhere but inside herself, in a churning, sickening dream she could not break. The rain came harder then, warm drops splashing her cheeks, her brow and lips, and the heat of it terrified her—she had always hated the summer, and here it came upon her, drizzling down its warmth when all should be cool and dry and quiet, and the screaming wind lifted her off the ground, off the slab, and she knew she was dead. She'd always hoped she would see her brother Pieter again when her life ran out, but instead she saw only the dark.

IX.

Jan never did anything right, never did as he ought, never, ever, ever. He was supposed to turn, was supposed to see and stop what he was doing and say he was sorry. Of course he didn't do that, but even then he was supposed to be quiet about it, to go silent and drop his arms and look mutely down at the tip of steel jutting out of his belly, a red drop suspended on its edge as a thin, dark creek began to ooze out around Glory's End. Jan was supposed to silently look at Sander, the rope falling from his fingers, and accept what had happened. Apologize, maybe.

Instead Jan freaked the fuck out before the sword had even passed through him, slithering forward and trying to escape the crypt, to wriggle into the water like a landed eel. His bare back was spurting blood as he fled and Sander stuck him again, trying to go deeper, harder, right through his heart, but Jan danced on the blade, bone scraping metal as he shrieked and shrieked, the noise so undignified, so unquiet, so utterly...un-*Jan*, that Sander stopped trying to stab him and set to slashing at the back of his neck with the sword, her thirsty edge winking between them as she fell again and again.

Jan managed to get turned halfway around, his eyes meeting Sander's as he babbled and thrashed, and in that moment Sander froze, realizing what he was doing, what the fucking fucking fuck he was doing. Without warning he was murdering his dear Jan, was what, but while he hesitated she did not, Glory's End diving down and through and deep, deep, deep, the hard man not so fucking hard as he thought.

That, then, must be the heart, Sander realized as Jan's face set and his eyes rolled back and his thrashing gave way to a weak shivering, the sword spearing him the way she had speared so many others, and she twisted in Sander's hand, widening her hole and bringing forth more of the frothy blood.

Jan was not begging. Jan was not moving. Jan was not even breathing. Jan was fucking dead.

This was enough, and not letting any more thoughts come into him, Sander went to the girl and dug his shaking, bloody fingers under the cord around her neck. It slid up with a noise like it was coming off a dry bollard. It had dug in so deep there was blood, or was that his? No, Jan's. She didn't move. She didn't breathe.

Sander knelt down farther and gave her a rabbit-punch to the bare stomach, and as if she were a dead spider, she drew her limbs inward at that, arms and legs coming together as she rolled onto her side, gasping so loudly it caused Sander to jump. He pulled the cord the rest of the way off her and turned away, as if embarrassed by her nudity. She might have pissed herself, but that could have been Jan, who knew?

Fucking stupid, was what it was. No, fucking *mad*. Why hadn't Sander asked, why hadn't he begged, why hadn't he threatened? *Oi, neuker, I'm not asking you, let the skinny little slut go, or I'll fucking kill you*. Why hadn't he said that? So he wouldn't have to say it? So he wouldn't have to stare blankly at his lover without any reason for it, other than he was a soft fucking cuntbitch himself, now that the Karnöffel cards were down?

No, he had done it because Jan was working with them, was— no, no, no, there weren't no fucking *them*, there wasn't nobody but him and Jan and this wee girl, and here they were. Sander had never really thought of himself as a murderer before, even after what had happened with his father, but the word came to mind now, yes it truly did. He looked at Jan and a rush of remorse and grief and fear and confusion flooded him, washing away all his thoughts and rationalizations, and he went to his man and lay down beside him and cradled him in his arms and wept and howled and whispered apologies to the sodden, mangled corpse.

The girl's breath had caught several times, turning to wet coughing, and now she began to groan. Fearful she would find him, Sander was on his feet so fast he almost slipped in the blood and went over the side of the crypt, but he caught himself, and wrenched Glory's End from Jan. The sword seemed reluctant to leave the scabbard she had made for herself in the man, and when she came loose, the sensation brought bile and booze up Sander's throat. He pushed the sickness back down, but only just. The girl was crying now, he could hear, but she'd brought her arms up to shield herself from the sight of him, and he could not see her face.

Quickly, then, right to the throat. It would mean going through her purple arms, but they were skinny things, and Jan had lined her neck for him with the ropeburn, like the first notch hewed from a log in need of splitting. Sander raised Glory's End, wondering just what the fuck he was doing. When in doubt...

"No!" he cried, and pivoting around, he hurled the sword high into the air, a steel windmill turning through the sky. The dead tree near the church spire was just there, ready to catch her in its trunk as she began to arc back down. Her point would skewer the wood all the way to the hilt, and there she would wait until he returned. Or, perhaps, he would grow old and withered and never again be fit to wield her, and the tree would keep her until some worthy man came a-questing for the legendary weapon and found her sleeping there amongst the birds' nests and eel dens.

He turned and was running then, running, but only for two steps, for the crypt promptly fell away. He leapt from the edge of the slab, up into the air like Glory's End, and with his back turned he did not see the sword splash into the meer far short of the dead tree. The flat of mud and rushes where they had first beached the boat was beneath Sander, but he would never reach it, he realized; his fall would last longer than his life, the price for his sin an eternity plunging down into darkness, into filth, with the bottom never reached, for he—

—Splashed into the mud with a rather unimpressive plop, twisting his ankle in the process. He sank near to his waist but wriggled deeper into the islet, intent on burying himself alive in the muck, but by the time he was up to his tits in the stuff, a different thought had caught his attention, and he sat in the mire contemplating his lot. It seemed very likely that if Jan thought the slut was a, what's it, a *liability*, he might have thought the same about Sander. Jan had given Sander a lot of reasons to doubt this, granted, but then the little bitch had seemed rather surprised by the turn of things as well. A man willing to do such a thing to a child might not shirk from doing similar to a lover, would he?

Maybe Jan had all sorts of his own black thoughts going on, and maybe Glory's End had directed Sander to save the bitch in order to save himself. Jo, he thought, squirming in the suddenly uncomfortable mud, he had saved *Jo* at the cost of Jan because she wasn't a bitch, a slut, an idiot, a whore; she was Jo. That was why. Jo. But there had to be something more, there had to be. Right? He had saved her for a reason. Now he just had to find out what it was.

X.

The only thing that hurt worse than Jolanda's pounding head was her throat. It felt like the shellfish hammers whaling away at the inside of her skull had splintered off bone shards that had fallen down her craw, jamming it full of sharp slivers, and even breathing made her eyes water from the pain of it. Her shift, she thought. Even more than a sip of water to wash down some of the hurt or the absence of the bloody body lying just there beside her, she wanted her shift. A strange truth, but then they often were. She squirmed over the damp, sticky crypt to the wad of soaked linen and pulled at it, untangling the clump of wet cloth from the bulkier gown. Evening was finally beginning to settle over the grave of Oudeland, and she was alone on the crypt with the body of...

She went to him, still not quite believing he could be...But no. He lay on his side, and she reached out her fingers to brush a deep gash that stretched from just behind his ear all the way across his shoulder, black lumps of bone glistening in the wound. He was already cooling, and he stank like something spoiled. She had the sudden thought to kiss him, but his eyes were like those of the fish she'd sometimes find before the gulls did on the strand, and the thought of touching her lips to his with those rolled-back eyes staring through her brought on a shudder of repulsion. There was so much blood she could scarce believe it.

Jolanda found herself crying, but she fought herself—not that there was anyone else on that lonely slab of stone to see and laugh at her grief, but the choking sorrow jostled all the splinters around her throat, making it even worse. Images of him assaulted her with each agonizing throb in her head, in her gullet, in her heart, images of him smiling that queer, crooked smile of his, the sight of him there in her father's hovel, standing up to her papa and all her shitbird brothers, his handsome face looking down at her on the Dordrecht quay as he said those words that had softened something long calcified inside her, the oaths that had brought a trickle of color into the gray world. She had been like some rocky sea creature, and he had worked her, first smashing her that earliest day on the beach, then cooking her with his heat, drawing out what was best in her...

And now he was...

But then he had...

Why, she wondered, the hurt of it worse than anything she felt with her flesh. Or so she told herself. Why? Then she hardened at once, the twisting, soft clay in her belly cooking to brick as her damp misery blazed into wrathful fury—because she was a stupid little bitch, that was why. Because she had let herself be used like a grub on a hook, cast in to catch something nice, and discarded when she landed it...assuming a big fucking fish didn't bite her in half first. Better ask why she wasn't dead herself, why Jan was lying there all hacked up.

Sander, of course. The madman. She got into a crouch, suddenly aware that no matter which way she faced, her back was always vulnerable, open to his sword. He wasn't in the boat, and wasn't on the crypt, and wasn't—

—She screamed, which she never really did, but there was a face watching her from the marshy island beside the crypt. Some slick toad-man or something, an eel-monster coming out of his burrow now that the sun was setting, his reptilian eyes staring at her the whole time, his lumpy brown hide blending into the marsh, and—

Sander, of course. The madman. As she watched, he began to drag himself out of the mud, which was almost up to his chest. It

would have been comical a day before, the stupid creeper cursing and grunting and becoming even filthier as he wallowed
in the muck, but at present it was positively chilling. Jolanda
weighed her options. Looking down into the boat and the impossibly long oars that stretched along its bottom, she realized she
had precious little choice if she didn't want to swim back to land.

"What did you do?" she heard him mutter, and though his
face was cast down into the clinging mud, he pulled himself up
and across its boggy surface. Toward her. "What did you do?"

Precious little choice is better than none at all, and though it
meant dropping down onto the flat before him, Jolanda made a
break for the boat. If she could get it free of the muck, she could
row, she could, she could use the quant to push herself along the
stones and then she could row. Lowering herself, she instantly
sank to her knees in the marsh, but before she had reached the
nose of the boat, he was upright and lurching over to her, free of
the mud and horrible as any catfish, long barbels of filth dangling from his beard.

She stared at him, wondering if all would come to naught, if
the lunatic was about to push her down into the mud to finish
what Jan had started. He extended his fingers toward her face,
the digits just beside her mouth, and she considered biting them,
taking the moment of surprise it would grant her to dive for the
shallows, to try to swim for it.

No. She was too tired for all that, too goddamn tired, and his
cold, damp fingers brushed her neck, making her wince. She did
not look away from his intense stare.

"Let's get him in," said Sander, his voice quiet and hollow as
he turned to the crypt. "We're not planting him here for that fish
to dig up. Let's take him home."

The tears came again as they loaded Jan's ruined body into
the boat, though she wasn't sure if they were for him or for her.
Sander washed the caked grime from his hands before slipping
the bloody ring off Jan's finger and putting it on his own. Jolanda

still hadn't gotten a proper look at the thing for which she had nearly died several times over, but now found that she didn't want to. It was a stupid ring, was all, and looking at the stricken, terrified rictus of Jan gazing up to heaven from the belly of the boat, she felt the splinters in her throat twist and grind as a sob heaved its way up from her depths.

Sander took his place on the rowing board and they were off, twilight blurring the lines between sky and water, mist and cloud. They heard a mewling cry as they passed between two crooked stones jutting out of the meer, and before Jolanda's heart could land after jumping up her tight craw, the Muscovite's cat had pounced into the vessel from her perch on a tombstone. She landed on Jan and limped across him to Jolanda, but other than keeping her right foreleg off the corpse, she seemed well enough, purring and nuzzling Jolanda as Sander mutely rowed on.

They reached the island of the manor a moment later, the gulf between house and graveyard she had swum in desperate, endless flight now seeming such a narrow passage. Sander nearly tipped the boat getting himself onto the marshy roof. He dragged Jan out after him, but Jolanda stayed in the prow, keeping her eyes on the gray tabby and continuing to pet her even when a splash came from the center of the island. Then Sander was hurrying back over the mire, muttering about hauntings and proper burials and ill fucking omens and all.

Then they were away from Oudeland, back the way they had come. Something large-winged and ink-plumed landed atop the church spire behind them, but both she and Sander pretended they didn't notice, and the scrapings against the bottom of the boat as they passed through the flooded willow wood were just old branches, that was all, nothing more. The gloaming slowly turned to night proper, but only when the mist thickened and the darkness deepened did Sander pull the oars back into the boat. Neither had said a word since leaving the manor house, but now his voice came to her from the blackness at the back of the boat.

"This is a good spot for the night," he said, and the utter stupidity of this statement caught her so off-guard that she burst out laughing. This did not sit well, apparently. "What's so goddamn funny?"

"Saw a better place...back there," she said, the strain that simply talking placed on her raw throat making her eyes flood. "By the...water."

Then he was laughing, too, and if his cackling also turned to sobbing, she could not tell in the darkness. Eventually it passed, and the moon came out from beneath the clouds. The meer was louder than she had imagined it could be after the solemn quiet of the day, and dark things flitted above them, cutting slashes of black across the jaundiced moon brooding overhead. The weight of an entire flooded house settled on Jolanda's arms and legs and ragged neck, but she had finally recognized the pinching, knotting, gurgling pain in her stomach as hunger, and in the gloom she easily found one of the satchels they had brought. Her fingers felt like wooden dowels jutting out of her hands, but when she numbly raised the first object she found in the bag, it was a loaf of bread, and she attacked it with something like love.

Sander slid off the bench, his full darkness hanging over her, and then he silently began picking through the bag as well. He removed a gibbous wheel of cheese, its wax glinting in the moonlight, and a jug of beer. Then they feasted, eating and eating and eating despite the tears it brought to Jolanda's eyes, eating as though they had just discovered what their teeth were for, and washing it all down with flat, malty beer that first heightened but eventually dislodged the spurs of pain from Jolanda's throat. A few of them, at least—it still hurt, but not so badly as it had, and at last she lay back in the clammy curve of the boat and let her exhaustion drown her, the cat lodging itself in her armpit as she drifted off. Sander was still sitting up, watching her as she went, but she had given up on doing anything about the shitbird—the worst he could do was kill her, after all.

Feast of Saint Servatius 1423

"Where the Gate Is Open, the Pigs Run into the Corn"

Poorter didn't recognize the knocking at his door, which wouldn't have been so strange if it wasn't clearly intended to be some sort of recognizable code—three quick raps, a pause, two slow raps, and then four more in quick succession. He straightened up slowly and carefully, as slowly and carefully as he had been shaving down the channel in the crossbow before him, but even still, staccato twinges fired off up and down his spine, a ragged line of archers shooting at will as the enemy bore down upon them. The knocking was coming a third time as he went to answer it, a vague disquiet filling him as he stared at the inside of his door—he found that he rarely liked his visitors these days.

Ah, well, perhaps it would be someone pleasant this time.

It wasn't.

The madman continued glancing up and down the street even when Poorter cleared his throat in the open doorway. Sander looked about as suspicious as one is able to without actively skulking in an alley with a bandit's mask in one hand and a bloody knife in the other. Next to the madman stood the moppet, who seemed every bit as silently wretched as she had proven in their early acquaintance, an ugly statue put out at having been brought to life. She held a squirmy gray cat. Having a workshop perpetually cluttered with half-constructed devices that did not respond well to being knocked onto the stone floor, Poorter was less than fond of cats, but given the circumstances he had to admit that the tabby was the most welcome of the guests on his stoop.

"Yes?" said Poorter, hoping that if he filled the doorway at just the right angle, the degenerates would get the hint that they weren't welcome. If such a pose existed, Poorter evidently had yet to master it—Sander pushed his way into the house without a word, leaving a cold, damp impression on Poorter's shirt as he did. The girl followed the madman inside, and shutting the door after them, Poorter trailed them into the kitchen. "Have a fine time of it, then?"

"No," said Sander, pulling out a chair at the table. "Let the puss go already, she's sick of your stink."

The girl tossed the cat onto Sander's lap, and the beast immediately bounced up onto the table. Presumably it had hooked Sander as it went, for he began to shout furiously, first at the cat and then at the girl, who was wearing the sort of smile dogs adopt just before they bite. The feline left muddy footprints on the freshly scoured table, and when Poorter moved to push it off, it hissed at him, sprang onto the floor, and disappeared into his workroom.

"—wretched ball-battering slut!" Sander finished.

"Well, then," said Poorter. "The cat can't stay, I'm afraid, so I'll just go put it out and—"

"I'll cut your fat face if you touch her," the girl snarled at Poorter, her glee at enraging Sander instantly turning to something similar to what the madman evidently felt at having his belly scratched by a rank cat. They were the first words she had ever spoken to Poorter. He believed them.

"Well, if it's just for the night..." said Poorter hopefully as he fetched two mugs. He admired his own craftsmanship as he filled them, the shelf he had built for the small keg just the right height for tapping without bending over. Turning back with the beers, he saw Sander rummaging around in his cheese barrel as the door of the privy closed behind the girl. "It will have to be, I mean. Family's visiting tomorrow, and much as I would prefer to have sufficient accommodations for all parties, I simply do not. If Jan—"

"Jan's dead," said Sander, turning back from the cheese barrel with a cloth-draped wheel Poorter recognized as a Gouda he had been aging for a special occasion. Dark stains were already spreading out across the white cloth from where the man's filthy fingertips gripped the cheese. It was a sad sight, this dirty-handed madman sullying a perfectly innocent Gouda, and Poorter set down the beers. He supposed it said something about his character that even with such dire news hanging in the air he couldn't help but imagine the intelligent supper guests who might have appreciated the cheese for what it was, as opposed to these grimy villains.

"Dear God, how awful," Poorter said with genuine emotion. He was still looking at the cheese. "My condolences, Sander, truly, I know you and he were very close."

"Yeah," said Sander, planting the wheel down before him and taking one of the mugs. "'If there's anything I can do,' right?"

"What?" Poorter blinked, as if the man's lack of clarity was something that could be brushed away with a diligent eyelid.

"'If there's anything I can do to help in your time of loss, Sander, I'll do it. For you and Jo.'" Sander raised his mug and eyed Poorter over the top of it. "Right?"

"What?" Poorter repeated, then caught on. Jo must be the girl's name. "Of course, yes, anything I can do. Within reason. I'll put you up for the night, and in the morning..."

Sander tilted the beer back and drained it in a series of gulps. The girl came out of the latrine, went directly to the table, and picked up Poorter's mug. He opened his mouth but thought better of it and rose to get another beer for himself. Giving her provocation to speak seemed like a losing proposition.

"In the morning?" Sander said to Poorter's back, and the man flinched as if snapped at the baths with a rolled-up towel.

"Yes, well, as I said, much as I would like to put you up longer..." Glancing over his shoulder at their twin scowls, he lamely finished, "I have family visiting."

"That's fine," said Sander. This relieved Poorter. "So long as you manage to do what I tell you 'tween now and then, that's fine as silk." This did not.

Poorter returned to the table, where Sander was using a

blackened, dangerous-looking dagger to slice the cheese. The madman waggled the blade at Poorter, a whitish chunk balanced on its end. Poorter took the cheese and popped it into his mouth, unhappy to find it slightly oily, and with a grit that it surely hadn't acquired in his barrel. This did not bode well, it did not bode well at all.

"Yes, well, it's already quite late, and—"

"This'll be simple," said Sander, and Poorter's frown deepened to see the girl dig her fingers into the wheel itself and break off a fat piece of cheese, leaving brown smears in the finger furrows. "You get what was coming for Jan and we'll give you your cut. Be on direct, then."

Poorter cocked his head at the madman. "What do you mean, 'what was coming to him'? He was going to, that is, his plan was to assume the person of Graaf Tieselen. That was his plan."

"I know about his plan, cockstand." Sander snorted as he got up to refill the empty mug he had pushed in front of Poorter without result. "What I'm saying is graaf has coin, aye? So you go and get it."

"And how do I accomplish that, without the graaf to whom it belongs?" Poorter said, trying so hard not to smile that his eyes watered. The madman was not to be provoked, and Poorter rightly supposed that taking pleasure in Sander's ignorance would ire him greatly. "'Excuse me, I'm here to retrieve the graaf of Oudeland's gold? Yes, yes, I know he drowned in the flood, but he had a secret nephew who's inherited it all, and upon whose behalf I'm retrieving it. He's just not around at the moment.'"

"You take the ring, you thick-pated sheephead," said Sander irritably, draining the mug he had just filled and sticking it back under the tap.

"'See, I've got his ring—all the proof you people who've been spending the fortune that is rightfully yours require in order to turn it over to me, yes?' Come on, Sander, think! Jan was the heir, official or not, and no heir, no graaf. No graaf, no groots. I can take the ring, certainly, and sell it for you, but anything else is—"

"You be the graaf," said the girl, cheesy white saliva webbing the inside of her mouth as she talked through her food. "Wear it and all, be the graaf."

"My dear child," said Poorter. "I am known! Broadly! No one would believe I am related to—"

"Not you," said the girl. "Him."

Poorter's laugh died on his lips as he realized the little idiot was serious. "Preposterous. Jan would have had enough trouble passing himself off, but Sander—"

"Sander what?" said he, his scowl giving way to an even more disturbing smile. "Sander what, you pudding sack?"

"Jan really was the graaf's son," said Poorter, hoping an appeal to the natural order of things would soothe the madman. "Bastard or no, Jan was of noble blood, Tieselen blood. He looked the part, could act the part, was—"

"—A fucking crook who would step on a baby in the street if it meant keeping his boot out the mud," said Sander. "How you know he weren't lying about being a bastard and all? How you know it weren't a story he cooked up to feed whatever lawyer he got writing down his lies, eh?"

"That very ruthlessness you speak of!" Poorter countered. "The true mark of the upper class, is it not? He—"

"My papa's ruthless as he," said the girl. "Worse, maybe, I dunno. And he's poor as they come."

"Sander, don't be foolish," said Poorter, deciding the best course where the child was concerned was to pretend she wasn't there. Answering her only seemed to deepen the hole, and he was already up to his ankles in seepage. "No one would believe it. The lawyer knows Jan, knows he's legitimate—no, not legitimate, obviously, but knows he's got the blood, yes? He's not likely going to mistake you for Jan, is he?"

"And you think this lawyer's honest?" Sander shook his head, refilling his mug once more. He was beginning to sway slightly in place. The girl kept tearing pieces from the cheese with her grubby fingers despite the dagger sitting right there beside it. "You think any of them what ran with our dearly departed was on the level? We're all foxes and cranes at the table here, Poorter, yourself included, eh?"

"Foxes? Cranes?"

"Means we're all throwing in with each other for our own ends, dummy. Or you been putting us up and helping Jan cheat them who's rightfully come into the holding of this Tieselen's business for some kind of higher purpose?"

"It's, it's idiotic," said Poorter, whatever patience his interest in self-preservation had mustered finally routed in the face of such unrelenting stupidity. "I'm not going to give you the name of the lawyer, nor where to find him, nor anything else. It's another flaw with even considering any sort of furthering of Jan's plan without the man himself—I am known here, and any attempt on the part of you two to run some sort of game will result in my being the one most easily found and taken to task for it when you are discovered. Which you will be! Immediately! As soon as you step out of this goddamn house! Look at you, man, you look like a gleaner! And what would you do with her, eh?"

"Tried to sell me off at a nunnery," said the girl. "After we was out of the meer and back up in Rotterdam. That old sister on the other side of the gate wasn't having none of it, but this loon kept saying they had to take me on, even if they couldn't afford to give him more than a few mites for his trouble. She went back inside, left him cold when he told her he'd rape me if she didn't take me in. Must've smelt the cock on his breath and known him for a lying fucking poot."

There was a brief silence as Sander finished drinking the most recent mug he had poured, and then he hurled it at the girl. At least, Poorter hoped it was aimed at her—it flew between host and child, foam spattering their faces as it shot past and exploded against the privy door. Shards of clay skittered back around their feet, and a crash came from Poorter's workshop that sounded suspiciously like a ten-groot commission landing on the stone floor.

Poorter and the girl were on their feet as one, but before he could find and throttle the cat or she could return fire with her mug, a clear knock drifted through the house. Poorter paused. The girl did not, her mug grazing Sander's shoulder and shattering against the keg. Then the madman was moving forward, an obscenely happy expression on his face, but Poorter's voice somehow arrested his charge.

"Please!" was all he managed, but seeing how well it worked, he reiterated it. "Please!"

The knock came again, three loud raps. Sander raised his eyebrows, whispering, "Let's just stay quiet till they go away."

"Stay. Quiet," Poorter growled. "I mean it."

He closed the kitchen door behind him. A quick glance confirmed that the commission had indeed been knocked from its joist and lay forlornly on the ground. He didn't want to look closer to see if the stripe running up the side of the ash butt was a crack or just a shadow, instead hurrying to the door. He paused, his hand on the latch, a dreadful thought occurring to him: He hadn't inquired how Jan had died. Or where.

What if they had murdered him? Much worse, what if they had murdered him and left witnesses? What if they had been followed?

This could be a very large problem. Poorter chided himself, as he usually did when people rapped at his door, for not having a peephole installed.

He would never actually spring for the expense.

Knock, knock, knock. Hellfire. Poorter flung open the door, taking a deep breath as he did.

And nearly choked on it. Count Hobbe Wurfbain stood before him, his brilliant crimson hose tucked into high gray boots, his magenta doublet wreathed by a lavender cape trimmed with vair that mirrored his florid complexion and neatly kempt, hoary goatee. A taller man, even by Holland or Zeeland standards, and a handsome one, despite his age, and, of course, a rather notorious one. He had a velvet hat of some foreign style that Poorter detested on sight, and before the crossbow-maker could recover from the delightful shock of having such a wealthy client on his stoop, that very ugly hat was doffed, the count offering a bow that was mirrored by his pair of footmen.

"Master Primm," said the count.

"My lord Wurfbain," said Poorter, finally remembering to bow himself. "This is an honor indeed, sir. Welcome to my humble shop."

"Yes," said Count Wurfbain, and there followed a silence that was awkward by anyone's standards. Finally, the count arched his pale brows and asked, "May I come in?"

"Ah," said Poorter, hoping his face didn't reveal his displeasure. It did. "At the moment, actually, it so happens that I, unfortunately, am indis—"

"Capital!" said Count Wurfbain, advancing fast upon Poorter. The count had clearly not listened to a word he'd said, and Poorter found himself stepping aside at the last moment to avoid bumping into the noble. This was absolutely bloody typical where Poorter's luck was concerned. "Now then, where is he?"

"Ah," said Poorter as the count looked curiously around the dim workshop. "Who?"

"My dear old friend," said Count Wurfbain with such warmth that even though he'd never officially been introduced to the count before, Poorter was a little hurt when he realized he was not the person in question. "Shut the door, Primm, you're letting in the damp."

Glancing back, Poorter saw the footmen had vanished rather than follow their master inside, but quick as he was to shut the door and turn back to his guest, the count was already flinging open the door to the kitchen.

Shit.

Shit, shit, shit.

Also: shit.

A voice was raised, but the anxious blood crashing behind Poorter's ears deafened him as he ran to put out a fire that never should have been kindled, a fire that might well burn his fucking house down.

"—So good to see you again," the count was saying, pumping Sander's hand. The madman looked, well, like a madman. A drunk, filthy, wild-eyed madman with a beard like an untended hedge and hair like rotting straw, and the count had his lily-white hands around one of Sander's brown ones, just shaking away at it like he was trying to draw water from the stunned lunatic's mouth. "Haven't aged a day, have you?"

"I haven't?" said Sander, confusion giving way to some darker glimmer in those beady eyes of his, and Poorter searched in vain for his voice to somehow forestall the impending disaster. It was Agincourt all over again, the sun blacked out by a rain of arrows, but this time there was no pleasant little Dutch river town to retire to once the day was miraculously won.

"Let me introduce..." Poorter finally got out, but it was a whisper, and he had absolutely nowhere to go with it. Let me introduce this mad murderer? Let me introduce this raving imbecile? Let me—

"The graaf and I are old friends, old friends," said the count, finally releasing Sander and turning to Jo. She had resumed her seat in front of the cheese while Poorter was answering the door and now stared aghast at the nobleman, a wedge of dirty Gouda smushed to paste between her fingers. "I have not, however, met his lovely daughter. No, no, please don't get up, pet."

The urchin had clearly not intended to rise, but as he sashayed toward her, the cheese slipped from her fingers. He knelt on one knee and reached for Jo's hand. She recoiled from him, her eyes huge as hen's eggs. Shrugging, the count rose empty-handed and looked to Poorter. Poorter gulped.

"My lord, there, there has, there was…" Again, Poorter was lost, and threw up his hands in frustration.

"There *is*," said the count, giving his flustered host a condescending pat on the shoulder as he pursed his lips and turned back to Sander and Jo, "an *enormous* amount of work to be done. We'll keep them at my estate outside Leyden until they're passable, which may take no petite span of time. Until then, not a word, Master Primm, not a word, but when they return, old boy, when they *return*…"

"Return?" Poorter gasped on the word, as though it were composed of noxious swamp vapors.

"When they return," said Count Wurfbain with a cocksure wag of his finger, "they will be Graaf Tieselen of Oudeland and his lovely daughter. Obviously. Who else could they be?"

Feast of Saint Alberic
of Utrecht 1425

"Casting Roses Before Swine"

The Bumpkins would be arriving in less than three hours, and the new girl had only just knocked, timidly, at the white birch door of the house on Voorstraat. Lansloet knew who she was but acted as if he didn't, standing with silent expectation to see if she was as mousy as her feeble knock. She was, and he knew her name was Quakeyshakes before she even told him her real one.

"Sir, I…I am…my name is. Lijsbet. And I…Griet told me to come. Sir." When Lansloet opened the door, Quakeyshakes had pulled her hood back, dislodging the white wimple beneath it in the process, and the rain was making her greenish-brown eyes blink like those of a landed carp. Lansloet leaned sideways in the doorway, out of the draft. As she rambled, he casually settled a hand at belt level and flattened his palm into something like a beckoning shape, careful to do so as slowly and subtly as possible.

Lansloet waited, silently gazing down at the bedraggled creature on his stoop. There were two thin ridges of mud on the lip of the bottom step where she had wiped her rag-swaddled shoes before knocking. The rain would take care of the mess, and it showed some small measure of wits on her part, but he would nevertheless take her to task for dirtying his stairs.

Quakeyshakes waited, her face now streaming, her sluttily exposed auburn hair wearing a net of rain beads. Her gown was clean, cut from a single piece of pale blue linen, and she had a white shawl around her shoulders—likely a folded apron. She must be very cold, her wide frame shuddering, and Lansloet wondered if she had a warmer but less presentable garment in the covered wicker basket weighing down one trembling elbow. She was perhaps sixteen or twenty, and thus fifty years his junior, but still he thought her far too old for such folly—she must know the position was hers, regardless of how ratty her cape was, and yet…

At last her eyes fell from Lansloet's imperious face. As she took in the frozen hand gesturing toward the interior, and the fact that he was no longer filling the doorway, her strained smile softened into something more genuine.

"Oh, right, sorry, sir." Quakeyshakes blushed as she took the steps, entering the foyer with a sharp wiggle that dotted Lansloet's shirtfront with droplets. He had once seen fleas abandoning an old dog, and the image sprang to mind now. Time to break the silence.

"You will not shake yourself like a wet bitch when inside this house," Lansloet said, careful as ever to keep his voice to a whisper despite his irritation. A soft voice kept people close at hand, and lord or lady, butcher or beggar, nobody was happy with a close-talker. Those who were ill at ease and keen to be away tended to give up more advantages than comfortable folk, and a low tone ensured he would be taken very seriously indeed should he raise his voice above a rasp.

Except the girl seemed not to have heard him, turning her head slowly from left to right, taking in the fine, fur-trimmed cloaks hanging on the rack beside the still-open front door, the brown and black pairs of high leather boots on the floor beneath the garments, the buffed stairway leading up to the second floor, the warm, bright hallway leading to the kitchen, the double doors opening to the parlor opposite the stairs, and then, at last, Lansloet again. She blinked. Her blush had faded to a pale rose, and then her cheeks blanched completely to something like the gamy yellow fat on an uncooked rack of lamb.

"I'm *so* sorry, sir, didja say something? To me?" Quakeyshakes had lowered the basket from her elbow and now held it in both hands.

"Yes," said Lansloet, and said no more. He was quite aware of how he must seem to this girl—a mean old beanpole of a man, with a face like a long, withered pod. So what if he was?

"Sorry," she said, the basket's handle creaking mournfully in her hands. "I don't always hear so good. My da was a smith, a real guild one, and the clanging—"

"I said do not shake yourself off like a wet bitch in this house. *Ever.*" Lansloet's chicken-bone fingers went to his chest and sharply flicked across the gray shirt, but whatever water she had moistened him with had already been absorbed into the cloth. Quakeyshakes flinched, stammering an apology, but he raised a hand and she fell silent. "Nor shall you dirty my stoop with your boot scrapings. This home shall neither be filthified nor dampened by your presence. Understood?"

"I . . . yes," she said, eyes falling to her basket. The woven willow had caught quite a bit of rain, and in silence they listened to it dripping onto the oak floor. Her face went from pear flesh-pale to cherry-skinned, her knuckles tightening on her load with a squeak. "If I may, uh, if . . . if I can take this to my quarters, I'll come and mop up in here. Sir."

"In time," said Lansloet. Over the many years and masters he had served, Lansloet had developed a method for letting himself smile without ever displaying it on his face. It was as if the grin spread across someplace so deep and dark that not even its faintest edge could be seen on his eternally frowning lips. He was smiling that secret smile now, wondering how long it would take her to notice he was again holding his hand at his waist, motioning toward the parlor door. About thirty heartbeats, as it turned out. The heartbeat was Lansloet's preferred method of timekeeping, his own being as reliable as finding frivolity at a feast.

"Oh! Sorry, sir, I'm . . . I . . . I don't." Quakeyshakes was moving for the parlor when he cleared his throat and directed his eyes to the still-open front door behind her. Throwing the mutts a bone from time to time was just common sense for maintaining respect and order. "Oh! Yes, sorry, sir."

After closing the door, Quakeyshakes took a step toward him

but paused, like a rumbled rat contemplating flight. He nodded, and she turned back to the door, fastening the heavy bolt into place. She would do well enough, he supposed.

"The parlor," he said, opening the double doors leading off the foyer and ushering her in. After her initial entrance into the house, he would never permit her to go through a doorway before him, except where the serving of meals was concerned. He should have enjoyed taking her upstairs first, so that her basket would drip all over them and he could then have her wipe them all down again, but there simply wasn't time. In the parlor, a dark rug, which would soak up the dribbling, covered most of the room—he certainly wasn't going to let her put her basket down until after the tour.

As soon as she entered the parlor she winced as if struck, the painting that hung above the hearth clearly affecting her as strongly as it did all who beheld it. Christ had never looked more alarming, the far-too-realistic style of the work making him look as though he were about to pounce from the wall and seize the unfortunate viewer in his long fingers. Lansloet had hated the painting when the graaf had first brought it home, as was natural given its ghoulishness, but upon realizing how uncomfortable it made everyone save for the master of the house, he had grown to love it.

"His lordship's chair is to be brushed with a *clean*, dry cloth every morning." Lansloet motioned to the cushioned, thronelike lounger in front of the fireplace and its stern guardian. "Then the other chairs, and the tiled table against the wall. The shelves and mantel will be wiped with a dry cloth every third morning. You *may* use the same cloth, provided the chairs are done first, and *then* the table. The vases will be removed from the shelves and placed upon the floor prior to dusting. They will then be wiped with the same cloth and returned to their original positions. In the spring and summer the functional vases will be filled with flowers, the decorative vases shall remain empty at all times. Under *no* circumstances are you to purchase cheaper flowers in the hope of pocketing the difference—I shall know, and you shall be released from service."

"I wouldn't!" Quakeyshakes cried, then blanched again from her own outburst.

"The girl before you was a sneak *and* a snatcher," said Lansloet, displeased with this exhibition of emotion. If her initial timidity was just that, he would be sorely disappointed, and not just because it would necessitate a new nickname. "After being punished, she was released. I will not suffer a thief."

In truth, Lansloet would suffer a thief, and did, most of the time. He would not, however, stand for a stupid one. The likelihood of finding an honest and intelligent servant was about the same as finding a master who was both rich and fair. No, the issue was that the girl in question had been an *obvious* thief, and that ruined it for everybody. If he had to choose between an honest, stupid servant and a crafty, duplicitous one, he would take the cheat every time. Unfortunately, Quakeyshakes already seemed the former, but so it went. They were shorthanded, and the Bumpkins were coming.

Lansloet knew Graaf Thirstybird would not have given a belch about appearances if the guests were old Dordrecht blood, but as the Bumpkins were new to the city and likely not yet aware of how lowly their hosts were, an efficient supper service was crucial. If Lansloet had known about the impending visit before this morning, when that troublesome Count Wolfmean had arrived unannounced, he would have further put off hiring a new girl until he could find a better advantage in it—as it was, he had been pocketing the discharged servant's wages for a fortnight without the graaf or Lady Greenplum noticing they were down a drudge, and now he was out of that, as well as owing his cousin Griet a favor for finding him this new girl so quickly.

Surely Wolfmean had his own designs in forcing the master to host a pair of out-of-town nobles on a day's notice, but the sly count was every bit as inscrutable in his machinations as Lansloet's employer was daft and obvious in his. And thank the saints and Mary and the founding fathers of Dordt for that—having served both sorts of men, Lansloet would take the addlepated lord over the cunning one every time. There were those who held that a man could not choose his master, but by Lansloet's reckoning, such people tended toward dimness. He had been around longer than the building itself, and took it as a point of private pride that no matter who he was bowing to at any given moment, the house was, now and forever, his in spirit if not in literal deed.

"The dining room is beyond this partition," Lansloet said, opening the gate section of the high wooden screen. "The table will be wiped clean and polished after *every* meal, and again before breakfast. After that you will crawl beneath to clean up crumbs and sop up spills. After *that* you will…"

"Lansloet!" Dribbling, the cook, was standing in the door to the kitchen. She was every bit as scrawny and old as Lansloet, but far less clever. He had her loyalty, but she was too cheeky by half. "She don't need to hear everything at once. What're you called, and where you from?"

"Lijsbet," said Quakeyshakes. "We were in Hoecke, but after the flood took it, Rotterdam, and then I come here with my husband, but he ran off and so I was working down—"

"Time enough for that later," said Lansloet, almost raising his voice but catching himself in time. "This is the worst day for you to come. We have guests. Noble guests, in a noble house, and being shorthanded—"

"Being shorthanded, this is the best day for you to come," interrupted Dribbling. "My name's Drimmelin, and I'm guessing Lansloet didn't introduce himself, but that's him, Lansloet. Now, you get with me, you'll share my bed in the pantry. We'll set those things down and put some food in you, ya?"

Quakeyshakes went to the kitchen without even asking Lansloet's permission, so thoroughly had the cook stripped him of his authority. Dribbling was getting revenge for his refusal to promptly replace the former servant, he knew it, as if her work were so hard that she needed extra hands. Between Dribbling and Lady Greenplum, Lansloet was up to his teeth in spiteful, unpleasant women.

"Yes, see that she's fed and comfortable, then put her to work," said Lansloet. "There's much to be done between now and—"

But the kitchen door was already swinging shut, the women tittering to themselves. Lansloet cleared a morsel of something solid from the back of his throat and hawked it onto the dining room table. Standing there for several moments, he watched the door swing back and forth on its squeaky double hinges, and then hunkered down with his forearms resting on the table, eyeing what he had spit there. After some reflection on the amber chunk, he flicked it from the board and straightened up sharply. There was much to be done, but first he really ought to have a nap in the attic while Dribbling got Quakeyshakes sorted out…

The rest of the day passed far too quickly, and before Lansloet knew it, the light beyond the garret window had faded. Rising with a yawn, he cocked his ear to the roof, confirming that the rain was still coming down. He retrieved the yellowing table-cloth that was his perpetual cover story for afternoon sabbaticals in the attic and descended to see if all was in order.

It was.

Count Wolfmean arrived first and settled into the parlor with Graaf Thirstybird, as was his custom. Quakeyshakes was sent up to fetch the lady of the house, who, as was her custom, took her sweet time coming down. Lady Greenplum and Quakeyshakes were chatting as they passed through the kitchen, which spoiled Lansloet's pleasant postsnooze mood. Fraternizing with the mistress was the first step down the steep stair of entitlement, and Lansloet well knew that entitlement begot sloth. He would have to find a way of destroying their relationship if it progressed beyond casual kindness on the part of Lady Greenplum.

Then, at last, a knock from the front of the house.

Lansloet knew the Bumpkins would be trouble from the moment he opened the door and got a look at the pair. Graaf Gauche wore a purple, pointy-collared suit of riding clothes highlighted with gold and silver thread that would have seemed ostentatious on a Turkish prince, and a brimless beaver hat of such pronounced ugliness that the servant had the momentary impulse to strike it from the rich man's head on general principle. The brittle pink crust edging the graaf's blond mustache was the finishing touch on the more-money-than-sense picture drying before Lansloet's eyes.

If the graaf was bad, his daughter was worse. The broad-shouldered child had been squeezed into what might have been a very handsome gown on a girl half her height. As it was, the effect was heinous, with the hem of the red-and-gray garment falling little farther than a fisher's tunic, and what *had* to be man's stripy hose protruding from the dress like taproots hanging from some awful serge grotto. Her bizarrely long gloves matched the hideous yellow clogs on her feet, clogs that clattered all over Lansloet's clean floor as her father half-dragged her into the foyer after him—Lady Foolsuit had seemed content to lurk on the stoop instead of coming inside from the sleet that plastered her dark hair across her unfortunate features where her bonnet had come up. What was wrong with girls these days, shamelessly displaying their tresses so? They'd be exposing their titties in public, next.

The Bumpkins were unaccompanied by servants, and both smelled like wet hay.

"You the graaf?" Graaf Gauche demanded, seizing Lansloet's hand and shaking it as though it were a hare he aimed to put out of its misery as quickly as possible. "Ha! I'm the graaf! You the other one? Where's Hobbe?"

"His Worship is in his parlor, sir, as is Count Wurfbain," Lansloet said, talking at a normal volume to shorten the duration of time spent in the troll's company. "If I may take your wet things?"

"Sure, Granddad," Graaf Gauche said, unclasping the copper brooch that pinned his cloak. He whipped Lansloet in the face with sodden fox-fur trim as he removed the garment with what must have passed for a flourish in whatever backwater Flemish duchy or fiefdom from whence this fen-lord had hopped. His Toadliness the Sixth Graaf of Froglandia, or whatever his full title was, proved unwilling to wait for a proper introduction. He made off down the hall, away from the parlor doors, calling, "This way, yeah? Hobbe, you back here?"

Lady Foolsuit rushed after her father, clobbering dark scuffs onto the freshly scrubbed oak and trailing an actual wake, so heavily was her oiled cerulean cape shedding rainwater. Lansloet mashed the graaf's sopping cloak in his long fingers for only a moment before smoothing out the garment and hanging it on the rack. A shout from the kitchen implied Dribbling had met their guests. Lansloet ambled after.

These two Bumpkins made Graaf Thirstybird seem cultured and intelligent, so at least Lansloet would be spared his master's usual after-guest raging about how everyone was always mocking him in his own home, as if he were too stupid to know what they really meant, et cetera. No, for once it seemed that Count Wolfmean had engineered a true meeting of equals—this ranine moron and his grotesque spawn might be richer than your average Dordrecht noble, but they seemed even less housebroken than the cook's courtyard chickens.

Following the muddy boot-and-clog prints down the hall, Lansloet ignored Dribbling's shrill blather regarding guests in her kitchen and made straight for the dining room. He stopped short of the still-swinging door and peered around the side, where the freshly oiled double hinges gave him furtive glimpses of the immaculately set table. Yes, there was Wolfmean intercepting graaf and daughter at the partition that separated parlor from dining board. Rather than follow them into the room, Lansloet took a step back, lest the count catch sight of him. Let him handle the introductions.

After watering down the wine far more than he did when filching mugs for himself, Lansloet added far less honey than he personally favored and mixed it all up with his crumb-caked ear-picking finger. He didn't even bother skimming the stray flake from the surface before placing the clay vessels on a polished tray. Quakeyshakes tried to take it, but he bared his teeth at her and strutted out of the kitchen—he wanted to make sure Wolfmean had the first cup he had dipped his digit in.

"—put the poltroon off the boat!" Graaf Gauche brayed as Lansloet edged the gate-section open, someone having closed the screen after them. Wolfmean, no doubt, in payment for letting the foreigners run amok through the house instead of being appropriately led in. Graaf Gauche's accent was even worse than his manners, the man sounding more like an especially daft laborer rather than a dignitary.

"Hilarious," Wolfmean said, following this pronouncement with an artfully executed chuckle. Yet again, Lansloet was impressed by the count's skill—he sometimes wondered what might have been had he served Wolfmean; if it should have made his life better or worse to have so crafty a lord. Worse, no doubt.

"Your Worship," Lansloet murmured, offering Graaf Thirsty-bird the first goblet. Lansloet's master took it like a drowning sailor seizing at driftwood, giving Lansloet a knowing, exasperated nod in the direction of Graaf Gauche, who was muttering something to his daughter.

The five nobles sat in a half-circle around the hearth, with Graaf Thirstybird closest to the fire in his lounger, Lady Greenplum sitting primly beside him, Lady Foolsuit to her left, Graaf Gauche beside her, and Wolfmean between him and the roaring fire. As usual, the tidy blaze Lansloet had painstakingly built had been heaped with more wood by his master, and everyone was sweating in their posh seats.

"Thank you, Lansloet," said Lady Greenplum, taking her wine. He winced at her. She was cunning, and without her constant whispering into Graaf Thirstybird's ear, the man should be utterly helpless. Had Lansloet been of a slightly more vicious temperament, he would have poisoned her long ago, but he thought himself a principled fellow and so he simply avoided her whenever possible.

"Thank you," said Lady Foolsuit, which was an unexpected bit of class. She seized the cup with both hands in a display of such nervous passion that she sloshed wine all over the long yellow gloves she had still not removed, despite the heat of the room. That was a bit more expected. "Arseling!"

Unsure if she were directing the insult at him or at herself, but not particularly caring, Lansloet smiled his secret smile as he said, "I shall fetch the lady a cloth. If you care to—"

"Go on, man!" said her father, leaping up and taking the two remaining glasses from the tray. "Clumsy chit will've spilt more by the time you're back."

Lady Foolsuit grumbled something unintelligible at this, and Lansloet caught Wolfmean stifling a smile. There was now no way of telling whether Wolfmean or Graaf Gauche would receive the earcheese-tainted wine, but that was all right. Plenty more would flow before this night was through, or Lansloet was a smoked kipper.

The supper was poached eggs with cumin sauce and a perch blancmange. The food was exquisite; the conversation, painful. The contrast between rigid hosts and thrashing guests would have been comical if the Bumpkins' deplorable habits had not started to rub off on Graaf Thirstybird as he lowered himself farther and farther into his cups, to the quiet but obvious chagrin of Lady Greenplum. Lansloet would have expected the opposite, the Bumpkins shamed into emulating their betters, but apparently he had underestimated both their obliviousness and his own master's coarse roots, which were forever coming to the surface like those of a young willow on a rain-ravaged riverbank.

When Graaf Thirstybird pronounced the Bumpkins the best

guests he'd ever had, even Wolfmean appeared embarrassed, a feat Lansloet would have doubted possible prior to this shameful occasion. The table looked like a flooded farmyard after the waters had receded, edible flotsam and cutlery jetsam cast hither and yon, a few half-picked drifts of bone lying forlornly in pools of grease and spilled drink. Lady Greenplum had spent the bulk of the supper futilely trying to put the anxious, ox-faced Lady Foolsuit at ease, but all this had resulted in was the increasingly tipsy girl asking ever less appropriate questions of the young noblewoman.

"My papa's got more money than the count of Burgundy," Lady Foolsuit was slurring as Quakeyshakes cleared the table and Lansloet served the cider. That Wolfmean failed to reprimand him for not waiting until the party had moved back to the parlor Lansloet took as a sign that, for tonight, at least, they had an understanding. The sooner this was over the better, for all concerned. "How much money does your papa have?"

"Ugh." Lady Greenplum coughed into her cider. Lansloet doubted it was an errant clove in her throat. She recovered quickly, dabbing at her mouth with a napkin. "He is… comfortable."

"I hate it here," said Lady Foolsuit. "It's too wet on islands. Don't you hate it here?"

"I find it…" Lady Greenplum sighed, casting a forlorn glance at the blathering lord of the house, who had scooted his chair over beside Graaf Gauche to better shout over him. "Comfortable."

"'Cause you don't know no better." Lady Foolsuit burped. "You come and stay with me this summer. You'll see, then."

Lady Greenplum sipped her cider to avoid answering, and Lansloet's secret smile bloomed wide and warm to see his lady squirm. How she must be struggling to bite that nasty tongue of hers! This had been a rather fun night, after all, seeing her and Wolfmean in such perfect misery.

"Papa will find you a husband," said Lady Foolsuit. "Then you'll never have to come back here. Why are your fingers purple?"

Lady Greenplum finished her cider and motioned at Lansloet for another. Then she darted her violet arms across the table, knocking Lady Foolsuit's mug to the floor and seizing her hands. Lady Greenplum seemed to be crushing the younger girl's gloved fingers between her palms, her mouth splitting into a wicked, wine-ruddy grin. For a moment Lansloet dared to hope she might bite the child.

"An angel held me." Lady Greenplum spit the words in the startled girl's face. "When I was a little thing, still inside my mother. I was turned 'round in her belly, and couldn't find my way out. An angel came and took my hands, just like I've got yours, and he led me out of her crack. Angels are fearful strong, so I've borne his mark ever since."

The two graafs failed to notice what their daughters were up to, but Lansloet noted that Wolfmean was watching the girls. Lady Foolsuit was staring into Lady Greenplum's large, dark eyes, a minnow mesmerized by the maw of a pike. Lansloet made a to-do of his age slowing his efforts to clean up the cider his lady had spilled, wondering if Lady Greenplum had lost her temper to the point of violence, as she sometimes did with the graaf, the two wrestling in the parlor like mad dogs or Flemish children. Lansloet dearly wished his mistress would strike the child, or something similarly entertaining that would also result in trouble for her even after the Bumpkins departed.

Instead, Lady Foolsuit burped and yanked her hands free, her eyes darting away from the older girl's. "Angels don't."

"They do," said Lady Greenplum, still sprawled across the table from titties to tummy like a stretching cat. "One came to you, when you were in your mother."

"No, it didn't," the girl said with a shudder, despite the dining room fireplace being every bit as hot as the one in the parlor. His Worship did like a good fire. "You're lying, Jolanda. I'd remember."

"No, you wouldn't," said Lady Greenplum, and Lansloet laboriously straightened back up with the fallen cider mug. It had a hairline crack running down it. "The angel told you to forget you'd ever seen him. But he was there, inside your mother with you. Watching you sleep."

Lady Foolsuit was growing upset, fidgeting in her chair and knotting her fingers together in her lap. "You don't know. How would you know?"

"I can see where he touched you," said Lady Greenplum, her wide smile every bit as mean and sharp as the ones Lansloet kept hidden inside his breast. She slowly stretched even farther across the table, and Lady Foolsuit leaned farther and farther back in her chair, until there was nowhere left to flee and Lady Greenplum's legs were up in the air behind her, her body flat across the board. A purple index finger settled just beneath the trapped girl's twitching nose. "Here. The angel watched you sleep, and he told you all the secrets of the world, every one, and then he touched you. Here. And his touch marked you, like it marked me, but he made you forget everything. Not me, though. He let me remember. I remember everything."

Lady Foolsuit, who was perhaps ten years old, looked as though she were torn between being sick and bursting into tears. Lady Greenplum squirmed back across the table and half-fell into her chair. Looking back and forth between Wolfmean and Lansloet, she shrugged. Checking her mug and finding it empty, she raised her brows at Lansloet, who bowed and hurried off to refill it. By the time he returned to the dining room, Lady Foolsuit had fled her chair and crawled into her father's lap, nesting there like some monstrous gosling. Graaf Gauche was cooing to the girl, saying,

"There, there, lump, it'll be all right. Best be off, she'll be retching it out before long, ho! Poor chit always gets like this from wine, it riles her guts. What do I tell you, lump, what do I tell you? Pace yourself!"

"I shall accompany you as far as the burgemeester's," said Wolfmean, getting to his feet. "It's not far from here, and close to where I am staying. Come, the night air will do her good!"

It was common knowledge that Count Wolfmean's mistress, Zoete Van Hauer, lived across the street from the burgemeester's, so common, in fact, that Lansloet wondered at Wolfmean not mentioning her by name. Unless of course he didn't want these two popping by anytime they should like. Ah.

"Yeah, well, come on back next chance you get," said Graaf Thirstybird, too drunk to rise from his chair but sober enough to know better than to attempt it. "Me and Jo'll put you up, you need it. And mind the grape juice you had this night—get you fair fucking prices, son, keep you well wet."

"It's been a pure pleasure," said Graaf Gauche, pushing his daughter from his lap. Lady Foolsuit grunted, landing like an especially clumsy cat and scrambling upright as her father hauled himself to his feet. "A pure pleasure, Graaf Tieselen."

"Jan," said the bleary-eyed Thirstybird, looking beyond his departing guests, beyond the looming shadow of Wolfmean, beyond his sour daughter Greenplum, beyond Lansloet, to something far beyond the sight of even his attentive servant. "You just call me Jan. Everybody else does."

Easter 1424

"One Shears Sheep, the Other Shears Pigs"

I.

After their unexpected introduction to Count Hobbe Wurfbain in the kitchen of Poorter Primm, the enigmatic nobleman immediately spirited Jolanda and Sander off to his house outside Leyden. They were to stay hooded at all times on the journey, but even from the depths of her cowl Jolanda saw more luxury than she'd ever dreamed of: velvet cushions on the board of the boat from Dordrecht to the mainland, private rooms at an inn in Delft, an enclosed wagon called a coach that was essentially a tiny house on wheels, and everywhere they went, wine and soft cheese and fresh meat. A lass could grow accustomed to such things, she thought, but Sander seemed more suspicious than ever, his eyes shining with the wide wildness of an overstimulated kitten. But then, he was mad, so such behavior was somewhat expected. The only downside was Wurfbain's staunch refusal to let her take the Muscovite's cat with them, but Primm assured her he would take care of Margareta until Jolanda's return.

"When's that to be, then?" she had demanded, refusing to relinquish the squirming cat from her arms despite both feline and count's obvious preference that she be dropped at once. "How long you putting us up?"

"Until you're ready," Wurfbain had replied with only a hint of annoyance in his gentle voice. "The duration of your tutoring depends entirely on how sharp a study you are."

"Little bitch doesn't listen to a word of her betters," Sander had said. "Reckon on having her until she's a crone, you're waiting on improvement!"

Which had led to a row. Which had led to their hasty ejection from Primm's house. Which had led to her failing, in her rage, to remember to smuggle Margareta out under her cloak. She missed the cat, especially when she arrived at the dark, foreboding house that rose from the harlequin fields bordering the banks of the Oude Rijn. Jolanda immediately disliked the place; it was altogether too reminiscent of another manse she had but recently quit, the dim halls as cold and lonesome as if they were filled with meer water.

Jolanda's bedroom was bigger than the hut where she had grown up, and at first she had preferred to sleep on the thick rugs covering most of the floor rather than the too-soft bed. Her handmaiden, Fye, insisted she get used to the latter, however, and so she'd given it a go. It was a bit like wearing shoes, she found—what was miserably uncomfortable for the first few months eventually became, well, still uncomfortable, but not so miserable. A bit like the rest of her life, come to think of it.

Staying confined to the rural manor for so long was maddening, but whenever the creepy count left on business, Sander let her accompany him on his walks through the countryside. The way he would wait until the two of them were out of sight of the house before stripping off his boots and hose and hiding them in the tall grass bordering the paths through the fields was one of the things that finally convinced Jolanda he was not entirely mad. For all his outbursts and strange fancies and obsessions, he too preferred the feel of dirt and grass under calloused heel and spread toe, and that, more than even his rescuing her from Jan, made the difference in her mind.

Not that he wasn't an obnoxious neuker most of the time, always trying to act clever when it was clear as the Oude Rijn on a calm day that he was even more mixed up about the world than her, and she'd been in it half the time as he—but still. Sander was all right.

Except he was Jan now.

That was something. Sander was Jan. Just as he always

should've been. That was, Sander should've been the one to try and murder her out in the swamps, and Jan should've rescued her. That made much more sense. Instead…instead something else had happened, and just thinking about it made her wish Jan had finished the job, that she'd never woken up to such a mad world where the very thought of taking a swim in the nearby river filled her not with joy and expectation but instead a sharp, bone-deep dread.

After leaving the submerged graveyard of Oudeland and becoming lost in the meer, it had taken them well over a week to find their way back to Rotterdam. Neither wanted to return to Dordt, at least not then, and that miserable voyage was the hardest time of Jolanda's life. Sander had barely spoken to her for the duration, and then ineffectively tried to dump her at a Rotter convent—*try those Beguine sluts*, the nun who had answered the gate had told them after Sander tried to sell her the girl. Not that Jolanda would have let the crazy bitches keep her locked up, but it nevertheless stung to be rejected by the old biddy, who'd stormed off after offering her enigmatic suggestion. That had been a curdled dram to drink.

Hell, beyond the obvious issue of Sander's idiocy and nasty nuns, it had been a struggle to figure out just what was going on, with her, with life. Jan had never cared about her except as a submarine draft animal, she knew that much from the moment he'd put the rope 'round her neck out on the crypt. But taking it in, really swallowing the lump of it and making it a real part of her, that had been rough. Nobody had ever cared about her before, so why did she care if they didn't now? What had she expected from a man who had near-drowned her the first time they ever laid eyes on each other?

Everybody just wanted something, was all—her father had only seen her for the work she could do, and then the groots he could trade her for, and her brothers had wanted the extra food they'd have if she weren't around, or the extra blankets, and even the most sheep-eyed of the fisherboys had only wanted her for what she looked like from across the waves: a half-furred fanny and a budding pair of tits.

But Sander, he could've left her anywhere, anytime, even after the nun had sent him packing. Instead, he'd helped her track down the stable in Rotterdam where Jan had said he'd boarded Mackerel, except that the horseman had played ignorant, even when Sander grabbed him by the hair and shouted in his face. As she lay in the colossal bed in the overgrown Leyden house, Jolanda wondered where she would be if they had recovered Mackerel and then parted ways as she'd originally planned, her taking the horse instead of accompanying Sander back to Dordrecht. Hurrying away from the stable before the proprietor could recover from the sucker punches Sander had liberally administered, he'd promised her a share of the fortune he'd been sure Primm would secure now that they had the ring.

It had seemed like such a simple thing to hear him say it, but even in the boat back to Dordt she'd suspected it was a foolish plan. Yet here they were, a few turns of the seasons later.

Nobles.

More or less.

A year before, she'd been an ignorant child, dodging work and the blows she earned as a result, and now she was a lady. Or so Wurfbain assured her—she didn't feel much different, although she was learning to fake that, too. Her instructor in these impossibly intricate matters was the Lady Zoete Van Hauer, a blond, bosomy noblewoman who called twice a week. Zoete could go from severe to silly in the blink of an eye, but the constant about the handsome older woman was that she never gave the slightest hint that she might suspect her clumsy pupil of being an impostor.

Still, other than Sander, there wasn't a person Jolanda met that didn't make her feel all stupid and obvious, a thief caught in the act, a hound trying to walk around on her hind legs and speak man's words with a bitch's tongue. Even when Fye turned down the bed for her and tucked her in, the elderly maid's eyes, for all their kindness and pity, seemed to dig into Jolanda, like a crow pecking at something juicy. She never felt at ease, not with the servants, not with the guests Wurfbain occasionally brought home, and certainly not when he made her go out in public.

"Church," Wurfbain said on Easter morning. "Something you've both been lacking, I think."

Sander yawned. Jolanda blushed. She hadn't been inside a church since leaving home, and the thought of the confession she'd have to make was horrifying. She looked up at Sander with sudden worry, thinking how much worse his impending penance must be than hers, for she had heard from the way the count talked of poots that to be a sodomite was as bad as being a killer. Which Sander also was, aye. Yet he didn't seem concerned by the prospect, and so she tried to allay her fears as well.

"That of course means unveiling you, but I think you're ready." The man's snowy eyebrows went up so often when he addressed them that Jolanda wondered why he ever bothered relaxing them. "I have decided, however, that your dear daughter will need to be ever present as you enter society. Considering."

"Considering what?" demanded Sander.

"Considering your mind, dearest Jan, is a sieve," said Wurfbain, scooping a runny piece of egg with his bread crust and popping it into his mouth. He never got any food in his mustache, Jolanda noticed. Never.

"That a fact?" said Sander in his quiet, calm, I'm-about-to-attack-you voice.

"It's something I noticed immediately upon meeting you, of course," continued the count, seemingly oblivious to the danger he was in. "Which is why I've spent as much time on Jolanda as I have."

Sander's eyes, the only part of him that gave away how furious he was at times like these, now shifted to Jolanda. Why the hell should he be cross with her? Fickle as the dawn, his temper.

"Spending time on Jo, are you?" said Sander.

"Yes. Tutoring her so that she can whisper in your ear when you're in danger of embarrassing yourself. The pretext of course is that being raised abroad, your Dutch is not as good as hers, and so she will occasionally need to translate."

"What?" Some of Sander's fury was edged out by his confusion.

"Who is Francis van Borselen?" Wurfbain asked breezily.

"Oh," said Sander, and the rest of his wrath departed, pushed out by the tongue he pressed into his cheek as he stared off into space. His lips began moving soundlessly. Jolanda glanced at the count but did not speak until he asked her.

"Do you know, Jolanda?"

"He's the Graaf of Ostrevant, in Zeeland," she said at once, and for Sander's benefit, added, "I think?"

"Exactly," beamed Wurfbain, his eyes closed, perhaps from the brilliance of his own sunny smile. "Borselen's a Cod, and thus no friend of ours. Your daughter will remind you whose favor we curry and whose toes we step on. Politically," he hastened to add, "only political foot-stomping, my boy. And in the event you forget to whom you are speaking, or the details of your country-mouse backstory, she'll be right there to provide you a cue. If you're separated and find yourself in need of her, simply feign confusion and hurry off to find her. '*Pardon, pardon, my daughter, she translate something for me.*'"

"Yeah, I get you," said Sander, warming to the plan now that he realized it would be less work for him, the lazy ball-washer. "Jo follows me around, keeps me out of mischief."

"So . . ." Jolanda suddenly felt rather ill, like she had after eating Primm's lamb that first day in Dordrecht. "So I have to, I, I'm to be with him all the time, around all the people? The nobles?"

"Absolutely. All the time." Wurfbain nodded, taking another bite of egg. Jolanda pushed her hardly touched plate away and dipped her hands in the finger bowl. It wasn't fair, having to pick up Sander's slack as well as studying the different knitting styles and points of etiquette and the names of a hundred people she'd never laid eyes on and still making time for the sword, which the count had only relented to let her learn after she'd agreed to do all the rest. Foolish goddamn neuker. Wurfbain waved them away, saying, "Change into something nice. The count of Holland will be at the service, so no shilly-shallying—better we queue up late to catch the right sort of attention, but we don't want to be *too* late. Tout de suite."

Toot sweet? Service? Oh—Church. Now Jolanda didn't think she would be sick—instead, she was sure of it. Count of Holland? Church? Bullshit.

She was nearly in tears when she got to her room, but Fye was waiting with a gorgeous new gown, a mantis-green-and-lamb-white damask affair with silver ivy embroidered across the chest. It looked like it was made for a princess or queen and not some dirty little fraud from the sea. The handmaid helped her into it and the matching veil, offering encouragement as she did—so far as the woman knew, Jolanda really was a noble girl from a distant land, and so in the servant's mind she shouldn't have anything to fear beyond embarrassment regarding her provincial ways. If only.

Looking at her reflection in the polished silver mirror Fye held up, Jolanda scarce recognized herself, a real lady looking back at her…until she noticed her purple hands jutting out of the sleeves, and the tears broke through. She was supposed to tell people they were birthmarks if anyone was rude enough to inquire, but she knew somebody would recognize the dyed skin for what it was, and then they would be unmasked and it would be all her fault and…

"There, there," said Fye, embracing Jolanda with her pillowy arms. "It'll be good to get it over with, miss, it will, and you'll get to see the church, which is no small thing!"

"Thank you," Jolanda muttered, her apprehension not so much allayed as displaced by the awkwardness of being coddled. Fye was all right, but was clearly trying to fill the mother-shaped hole in the girl's life—a void Jolanda was not in the habit of noticing until it was pointed out to her. "I'm...that's good, Fye. I'm good now. Let me go."

"Bah, such a tough thing!" said Fye, releasing her. "Keep your father quiet in there if you can."

"Yes, ma'am," Jolanda said with a sigh. Babysitting Sander was bad enough in the manor, but doing so in a church, and in front of a pack of kingly men all looking down on them...that was some dumb shit, right there.

A knock came at the door; Sander was there in a baby-blue doublet, a moss-green mantle, and bright white hose, looking as itchy as a flea-plagued hound in the finery. Jolanda realized he was even less comfortable about all this than she was, and she accepted the trembling palm he extended with a little thrill of pleasure at his nervousness. Hard man like him scared of going to church!

Wurfbain was waiting in a carriage before the manor's impressive portico, the coach's latten trim gleaming through the light morning drizzle. The four horses and driver behind them waited stoically, already soaked themselves, but the count impatiently waved at Sander and Jolanda from the window of the box. Jolanda was down the stairs in an instant, eager to see the interior of this new, ostentatious coach, but at the edge of the muddy drive Sander swooped her up from behind, an arm hooking under her armpit and the other catching her behind the knee. She barely stopped herself from planting an elbow in his throat—old habits and all.

"Ruin your gown, idiot," said Sander as he carried her to the coach. "Some lady, prancing around in the muck like a suckling pig."

"Why, thank you, Graaf Jan!" she said with a laugh, the priggish expression on his face almost convincing her they might pull this off after all—he certainly looked tart and stodgy as a nobleman. Quite before she realized what she was doing, she kissed him on his cheek, which caused him to jerk his face back and grimace.

"No need for all that," he said, pushing her through the door of the coach.

"Sorry," she said, falling over the count's long knees. The inside of the box was tight and rather flimsy-looking, with only the single padded bench to sit on. How had she ever thought these vehicles spacious? Wurfbain helped her across him and she flopped onto the seat, damp and jittery, as Sander inserted himself on the other side of the count and closed the door. The chains rigging the contraption together jingled as the driver cracked the reins dramatically, and they bounced off at a fair clip.

The drive was so rocky that Jolanda later marveled at her strength of guts in not losing what little breakfast she'd managed, though part of the credit there was probably owed to the count's endless quizzing, which kept her mind off her queasiness. Sander was quieter, and twitchier, for the duration. At first they followed the thick row of brilliant green reeds bordering the Oude Rijn, but before very long the stomach-churning bumpiness of the road through the outskirts gave to clattering stones as they entered Leyden proper, the stone walls scintillating silver in the rain.

"Right-ho, Graaf and Lady," said Wurfbain as the coach slowed to a stop. Jolanda stuck her head out the window, braving the wet to get a look at the church. She saw only rows of ordinary brick buildings on either side of the road, and the back of another halted carriage in front of them. Sander pulled her back into the box, having leaned across the frowning count to reach her.

"Neuking bumpkin," Sander grumbled. He looked a little better since they had reached town, but still far from hale—his sickly verdancy had faded to a complexion devoid of any color at all, like grass bleached by the sun; a pale noble in bad need of a crap or a nap. Or both.

"Sir Jan Tieselen," said Wurfbain. "Bow before your sovereign."

"Eh?"

"Your sovereign's name being..."

"John, everyone knows it's Count John," said Sander, turning to the window, where a steady throng of chattering peasants drifted past, their spirits apparently drier than their coats. "John, the *cunt* of Holland."

"John of…"

"John the Cuntbitch, Cunt of Holland."

"Very funny. No, John of—"

"Bavaria," said Jolanda, forgetting not to interrupt. "John of Bavaria."

"And how, then, did a Bavarian barbarian come to oversee we free people of Holland and Zeeland?" Wurfbain asked her, but he was looking at Sander.

"He put Countess Jacoba on the run, and—"

"Earlier," said Wurfbain. "Start earlier."

"Earlier?" said Jolanda. "Aye, soooo…when the old Count of Holland, William, when he died, his daughter Jacoba was supposed to rule beside her husband, John. John of Brabant. That early?"

"Which John?" asked Wurfbain. "There are an awful lot of Johns, in Brabant as elsewhere. And no ayes, remember, no ayes."

"Aye. Yes. Sorry. The sixth," said Jolanda. "No, shit, the fourth. Anyway, John's in the Hook party, like us, but he's weak, and people took issue with him and Jacoba, particularly folk in Dordrecht, which is where the couple was when things went sour. John, not the Brabanter she married but our uh, steward, the Bavarian, he's Jacoba's uncle, and a Cod, and he stole his niece's birthright, making himself count of Holland. So they've been fighting ever since, Jacoba's Hooks and her uncle John's Cods, and he's mostly won out, despite being an enormous arsehole."

"Very tidy," said Wurfbain. "We might make a lady of you yet. But never, *ever* refer to John of Bavaria's theft as such—don't forget, we Hooks are in a delicate spot, with our Jacoba on the run. Ah, and those from Brabant are Brabançons, *not* Brabanters. As for you, I wouldn't advise that."

Sander put the stopper back in the small bottle he'd been drinking from and tucked it into the fold between the bottom cushion of the seat and the brocade backing. He muttered, "Shouldn't be here. Won't work."

"Nonsense," said Wurfbain brightly. "Why, with Jolanda's wits and your credentials, you're—"

"Getting out," said Sander, fumbling with the latch on his door. "You lot get hanged if you want. Not me. Getting out. Forget it, the whole thing. Keep my coin, I'm out."

"*No*, you are *not*," said the count, rapping Sander's knuckles with the gilded cane he had hereto steepled his hands upon. "If you leave this carriage you will be caught by sundown and tortured through Pentecost, do you understand me?"

"Dare threaten me, you cunt?" said Sander, the reddening hand Wurfbain had struck shooting out to the count's throat, the chains of the coach jangling and the whole box shifting as Sander fell upon the man. Jolanda found herself incapable of moving, half-buried as she was under the uprooted Wurfbain. Over his shoulder she saw that several passersby had stopped to peer through the window, evidently delighted to see the noblesse throttling one another. And on Easter!

"I do, *Sander*, I do, indeed," whispered the count. He had never before called his pupil by that moniker; even when he was acknowledging the ruse, which was not often, he never used the man's real name. Wurfbain went on, as though they were continuing a pleasant conversation postponed by the refilling of glasses. "You murderous sheephead thug, you listen to me, with both ears. I know all about you, and I have men who can find you wherever you go, and—"

"All about me?" Sander faked a laugh. It sounded painful, desperate. "What's there to know, fancy man?"

"All your secrets." Wurfbain's lips had pulled back, his mouth resembling a deep wound, all blood-red gums and bone-white teeth. "We both know what I'm talking about."

"Secrets…" A shadow of fear passed over Sander's face, like the pulsing current of a winter stream momentarily darkening the thin ice atop it, but quick as that it was gone again. "I haven't got any secrets."

"No? What about Sneek, you mad buffoon?" asked Wurfbain, still pinned to the seat beside Jolanda. "What about *that*?"

The color returned to Sander's face, and how. He looked purple as Jolanda's arms, and she wondered if his eyes would pop out like those of a sunbaked fish, so wide did they bulge. She didn't understand what was happening—Sander should have punched in the count's face for continuing to take a tone after being warned, but instead the larger man released Wurfbain and fell back, blocking the window with his wide shoulders and earning boos from the small crowd of townsfolk who had gathered beside the coach.

Then, just as quickly as it had struck, Sander's terror palpably withdrew, leaving him bristling mad again. "Jan was there, that cunt. Helped me get away. He told you about it."

"Ah, yes, he brought you your sword as you were fighting your way through the mob," said the count, his voice never rising above a whisper. "But what about after? When you went into the canal? When you went under? And all those long weeks and months after? Whole seasons, Sander, gone—did you tell your beloved Jan about where you were that Christmas? That Shrovetide? That Easter? Do *you* even remember?"

"I told him." Sander choked on the words, clearly trying to convince himself of something. "I told, I told about losing them months, about—"

"Belgium?" Wurfbain said lightly. It was an odd, ugly-sounding word that Jolanda didn't recognize. Based on Sander's appalled expression, it wasn't the sort of word you'd want to recognize. "Did you tell him about your Belgian playmates, you nutty bastard?"

Sander's face fell and his shoulders slumped. His eyes were brimming with tears. Strange as it was, this relaxed Jolanda, even as she wondered just what in heaven they were talking about, wondered at Sander letting somebody other than Jan call him mad to his face.

"Nobody gives a quick shit that you murdered a Frisian, and then murdered some more when they tried to hang you," said Wurfbain, leaning toward Sander and patting the man's trembling knee. "Sneek's a long way behind us. I don't bring that up, or the Belgian business, to threaten you. I simply mention them so that we understand each other, *Jan*. I know who you were, who you are, and rest assured, if you ruin what I've worked so hard to achieve with your... cowardice, then I will have you tortured to death. Slowly." Perhaps as an afterthought, the count turned to Jolanda and smiled as he added, "And the dye-maker's daughter. Slowly, Jan."

Sander was silent. Jolanda was silent. The coach lurched forward a few dozen paces and stopped again.

"Or you can both be filthy, filthy rich until the day you die, old and happy," Wurfbain said, looking back and forth between them. "Your choice!"

"He really say all that?" Still smashed against the door of the carriage from the weight of his fear, Sander looked over the count's head, at Jolanda. "You hear him say that, 'bout...'bout Sneek, and afterward and all? He say that?"

Jolanda nodded, and Sander put his hand in his mouth, biting down and closing his eyes. Wurfbain swatted her arm lightly, winked at her. She flinched, a burst of hatred burning through her—she wasn't sure what he had meant with his speechifying, but he had clearly intended to hurt Sander with his words, and succeeded wildly. To say fuck all of threatening to torture her if Sander ran off.

Eventually they began moving again, Wurfbain testing her on the differences between Leyden's old Pieterskerk and the new Hooglandse Church until the latter came into view through Sander's window, which he was no longer blocking, having finally slithered back down onto the bench. After that, Jolanda forgot to keep offering Sander reassuring glances as the coach came around the side and then the front of the mighty building. It was the biggest thing Jolanda had ever seen, so large it hurt her eyes to look upon it—squinting at the spiny spires cresting the front of the church far, far overhead, she felt herself grow dizzy.

They slowed to a stop as a man and a woman draped in fur-trimmed, well, everything, ascended the stairs, the open doors of the church flanked by militiamen whose attire was nearly as fine as that of the noble couple entering the building. Sander leaned forward, sticking his head out the window and spoiling the view, but before Jolanda could tell him to move his fat head, he puked down the side of the coach.

"Jesus fucking Christ," said Wurfbain, his constant smile straining so hard Jolanda wondered that he didn't pull something. Sander retched again, and as he hung farther out the window, Jolanda saw that the couple on the stairs had turned and looked back at them with disgust—justifiable, she had to allow, and she sank back into her seat, wishing she could blend into the soft cushions and be left behind. Wurfbain put a white-gloved hand on Sander's heaving shoulder and murmured, "There we are, as noble an appearance as any I've witnessed. Now, get the hell out there, Jan, before we slow things down any more."

Jolanda closed her eyes, told herself it would be all right. In the precious blackness she heard Sander spit. Then the door of the coach creaked, and crockery shattered, startling her eyes open. Sander had knocked the bottle he had tucked into the seat cushions onto the ground, and as he stood blinking miserably beside the coach, Jolanda realized it had stopped raining and the sun was out, shining upon their entrance.

"Come then, m'lady," Sander said, leering at her as Wurfbain surreptitiously wiped off the madman's face with a handkerchief. The count resembled an embarrassed mother cleaning up her boy with a washrag in front of unamused company. "The cunt of Holland awaits!"

II.

The sun might have finally showed its craven face, but outside the coach it was still damp as a used whore's thighs. Or so Sander had heard; he'd never lain with a woman, bought or free, in all his life. His stupid, overlong calfhide noble shoes slipped halfway up the wet stairs of the church, but he regained his balance and advanced on the massive double doors. He offered the crowd of peasants fanned out in the square on the far side of the line of carriages a knowing nod. People were laughing. Lots of them.

Fuck 'em. He was Graaf Jan Tieselen, and he was going to fucking church on Easter.

Except now the ruse, the meeting of predominantly Cod nobles who would hate him for being a Hook even if they didn't suspect his fraudulent nature, all of it was eclipsed by a much greater and more pressing concern: *Hobbe fucking Wurfbain.* It was only through the most steadfast concentration that Sander had kept thoughts of that aquatic Frisian nightmare from his mind over the last year, and now the count had dredged it all up, rubbing his nose in it. The ponce wasn't just a ponce; he knew more than anyone, he knew about Sander's dream about Belgians and—

But what if it wasn't a dream? Shit, fuck, piss, if Hobbe knew about it, then it couldn't just be a dream, could it? How would he know about it if that were all that had happened, a knock on the head when he went into the canal, a prolonged dream-fit or something—Saint Lizzy's crack, had he really just pretended it hadn't happened? That it wasn't a big deal that he didn't know where he'd been or what he'd done a year ago? Or for months on either side of last Easter? Well, he knew that somewhere in there he'd been down in the world's biggest cunting well with a pack of demons. No, worse, a pack of *Belgians*, whatever the shit a Belgian was, but that hardly made up for all the time he'd lost. He—

—Had entered the church without even noticing, the vaulted ceiling stretching high as heaven above him, rich people everywhere, staring and covering their smiles with kidskin gloves, Hobbe whispering something behind him as Sander strode forward up the aisle of the packed church. It was white, the church, white walls and white chapels and white pillars and white statues. Too white, it was, the sort of white that made filth stand out all the brighter.

Sander must have met Hobbe during those now-forgotten times and then told him all about his Belgian dream. Yes. Sander imagined the scene, bearing down on it, hammering the fantasy into a memory—it might not've even been Hobbe, it could've been any random asshole, the story eventually finding its way to the count. Saints knew, each and all of them in heaven, that the first thing Sander would do after having a dream like that would be to tell anyone who would listen, especially if he was out of his head from… whatever it was that made him go out of his head, and—

—Hobbe snared Sander's elbow, which almost led to the ponce catching it in the chin. But then Sander saw the count was trying to pull him over to a gap in a row of churchgoers, Jo hissing at him to step out of the aisle, but he couldn't hear her over the coughing, scraping, squeaking, rustling riot of the church.

Sander continued to sift through his convoluted theories throughout the service, only coming back to the church when the bleating jester at the front hit an especially high note of Latin. There was so, so much for Sander to riddle out, and stretches of warm relief were bookended by cold flashes of panic as he vacillated between a calm certainty that Hobbe was simply playing on his fears in order to manipulate him and the mind-rattling terror that each and every member of the noble congregation was in cahoots with Hobbe *and* the Belgians. That the monsters and the counts of Holland were collaborating to get Sander's fucking ass was a shit prospect. By the time Hobbe leaned over and whispered in his ear, Sander was drenched in sweat.

"That's it, Jan, we're off," said the count. "Now as we leave, I'll introduce you to whoever happens to be about, so I need you to pull yourself together. Now. Or you and the girl will pay for it. Simply be a good boy and we'll have a private chat later, you and I, but if you're bad . . ."

Sander awkwardly stepped in place, getting the life back into his dead legs until Hobbe let him enter the stream of nobles leaving the church, Hobbe and then Jo following him out. As they moved slowly toward the open doors, through which Sander could see that the rain had begun again, the count chatted with an older woman draped in fancy pelts and another lady Sander recognized as Zoete, the noblewoman who came around the manor to tutor Jo in the arts of being a rich female. Hobbe introduced the dowager to Sander, but her name swum away even as he heard it and he made no effort to net it again.

Thankfully, the ladies seemed more interested in Jo, and so Sander was free to further ruminate on the possibilities— whatever the means, the end seemed to be that Hobbe was a conniving motherfucker who knew more than he ought to, and thus a dangerous enemy. Stupid cunt thought he could control Sander, though, which was something Sander could use to his advantage—meant he didn't have to be in a hurry, meant he could bide until he found out what he needed to, until he found a way to get Jo safely away from the evil nobleman.

"Something amusing?" Hobbe asked after the women parted their company at the door. Sander realized that the fantasy of smothering Hobbe with a pillow on the night he and Jo escaped the manor had caused him to grin like an idiot. They were atop the stairs just outside the church, at the crest of a velvet-and-satin wave waiting to break down upon the line of carriages as soon as the rain let up or one's personal coach was sighted in the queue.

"Nay," said Sander. "Just thinking 'bout what you said."

"Papa?" said Jo, taking his hand and giving it a squeeze. "Are you all right?"

Nice of her to ask when she was clearly the one shitting herself, the girl washed-out and trembling as a water lily on a choppy day. He squeezed her fingers back, but must've done so a mite too hard, for she scowled and yanked her hand away. Her anger brought some color to her cheeks, and he smiled at this. "Just fine, Jo, just—"

"What is the meaning of this?" A squirrelly young man in a red cape had appeared on the steps before them. "Who the devil are you?"

It took Sander a moment to realize the lad was addressing him, but when he did, he comported himself pretty damn well, he thought. "I'm Jan Tieselen—and whose honor I got?"

"*What?!*" The man's thick blond mustache made Sander think he might be a decent sort, his odd response notwithstanding. "*What?!*"

"Damn," said Sander, realizing he must have bungled his introduction. Taking off the hat he had mauled between his fingers into an orange velvet lump during the service, he bowed as best he could without this worked-up twit giving him space to properly do it. "I am Graaf Jan Tieselen, at last returned from my, uh, *tenure* in the East. Whose, ah, acquaintance I got the credit of making?"

"Bullshit," the nobleman sneered, turning to Hobbe. "Who is this man, Wurfbain, this, this—"

"Jan Tieselen," Sander said a third time. The fancy-caped fellow was now giving him his full attention, probably due to the fact that Sander had darted out his hand and grabbed the man's cock and one of his balls through the puffy junk-pouch of his hose—fashionable or no, this ponce was going to learn the value of a real codpiece. Sander squeezed hard enough to blanch the man's face, but not enough to make him collapse. Yet. "And I'm a graaf you don't ignore without result. Cunt. Now tell me your fucking name 'fore I geld you."

"Simon," the man gasped. "Simon Gruyere, please, I, I meant no—"

"'Course you didn't," said Sander, releasing the ponce—the last thing he wanted was to hold on long enough for one of these other assholes to notice and make a scene. "Now that we're met and all—"

"You mad cur!" the ponce hissed, slipping backward on the stairs. "You have no, no *concept* of whom you've made an enemy!"

"That's where you're wrong," said Sander. "Simon Gruyere's the name of the cunt, and I don't aim to forget it."

Jo giggled behind them, and to Sander's surprise Hobbe laughed as well, the count taking a step down the stairs to put himself between Gruyere and Sander as he addressed the offended noble. "Tell your brother to start packing. You boors have just been hooked!"

Gruyere abandoned whatever retort he had been levying at Sander and stared dumbstruck at Hobbe. The rain dribbled off his tremulous mustache, and Hobbe descended the stair past him, wiggling his fingers in a silly little wave as he did so. Sander followed the count, imitating Hobbe's gesture. Jo caught up with Sander and took his hand, smiling up at him.

The exhilaration of barking down that Gruyere bitch had cheered Sander considerably, but clambering back into the coach to sit beside Hobbe, he was well reminded that not everything was so grand. The count was giving him a peculiar look that might have been either annoyance or pride, Sander wasn't sure which. He decided to be optimistic:

"That went well, eh?"

Hobbe laughed until he wept, then regained his composure, wiping his face. Looking back and forth between Jo and Sander, he started again, hooting with mirth as he shook his head. Finally, he managed,

"No, no, no, not at all. That was *dreadful*. Dreadful. You grabbed his pouch!"

"He learned a lesson from it," Sander said defensively. "Won't happen again, tell you that."

"Aye, he had it coming," said Jo. Sander's victory was short-lived as she added, "But that don't mean you ought to give it to him."

"Exactly," said Hobbe. "John fancies himself a knight of legend, despite his picking fights with his own niece. Grabbing another noble like that at court where he might see is about as stupid a thing as you could manage without special instruction. Jolanda, on the other hand, did wonderfully. Did you enjoy yourself?"

"It weren't so bad," Jo allowed. "Zoete's friend was nice enough."

"Lady Meyl Von Wasser? She's the evilest Cod in Holland. Charming enough to exchange pleasantries with at an Easter service, certainly, but Hook women like you and Zoete will never be invited to join her sewing circle, even when you're all neighbors in Dordrecht."

"And when's that, anyway?" said Sander. "When we get our own place?"

"Very soon now. Even sooner than I would have preferred, but your inspecting the Gruyere jewels so thoroughly will necessitate a hastening of plans—Simon will be back in Dordrecht to warn his brother in no time at all, and we don't want them getting too far ahead of us."

"His brother?" What the fuck were they talking about? "Whose brother?"

"Jesus, Sander!" Jo shouted, the little bitch pissed off at *him*, now. "Simon's brother is Braem, the elder son of Jan's father's wife's brother, Rutger Gruyere. How's that hard to remember?"

"Wait, him?" Sander recognized the name Gruyere now. Well, it sounded familiar, anyway. "Yeah, I knew *that*. Obviously. The one I grabbed, that Simon, he's…he's who, now?"

Hobbe groaned theatrically.

"You need to keep this straight," Jo said. "Simon and Braem are Jan's cousins, and since every other heir died in the flood, they've received everything that was Jan's father's—the Tieselen house in Dordrecht, the wine importation business, and, if the waters ever recede, all of Oudeland."

"Sure," said Sander, remembering now. "Gotcha."

"You've had almost a year to learn this stuff," said Jo. "You at least need to remember who it is that's going to want to kill you when we're done with this."

"No worries there," said Sander, trying his damnedest not to glance at the count seated between them. "I got that part firm in fist, daughter dear, and it ain't the tail I've a hold of, neither."

"Jan," Hobbe said patiently. "I don't want to kill you."

"Provided I do as you say," sneered Sander.

"Correct. I hope you're not still sore about our tiff during the drive?"

"Me? Nay, I ain't given it another thought." The cobbles ended and the coach began to rattle over the rough road. Sander felt like he might throw up again.

Hobbe sighed. "You'll have calmed down enough to realize it was Jan who told me about your nightmare, yes?"

"Yeah, my—wait, he what?" It was disorienting enough, having a conversation with someone all up on you with the seat cramped like this, but this particular conversation...

"When I met him in Dordrecht, just before you set out to Oudeland for the ring. He told me everything. He said you fell into a canal during your escape from the gallows in Friesland, and disappeared for ages and ages. When you found him again, you told him you couldn't remember what had happened."

"That so?" Sander's heart began to imitate the carriage wheels, bouncing around his chest as it picked up speed. The count was lying, obviously—Sander had told Jan that much, sure, but nothing more, certainly nothing about the Belgians.

"Jan said you took to talking in your sleep after your reunion in Rotterdam," Hobbe went on affably. "He said that when you awoke, you claimed not to remember anything, but while you dreamed, you muttered quite a bit, and from that he pieced together what had happened. Belgians from Belgium and all that."

Sander just stared, not sure what the devil was going on. Jan had told Hobbe *what*?

"Jan said it sounded like you'd washed downstream from Sneek and were rescued by some exceptionally ugly lepers. Peat-cutters, by trade, an old man and wife and their children. Apparently these poxed peat-cutters nursed you through the winter—you were very sick, having fits, but they did their best to keep you warm and fed, being good Christians. Even in a fever-state you ate them out of house and home, it sounds like, until the end of spring."

"…What?" Sander finally managed, concentrating on that black stretch of lost time and imagining dim glimpses of dirty, deformed faces looming over a pallet, where he lay shivering. He shivered again, there in the coach. This was bullshit. Had to be.

"And *then*," Hobbe continued, turning to Jo and waggling his eyebrows, as if he'd hit the good part of a favorite story, "and then, it seems, you had a different sort of fit entirely, mistaking your saviors for monsters. Belgians, you called them. Belgica is the old Roman name for Holland, of course. I have heard that in the wilds of France some peasants still speak a bastardized Latin—it seems likely to me that your lepers similarly retained some of the old language, and you overheard them speaking this gibberish."

"No," Sander whispered. He envisioned a misshapen man on a dark stream bank holding up a sputtering rushlight, searching the moonless night for Sander, who had sleepwalked away. So the husband—call him Belgian, sure—had come looking for Sander, and then Sander had wrestled him to the ground, beat him, stabbed him with a piece of bone. Then he had gone looking for the wife. For the kids. "No."

"It's not your fault," said Hobbe, patting his shoulder. "You were out of sorts, sick in the pate. I was curious, so I investigated a little, and it seems that there was indeed a nearby familial leper colony that was eradicated by an assailant or assailants unknown. No survivors, you understand, or I should be able to provide you with further details."

Sander stared with unabashed horror at Hobbe. This was worse than a conspiracy of monsters, worse by fucking *leagues*. He could picture it all too well, lepers old and young leaping on him with their peat blades, croaking their damn Friesland-talk as he killed any he could lay hands on, until they pushed him back into the black water, their tools crack-crack-cracking into his already feverish skull, driving him into the current that would take him downstream...

"Maybe it's unrelated," said Hobbe, his voice coming as if from a great distance, a great depth. "Maybe the massacre was unpaid mercenaries raiding, I don't know, the peat supplies, or just someone who hates lepers. All that I can be sure of is that Jan claimed to put together such a story from your sleep-talk. He said he would talk to you as you muttered away the night, trying to help you preserve the memories when you were awake as well as dreaming, but in your sleep you insisted you didn't want to. He said when you were awake, he would fish about to see if you could recall anything, but it only annoyed you."

Sander certainly remembered Jan getting on his nuts in that regard, badgering him about where he might have been and what he might have done between Sneek and their reunion. The notion that all along Jan had known or at least suspected what had happened but not volunteered the information stung like a wasp to the asshole. Of course, that meant that Sander had known all along, too, that he had simply kept it locked up deep inside and refused to let himself see it.

It might not be the first occasion Sander had done it, either, remembering how firmly he had convinced himself that he was leaving home for good simply because he wanted to and not because he had tossed his drunk father into the shallow well and locked the lid in place. It was only from the dreams that began long after he fled that Sander really remembered what he had done that night—the sounds of his father scratching at the soft wooden walls of the well, the splashing and crying bubbling up through the darkness of slumber.

"I apologize for using the information to frighten you earlier, but you must understand that I couldn't have you running off on me at the last moment, not when we're so close to success." Hobbe yawned. "That was one of Jan's suggestions, as it happens. *'If you ever need to really get Sander's attention, just tell him you know about the Belgians.'* I didn't anticipate it having quite such a strong effect, so I thought it best to come clean about everything sooner rather than later—it occurred to me during the service that my mention of it might lead you to think something, I don't know, *unnatural* had happened, and not—"

"Shut it! Just...shut it! Cunt!" Sander exploded, clenching his fists until they ached. Jo had squirmed around in her seat and was looking at him with the wide, stupid expression she sometimes wore when she was upset, like when she'd realized what Jan was about as he strangled her. Sander turned away to the emerald blur of reeds outside his window. He put a hand on the door. "I'm walking back. Or you got something smart to say 'bout that, too?"

Hobbe didn't reply other than to lean forward and bang his cane against the fore wall of the coachbox. The vehicle slowed, and Sander fled into the rain. Jo tried to follow him, but he waved her off, and then the carriage was moving again, the manor lying somewhere beyond the storm that seemed to pick up the moment he left the carriage. Fuck-knuckles. Looking over the empty fields to one side and the Oude Rijn beyond the rushes on the other, Sander felt his throat constrict even as his fists finally relaxed, clubs becoming hands as if thawed by the warm rain.

What was better, being a mad killer or the world being full of monsters? What was more likely, Hobbe telling the truth before the service, or after? It would be the tidiest trick of all, if Hobbe was working for them, to make Sander think he was mad, when really he hadn't killed anybody at all, just demons.

Other than the people Sander knew he had killed, of course, there were plenty of those, but as for leprous peat-cutters that even now he could only half-remember...

Remember or imagine?

But no, that was just an excuse, wasn't it? Something to keep him from saying to himself, *all right, Sander, you were a little barmy there for a little while, but you're better now,* anything to avoid the unavoidable, to prolong the inevitable.

And they always had an excuse, didn't they? They, them, those—the rich men, the graafs and their bullyboys, the free-men, the knights, the mercenary chiefs, the militiamen, the lords and ladies...

And now he was one of them. Would that he hadn't drowned his old da, so the wicked asshole could have seen his son become a graaf before being hanged for whatever crimes Sander saw fit to charge him with. Sander smiled to himself and set off down the road after the coach, thunder rippling across the sky as his stupid noble's shoes filled with mud.

Autumn 1425

"The Best Straps Are Cut from Someone Else's Leather"

I.

The day after the Feast of Saint Alberic, when Graaf Tieselen and his daughter had entertained a remarkably vulgar Flemish graaf and his brat as a favor to Count Wurfbain, the Lady Jolanda spent her afternoon taking her new servant around to the various markets. This sat predictably poorly with Drimmelin, for the cook preferred to do the shopping, but the sun was out and Jolanda would be damned before she would sit inside just so the older woman could get her haggle on. No doubt Drimmelin turned a pfennig or two for herself in the process, but that was just one tough tit—Jolanda liked the market on fall days like this, with the breeze akin to cool hands on a warm cheek rather than the slapping palms of winter.

Mistress and maid set off with baskets in hand, toward Groenmarkt. At this time of day Varkenmarkt would be less busy, but the grain market was closer, and Jolanda preferred to get the meat last to prevent it from leaking on everything else. The crowds were certainly out in Groenmarkt Square, necessitating a clumsy dance through the stalls with five new partners popping up for every step a lady might take. Jolanda was glad to be in the midst of the madness—she was never quite sure how to behave around new people, and Lijsbet wasn't making things any easier by keeping her own mouth shut. Better than a blatherer, aye, but it made it difficult to get a feel for whether the girl was smooth or coarse, coming from a softer situation or a harder one.

"What did Drimmelin want, rye or barley?" Jolanda asked

the girl when they broke another wave of townsfolk and found themselves pressed against two sizable bins of grain.

"Don't you decide such things?" Lijsbet replied. Was that a sly smile turning up her plump lips as she said it? Jolanda wasn't sure if the girl was being cheeky or genial, and she felt her cheeks flush with the heat that always seemed to be a puff of breath away from flaring up inside her, everyone from count to kitchen-hag putting her on edge. This was some test, the servant trying to feel out the parameters, find out what she could get away with, how far her new mistress was going to let her stray from prim silence. Which meant it was on Jolanda to play her back, depending on what advantage she saw in—

God's wounds, not every wee thing needed to be thought to death. Jolanda had spent so much time pretending to be a rich arsehole, she was beginning to think like one. If Lijsbet turned out to be a scheming cuntbitch, they'd just sack her. Still...

"I am of the mind that it is always efficacious to let a servant choose what she might, so that one may judge her true worth accordingly," said Jolanda, raising her eyebrows severely at Lijsbet. "I put it to you, then, and caution that your response will dictate whether your services are further required in my house— rye or barley, girl, barley or rye?"

The servant cocked her head at Jolanda, that hint of a smile returning for an instant before dropping away as her mouth opened and hung there. Lijsbet's cheeks colored furiously, and her basket squeaked in her hand. She'd doubted at first, but Jolanda's hard expression had convinced her.

"I'm just riding your tits," Jolanda said with a grin. "I don't care what's in the bread so long as it's soft, aye?"

The servant's blush darkened and her eyes widened, and then they were both laughing.

"Tell you, it's a relief," Lijsbet said as they gained a quiet alley after loading her basket with rye flour. "I was in a house off Gravenstraat afore, and it was awful. Lady was cold as February ice, and the master, well...was glad to be rid of there. But then that Lansloet, he made me think, I don't know, there weren't no smiling to be had in your house, neither."

"He doesn't think there should be," said Jolanda, swinging her empty basket before her. The rains had cleaned these narrow avenues of some of summer's overripe filth. "He's as withered a piece of drift as ever washed ashore. Thinks Jan and me indulge ourselves overly much."

"Oh no, he never said nothing like that," Lijsbet said quickly, and with a bit more seriousness. Clever enough girl to know better than to gossip about other servants to the lady of the house. At least, at first. "He and Drimmelin only ever say the nicest stuff about you and the graaf. On my honor, they think nothing but the best of you two."

"And what's your honor worth, then?" Jolanda hoped it came across as teasing rather than insulting.

"Why, m'lady, I wonder how you come to suppose I was some slut—and here I thought you's unaware I was turning extra mites sneaking up to the attic with Lansloet!"

Jolanda shuddered at the thought, and then they were laughing again. Jolanda couldn't stop herself from wondering if this were all some ruse on Lijsbet's part to insinuate herself into her mistress's confidences....or could be she was just a pleasant young woman. Not everyone was like Wurfbain and his friends. Or herself, Jolanda supposed. Not everyone was a fraud.

"—*such* a pervert!" Lijsbet was saying, and then, realizing they had just stepped from the empty alley into the teeming De Waag, burst into another giggling fit. The servant was a blusher, all right, once more turning red as the lamb shanks they would be bringing home, provided the cuts weren't too pricey. Jolanda laughed along with her servant, but now she couldn't be sure if she were faking it or not.

The leeks were nice and thick, and greener than the last time Jolanda had been, but the almonds were positively desiccated.

She clicked her teeth as she ran her fingers through a nut bin, the proprietor standing firm on his price even in the face of her displeasure. Lijsbet stepped in and talked him down, not with the fierce indignation that Drimmelin, or, fair enough, Jolanda herself would have employed, but instead with a sweet, pleading tone that revolted Jolanda but got results. The ginger was white rather than yellow, and the parsley yellow rather than green, but what could you expect with the first freeze already here? It's always the worst guest who arrives early, Sander often said, which was no doubt why he was always the first at the table. The last thing to procure before moving on to the Varkenmarkt was a jar of amylum, and again Lijsbet took charge of the bartering, this time adopting a harder edge to get the seemingly intractable crone to lower her price on the starch.

"Don't look now," Lijsbet said as they wove their way across the plaza, "but there's a handsome fellow over by the onion-seller who's got his eyes stuck on your veil, or I'm blind myself. You wouldn't have a sweeting, would you?"

"Certainly not," Jolanda said, her heart kicking in her chest at the prospect of being spied on. She hated how the men of Dordt would ogle a woman as though she didn't have a stitch on, regardless of her position or escort, and she hated feeling as twitchy as Sander acted. A year and a half in the clear as Graaf Tieselen and he was still imagining shadowy figures watching him from every dark alley, but Jolanda wouldn't be sucked down into the mad bog where her ersatz father typically dwelt. She kept her face set even as her eyes darted from booth to stall. There were two rooters that she could see from here, but neither had even a halfway-decent-looking man near their stall. "Which one?"

"He's gone," said Lijsbet, frowning. "An older chap, maybe the graaf's age? Hair the color of my basket."

"Narrows it down enough," said Jolanda. "Brown-haired old creeper. Not many of them out."

"Smooth-cheeked, though," said Lijsbet, dropping any pretense of subtlety and craning her neck all around. "And prettier than most sheepheads."

"Oh," said Jolanda, looking about as well, despite how foolish it made her feel. "Wish I was allowed to carry my sword. Poots wouldn't stare if they thought I'd give them a poke instead of the reverse."

"I don't think he was a poot," said Lijsbet. "Nobody'd take you for a boy, m'lady."

"Christ, shut it!" Jolanda said, hurrying the last few paces out of the square and starting down 'S Heer Boeijenstraat. Having the tall stone buildings lean over them put her more at ease than how they hung back at the edges of Grote Markt Square. "And everyone's a poot to me—really gets on Jan's sack to call folk that."

"Your father doesn't like you using such language?"

Jolanda snorted. "Goddamn poot can burn in hell, he tries to tell me how to talk. No, he's sore for the obvious reason."

"Which is..." Lijsbet's hazel eyes were sparkling in the shadow of her wimple, little licks of auburn flame wantonly curling out to frame her face. Again, Jolanda found herself wondering just what was going on behind the girl's pale, pretty face—was she merely angling for gossip, or after some bigger, more elusive catch?

"You ever meet the man likes to get called a poot? Or anything else but *your strongly handsomeness*?" Not a bad save—not the best, but not the worst, either. Sander might insist that nobody cared, that two men could even be married-like, down in France, but then Sander was a moron six days out of seven and Jolanda had overheard enough in her day to know that wasn't the sort of thing you wanted getting out lest you have your head busted open. Even Sander, for all his noise about not giving a toss who knew what wax he liked dipping his wick in, kept things as close to quiet as he was capable, being a raving fool and all.

"Do you really have a sword?" Lijsbet asked. The girl seemed to possess the attention span of a spastic puppy. "What do you do with it?"

"Got a couple," said Jolanda, happier to be on such topics. "My main one's made of Spanish steel, long as my arm. Call it my Tongue, for a laugh, and 'cause it bothers Jan, my giving the weapons names. Says he's the only... ah, never mind the why of it. The other sword, my Tooth, is dull on the sides and tip—use that for practice, since the weight is good. Fucks up my sparring mates something awful. Broke two arms and twice as many fingers with it, training."

"No!" cried Lijsbet. "Whose arms? Whose fingers?"

"Jan's arm the once, and all of the fingers on a couple of occasions. He's the one who taught me to go for the hand holding the sword, you get the chance, but wasn't too happy to find me a quick study!"

"Has he ever hurt you? Practicing?"

"Sure." Jolanda held up her purple left hand, her right easily holding the basket with its light load of amylum and leeks. "See the white line there on the palm? And the way the pinky lists out halfway down? That was two different times. Got scars on my shoulders and arms, and you felt around in my hair you'd find all sorts of hills and valleys from that brute's beatings. We're out in the courtyard near everyday there's not rain."

"Whoa," said Lijsbet, impressed. She stopped walking and Jolanda paused as well, and Lijsbet set down her basket to take her mistress's hand and inspect the scars. "Didn't know noblewomen did that. Any women, really."

"Do anything I want," said Jolanda, pulling her hand away and resuming her pace. It had gotten later than she'd thought, and lest Drimmelin need some of their shopping for that night's supper they had best hurry. "Who's going to make me spend all day weaving? Jan? I don't think so."

"I suppose not," said Lijsbet, her laden basket held in both hands. "Seems to give you your own berth, does the graaf. Lucky. Most ladies like you'd either be married off by now, or have your mother—"

"That's enough talk for now," said Jolanda, hoping it came across as hard as she intended. The servant needed to learn to shut her goddamn mouth once in a while. They were being followed, Jolanda was sure of it, a man about a block behind them taking his sweet time going wherever he was going, which, ever since Grote Markt Square, seemed to be the same destination as theirs.

"Right, sorry," muttered Lijsbet, casting her eyes down. Jolanda didn't reply, moving even faster toward the Varkenmarkt—she might just be imagining that the creeper was actively following them, but the sooner she was done with the shopping and headed home, the sooner she would know for sure.

The chops were as pink as the sunset over the new harbor, with only a faint, algaelike patina on the ends of the bones. Lijsbet commented on this verdigris before a final price was set, and as a result they got off lightly with the lamb. As with any meat, its worth wouldn't be known for several hours after it was eaten, but it certainly shone prettily enough in the fading light. Most of the carts were being wheeled away and the stalls taken down as they left the market, and Jolanda sighed. Whoever creeper had been shadowing them had evidently cleared off, Varkenmarktstraat empty in both directions, and now she had no more excitement to reflect on than a supper with Jan, Wurfbain, and their lawyer, Laurent. Ugh.

"I am sorry for talking too much," said Lijsbet quietly. "I'm . . . well, I really like being in your house. I'm not used to that. Not used to really, I mean, *really*, liking the lady I work for. So I ran off at the gob. Won't happen again."

Jolanda sighed again. "We'll see how much you like it in a few weeks. Jan's awful, and, well, I'm not so good at this, either. Talking with people, I mean. Or anything, really, other than beating on him with a piece of metal every chance I get. Everything else . . . I dunno. But I want you to talk all you want, Lijsbet, so long as you don't take it too sore whenever I tell you to shut it. Which I will. Sometimes I just like the quiet."

"Yeah, of course, absolutely," Lijsbet said enthusiastically.

"And I think you're wonderful at talking! Truly, never met a lady like you—you're great!"

"Shit," said Jolanda, smiling to see how similar their long shadows appeared on the lane before them. "Well, I don't know about that."

"I do," said Lijsbet. "And you're better than the rest. Don't have a stick up...well, I'm sure I don't have to tell you!"

"I guess not," said Jolanda. "Here, let's trade baskets, mine's light as down."

Lijsbet protested, but Jolanda soon wrested it from her. It was a fucking heavy thing. Small wonder the servant was lustrous with sweat despite the chill of the evening—Jolanda would have to make sure the girl didn't overexert herself in her desire to impress.

"Can I ask you something, about the arms?" said Lijsbet as they turned on Voorstraat, and Jolanda felt a mug or two of her goodwill slosh out. Just like that, this slattern was going to ask about the purple? Too goddamn cheeky... "You said you broke two while practicing with your Tooth-sword, but then only mentioned the graaf—who was the other person you hurt?"

"What?" Jolanda said, though she knew what Lijsbet was talking about—it had simply caught her off-guard. "Oh, aye—it was Simon Gruyere."

"Who's he?" asked Lijsbet.

"A dashing youth of better looks than luck," said a patch of shadow as it broke from an alley between the houses bordering the lane. The shadow wore a greasy-looking hooded cloak, which it pushed back to reveal a bad-toothed smile and a stubbly chin. Simon Gruyere wasn't a bad-looking man, if you went in for the poncey sort. Jolanda didn't. Not anymore, at least.

"Simon." Jolanda nodded, stepping around the bowing man to continue homeward. "How's the life of a son of Dordrecht?"

"Improved by your, uh," Simon began walking backward to keep up with Jolanda, dropping painfully obvious glances at

Lijsbet as he went. "Presence, Lady Jo, improved by your presence. Might I have the honor of escorting you home?"

"Nope," said Jolanda. Simon fishing for an invitation inside was just what she needed, on top of Wurfbain and Laurent—how did every annoying acquaintance show up on the same day? Never rained a little in Dordt, that was a fact.

On the other hand, Wurfbain positively hated that Sander associated with the very noble whom he had disenfranchised by pretending to be Jan Tieselen, Laurent didn't like being polite to those he'd legally mauled, and Lansloet clearly felt nervous having his former master visit his old house, even for a short duration…And besides all that, Simon wasn't such a bad sort. Jolanda stopped short, and Simon almost slipped in a puddle as he paused his retreat. "Simon, were you at the market?"

"Which market, dear lady?" Simon batted his eyes at her. Was he drunk? Better than his simply being stupid, she supposed, but a combination of the two seemed most likely.

"This the letch was giving me the eye?" Jolanda asked Lijsbet, who was biting her lip in an attempt not to laugh and shaking her head. The girl couldn't have the faintest idea why Simon was trying to toady himself, let alone so blatantly, but was delighting in it nevertheless. Jolanda held out her basket and said, "If you're going to follow us about, at least offer to carry these before we're within sight of the house. Lazy poot."

"Madame," Simon said, "I assure you I would never—"

"Take our baskets, Simon, and I'll see that you're fed."

Simon displayed his jacked-up teeth and offered Jolanda a cocked-eyebrow expression that was likely meant to be enticing but instead came off as insane, like an otter trying to seduce an otterhound. Jolanda's basket weighed down both of his arms, and he looked pleadingly between her and Lijsbet's proffered load. Jolanda was merciless. A basket at the end of each taut arm, Simon stumbled up the street after the two young women.

"Lijsbet, that is Simon." Jolanda made sure to enunciate clearly since he was behind her. "He used to live in our house."

"Oh," said Lijsbet. "Was he the old master's dogsbody?"

Simon gave a stricken cry but did not otherwise interrupt. Jolanda decided that she really liked Lijsbet. Her good mood restored, she slowed her pace—partly out of pity for Simon, and partly to delay her return to the house where Wurfbain and Laurent waited.

"Nay," said Jolanda. "Simon is my cousin. He stewarded our estate following the death of my great-uncle, the late Graaf Tieselen, until my father and I arrived to claim our birthright. Simon and his older brother were very reasonable about the handover, despite their somehow being unaware of our existence prior to our arrival—we had to find out about old uncle's death years after it happened, and from a third party, since our dear blood relations were somehow entirely ignorant to us."

"How wonderful you're all reunited," said Lijsbet, looking back to Simon. "You must have been chuffed to meet your cousins!"

"The emotion." Simon gasped. "Cannot. Be described."

"Now we let him live in one of our warehouses," said Jolanda. "His brother was too proud to accept the invitation, but not our Simon. He earns his keep by scaring off the rats that swim over from that island of garbage just outside the walls, where the water's going back down."

"A ratman!" said Lijsbet. "I never would've guessed it!"

"The smell gives it away," confided Jolanda. "You'll notice a faint rodentlike aroma whenever Simon—"

"Enough!" cried he, and they turned to see him beet-faced and sweaty, the baskets set on the cobbles beside him. "Enough!"

"Enough what, Cousin?" Jolanda flicked her lashes at him in imitation of his own affectation.

"Enough..." Simon panted, and then the passion left him, his shoulders slumping. "*Not* enough, rather. Not enough time. Not enough time to join you for supper after all. I must away, and—"

"Nonsense," said Jolanda, going to his side and picking up her basket in one hand. She hooked her free arm through Simon's, and was pleased to see Lijsbet doing the same without being prompted. The three resumed the walk home, Simon now grinning to have a young woman on each elbow. God help the fellow, he really did smell like rats. "A lovely evening, is it not?"

"Lovely," agreed Lijsbet.

"*Most* lovely, Cousin," said Simon. "What are we having?"

"Sheep for the sheepheads, and—" Jolanda began, but whatever barb she was going to follow her opening with was lost as an unexpected wave of frigid air broke on her back, stirring her veil around her face and distracting her from idle taunts. Even as the breeze fell away, its chill soaked through her heavy gown like seawater, and she felt the deep, unmistakable sensation of being watched. Much as she wanted to stop and look behind her, she marched on, refusing to give in to the impulse. She wasn't some desperate animal, to always be checking over her shoulder; she wasn't *Sander*, for the sake of all the saints—she was the Lady Jolanda Tieselen returning home with her handmaid and her cousin, and so she walked on, head held high, and tried to ignore the shiver trickling down her spine.

II.

Hobbe had been sour as kitten piss soup about Simon Gruyere crashing their supper, but Sander was glad to have his warehouse-man drop in, as it enabled him to schedule a matter of urgent business that was long overdue. Made the rest of the night tolerable, even with all the paper-signing and business-plotting that were endemic to Laurent's visits. He was the lawyer, sure, so that was to be expected, but listening to Hobbe and Laurent blather on about whatever document they'd put in front of Sander to stamp and sign was the worst part of being a merchant—the best part of being one was what he'd had a word with Simon about, a very particular appointment out at the Tieselen warehouse...

"Got the bastard!" crowed Sander, triumphantly pumping his crossbow in the air. "Like eating crates, you cunny-licking vermin? How you like *that* bit of ash wood, asshole?! How! Do! You! Like! It?!"

"I would *hazard*," said Simon with the air of a man not quite ready to commit himself to a popular opinion, "that he does not care for it. Just a thought."

The rat writhed, as well it fucking might, but then, beyond all laws of man and God and rodent, somehow righted itself and began crawling through the mud, the sheaf of the quarrel protruding from its back. As the rat jerkily dragged itself along, the arrowhead emerging from its guts left a trench in the muck, the channel streaked with black blood.

This miraculous escape presented a serious problem, as all of that asshole's rat friends would go into hiding if Sander charged across the mudflat to retrieve the wretched rodent. But then if he didn't, the fucker would get away. Beyond the obvious problem of being down both a rat and a quarrel, there was a deeper, darker possibility: what if the wounded rat became some symbol of resistance to his verminous kin? What if he became their king, and led a murine insurrection against the good men of Dordt? What if he—

—Split apart at the neck as Simon's bolt struck him dead-on, ending his pretensions of rattish glory. Sander grinned at Simon, who saluted him with his still-vibrating crossbow, and Sander had to stifle the impulse to kiss the man hard on the mouth. Simon didn't go in for that, which was total bullshit—the man acted like the pootiest neuker Sander had ever met, but made it clear as well water he only went with girls. Still, a good friend was better than a lover in some ways; safer, too. For all the clouds of ill wind they'd had to fan away to get comfortable around each other after Sander displaced the younger noble in the Tieselen chain of inheritance, now they were all right, were Sander and Simon. Or rather, Jan and Simon.

Point was, Simon knew without being told when to hold off on putting another bolt in a stuck rat and when to tap it twice, knew when to pass the bottle and when to pull the rag on a new one— Sander had no stomach for the sand at the end of a wine. Sander very much did have a taste for being outside in good weather with Simon, lounging on the end of the dock and picking off the rats that swarmed through Trash Island.

Trash Island was, well, an island of trash. It was formed where the currents of the River Maas and the tides of the meer conspired to bring all manner of drift together into a massive rotting mound right outside the city walls. As the sheepheads had done a bang-up job reclaiming some of the flooded countryside surrounding Dordrecht, the garbage heap was now accessible by foot, when the tides were out—the inland sea retreated to the south, the river proper lay just to the north, and here they were on a strip of tideland between the two. Almost hard to believe, wide as the mudflat was, that every night this place became a single expanse of dark, unbroken water as Maas and meer, man and wife, were reunited.

Sander had, at Hobbe's prompting, built a second Tieselen warehouse out here, where no honey-handed officials could lay tax on the wine coming in and out of the ledgers. More than one of said grubby grabbers had tried to talk Sander out of it, had told him it would be too risky to build on the mud until it was further drained, and too expensive to try. When that hadn't dissuaded him, they'd appealed to the reasonable fear of breakers any merchant in that sunken place harbored, the concern that outside Dordrecht's walls the Tieselen warehouse would be vulnerable to freshwater pirates. Better an honest thief than a city taxman, Sander had told them, and now, half a year out, the worst that had happened was the odd headache arising from juggling the logistics of the tides—a warehouse that was only accessible by boat half the time was a tricky affair to manage.

And yet, a highly profitable one—the old Graaf Tieselen had sold off most of his farmland around the family seat in Oudeland to get his wine importation business in the water, and while the neighboring graafs and hertogs who had snapped up the property had considered him mad to give up solid land for airy schemes, the landholder-turned-merchant had enjoyed the last laugh. Or rather, he would have, if he hadn't drowned along with thousands of his countrymen when the Saint Lizzy Day Flood had taken the Groote Waard. Sander was laughing that figurative laugh, was the more accurate view of things, and laughing all the harder since this city-free warehouse had established delivery timetables with guild-run ships in Rotterdam and beyond—really drawing in the groots now.

Other Dordt entrepreneurs had followed the Tieselen model, so there were now several other stilt-raised warehouses poking out of the tidal flat like a pack of giant wooden waterbugs. On this side of the city walls, though, there was little else—brown marsh when the moon took out the waters, and brown shallows when she brought them back in, far as the unsquinted eye could see. There wasn't even the odd dead tree to pierce the flatness, just Trash Island and a lot of mud.

Simon kept house and guard of the stores, only rowing his dinghy into the city to pick up Sander for a rat hunt, or to retrieve supplies. And probably visit whores and his brother Braem, sure, but what he did in his own time was his own business, so long as no meer bandits made off with the wine and no rats made off with the packing hay.

The tide was out now, obviously, but the two men sat where the red came and went, dangling their legs off the end of the warehouse dock. Whenever they called it a day, they'd march through the mud to retrieve their trophies, but for now best to keep the feet dry and the tongue wet.

"I declare, Coz, this is the life," said Sander after a long pull on the finest of the last shipment's Burgundy. Spicy and nutty, with a delightful sting to the mouth that was like climaxing after a serious case of woad nut. He'd never cared for wine before getting into the business himself, especially not unwatered stuff, but now he hardly had a taste for anything else. Remembering the days of mashing berries into his spoiled beer to mask the taste, Sander grinned and took another drink.

"*The* life, Jan, or simply *a* life?" said Simon, reloading his bow with a bit more vigor than he usually applied. The lad have some kind of pea stuck in his pisser all of a sudden? How could anyone be raw after nailing a moving rat at fifty paces?

"Tell you, Simon, you don't even know," said Sander. "You don't. I've lived more than one, and this, *this*, right here, with you, and this wine, and these rats, this is the one to keep, the one to cherish."

"And how do you think the rats feel about being included in your perfect life?" said Simon, an errant yellow canine protruding in that fetching way it had of escaping his wine-purpled lips.

"Rats?" Sander considered this with more care than the

question perhaps deserved, but then he was...what's it...magnanimous, these days. "I was a rat, I wouldn't very well blame the man with the cross for taking me out. Couldn't look myself in my ratty little mirror and pretend to be truthful. Hell, I can't blame people too much for hating me, and I'm not even a rat."

"No," said Simon as he aimed his weapon, but it sounded an awful lot like "No?" for Sander's liking.

"Shit, no," Sander said vehemently. "Hate is normal, normal as breathing. No, wait, hate's not it—I don't hate rats, not at all."

"Really?" said Simon, and fired. Not even close—the quarrel spit up mud a good ten steps from the nearest rat, which went scurrying into the jumbled mass of refuse. "That raises the question, then, of why you take such delight in their slaughter."

"Slaughter's fun," said Sander, loading his bow. Time to remind this lippy little terrier who was king of the rat-killers. "No. *Shooting* is fun. I can't begrudge a rat being a rat any more than a rat can blame me for popping him with a bolt any chance I get. All part of the plan."

"Whose plan?" Simon said, spoiling Sander's shot. His missile sailed clear over the top of the island, which rose a dozen feet above the slime. The thought of plans dictating events pushed Sander toward familiar paranoid flights, but he gripped the railing rather than descending. "I said, what plan?"

"Huh?" Sander blinked at Simon. Where'd he get off, asking such things? "Yeah, I got plans for the rats. Not out here just to be an asshole, killing rats for no purpose."

"And what plan might the humble rat play into, pray?" asked Simon, picking up the bottle.

"Kind of plans don't concern you," grumbled Sander, his mood as bitter as his belly had turned. Needed to remember not to drink past the halfway mark on the bottle, leave the sediment for Simon. "Go on and fetch the kills, I'll pack us up. It's gotten cold out here for my taste, and I'm inclined to return home."

"If we give it another bottle or so, Coz, the tide will be back enough to row out rather than—"

"Go on, you lazy dastard!" said Sander, giving Simon a hard enough slap on the back to send him off the pier. The mudflat swallowed the contrary fucker to the knees as Sander laughed and laughed, getting wearily to his feet. "I'm cold *now*, Simon, so get the rats and I'll grab another bottle for the row back. And take care you don't tear 'em up getting the bolts out—I got schemes for those rats, I do."

Simon squirmed out of the mud by clinging to one of the pier's posts, forcing a dreg-speckled smile up at Sander. The graaf hurried him along by fumbling with the silver-braided laces on his codpouch and freeing his cock, whereupon he pissed down at his cousin. As Sander watched Simon make his heavy-footed way across the mire, he let out a long sigh and savored his urination. If this wasn't the life, such a thing didn't exist. Long way from Sneek, long way from the well, long way from the flood.

As if contradicting him, the glimmering edge of the meer caught his eyes to the south, where it came crawling back home like a guilty dog. The goddamn meer, cloudy as a tempest, dark as the tideland he was cutting into with his piss; molten gold transmuting to bubbling lead. The tide itself wouldn't bring in much more than a kingdom-wide puddle, but beyond that, out where they hadn't been able to even half-ass the drainage project like they had on this side of Dordt, *there* was the real meer. Somewhere out there rose a church tower and a graveyard, and a dead tree standing sentinel, guarding the weapon Sander had no longer been fit to wield, a relic of battles exceeding his ken, the one queen he'd ever bowed before: Glory's End. That drowned village was also the grave of his once and forever king, though, wasn't it, the putrid bower of his—

"Jan!" Simon cried, and Sander shuddered, as he sometimes did when people called him that instead of Graaf or Your Worship or what have you. He blinked at his cock, and put it away without shaking. Stupid thing had just been airing out there for saints knew how long, yet it still set to dribbling soon as it was back in warm, dry linen. Fucking Simon was likely bogged down in a patch of sinkmud and wanted a hand out, the wretch. "Jesus, Jan, Jesus!"

The mud was only up to Simon's calves, what was he whinging about? The fool was at the edge of the heap, where the solid flotsam and gelatinous jetsam merged into the walls of Trash Island's rat city. Unseaworthy bits of boats, lost planks and bolts of cloth, the errant drowned sheep or cow, and all manner of random, unidentifiable filth pushed together to keep the rats dry in beds lined with stolen hay, where they fucked out a hundred rat babes a night and dreamt of inheriting a nicer hole, perhaps a wine-crate manse in Tieselen Town, where—

"Jesus, Jan, Jesus!" Simon called again, and then hunched over. Usually Sander was the one with stomach complaints, but there was Simon spitting up in the muck. Jesus, indeed. Sander lowered himself onto the tidal flat, sucking his teeth as he let go of the edge of the dock and sank almost to the tops of his boots.

"What?!" Sander bellowed, hoping to avoid the march, but the man just kept hurling out the dinner he hadn't even paid for. No doubt he'd be wanting another supper invitation now, Sander thought coldly as he began to sticky-step it across the bog. Sander wouldn't be surprised if the cunt had put his own fingers down his throat to effect the result, get a pity feast. Ah, wonderful, there was icy mud sliding down around his ankles, how lovely. "I said! What?!"

Simon was wiping his mouth as he straightened, and pointed a shaking hand at the piled garbage. The lad really looked rough, his face near as milky as Jo's, except of course she was supposed to look like that, whereas Simon was normally a shade duskier, and here he was, ashen and quivering. Huh. Sander felt his palms get itchy, felt himself wishing he hadn't cast his mistress into an arboreal scabbard many leagues of water away—the poncey sword at his side might have fine etching on its blade and a rope of velvet wound through its hilt, but he'd yet to draw real blood with it, and an unproven sword was the only thing worse than a flood, a strange dog, or a bloke who thought himself wise. Was that how it went?

Trash Island had grown since the last time Sander had actually hiked or rowed out here instead of sending Simon to collect their quarrels and trophies. It hadn't expanded up, but out; the walls of current-compacted drift looked tight as ever, but now whole villages of rats and marsh-roaches bordered those edges, their oily ponds shining with rainbow sheens, their fields of refuse pushing up a bumper crop of water maggots. Just for a moment, Sander imagined an awl-toothed Belgian devil hunkered down in the heart of the island, waiting for him. Poncey steel or not, the sword was in hand as Sander picked his way around the pools of shitwater and piles of rubbish, now stepping into the shadow of the rearing mound of stinking, wet corruption.

Then, as he stared, the whole fetid mass began to slowly pulse, like the side of a sleeping sheep.

What the wounds was going on out here?

Sander squinted until he was near-blind, willing the heap to stop breathing, to go still as filth ought, to leave him to his wine and his rats and his Simon. It obeyed, thank each and every saint in heaven, but he knew that couldn't be the end of the weirdness out here. Taking a deep breath, a swimmer's breath like Jo would've took, he committed himself to seeing whatever the world had to show him. Beyond, the sky was the same pale bluegray as his eyes, wisps of white drifting overhead like angels on wing, but down here in the meer flats it was all green and brown and black, rats rustling through the mountain like demons in some hellish keep, like black—

—White. Bluish-white flesh, there, in the churned-up mud at the edge of the main junk pile.

Sander leaned in for a better look. Well. Shit. Then something too awful for words shot through him, hot as fire through dry hay, sharp as steel through warm fat, and his breath caught.

Jo.

"It's a girl," Simon's voice was quavering. "A girl, Jan."

"Yeah," said Sander and made himself take a closer look. It was the hardest thing he'd ever done, and he did more hard things before breakfast than most cunts did in their lives. He looked, and he saw her clawlike hands were pale as fresh grubs. He let out his breath in a low whistle.

Obviously this girl was too young to be Jo, but Christ's crown, for a moment there...How old could this poor chit be? She barely had any fat on her, tits included. Though it pained him, he glanced down between her splayed legs. Barely a hair. Christ. He closed his eyes, trying his damnedest not to pull a Simon impression.

"She's naked," Simon said, barely audible over the racket the rats were making in their castle. "Where are her clothes, Jan?"

"Her clothes?" Sander's incredulity temporarily settled his guts. "Her *clothes*, you clot?"

"Yes," Simon gulped, but Sander saw he wasn't looking at the girl, he was staring back at the cluster of warehouses, at the city walls beyond them. "Her clothes. It's too cold to swim, too—"

"Where's her fucking head, is the question," said Sander, turning back to the corpse. "Her *clothes*."

"*What?*" Sander wouldn't have thought it possible, but Simon sounded even more distraught. "Buried in trash, or, or under the mud, she—oh, *Jesus!*"

Simon had stumbled closer, and Sander saw by the unbroken mud between the girl and the fop that Simon really hadn't gotten close enough to see before. He saw *now*, that was certain. The lad didn't have any further alms to give to the rats, but that didn't stop him from trying, gagging on his own breath and nothing more as he hunched over in the muck.

"Jesus? No, not him," Sander said. He nodded to himself as

he stared down at the girl. "Jesus didn't do this. No. Nor no Belgians, nor no catfish, nor nothing else but what you'd expect. A man did this."

Sander stared at the corpse for a long time, willing himself not to speculate how she might have gotten here but doing a shit job of it.

"You think she's murdered?" Sander's heart jumped at the sound of Simon's voice; he'd almost forgotten he was there.

"No, Simon, I think she died of plague." It was harder for Sander to take his eyes off the girl than he'd expected, so he didn't even try. She was tangled in the mud, in herself, her limbs all wrong, that sallow skin seeming to turn bluer the longer he looked at it. At her.

"No, I…" Simon sounded like he was going to cry. "Why would someone… how could they…"

They. That was certainly a possibility. If… *No*, Sander bolted down that particular box of horrors, lest he never get a good night's sleep again. No Belgians, no conspiracies, no plots of men or monsters. Not *They*, not *Them*, not nothing, save *Not His Business*.

"Come on, then," said Sander, trying to reassure himself as much as Simon. "Nothing more to be done here. We're going home to get dry and warm. And drunk."

"Don't we have to tell the militia?" Simon said, his voice cracking. "Or bring her with us, or—"

"Certainly not!" Sander couldn't believe how thick Simon was. "There's not a militia in the world lazier and shadier than the Dordt watch! We tell them we found a body, at best they'll be on us like stink on shit for weeks and weeks, poking around our business, getting their touch on our warehouse, seeing if we're involved. That's best case, mind, worst case is they just blame us and hang us, end of story."

"No," protested Simon, "they wouldn't, we didn't, we—"

"We didn't find nothing out here, Simon!" said Sander, trying not to shout. "Militia does *not* need to be sniffing around me, and that's all they'd do. Think about it, Simon, think for once—what can they do that we haven't? Poke it with a fucking stick? She's dead, so it's a little late to help her, and she don't have a head, so it ain't like they can tell who she is, so where's that leave us?"

"I don't know," whispered Simon. "Where?"

"Doing the gallows jig, we tell anyone 'bout this!" Sander told himself Simon hadn't lived a real life, that the lad couldn't know how wicked the Dordt militiamen could be, given the chance. "They think I'm a Hook, Simon, everyone does, 'cause I'm in good with Hobbe but none of the Cod nobles, save you. Believe me, man, they're just looking for an excuse to bring me down—best case, *best case*, I bribe them to let me walk, but what if they decide to just hang my ass and turn out my pockets when I'm dead, eh?"

Simon was wincing from each pronouncement, and Sander really was shouting now: "I'm hanging dead from a gibbet in Grote Markt Square, pants full of spunk and shit and piss, I've bit my own tongue off, so blood's everywhere, Jo's reputation's ruined, if they ain't hanged her, too, *you're* out on the streets if you're not swinging beside us, and why?! Why, you cunt?! Because Simon had to tell the militia 'bout something nasty he found by the wineshed?!"

"I'm sorry," Simon whispered, tears rolling down his cheeks as he stared at the corpse. "I . . . we'll just leave her, then."

"Good," said Sander, turning to his task before Simon's spine lost its stiffness again. Sander wrinkled his nose as the piece of moldy canvas he was tugging out of the mound melted between his fingers. "Now, come over here and pull this crap down on her, cover it up like we couldn't even know she was out here."

Simon trudged over, defeated. "Why?"

"What's wrong with you? This jacket's fawn, Simon, fawn—I get corpse-grease on it, I'll never get it clean."

"No, why . . . why cover her?"

"Just 'cause we're too smart to report this doesn't mean some other cunt won't be, they stumble on her," said Sander, pleased with himself for being so sharp. "This heap's a bow's shot from our warehouse, and folk know we rat out here—we don't want it looking like we must've seen her and not told somebody. That'll look even worse than telling the militia in the first place."

"So if it's bad either way, let's just tell—" But Sander was done with Simon's bullshit, and cut him off by tugging at a board protruding from the mountain of refuse. He danced back as an entire layer of Trash Island sloughed off, burying the corpse in an avalanche of waterlogged wood and the reeking gray sludge that mortared the waste pile together. After frantically checking his jacket and seeing it was relatively spotless, Sander looked up to see that Simon was splashed with foul mud from his mustache on down. It would have been hilarious in different circumstances, but even now it was pretty funny. Sander waved toward the warehouse and began picking his way back across the flat.

Fucking tide had come in while they were messing around, and Sander's boots were sloshing-full before he got ten steps. It was only when he settled into the dinghy that he realized Simon hadn't brought the stuck rats and stray bolts with him, meaning the lot was taken by the meer by now. Goddamn Simon.

They returned to Dordrecht in silence, other than the occasional reiteration that Simon not tell a fucking soul about what they'd found. Shouldn't have to say it even once, but, considering the greenness of Gruyere, Sander felt the need to repeat himself. Simon rowed and Sander looked behind them, to where Trash Island and the cluster of warehouses jutted out of the marsh like tombstones, the sunset turning the surface of the meer to blood. Or maybe just watered-down wine. Sander sighed. Some life.

III.

Jolanda never thought she would miss the smell of putrefying sea snails, but the purple pots of her youth were veritably fragrant compared to the stench that woad gave off. The herb itself was not so bad, but to get the color from it, she had to dry the leaves and pack them in piss and sheep shit, and then wait and wait and breathe through her mouth whenever she went up to the attic to check on the rot's progression. How Lansloet could stand to keep his nest up there was beyond her—Drimmelin's bed was more than wide enough for him, even with Lijsbet sharing it, but no, the bald ferret liked his attic, and kept to it even when the woad was eye-wateringly close to ripeness.

Jolanda also had to mix a bit of madder into the finished blue dye to get a comparable shade, but the reddish root was nowhere near as odiferous as the fermenting woad. The result was a far duller purple than what she and her family had manufactured, and every bit as time-consuming, but she had been unable to find the particular spiral-shelled snails in any of the markets she had visited during her tenure as a lady. On the one occasion she had found a merchant in Gouda who claimed to be able to procure for her a purple dye made from shells, the price he had quoted her was so outlandish she had laughed in his face. If the purple was worth that much, she sure as Mary's mercy wouldn't have starved most of the year in a shitty shack with a perpetually skint father.

Unless her father was too thick to realize the worth of his product, of course. The thought had come to her before, but it was only when she was dyeing her hands that she really worked it over. It was actually quite funny, in a mean-spirited way…just like remembering that the most her father had ever been paid in his life was the four groots Jan had given him in exchange for Jolanda, and those groots had been every bit as false as the man who had paid them out. Counterfeit coin for a genuine daughter—Jan had certainly got his money's worth out of the old dye-maker!

The wide bowl balanced between her knees, her cold hands long since asleep in their shallow bath, she sat in the dark of her room, the stinking dye making her eyes flow like those of some more merciful creature, some more loyal daughter. Her father had a traveling merchant he sold to, the man visiting Monster once a month or so during the peak season to take what the purple-maker had produced in exchange for a handful of pfennigs, and oh, how her old man bragged to be paid! Since becoming noble, Jolanda had taken to letters more than numbers, but even without a firm grasp on arithmetic she figured the traveling merchant had to be reselling the purple they made for a hundred times what he bought it for, if the figure the dye-seller in Gouda had listed was remotely accurate. How in heaven's name her father had learned his trade but not its value she could hardly imagine…

A wicked thought came to her, and she smiled, turning her hands over in the bowl. It would be easy work to undercut the merchant who bought the dye from her father and then resell it at a substantial profit to a dyer or guildsman in Dordrecht or Rotterdam. All she had to do was hire some goon to go proposition her father, maybe with a comparatively large onetime payment to have him sever all ties with the old merchant, lest some bidding war gain traction. Her father was thick, but not so thick that he wouldn't grow wary if his old contact and Jolanda's agent kept raising their offers.

Aye, best to concoct a story about her man being a relation of the old merchant but having had a falling-out, I'm-the-one-you-should-be-dealing-with-and-here's-five-groots-if-you-never-talk-to-him-again, that sort of thing. The old dye-buyer wouldn't like it, of course, but devil take that fraud—she had half a mind to pay her imaginary representative to rough the merchant up a bit, taking such cruel advantage of her family.

Granted, the plan would involve making her shitbird brothers and slaphappy father more financially comfortable, but the time away had somewhat softened her animosity toward them. Somewhat. After she'd bought a few batches of purple and made sure that the old merchant was gone for good, she'd have to go back there, all dressed in fine attire, with a retinue of servants, and seriously flaunt her shit in front of those sandy arseholes.

That, thought Jolanda, was a plan. She had enough pocket money stowed away in her dress chest to finance the venture without consulting Sander, which was just as good—never knew if the old poot would start to listen to Wurfbain's insistence that she be married off, and soon, and it would do to have a substantially larger nest egg before quitting the Voorstraat nest. The purple-maker's-daughter-turned-graaf's-child-turned-wealthy-independent-purple-merchant—not bad for a lass of some eighteen winters.

She began working her tingling fingers in the dye, trying to wake her hands back up. It had been midafternoon when she'd set to work, and dark as it was, it had to be long past suppertime. Sander still hadn't come back from ratting with Simon, but to hell with the both of them, she was hungry.

As she shifted her aching thighs a bit, the bowl rocked and some dye dribbled over the side, shudder-inducingly cold on her knee. She was naked, having learned from experience, and the carpet was pulled back—her bare floor was spotted with blue and red from the mixing of the stuff. Not for the first time that night, and not for the hundredth time since Wurfbain had issued the mandate that Sander had been too chickenshit to override, she cursed the meddlesome count.

A miracle, she'd offered, which, sure, was what it seemed like to her when the purple began to fade from her skin with the slow-but-certain pace of seasons passing, so why should anyone else doubt the explanation? The son of a purebred bitch wouldn't budge. It would arouse attention, Wurfbain had said, it would raise questions. Bad enough they'd had to initially tell everyone she had such extensive birthmarkings, but to then claim they were going away, lightening and lightening on her hands and arms—whoever heard of such a thing?

No, the only thing for it now was to re-dye her limbs when they began to fade, which, when all her raging had come to naught, led to her discovery that the dye that had originally marked her could not be had without a large fortune.

How she'd love to pour the hated woad into Wurfbain's wine, or Sander's, the coward, always relenting to the count for fear of being exposed. Sander always asserted they owed Wurfbain, for putting them up and teaching them to be nobles and working out the Tieselen snatch of the Gruyere fortune, but Jolanda suspected the mad poot had other reasons for being loyal to the silver fox. Reasons that involved gobbling cock, though she'd never substantiated this suspicion. And thank all the saints for that singular mercy!

She lifted her arms from the basin, dye dripping from elbows to fingertips, and delicately shook herself off so as not to send any drops over the rim of the bowl. This took some time, and even when she was done shedding purple spots, she still couldn't wipe her arms off—the dye set better in her skin if she let it dry on its own. Her room had grown much colder now that her numb arse and legs and hands were waking back up. Leave it to her worthless skin to feel the chill more when her hands were out of the pot than when they were soaking in frigid soup. A little moonlight was coming through the open window, but she'd rather be blind than freezing, and so she set the basin down beside her and stood.

Well, actually it was more of an upward lurch, one leg still nettle-riddled, the other awake but seemingly hungover, and she smiled to herself as she stumbled across the room. She nearly tripped over the rug she had rolled back to protect it from the dye, and thanked her past self for having the foresight to keep her chests, table, and wardrobe all lined up against sundry walls rather than out here where she could stub her toe on them in the gloom. As sometimes happened, the black shadows of the room suddenly seemed denser, cooler, as though she were back in another benighted noble house, holding her breath as she floated toward another hazy window.

Then she was in the patch of moonlight proper, and drove the thought back under to admire the sleek, dark sheen to her arms. There was something about the purple tint that she'd come to almost like, just as she'd grown to appreciate the bittersweet taste of horehound tea. Maybe it was just that the purple kept her separate from all the ponces and bitches she dealt with, that it reminded her she'd worked more as a beach sprat than these lords and ladies would in the whole of their lives. Maybe. Or maybe—

"Oi, cover your tits!" came a cry from the street below, and Jolanda, too shocked to do anything but obey, slapped a hand over her modest bosom. Peering down, she saw Sander standing in the middle of the dark road, staring up at her like some besotted paramour gazing at his lady's window. How long had the creeper been down there, getting snowed on, sheep-eyeing his own house like the barmy coot he undoubtedly was? "Simon's not coming tonight after all, so you can put 'em away!"

Snow? Her eyes floated up from the still-shouting Sander. The upper stories of the houses across the way were dark, and above the unlit windows and pigeonless gables she saw that the jumbled nightscape of Dordrecht's rooftops had a fine salting already settling against its cliffs and ridges, upon its hills and hollows. The powder was drifting through the air like goose down or dandelion fur, lightly falling yet, but the sky was the color of her sword blades, harkening a heavier snow by dawn. The waning

moon was sinking deeper into the gray clouds like some bur-
nished piece of metal dropped in a lake, a silver horseshoe casting up pale flakes of sediment as it sank. It was like glimpsing the
sun from the bottom of the meer.

Jolanda shivered. No wonder it was so damned cold in her
room, first snow of the year sneaking in when she wasn't looking.
The front door banged beneath her, and looking back down, she
saw that Sander had gone inside. Smart. She shut the window,
her skin burning where her sticky arm had briefly bonded to her
chest. Supper, then, and a word or three on his calling attention
to what she may or may not be doing in her own window under
cover of darkness, and the added insult of alleging that she'd display herself for *Simon*.

Much later, after Sander had acted even queerer than usual at
the supper table, muttering about landing the biggest rat of them
all before turning terse and mean, Jolanda lay in her cold bed in
her cold room and stared at the black beams striping the white
ceiling. She had left the shutters ajar, thinking it better to be cold
than blind after all, and wished she could have Lijsbet beside
her. Yet she knew that having the maid as a bedmate so soon
after dyeing herself would lead to questions arising from the pungent woad smell, questions Jolanda wouldn't be able to answer.

Lansloet, beady-eyed old baddie though he was, did not ask
questions, not even when his attic became the rank aging cave
for the dyes, not even when he saw Wurfbain treat Sander less as
lord of his own home and more like a servant, and not even when
a drunk, weeping, and naked Sander had to be helped up the
stairs to bed after stripping to his skin and burning his fine clothing in the parlor fireplace, as he'd done twice since becoming
graaf. Of course, sooner or later Lijsbet would notice the dye,
either the smell of the stuff or the fluctuating shades of Jolanda's
hands, and then she'd have to be told *something*, but for now
Jolanda couldn't think of a lie, and so a cold bed it was.

A draft pushed the shutters farther open, making them groan, and Jolanda's heart skipped at the noise. A puff of snow fluttered in, wide flakes swinging slowly down to fade into the rolled-back rug. Jolanda was out from her sheets like a spooked ray quitting its sandy bed, bare feet barely touching the cold floorboards as she danced to the window.

The breeze that had set her on her course died off, perhaps hoping she'd change her mind, but it was too late for reprieve—latched shutters, then a pile of blankets so deep they'd need a team of clam diggers to excavate her come dawn. The snowy roofscape of Dordrecht again shone before her, and she paused, a hand on each shutter, grinning out at the frozen city where a few lights still burned in garrets and towers, twinkling like stars in the night sky or sun-kissed shells in the morning surf.

Pretty enough, but cold enough to freeze a Frisian. Before she could close the shutters, though, something caught her notice, and set its hook well. She was focusing on it even as every part of herself save her eyes was cautioning against it, telling her to dispense with shadows in the night and return to bed. Ignoring this urge to slam the shutters and flee to the covers, she squinted down, and for the second time that night her heart iced over as she stood in her open window.

Sander was down in the street again, looking up at the house. At her. At least he couldn't complain about her tits this time, the night air billowing her shift around her like a jellyfish's mantle as it pushed itself through the abyss. But no, he wasn't looking at her, or even noticing she'd come to the window—he'd have said something by now if he'd been eyeing her casement.

She leaned a little farther out into the moonlight, half-trying to catch his notice so he'd break the stillness of the night, half-trying to get a better look at him, see if he had a bottle he could toss up. He wore a hooded cloak, everything about him black except for his upturned face, which was as white and faintly luminescent as the snow falling upon it. It would have been downright creepy if she didn't know creepy was simply a matter of nature for Sander.

Shadowed though the ivory-dusted lane of Voorstraat was, Jolanda could see no tracks coming or going from him, meaning that the lunatic had been out there for no small time, getting snowed on and gawping up at his own fortune. Her mind turned over, trying to till up something clever to needle him with, but just as she settled on an excellent jab, a knock came at her door.

Jolanda lurched back from the window, out of the moonlight. The knock had startled her, frightened her even, for some stupid, indefinable reason. No doubt it was Lijsbet, here to complain about Drimmelin's night-gas and beg to share Jolanda's bed. No doubt. From her cover behind the shutter's shadow, Jolanda saw Sander hadn't moved from his position, still clueless to his being observed. Better to let Lijsbet in quickly and then bring her to the window so they could both have a quick taunt of Sander before bed. She scurried to the door, careful not to step in front of the window, wondering if there was enough snow on the sill to pack a snowball to volley down at the mad graaf.

The knock came again, louder and harder than the maid had any right to rap in the middle of the night when she was not expressly invited, and Jolanda threw open the door. For a moment the candle in Lijsbet's hand blinded Jolanda, and she blinked away the tears, holding a finger to her lips lest the servant set in with her constant blathering and spoil the ambush.

Except it wasn't Lijsbet. It was Sander.

"Hey." He looked ghastly, his nightshirt a collage of stains, his unwashed body giving off the moldy scent of stagnant mud and standing water. He looked, in a word, like Sander, instead of Graaf Jan, respectable nobleman and merchant. He also had no cloak nor boots, no snow in his hair, and Jolanda hated him more than she'd ever hated him before, which was saying quite a lot.

She was too upset to speak, and so she sucker punched him in his paunchy gut. Nasty goddamn poot, nasty, nasty, *nasty* man. Back when they'd first met, he probably would have expected that, maybe caught her arm or at least tensed for it, but since becoming a noble, he'd grown lazy as an eldest son, stopped respecting her ability to whip his arse at a moment's provocation. Stopped being so crazy, too, aye, but what—

"—the fuck?!" Sander was gasping, stumbling back. Instead of swinging on her, the ponce grabbed his belly in one hand and held the candle between them with the other. "Why?"

"Not funny," she said, her fists tight, hoping like she'd hoped for few things in her life that he'd make a move on her instead of sniffling there in her door, the caitiff.

"What?" Sander looked so stupid she could laugh. She didn't.

"Teach me about standing in my own window?" She suddenly felt like crying, wondered if she was getting sick. "That why? You put Simon out there, teach me…"

She trailed off. Sander had no idea what she was talking about, she could see that, his eyes narrowing, angry-dog-like, his overgrown head listing to the side as though he couldn't quite hear. It was how he looked when he suspected, often correctly, that she was taking the piss. She shuddered, her mind struggling to make sense of it, glancing at the window to make sure nothing was there, nothing but the moon…

"Simon," she settled on him quickly, desperately. "Goddamn letch. Don't know what he wants to get up into more, his old house or my thighs."

"Simon's gone back to the warehouse," said Sander quietly, and blew out his candle. "You seen someone out your window?"

"He must've stayed in town the night, not gone back after dropping you—"

Sander said nothing, stalking across the dark room. He stumbled over the bunched-up rug, then flung the shutters fully open, jutting his head out into the snow. He stood there for so long Jolanda was sure he saw the man below, was trying to make out his features, but when she bit her cheek and joined him at the window, the street was empty, the clouds now too thick to make out any tracks leading up or down Voorstraat.

Sander looked cadaverous in the snow-thrown brightness, jaw set, brow shiny, breath held, flakes settling on his sweaty face like ashes on a corpse. Like the priest's censer dumping ash into her mother's open grave, Jolanda thought, the unexpected resurrection of that particular memory making an already fun night positively euphoric. She grabbed her upper arms and rubbed the pimply flesh, just as she used to when quitting the sea.

"A dream," Jolanda said, not believing it but hoping Sander would, that he could talk her into believing. "Stupid dream, was all. Sleepwalked to the window, and you woke me up when you knocked."

Except that even after the knock had come the man had still been right there, sizing up the house—she remembered looking down to see if he had heard the noise. Sander finally pulled his head back inside and closed the shutters. Little light came through the slats on a clear, full-moon eve, and on a night like this the room was dark as the bottom of the meer.

"You can dream when you're awake," Sander said, quieter than she'd thought him capable of speaking. "Dreams like that, they're impossible to tell from real life. Not like sleep dreams at all. So real you can feel everything, taste everything."

"I've never heard that," Jolanda said, teetering on the rim of belief, hoping he could push her the rest of the way. *Had* she heard that before? She thought she had, now that he said it—it was maddening, like a smell she couldn't quite place drifting from the kitchen, taunting her with its familiarity. A memory bubbled up, then, of another occasion when she had beheld a vision that defied comprehension, back in the sunken house in Oudeland...but she forced it back down, trying to fulfill the promise to herself to never again think of what she had seen there. That had been completely different; she had been drowning and imagined—never mind, she told herself, never mind, never mind.

"Used to happen to me a lot," Sander said morosely, and with such casual conviction that she believed him at once—he was an even worse liar than her, and if he'd been bluffing, she'd have known it. She was so relieved, she threw her arms around him, hugging him tight. He tensed at her touch and she almost gagged on his redolent shirt. Then he relaxed and she turned her head to the side, and they stayed that way for a moment, her blindly holding him as he just stood there, slack armed and stinking. It was, surprisingly enough, comforting, but then he spoiled it by adding, "Or could be you were awake, and there was some hentoucher down there what heard you air your charms in the window, came by for a peek."

Rather than releasing him, Jolanda squeezed him until he groaned, really digging into his ribs. "*Charms?* Don't call 'em that again, it's awful. Only reason I didn't have anything on was the dye. You want me to ruin something nice on account of modesty in an empty room?"

"Could be a suitor, though, yeah?" said Sander, doing that annoying thing where he only partially responded to what she'd said, too caught up in his own harebrained thoughts. "I've heard you're not as bad in the face as some of those rich bitches, and that counts for a lot with young lads."

"You're a charmer yourself, Papa," said Jolanda. "Maybe it was some lovelorn poot working up the courage to knock at your backdoor."

There was a pause, and Jolanda wondered if he was smiling or frowning. She could barely make out his silhouette, even with her eyes somewhat accustomed to the darkness of the shuttered room. He muttered, "Something about a canal."

"What?"

"Canal runs behind the house, should've done something clever about canals and backdoors. Too tired to think straight. To bed with you."

"Aye," said Jolanda. A thought came to her, inspired, perhaps, by the general peculiarity of the night, and she blurted it out before she could stop herself. "We should go ratting sometime, you and me. Sounds like fun."

"Not what you've said about the practice before," he muttered, the mad bastard sounding all stiff and awkward again. "Besides, we need to start thinking about your future. I won't live forever, and we'll never marry you off if you get a reputation for being moon-touched as your old da."

Well, that was one sure way of making sure the evening was ruined after all—the prospect of marrying some elderly bachelor was about as appealing as eating fishhooks. One thing she'd learned from all those bad times that had come before her current situation was that older men were only after their own interests. Of course, Simon's arsehole older brother, Braem, was proof enough that younger fellows could be pretty much the same. "I've told you once, I've told you a—hey!"

Sander had swept her off her feet, and she was too startled to fight back—how the hell could he see her well enough to pull that off in the dark? He had one hand behind her knees and the other sweaty paw 'round her back, and was making for the bed, she guessed. She tensed an elbow, ready to jab his collar and set to squirming free if he didn't drop her at once, when he spoke in that odd, quiet voice again, "Told me a hundred times. Like I could make you do something you didn't want to."

"Well," said Jolanda, not sure how else to respond. This was a different sort of Sander than she was used to, and it unnerved her a great deal more than his usual bluster and crank.

"Do me a boon, though," said Sander, leaning forward a bit and depositing her with an almost tender clumsiness on the bed. "When you go out, take that new Lizzy girl with you."

"When?" Jolanda asked as Sander pulled the blankets up around her. Although it did not occur to her until after he left and she lay alone in the dark, unable to sleep, no man had tucked her in since her brother Pieter had left home.

"Anytime," Sander said. "From now on, anytime you leave.

And carry a blade tucked away with you. Villains everywhere, looking to get their grope on."

"Nice," said Jolanda, trying not to let him spook her out again after the night she'd had. "Goodnight."

"Night," he said, and a few moments later the door opened, letting in the hint of whatever light he'd left burning in his room down the hall. Seeing him outlined there, his figure somehow blacker than the room had been before he'd opened the door, she suddenly remembered what had sounded so familiar about Sander's claim of dreaming while awake. He and Wurfbain had talked about just that during the coach rides to and from the Easter service in Leyden, something she'd written off at the time as just another example of a madman's folly. It had been a dreadful, tense exchange, something about Sander maybe hurting, no, *killing* a bunch of lepers up in Friesland. A family of them. How they'd nursed him when he was sick only to have him murder the lot.

Jesus Christ preserve her.

"Wait," she called, anxious for an answer, any answer. "Those dreams, where you were awake when they were happening? How did you wake up from those? How did you make them stop?"

"I couldn't," said Sander, closing the door behind him and leaving her to the dark.

IV.

Sander had evidently found a wee pox along with the mutilated corpse, and so spent the next three days in bed. The lengthy haze of aching limbs and pitching around in sweaty covers was occasionally punctuated with leek-and-garlic soup, horehound tea, and fever dreams of decapitated children, prancing Belgians, and, of course, a covered well, from which floated the admonishments of his father and Jan and all the other men Sander had ever killed. It was even worse than it sounded.

Eventually the illness passed, but the first afternoon Sander quit his bed Simon showed up, pasty and stammering to have a talk—so much for rest. The last thing Sander wanted was Lansloet eavesdropping on their conversation, and so he led Simon to the White Horse; the best place for a quiet word was a loud tavern. Jo and that Lizzy girl accompanied them, which rather defeated the purpose of leaving the house for privacy, but Sander was too weak to fight the girls on it. On the walk Sander would've sworn they were being followed, but that was surely just the fever shadowing him.

"That so?" Sander asked, keeping his voice to a whisper even with Jo and Lizzy across the tavern, fetching the ales. He'd told them four, but having Simon acting the donkey put Sander in a mood to keep two for himself.

"Haunted," said Simon, with a sincerity that gave Sander chills in spite of himself. Or maybe it was just the chills giving him chills; goddamn pox. "Every night since we found her, she comes to me, begs me to tell someone!"

"How's she do that?" said Sander, truly curious.

"I told you, in my dreams. I cannot rest, and when at last my eyelids shutter, I—"

"I got that," said Sander. "I mean how does she beg you to do anything, not having a head?"

"Oh," said Simon, pursing his lips. "Well, she has one in the dreams."

"Then how you know it's the same dead kid you're dreaming of, eh?" said Sander, something of a savant these days at using his wits to trump his fears.

"Jan, she…" Simon lowered his head. "Pray, Cousin, do not be cross, if I confide something to you."

"So long as you hurry up with it."

"She…sometimes, the girl, that poor, naked creature, she…"

"She gives you a hand job?"

"No! It's just…it *is* her, the girl we found, I have no doubt that it is she, but sometimes…well, she looks like Jo. She possesses Lady Jo's head."

Sander leaned in, motioning Simon to do the same, and when they were close enough to kiss, Sander rapped his hairy knuckles on Simon's brow. "I don't want to hear another word about this, Simon."

"But—"

"Shut up," said Sander. Jo and her maid were taking the beers from the bartop and turning back toward the table. The White Horse was as mobbed as the dive ever got, the usual threesomes and foursomes of flood-ruined nobles, coin-loaded merchants, and so-so guild members crowded around the boarded-over spokes of the tavern's cart-wheel tables. Sander recognized more of the merchants and boatmen than he did Simon's peers, but the broke snobs certainly knew him—the hatred in their eyes as the Cods glanced his way was about as subtle as a sick dog's fart. "Not another word. Not to nobody, and certainly not to Jo and her girl."

"But—"

"But nothing," said Sander, though he'd come to realize that only one thing would appease Simon. "Winter's come in the last couple of days; I'm sure you noticed that out at the warehouse. Say you tell the militia now, with fresh ice covering the mud and meer, and they manage to get out there. They'll see the ice ain't cracked, see you've been sitting on this 'stead of telling them right away."

Simon stared blankly at him, the thick plug.

"Meaning you look even more suspicious. Like you found out days ago but waited to report it. Anytime you wait to report a thing, it looks suspicious. Like you didn't want to tell."

"But we *did* find her days ago," protested Simon. "And—"

"*We*, nothing, cunt, we *nothing*—you want to get the crow eyes of every hungry militiaman in town directed on you and what you might have to steal, go ahead, but leave me out of it. I won't tell you another word on the matter, save this: you want to tell someone, do yourself a favor and wait 'til the ice breaks up. *Then* you pretend to find her, otherwise you'll look even guiltier."

"I can't wait until spring! I am benightmared by her nightly hauntings, and—"

"Shut it," said Sander sharply. "Oi, that's two for me and two for Simon, didn't you lasses get nothing for yourself?"

Lizzy giggled, placing both of her mugs on the table in front of Sander. "Here you are, sir, and I'm glad you're feeling so hale as to dare two whole water-thin ales."

"Lippy trull!" Sander cried, hoping to disarm the girls with his charm and send them off again so he could finish up with Simon and set to getting properly drunk. "I'll have a third, Lizzy, but this time buy yourself something wet while you're up."

"My name is Lijsbet," she lightly replied. "Lizzy is what you call a very old aunt or a very young child, and being something between, I would beg the courtesy of a proper name." Almost as an afterthought, she added, "sir," but with none of that edge that

Lansloet honed onto the word. She curtsied, the soiled end of her gown flipping a little of its icy sludge onto Simon in the process. She weren't so bad, this girl.

"The hell with that," said Jo, sitting down at a stool beside Simon but not relinquishing either of her ales. "These are for us, bought with my own coin. Let the gentlemen prove their gentility by stepping their fat arses to the bar themselves."

"Lady Jo, I should be honored to enjoy the privilege of purchasing you a refreshment, if only you did not already have a pair before you," said Simon, flicking off the slush Lijsbet had deposited on the thigh of his hose. Credit where due, the ponce pulled his shit together fast. "Perhaps next round?"

"Come on, Simony," said Sander, bumping the table as he stood and causing both the beers before him to slosh foam onto the table. "You can buy me one."

"Alas, I fear I may have spoken in haste," Simon said, following Sander to his feet. "And so it is a question of credit rather than coin, but nonetheless I shall be—"

"Shut it," Sander hissed, as they were sidling up to the bar. "Let's get this straight, Coz, and now—you tell who you want, when you want, but I was never there, and you never told me nothing. Or did you already tell that cunt brother of yours about it, tell him I was out there with you?"

"I—" Simon looked as ill as Sander had felt all week.

"I'll know if you're lying." Sander put an arm around the smaller man and squeezed his shoulder, lowering his voice even more. Old blubbertub Eckert was coming toward them—leave it to a barkeep to only be prompt with service when you're hoping he'll be slow. Sander held up four fingers to prevent the fucker from getting his pendulous jowls any closer. "I don't care if you told Braem or not, but if you lie about it now I'll know, and I'll put you out on your ass. You'll be dead to me, Simon Gruyere, I mean it."

"I haven't told him yet," Simon whispered. He looked earnest enough, and handsome, his eyes shining in the light of the smoking oil lamps behind the bar. "I haven't told anyone yet, not even a priest. That's why I came by, I had to talk to some—"

"Good boy. You really want to tell, you wait until the ice thaws a bit, and then you find her body."

"I find her when it thaws?" Simon asked as if it were a difficult concept to grasp.

"Yeah, thicky-Simon-thicky-cousin. It's too early for this weather to hold, so don't worry about being night-haunted all winter long. When it warms back up enough to get a boat out there easy, you pretend to find the body and tell your brother and the militia and God and anyone else you want. Point is, you go tonight and tell them you just found her today, they'll know you're lying, as she'll be under ice by now, and if you tell 'em you found her three days ago, they'll wonder what took you so long to bring it up. Get it?"

As Sander whispered all this to Simon, a table of boatmen beside them roared with laughter, and Sander wondered how much his dim-witted friend had heard. Enough, it seemed, as Simon nodded and whispered back, "So when the ice is broken up enough to row over to Trash Island, I report her?"

"Got it. But I mean it when I say I don't know nothing about it, here on out. I've got enough to worry about without the militia sniffing around 'cause you said I was with you when you found some dead girl. Get me, Simon? You and me, we never found nothing out there. It gets warm enough, *you* go and pretend to find her, stir up the mud and all, then *you* go to the militia, and then, *only* then, you come and tell me, your boss, like you'd report anything else of note you found out near my warehouse. Got it?"

"But—"

"Got it?" Sander squeezed Simon's shoulder hard enough to make the fop grimace. It was an easy-enough scheme, why the hell was Simon so soft in the head?

"Yes, yes, I have it," Simon said quickly, and Sander let him go, digging into his purse to pay for the beer Eckert was bringing them. Finally.

By the time they'd navigated back to the girls, Jo and Lijsbet were each down a mug and whispering to each other. At Simon and Sander's return they broke into an awful snigger that echoed from one mouth to the other and back again. At least Simon's spirits were restored, having some foolish chits to flirt with.

Sander settled down on his stool and drained his first beer in two long pulls. He still felt sore in the throat and brow, and drinking the tart, malty piss in as few swallows as possible seemed expedient. Goddamn Simon. Like it was so hard to understand. Militias were corrupt, as a rule, and none more so than Dordt's. If anyone knew it was Sander, having had more than one run-in with the fuckers during his youthful oat-sowing on both sides of the city walls. Wouldn't that just make some graybeard militiaman's day, recognizing Sander Himbrecht after all these years?

Even a pack of plaguebitches like the Dordt watch would've figured out it was Sander who drowned his father in the well before hastily quitting the Groote Waard way back when—no doubt whatsoever their shitheel neighbors had gone straight to the city to report the crime once they found the old man's body. Any one of those old assholes on the milita identified Sander and they could hang him twice: once for the patricide and again for impersonating a noble, to say fuck-all of some headless corpse at Trash Island.

What the devil was wrong with him that he'd agreed to come back to this place with Jan in the first place? That he'd never considered how easy it would be for some old-timer to take one look at his face and pin him for murder? He must be as mad as they said, to take the risk of setting foot in Dordt for a single day, let alone permanently settling down here...

No matter, because he wasn't going to be talking to any damn militiamen. He would forget he ever saw the body. He could do that. Forgetting was becoming something of a specialty of his, and top of the list was forgetting he ever gave himself the sweats worrying about being fingered for an ancient crime—he was safe here. Safe.

"A Rotter, eh?" Simon was saying to Lijsbet. Sander forced his attention to their conversation, dull though it was destined to be. Dull beat deranged any day. "A fellow Cod through and true, or did you perchance flee to Dordt for our reputation of harboring the odd Hook?"

What the shit was Simon even talking about? Something about his gibberish rang a bell, but it wasn't a very big one, about the size of the hand ringer Lansloet shook to announce dinner and supper. Sander enjoyed wordplay as much as the next cultured noble, but also like most of his peers, hated few things more than ones that went over his head.

"Simon Gruyere," Jo answered before her maid could, "I imagine if you spoke a bit louder, you could ensure that our continued association with your person fully ruined our good standing in society, instead of only partially so. I'm *sure* there aren't any Hooks left on the island, unless you know something the rest of us don't."

Ah, that was it, Hooks versus Cods, as in loyalists to the exiled Countess Jacoba of Hainaut versus supporters of Good Philip of Burgundy, steward of Holland, Zeeland, and all the rest, regardless of what the countess and her coterie of broke-ass nobles, Hobbe included, might think. Sander hadn't caught the drift at first, thinking Simon was talking about cod fishing. Would that he was—politics were infinitely less interesting than how to properly bait a line.

The thought of fishing reminded Sander that he still needed to take a boat out to Oudeland and go after that catfish, the biggest beast he'd ever seen. Thinking about the monster churned up other memories of that affair, however, and Sander ruminated on the same grim thoughts that had colored his nightmares of the days before.

He was slipping, Sander thought glumly as he finished his second beer, he was slipping. Where? On what? Slipping at the top of a staircase, on the edge of a well, in the mud of Trash Island. Strange fevers where whole days passed with his scarce noticing, save for the waking dreams that seemed so real yet couldn't be, unfounded fears that unknown conspirators were out to get him, that he was being spied upon and followed everywhere, that any moment the militia was going to pinch him… those were all faults of the old Sander, not Graaf Jan Tieselen. He had to hold on, had to dig in, set his heels, say no to madness—he'd done it before. Hadn't he? The past was the past, and this, *this*, he thought as he knocked a knuckle on the table, this was real.

Good.

Except a ghost drifted by him just then, and Sander felt his head begin to float at the end of his neck.

Jan.

Jan Tieselen was right there, in the midst of the throng of living men. Sweet Jan, the real Jan, not himself, the impostor, not Sander pretending to be Jan, but the man Sander had kissed five hundred times if he'd wept for him once. The man Sander had loved. The man Sander still loved. The man Sander had killed.

Jan.

Sander couldn't breathe, couldn't move.

Jan was back.

V.

Fast as the ghost of Jan appeared before Sander, it was gone. Or rather, past Sander's table, the black cloak it wore rippling across its shoulders, an empty mug hanging loosely from each hand. It picked its way around two tables instead of floating through them, and rather than disappearing into the rear wall of the tavern it placed the mugs on a table where a young woman sat, alone. The ghost scooted around the edge of the wheel to sit beside her on the bench that ran along the wall, smiling good-naturedly at the sloshed merchant he bumped in the process.

Jan.

The ghost winked at the young woman, who, from this angle, Sander could only make out in profile. Then the specter looked straight at Sander, and the woman turned slightly, following Jan's gaze, to look at him as well. It was Jo.

What devilry was this? What witchcraft? What madness? Sander felt himself choking on his tongue, the whole tavern beginning to shimmer and waver. What was happening to him?

"Come on, Papa, time to go," Jo was saying, putting her hand on his shoulder. He flinched, did a double take. She'd materialized at his side, Lizzy and Simon staring at him with unabashed curiosity. Lowering her voice to a plaintive mutter, Jo pressed a napkin into his shaking hand and said, "Wipe your face, man, you're crying. Must still be a little sick, huh?"

"Jo," he gasped, glancing between her and the other Jo that still watched him from the back wall. He'd expected the second Jo to have disappeared when he looked back, and the spectral

Jan as well, but no, the pair of impossibilities sat there, watching him, as if ghosts and doppelgängers had just as much right as any grain-seller to swill an ale at the White Horse on a Saturday eve.

"Jesus," Jo said, his Jo, and her voice sounded as strained as his must. He saw that she was now staring at the ghosts as well, her eyes wide. She could see them, too. They were real. He was so relieved, he could kiss her. The warm flush of relief only lasted until she turned back to him and said, "That man there, is he your brother? You could be twins!"

What? Sander blinked at her, wondering just what the hell was wrong with her shit-brown eyes, and almost asked as much. Instead he looked back at the two mysteries and saw that the man wasn't Jan, after all, and the woman definitely wasn't Jo. She was too young, and too pretty.

More importantly, though—all importantly, even—did the man's face resemble what Sander saw in his polished mirror on mornings when he could be bothered to look at himself? Maybe a little. Yeah, sure, maybe a lot. That must have been why he looked so familiar—he looked like Jan, all right, just not the old one! Mostly: the wavy frame around the dashing stranger's face was much darker than Sander's hay-colored coif, and peering closer, he wagered his own mustache and goatee weren't so neatly trimmed, nor his hair so well brushed and shaped. The fellow looked good all around, and not just in a not-actually-a-fucking-ghost-set-loose-from-hell-for-vengeance sort of way.

Shit, the man had noticed Sander staring and was getting out from behind his table. Not good. Jo was running her mouth, but all he could hear was his own voice shouting in his brain's ears, telling him to run like fuck—given the alarming omen he'd just witnessed, what good could come from sticking around? Yet Sander felt rooted to his stool, stuck fast the way that poor headless bitch must be welded to the icy mud of Trash Island. Do something, man!

Nothing. The handsome stranger bore down on Sander, a stormy force of nature in all its inescapable, idiot fury. The woman who wasn't Jo remained seated, but Sander could see her watching the man's approach, which somehow made it all worse—she was like some saint bearing witness to a miracle. Or a divine massacre. The room spun, but the man remained upright, and then he was there and—

"Monsieur? Sorry, *sir*," the man corrected himself, and all at once Sander felt the fear flee his bones. This joker might look a little like the new Jan Tieselen, but he didn't look anything like the old one, and on top of that, the day Sander got tail-tucked by a Frenchman was the day he deserved to be haunted. "My companion and I could not help but notice that you and I, perhaps, are sharing some resemblance?"

Why the fuck was everything a question with grapesippers? Out of sheer instinctual surliness, Sander would have liked to refute the Frenchman's claim, but his tongue was still soldered with bitter drool to his palate. Jo was saying something, but Sander's ears were suddenly ringing like the final peal of the Saint Nicolaas Church's bell, and so he didn't hear what she said. It had the right effect, though, the handsome stranger smiling slightly before he spun around and left without another word. Nicely done, Jo, send the asshole packing! He'd have to thank her, soon as he was able, and—

Wait a tic, what? The Frenchy had reached his table, but rather than sitting his ass back down, he took his two empty mugs and then offered a hand to his lady. Ah, they were leaving the tavern altogether, good, better, go on back down to grapetown, fuckers, get on the next Tieselen hulk and piss off back to—

Fuck. Simon appeared out of the teary blur that was Sander's periphery and set two stools down between Sander and Jo. God-*damn* Simon. Jo was scooting her stool back, standing up, curtseying, and no no no, what had she done, the stupid bitch, what had she done? Unbidden by his whining, bestial brain, Sander snapped to his feet so fast he nearly upended the table. The horizontal wheel rocked back down flat again without a single mug falling over, which had to be some sign, didn't it, that not everything was fucked?

"My thanks to you again, Lady Jolanda," said the French ponce, bowing. "This is my cousin, Christine, and I am the Baron de Rais, Gilles de Montmorency-Laval."

"My father," Jo said, her voice soft as a baby bird in a nest of wool scraps. If he could bullshit half as good as her, Sander would have been pope instead of just—"the Graaf Jan Tieselen. He is recovering from a malady, and, alas, his voice has been slowest to recuperate from—"

"We do look alike, don't we?" Sander blurted out, which was admittedly true, aside from this fop's jet hair. He willed himself to not be mad anymore. Was he really so out of his gourd that something as commonplace as resembling a stranger, albeit a Frenchman, sent him into fits? Best not to answer that, especially considering that at first he'd thought this man looked like someone else entirely—what kind of a gentleman doesn't know what his own face looks like?

"Yes! I saw you looking, and it was like the mirror looking," said the Frenchy, and holding up his gloved hand, he waved it slowly through the air. "Yet not a mirror, I see now for myself!"

Sander felt the madness draining out of him at the Frenchman's mundane attempt at humor. "Right, you see now. Not a mirror. So…"

"So we must be friends!" The Frenchman mistook Sander's dismissive wave as an invitation to sit, and his cousin did the same. Now that she was closer, Sander had no idea how he'd mistaken the girl for Jo—or for a lady. Unless his eyes were betraying him anew, this strumpet was cousin to a different patron or three every night Sander braved the White Horse. Considering how hard she and Simon were trying not to look at each other, she'd been his cousin a time or two. She couldn't be fifteen years old, the dirty sod.

"More fun not to drink alone," Gilles said, and with a cluck-

ing sound and a wave of his hand, he effected the impossible—
he brought Eckert waddling out from behind the bar.

The barman had his whores working the room, but no wenches
and no runnerboys, preferring to make everyone crowd up to the
bar—no doubt to keep folk from ever getting settled enough to
notice how uncomfortable his stools were, or the damp draft that
plagued every wall and corner. Yet here Eckert came, oily sweat
clinging like a diadem to his fat brow, a bottle in each hand.
Sander saw with some satisfaction that the bottles bore the Tieselen
seal. The greedy filcher had no doubt drained the good wine out
and replaced it with equal parts water and pigeon blood, but the
fact that he was promoting Sander's business warmed his heart a
bit toward the miserable fucking asshole.

"Sire," huffed Eckert, placing the bottles on the table. The
fatty hovered, as fatties are fucking wont to do when they suspect
a crumb's about to fall, and Gilles offered up a gold coin.

"Are you a knight, then, good master, or do old Eckert's good
manners exceed his vocabulary?" Simon asked, breaking the
seal on a bottle, pulling out the rag, and filling his empty mug to
the brim. Good dig, Simon, put the Frenchy in his place!

"Indeed I am," said Gilles, which spoiled things a bit. "A son
of France, away from home. I go to war, good stranger, whenever
she shall have me, but for now...foreign education. Are you a
knight of Burgundy, then, or some other place? Forgive me, I
have traveled far and cannot recall who, at this moment, you
bow before—who is the present swamp lord?"

"Good Philip of Burgundy is indeed our current steward,"
said Jo as Simon fumed. "But an heir of France such as yourself
can surely appreciate that, as with a violent bowel ailment, the
pain and indignity of having a Burgundian usurper is but a tem-
porary complaint, even if it seems eternal at the time. On an
utterly unrelated note, how is your Dauphin these days?"

Sander had no fucking idea what Jo was saying, but Simon
turned an even deeper shade of scarlet and the Frenchy laughed,

so it was probably something bad about Duke Philip. As far as Sander was concerned, a little idle shit-talking about the Cods and their champion sat just fine—the Hook allegiance Wurfbain assigned Sander and Jo had proved a comfortable enough fit, once it became obvious that every other noble in Cod-loyal Dordrecht despised the new Tieselen heirs sight unseen.

When Count John had died they'd had the perfect opportunity to hand things over to his niece Countess Jacoba, put an end to these civil wars for good...but of course the Cods couldn't have that, hence this Burgundian bullyboy taking over. Not that Sander thought it was as simple as Jacoba versus Philip, Brabançon versus Burgundian, Hook versus Cod; you'd have to be thick as Simon to buy into all that. No, it was all about rivalries between neighboring cities, desperate nobles fighting hungry merchants, rich pitted against richer, same as ever—the war was a justification for every brawl that blew out of proportion, every dispute that came to blows, from a pair of Papendrecht peasants fighting over a pasture all the way up the Netherlandish ladder. If anyone asked Sander, he'd have set them straight...

"In response to your query, *sir*, I am a son of Dordrecht," said Simon, with a tad more pride than Sander would have expected from a warehouse-dwelling ratman living off the scraps of his faux cousin. "As for the homage I pay, you need look no farther than to your right, where the wealthiest graaf in the city has offered you a seat at his table."

"That would be me," Sander offered the smiling knight. Not too shabby at all, this one, and if what they said about Frenchmen was true, Sander might have a decent chance. What they said about Frenchmen being that they'd fuck anything with an opening, of course, mossy knotholes and pig snouts included. "Nice cloak."

"Thank you, Graaf," said Gilles, touching the drape of charcoal velvet clasped around his neck with a fat gold chain. "I like your wife's, it is very...blue."

"Daughter," Jo said quickly. "Daughter, not wife. But thank

you, monsieur, you are too kind—it is an old thing, more warm than pretty."

Glancing at Jo, Sander saw she wore the cloak Jan had given her back in Poorter's kitchen, a lifetime ago. Two years, was that all? Ever since they'd come ashore after . . . the incident, he hadn't seen her wear it once. He would have remembered. That damn cloak had caused a rather tremendous row between him and Jan before they'd met up with the Muscovite, though of course Jo wouldn't know that, Sander having waited until she was out buying supplies with Poorter to bring it up, and—

—Christ, what a life they'd lived! Jo was staring at him, and he tried to smile at her. Even he could tell it probably looked more like a sickly grimace.

"—war with the English?" Simon was asking, his usual joie de vivre apparently restored. Taking a sip from the wine that the now respectfully silent Lizzy had poured him, Sander understood why—this wasn't watered-down dreg-drippings after all, this was actual Tieselen Orange, and somebody other than Simon was footing the bill. In all his nights of swilling under Eckert's roof, Sander had never been served a drink half as good as the cheapest stuff he imported, and yet here it was in his mug. Just how much had that French gold coin been worth?

"But of course," said Gilles. "It is what we excel at, defeating the Englanders any chance we receive. And you? It is much . . . funny, much funny, your Jacoba running to London, begging help with the Englanders to win again her crown. She is marrying one Englander, and already she has one husband here, yes?"

"She would do nothing of the sort!" Jo protested, which was stupid—of course the disenfranchised countess would, if she thought it would help restore the power that had now been stolen by two consecutive usurpers. She was too smart not to, by all accounts. Women had it hard enough without trying to play fair when everyone else was cheating. But then the righteous-lady-done-wrong line Hobbe had fed them had always appealed to Jo, and so the girl no doubt had an idealized perception of the Hook's deposed leader.

"It is the word of all who listen, as well as all who speak," said Gilles, making Sander wonder if this was some new proverb or just a clumsy translation. "Watch out if she does—the Englander foolish enough to wed a married countess is foolish enough to go to her house to look for the dowry, even if everyone else knows the Burgundians have already stolen it."

Simon laughed at this, his Cod ass forgetting he was drinking Hook wine, and Jo didn't fire back a retort this time, though she looked upset—might've been an etiquette thing, her not being able to sass back to a froggy knight without three maids to hold a pink veil between them, something like that. Sander was once lucky that as graaf nobody could really think less of him for the odd lapse in manners, and twice lucky for not giving a shit even if they did. He supposed since he and Jo were already pariahs amongst the local nobles for their obvious if unproven Hook sympathies, he should at least reap the benefit of now having an excuse to fight this mouthy Frenchman on account of his slandering Jacoba…

But the truth was, Sander was having a hard time getting excited about the prospect. What the hell was wrong with him these days, where brawling a French ponce didn't fill his cup?

"Men have been executed for talking of the countess in such a fashion," Jo finally said, glancing at Sander—was she signaling that she wanted to go home, or that she wanted Sander to stick up for the exiled liege they'd never laid eyes on?

Simon refilled his glass and said, "Only because the dirty bitch had them killed for daring to speak the truth. She's a tyrant. I swear that even in the unlikely event of an English invasion, this defender of Dordrecht will be the first to lay down his life to ensure the ignoble Jacoba never again sets foot on our lands."

"We would appreciate the sacrifice, Simon," Jo said coldly.

"Even a dead man's hand has more use than the all of a living coward," said Gilles, winking at Jo over his mug. Taking a sip, the Frenchman made a face and said, "This is the worst wine I have ever tasted, and I have been to Champagne."

"That's where we get it from," said Sander. He should be dueling this cunt over such a remark, but prideless for a pfennig, prideless for a groot. Or something. Besides, he quite liked that line about dead men and cowards, seemed like you could start a really good fight, saying that to somebody. Didn't make a lot of sense, though: "What use is a dead man's hand?"

"Pardon? Ah, a dead man's hand is—no, not just a dead man. A dead man who..." Gilles furrowed his brow and silently moved his lips. Then he brightened a bit, and holding a fist over his head, jerked it in the air and stuck his tongue out. A lot of folk might've been flummoxed by the display, but not Sander.

"Hanged, yeah? Hanged man?"

"Yes, a hanged man's hand is...special. For a witch, yes? Such a hand is called...*gloire*? You have gloire here in Holland, yes?"

"Glory, yeah, glory is glory," said Sander, now really feeling the eels of anxiety nipping at his nerves—first there was talk of hanged men, and now his old sword came to mind, waiting for him in that tree in the meer...Wait, was that an insult about not having glory in Holland? Probably.

"A witch will take a hanged man's hand, yes? Chop chop." Gilles placed his own on the table and mimicked hacking it with his mug, which led to wine splashing all over his glove. The stuff would leave a stain, Sander knew from experience. The Frenchman removed his soiled glove and held it up, then crushed it in his fist as he continued. "Taking the hand away, the witch, she mashes it up. Like a *charcutier* turning sausage, yes? Taking the fat. Then she uses the fat, the fat and...everything, to make a *chandelle*."

"A candle? Why would anyone do such a thing?" Simon looked a little peaked, probably thinking of a different missing body part on a different sort of dead person.

"Candle is—Merde, apologies!" In shaking his glove back out,

Gilles had spattered droplets of wine on the faces of everyone at the table. Sander licked a sticky pearl from his lips. "This candle is Hand of Glory. You have Hand of Glory in Holland, yes?"

"No," said Sander. If they did, he sure as hell for the wicked would have heard of it before. The thought of such a thing made his teeth hurt, he couldn't say why. "What's the candle for, spells and evil rites and all?"

Gilles shrugged, slipping his pale hand back into the glove. "Different things. You light the candle in the house, and all of the...not-sleepers, those people in the house will go to sleep. Or you hold the candle, and people will not see you, even if you stand before them. Different... *stories*, yes, different stories, but the same is hanged man's hand for candle, candle for sneaking inside and outside of the house. Good for the thief, maybe. Hence, even a dead man's hand has more solid use than the all of a living coward."

"Witchcraft is not, nor shall it ever be, more useful than a God-fearing man, coward or not," said Simon, making the sign of the cross. He seemed to have swung back around to being disgusted by Gilles. Probably from the realization that he'd just spent some time insulting the politics of his only wealthy friends in the service of buttering up a foreigner whom he'd probably never see again.

"Maybe," said Gilles. "Dead man's hand being better than the whole of a coward is only a...saying? Something that is said?"

"I think you have *said* quite enough. *Monsieur.*" Simon spit the last word like a grapeseed. "Unless—"

"*Simon,*" Jo said in exasperation. "You've already annoyed half the table, and insulting the baron won't take back all the nasty things you've said, so just—"

"Unless you care to have those blasphemous lips shut for you," Simon concluded, crossing his arms across his chest.

"Blasphemous?" The Frenchman seemed more bemused than insulted by Simon's challenge, thank all the saints who listen. "What is blasphemous? Do you not tell tales here in Holland? Did you not disparage the Countess Jacoba for punishing those who merely speak their minds?"

"Speak their minds?! Why, I—"

"*Simon*," Sander said, having had more than enough of the punk's flip-flopping for one night. "Shut it. Have a word outside with me, Guy."

"Gilles," said he, raising an eyebrow. "But of course, Graaf."

"Jan," said Sander, leading the Frenchman to the door of the tavern. The name burned acrid as ever on the tongue, but you got used to it, like wine. The White Horse was right full, but it was cold enough that there wasn't a lot of overflow on the street—people who couldn't cram inside simply went somewhere else. Out on Kuipershaven there wasn't much wind, but it was still snowing. Sander tried to get excited about what was coming next, but simply felt cold.

"What is it, Jan?" asked Gilles, snowflakes falling onto the frozen wave of his hair and sticking there like freshly ground salt caught in the crust of a pudding.

"It's like this, you frilly fucking ponce," said Sander, the words suddenly warming him in a way no fire had down the many long winter nights in the Tieselen house, reviving his strength like no tea nor philter ever could. Gilles was staring at him, his eyes dark as his hair, dark as all the hidden devils of the world, and Sander went on, happier than he could remember feeling. "I'm going to take you into an alley and you're going to suck me to the root. *Or*, and you have a choice here, *or* I'm going to beat the ever-loving shit out of you, and *then* you're going to suck me to the root. Your choice, you French pansy, your choice."

Gilles's lips pulled back so slowly it was goddamn sinister. Sander half-expected them to just keep receding forever, all the way to the man's ears, revealing...he didn't know what. Eel's teeth, maybe, or a dog's. Finally, the Frenchman said, "Where is this alley, Graaf?"

"Good answer," said Sander, feeling his heat rise instead of diminish at this unexpected but very welcome response. Come to it, he wouldn't have exactly been at his best in a scrap, getting over a fever and—

—Gilles came at him like Sander didn't have time to think of what, something fucking fast and mean, and then both men were on the ground. The cobbles were frosted, and cracked Sander's skull something fierce, even though he'd angled his neck during the fall to prevent just that. Gilles's fists were pummeling Sander's innocent guts into porridge, left and right, left and right. He was just fortunate the man hadn't been of a mind to stick him with a dagger or he'd already be dead, or close enough.

But what if Gilles did have a knife, what if Sander's belly was just too stupid to feel it? That moment of terror was what truly brought Sander back to life, the old Sander, the true Sander. He could feel the Frenchman's muscular thigh grinding between his legs, through his ornamental codpouch, could see Gilles's snarling face above him, sheer delight painted across the knight's face. Nice, thought Sander, *very* nice, and cock and man shot upright in the same burst of excitement.

Sander would have bit Gilles's face if he hadn't have been so pretty, but in his time as graaf he'd come to appreciate beautiful things for more than the pleasure their destruction brought. So, instead, he bit the bastard's shoulder, gagging on velvet cape as he wrenched a hand loose from under the Frenchy and punched the fucker in the throat. They were rolling then, over and over, the frozen street clobbering one side and fists clobbering the other, and Sander laughed a mad, desperate laugh as Gilles hissed a stream of furious French at him. They sounded good, those incomprehensible words coming out of Gilles's bloody mouth, and Sander kept trying to kiss his opponent. This only incensed the man more, which in turn only got Sander to burn the hotter.

Best night he'd had in ages, and it was only getting better—ten pfennigs said he sweet-talked the Frenchy into going home with him, once the brawl was resolved. Good night, indeed.

Januari 1426

"Holding an Eel by the Tail"

I.

Christmas and the Festival of Fools took too long in coming and then quickly fled, and since Zoete had quit the city to stay with Wurfbain somewhere abroad, Jolanda was not invited to a single feast that season. She was accustomed to being snubbed by the local nobles, of course; even Lady Meyl Von Wasser, who had seemed so friendly when they'd met at the Easter service in Leyden, expertly avoided eye contact during worship at Dordrecht's Saint Nicolaas Church. Hooks weren't welcome in the noble houses of the Cod-ruled city, Jolanda got that, but she had hoped for a pity-invitation over Yuletide, even if it came from a guildsman's wife or a merchant's widow instead of a proper lady.

She wished she possessed Lijsbet's easygoing demeanor that earned the maid friends wherever she went regardless of circumstance, but since she didn't, she was glad she possessed Lijsbet herself—they went to the baths twice a week and skating nearly every morning and spent the afternoons telling stories and playing cards and flirting with lads at the cider and chestnut stalls set up in Grote Markt Square. Just the once, Jolanda gave Lijsbet a sword lesson in the courtyard, but aye, just the once—Lijsbet was a comically bad pupil.

Then war came and ruined everything, as Jolanda supposed wars were prone to do. The local Cod wives Jolanda occasionally encountered at the markets were snootier than ever before to her, and Wurfbain came to visit more frequently than usual, updating Sander and Jolanda on political gossip. He also lectured them ad nauseam on the importance of avoiding any public conflict with even the lowliest Cod in Dordrecht, for the hated rivals were seeking excuses to ruin the Tieselens and any other Hooks they could finger. The count knew far more than he let on, as usual, but Jolanda gathered that Countess Jacoba had indeed wooed a powerful Englishman to her cause and that all of Britain was poised to crash down upon Holland, restoring the countess to her rightful place. When that happened, the whole world would turn upside down, and the Tieselens, as well as Wurfbain, Lady Zoete, and any other secret Hooks, would be the ones on top.

One afternoon in mid-January, they received word from a footman that Wurfbain had again returned to Dordrecht, and while Lijsbet combed Jolanda's hair in her bedchambers, the women speculated on what news he might share at supper.

"I have a pfennig that says nothing's changed from last time," said Lijsbet, working the boxwood comb with a practiced arm. In the time since she had become a lady, Jolanda's hair had grown well past her shoulders. It looked much better than she had expected it would, falling around her face in a surprisingly handsome fashion, as even Sander had remarked. Yet she still sometimes longed to cut it all off, to not have Lijsbet run her brutal comb through it ever again, as she did now while doing a passable Wurfbain: "*I bring the exciting news that Jacoba is still in London mustering her forces. Now, please pass your best wine over here, and some of that lamprey, too.*"

"Wurfbain's not Simon," said Jolanda, and then in unison, they both added, "unfortunately!"

Ever since the night when Sander had dueled that disquieting French baron in the street and then, to Jolanda's mortification, accompanied the Frenchman back to his lodgings, a transformation had come over Simon. He was every bit as flirtatious and painfully obvious as ever, but a certain seriousness had replaced his formerly chronic frivolity. He had also taken to church in a way he never had before, and seemed actively concerned with the state of the poor children of Dordt—what charity the orphans of the flood had received immediately after the catastrophe was long since used up, and while most people seemed content to pretend the young beggars didn't exist, Simon was constantly talking of the need to protect the wretches from the ravages of weather, starvation, and the obvious perils of living on the street. Considering how rough affairs were for nobles left landless and destitute by the flood, he would point out, imagine the state of their serfs, especially the young ones who had survived flood and famine only to be left adrift on the cruel streets of Dordrecht.

Mind, he was still a mooch and a cad, forever emerging from the crowd to join Jolanda and Lijsbet just after they'd purchased mulled cider or candied almonds from a stall, rather than before they'd laid down their coin, but there was something almost charming about this flagrant behavior. Combine his looks with Wurfbain's politics and fortunes and you'd have the perfect suitor, Lijsbet has said more than once, but then the maid took her Hookishness much more seriously than Jolanda.

If only Simon didn't have such an obvious motivation for being sweet to her, Jolanda might have let herself indulge in daydreams of his genuinely having changed, having become a more serious sort of fellow—as it stood, she was wise enough to recognize that he was simply changing his wooing tactics. Probably. It also would have made things easier if he would stop following her from afar, as he sometimes did—he no doubt thought it was gallant, minding her from the shadows to make sure nobody gave her trouble, but instead it was downright unsettling, forever feeling eyes following you from an alley, constantly catching glimpses of a hooded figure ducking around corners when you checked over your shoulder. If she hadn't confirmed it was him by once dodging into an alley and then lying in wait until he came rushing along after, it would have been truly disturbing, having a watcher always at your back...but aye, it was just Simon.

"I tell you," said Lijsbet, "we ought to find a way to get Simon down here for supper. Nothing's better than watching him and the count squirm at each other's company."

"Anything's better than Wurfbain's sermons to us novices," said Jolanda. "Been left out of every feast and court dealing since we arrived on account of our politics, but he still talks down to us, like we might turn on the countess if he wasn't here to remind us not to."

"Dull as it is to hear it over and over, m'lady, I'm glad you've got a friend like the count—I've served in a few houses, as you know, and it's saddening to know how many otherwise witty lords and ladies are swayed into folly by the counsel of Cods."

"Be that as it may, I can understand their outrage about Jacoba's double-marriage business," said Jolanda, bored enough that baiting her maid seemed like a worthy diversion. "It would be bad enough, marrying an Englishman, but when you've already got one husband here—that's an awful way to go about winning local support."

"That Brabançon she married before was jelly-boned as a pickled herring," said Lijsbet. "He'd been a good husband and protected her claim, she wouldn't have needed a new fellow—believe you me, m'lady, I know what it's like to have a husband abandon you to your own wits, and it changes a girl's outlook. Besides, it's not no double-marriage, or it shouldn't be; whatever that Cod-bought pope says now, he promised her a divorce ages ago!"

"Oh my," said Jolanda in mock surprise. "Besmirching the holiest man in the world as well as praising the villainous countess—you're on quite a tear today, aren't you?"

"Yes, yes, she's so villainous, asking what's owed to her by birth. She was cheated, as everyone knows, cheated and run off like a stray dog by your so-called local support. Only thing the countess did wrong was put her trust in courts and church, in her friends. Can you imagine what she must be going through? To be born to greatness, only to have some, some *fraud* come in and take everything? She's right to be mad, and right to rally any army she can, even if they are a pack of Englanders." Lijsbet had stopped combing in her passion.

"*Really*, Lijsbet," said Jolanda, trying to enjoy the ire she'd raised in her maid, but rather put off by some of the character of the girl's speech. "You ought to be careful about who you say that to—most of your sheephead friends at market wouldn't take kindly to your advocating for foreign armies fording the Maas!"

"So they say, but they're eager enough to tongue the ass of a Burgundian like Duke Philip! I'll take a woman of this land, born and bred, with foreign support, to a foreign man forcing his way into ruling us with the support of greedy locals."

"But Philip never would have been able to if her uncle hadn't chosen him," said Jolanda, remembering the last supper where all this had been discussed at length between Wurfbain and Laurent while Sander dozed in his chair at the head of the table. "Old Count John's grave is barely cold and already you're lamenting Philip's succeeding, when all he's done is—"

"John was Bavarian," said Lijsbet hotly, "meaning he had just as little claim to us as Philip. None, I mean, none at all."

"Bavarian or not, he was Jacoba's flesh and blood," said Jolanda. "A good ruler is a good ruler, no matter where he is born."

"Ha! How good was he, to steal his niece's crown and end up murdered by his own knight? John the Pitiless, they called him, and that sounds right to me, as I don't pity his passing. Problem with those foreigners is they're like rats, you can't just kill one, you need to burn the whole nest. Kill a Bavarian, and a Burgundian grows in his place. If the flood hadn't come, they never would have got away with it, mark me, it's all these corrupt merchants with their blood-dripping riches coming in from dirty foreign deals, all this, this, jamming a lever under the world and wrenching it out of joint, until—"

"*Lijsbet*," Jolanda said, now every bit as enflamed as her maid and turning in her chair to face the haughty servant. "I will remind you that the house you serve, a house that has supported Countess Jacoba unfailingly ever since my father and I came here, *this* house, stands, as a matter of fact, on the fortune brought in through the importation of foreign goods. Or were you unaware that the Tieselen farmlands are now, as they have been for some time, under fucking water, and that our breeding has much less to do with our situation than the foresight of the old graaf in transitioning himself into mercantile interests?"

For a moment Lijsbet defiantly stared down at her mistress, and then, abruptly, both women burst out laughing. They sounded like a couple of cranks at the White Horse, coming to blows over the affairs of people they'd never met nor seen, over events that had less to do with their lives than a sudden storm when they were swimming or a run of luck at the Karnöffel table. Lijsbet sobered first, and knelt down in front of Jolanda's chair. She suddenly looked on the verge of tears, and Jolanda wondered just what in the name of the nine valiants had gotten into her maid today.

"I'm sorry, Lady, truly I am. You're right that I forget my place, but I hope you know me well enough to see that it's not through pride or scorn, but just my silliness—I love you like a sister, though I know it's presumptuous to say it like that, but I do, and sometimes I just… well, act stupid as I would around a sister, instead of minding myself better, the way I ought to around someone of your station. I promise, *promise*, that I'll never say such foolish things again, nor take such a tone. I—"

"Oh, shut it," said Jolanda, pushing back her maid's veil to tousle her auburn hair. "I've never had a sister, and until meeting you I never wanted for one. Now I know better. I'm lucky to have someone who will tell me what they think when I ask, instead of what they believe *I do*. Now, turn 'round so I can do yours, it's tangled as I've ever seen."

Lijsbet obliged, pulling her wimple the rest of the way off and shaking her hair out. "You've spoilt me, m'lady—I never dreamt I'd work for good, righteous people in this den of Cods, and I get so carried away, I offend even those I love, those who're doing more to help the countess than a wretch like me ever could. Say you'll forgive me, Lady? Please?"

"Already done," said Jolanda, and meant it. Removing the comb from where it was lodged painfully in her own hair, she set to working it through her maid's. "I provoked you, Lijsbet, and cruelly—I meant to tease you, knowing your passion for the countess. I'd be a fool not to know by now that you have some love for the woman exceeding even what the graaf and I possess for her."

"Well, it's in my bones—my mother came from Hainaut, and my da's brother Bertie died at Gorinchem, trying to win the day for her. Now that things are getting hot again, I truly wish she triumphs, drives those Burgundy bastards back to where they came from. Even if she did marry an Englishman. She reminds me of Griet," said Lijsbet wistfully, resting an elbow on Jolanda's blanket-draped knee. "Just like you do. Women who won't stand for nonsense."

"Griet's your friend who put you in touch with Lansloet, about working here?" asked Jolanda idly.

"Her? Nay, never a woman less like the two of you. I mean Griet from the tales, her who raided hell itself—Mad Griet."

"Oh!" said Jolanda, as flattered as she'd ever been. "I don't know how I've given you such an impression of me—I'm just a girl of Dordt, same as any other."

"No," said Lijsbet with the hard certainty of rain coming after a red dawn. "You're not."

It felt good, sitting there in her bedroom with Lijsbet, combing out her maid's hair and talking through all the troubles, big and small. In that moment there was nowhere Jolanda would rather be, nothing she should prefer to be doing. Which meant she should do something to screw it all up, maybe. "I'll tell you a secret, Lijsbet, if you promise not to hate me for it."

"I don't think I could hate you, m'lady," said the maid, though there was something to her voice, some note Jolanda couldn't quite pin down. Not with Lijsbet facing the window, anyway, the backs of heads being a wee bit less emotive than faces. Time to tell her, then, the spilling of the secret as queer a mingling as hunger with nausea, desire with disgust. It felt good to tell.

"It's just...I really wanted to..." Jolanda stopped combing lest Lijsbet lose her temper again and do herself some mischief. "I wanted to go to war. Not against the countess, of course, but even if it had been her we were fighting, I wouldn't have declined...I mean, ever since Jan first started teaching me the sword, I've daydreamed of using it, you know, really using it, to do some good with it. So I'd hoped we would, me and him, go to some battle, some war, and truth be told, one side's as good as the other to those who are just in it for some sport."

"No good ever comes from spilling blood, and I think you'd find it other than sport," said Lijsbet, though not in the icy tone Jolanda would've expected—she sounded easy as ever, and Jolanda relaxed as the maid continued. "And go on with the brush and get it over with, unless you're prolonging my agonies to a purpose. But no. Or yes, I mean yes, of course you want to go to war. Not much of a secret, that—swords on your wall, daggers stuffed under your bed, that absurd jester's suit you like dancing about in—you thought I'd forgot!"

"I wish you would!" said Jolanda, and then they were laughing together at the memory—the sparring lesson Jolanda had given Lijsbet was doomed to giggly failure from the moment the maid had caught sight of her mistress's brigandine armor. Silly to behold, maybe, but practical—if Jacoba and her Englanders actually made it to Dordrecht, as Wurfbain insisted they eventually would, it would be incumbent upon the Tieselens to drop any pretense of neutrality and help the Hooks take the city. Wurfbain implied there were even more Hooks in Dordt than Jolanda and Sander knew about, that admitting an invading army might be easily done if sympathetic militiamen were manning the gatehouses...

"So no, Lady Jo, I don't hate you for being such a bloodthirsty brute," Lijsbet said when they had both settled down. "But I'd be lying if I said I wasn't glad you and Master Jan are loyal to the countess, and don't deny it, I know you are, even if you can't admit it out loud for fear of Codfoolery. I'm sure those crooked Cods have got Graaf Jan paying his due, but a lot of the nobles, they make quite the show out of being on the field themselves, as I hear it. I offer my thanks every Sunday that this house hasn't gone to war."

The walls of the house shook around them, as if God himself were leaning on the building. Or the devil. Sander on the stairs. The door burst open, and there was the mad graaf, red-faced and wild-eyed as any hanged man on the end of a noose. Instead of his usual, perpetually dirty hose, he wore thick leather pants and a massive steel codpiece in the shape of a ram's head.

"Jo!" he shouted, though she was five paces away. "Get your kit!"

"My kit?" She hadn't seen him look this crazed since his exchange with Hobbe in the count's coach that fateful Easter morn. "What kit, what are you—"

"War!" He hooted, and she still couldn't be sure if he was terrified or elated. "We're off to war! Now! Now, now, *now*, we'll miss the boat!"

Lijsbet seemed to be shriveling up into her gown where she sat on the floor. Looking back and forth between her maid and Sander, Jolanda asked, "When? With who?"

"Now!" Sander looked like a child trying to mollify his bloated bladder by hopping from foot to foot. "With, uh, Jacoba—her! We've flipped, Jo, we've flipped, and to hell with Hobbe and his precious countess—we're Cods now! Hurry, hurry, or we'll miss the boat! Put your kit on, big cloak over it, something hooded— they won't let you come if they know you're a girl, so big hood, and you'll wear the helm from my suit—saints know I won't stick my head in a jug, metal or no, for count nor country! War! Shit!"

Then he was gone, banging down the hall to his room and

hollering for Lansloet. Jolanda stared at the empty doorway for a long time, not wanting to look back at Lijsbet. She didn't want to see the sorrow on the maid's face, nor have the maid see the excitement on hers. Not for their turning into Cods, whatever that might entail—Jolanda had nothing but respect for the indomitable countess, and becoming her adversary would have chafed, had it not been for what Sander had said about their turning on Wurfbain. Jolanda knew she couldn't have it both ways, and if going against Wurfbain meant going against Jacoba, then so be it—she'd never met the countess, of course, so couldn't say if she was undeserving of such treachery, but she knew Wurfbain, the sinister, selfish poot, and was thrilled that Sander had finally bucked from the tight reins of the count. When she'd given Sander a hard time at the supper table about sitting out every interesting conflict instead of rebelling against Wurfbain, she had never dreamed he would invite her along even if he did get off his increasingly fat arse to join some foreign fray.

"M'lady," said Lijsbet, resting her hand on Jolanda's shoulder. The maid had risen as silently as the sun, and now stood behind her mistress just as she had when combing out Jolanda's hair. Once again neither could see the other's face, and Jolanda let out a long sigh. Before she could think of something to say, Lijsbet put on a chipper tone and said, "I'll fetch some ribbon to tie your hair back, if it pleases your knightly sensibilities, and then array Sir Jo's jester dress for inspection."

"No, no," said Jolanda, jumping out of her chair. "I won't have you help me with such a task. Why don't you..."

"Make you a flask of horehound? It will be cold as I don't know what, going anywhere in a boat this time of year." Lijsbet's smile looked almost genuine.

"Thank you," Jolanda said, and meant it. Her maid vanished down the stairs, and Jolanda stared out the window, trying to sort it all through. They were really going against Wurfbain and the Hooks...

Sander had apparently meant what he said about leaving *now, now, now*, for Jolanda had only just stopped cogitating and laid out her armor when he burst back into her room and demanded to know why she wasn't ready yet.

"I didn't have Lansloet to help me dress, for one," she said, too annoyed to be properly embarrassed at his barging in when all she wore was an undershirt that barely reached her hips.

"Where's Lizzy?" he asked, clanking over to her. He hadn't slipped his surcoat over his plate yet, and his sparkling cuirass, greaves, and gauntlets made him look like some bastard son of lobster and tankard. She suspected that a solid shove would result in his falling onto his back and remaining there, tortoiselike, until somebody helped him up. She would have tried it, too, just to see if she was correct, but lest he rescind his invitation she held her hand. For now. "My mother's mussel, you don't even have underwear on, idiot! You'll chafe your chafables, you don't—"

"Look away," she said, blushing and snatching up the linen sling she had been about to step into when he'd clattered into her room. Getting it into place, she turned back to see him rooting through her chest, flinging clothes up in the air behind him like a dune rat excavating sand from a burrow. "Oi, get out of there!"

"Getting your shit together," said Sander. "Might be on campaign for months, need to have plenty of warm—what's this?"

He turned, the sack full of her savings dangling from one gauntlet. Arsehole. She snatched it from his hand, but the cloth caught on the jagged edge of his finger, sending a spray of coins across the floor. For a moment they both stared in silence as the groots went spinning, but then Sander held up his silver palms.

"Sorry, sorry. But gather all that and bring it with you, we might need it."

"*We?*" Jolanda's initial relief that he wasn't giving her a hard time over hoarding any and all money she had lain fingers on since becoming a lady was somewhat mitigated by his casual appropriation of it. "Why don't you bring your own coin, eh?"

"I'm bringing what I've got, yeah," said Sander. "But I don't keep a lot here. Burglars. And we don't have time to go by Laurent's and free up more, so just keep track of what we spend and I'll reimpurse you."

"Reimburse," said Jolanda, hefting on her plate-lined leather doublet. "Every pfennig."

"Yeah, yeah," said Sander, and lodging a gauntlet under either armpit, extracted both his hands in one tug. "That's not going to hold, let me, let me."

Jolanda awkwardly raised her arms to let Sander tie off the laces on her doublet. His fussiness about knots would be comical if it didn't border on the totally obsessed. "If you die in battle, I'll never get this thing off now."

"Cut it," said Sander, straightening up and admiring his handiwork. "Best-kept secret about ropes, you can cut the buggers in a pinch. Now, hurry it up and get the rest've your kit on. Christ, but you're slow as rent from a farmer. I'm going to go see that the servants are readying themselves, and we'll be off." Sander turned to go, but this last made Jolanda pause midway through donning the next piece in her complicated puzzle of armor, a splinted vambrace for her left arm.

"What do you mean, readying themselves? Lijsbet and—"

"Everyone's coming," said Sander, but while he'd looked back at her, he wouldn't meet her eyes, the dirty neuker getting all gruff again. "Everyone."

"Why?" said Jolanda. "Don't servants usually stay behind and mind the house? Who ever heard of bringing a cook to war, or a handmaid?"

"Everyone comes!" Sander bellowed, the mad bastard going crimson. "I don't *care* what's *usually* done, we ain't leaving nobody!"

"Lijsbet's not coming," said Jolanda, immune to his raging idiocy by this point in their relationship. "If you make her go, I'll stay behind."

Sander sputtered, but no actual words solidified from the froth.

"I mean it," said Jolanda, tossing the tubular arm guard back onto the bed. "She won't want to go, and I won't make her."

"None of them *want* to come," Sander growled, his jaw set. "Lansloet and Drimmelin are giving me grief aplenty without your meddling in—"

"End of story, *Sander*," Jolanda said, satisfied to see him wince at his real name. "She doesn't go."

"Fine!" Sander shouted. "Fine! But don't tell me! Don't you tell me nothing, you come to regret that! Nothing!"

Then he was clomping out of her room, kicking coins as he went, and Jolanda asked the eternal question of just what in all the names for sex was wrong with the man. She would regret not having Lijsbet with her, she knew, for any number of reasons, but she would be dead before she'd make her friend march against Countess Jacoba. Glancing at the sundry articles of clothing Sander had scattered in his eagerness to hurry her along, Jolanda's eyes settled on the blue cloak Jan had given her back before everything went to hell.

Picking it up, she ran the cloth between her fingers—the weft felt much rougher to her now than it had when she'd first received it, back when the serge was the softest garment she'd ever felt. So long ago. Jolanda sighed. It was too small to properly conceal her face and armor and all, so she would have to borrow one of Sander's cloaks for the passage. Tossing it onto the bed beside her swaths and straps of reinforced leather, she resolved to give it to Lijsbet as a parting gift—the girl had often commented on how much she liked it, plain though it was. Something to remember me by, Jolanda thought, and then put such sentimental thoughts aside to properly fashion herself for war.

II.

By the time Sander had herded everyone out of the house, he was ready to burn the place down and be done with it once and for all. For a moment he'd thought Drimmelin meant to murder him with her cleaver rather than quit her kitchen, and who knew, if he hadn't been wearing armor, she may well have made a go of it, the cow. Whereas the cook had been wrathful as a riled angel, Lansloet had seemed on the verge of utter despair when Sander told him to pack his shit and meet them out in the street. There had been flustered protests, but no begging, thank the saint of girls and bitches. When the two older servants realized Lizzy would be staying behind to keep house, there would no doubt be a fresh wave of tears to crest or be drowned under, but for now it was steady, steady as guiltless prayer. At long last Jo and Lizzy came out on the stoop where Sander was waiting, the latter meaning to accompany her mistress to the boat, and then Drimmelin arrived, dragging a trunk of crockery and provisions. Still no Lansloet, though.

It was possible the old ferret had gone out the courtyard and through a neighbor's window to hide, or jumped into the canal to make a swim for safer harbors. If he had done either, he might have been saved, but instead Sander found him lamely hiding behind a crate in the attic. Given the option of walking out on his two stork's legs or jumping from the garret window, Lansloet took the stairs, head held high, and then, at last, they were dealt with. The events of the day had kept Sander busy enough to avoid thinking about the bottomless pit of excrement he was rapidly sinking into, but as he locked the front door and slyly slipped the key to Lizzy, everything began floating to the surface again, like a lump in the throat.

No matter, no matter, he told himself as he led the motley procession down the street, the afternoon sun sparkling on the ice-paned windows of the houses flanking them, the slick cobbles gold as groots. No matter. He was getting them out of Dordt, and *now*, goddamn it. They crossed the channel at Wijnbrug and there lay the old harbor, the green waters as calm as his heart should be, if only the stupid chunk of meat should listen to him.

Simon and his mussel-mouthed brother, Braem, sat in the dinghy pulled up to the stairs at the start of the quay. Theirs was the only vessel taking to the meer this late in the day, the Gruyere brothers looking sullen as plague-stricken paupers. Simon in particular appeared the color of the water, but nowhere near so bad as he had earlier in the day, before everything had gone straight to the devil's doorstep. Amazing, what the twin forces of wine and wisdom could effect—he'd been in a bad way when he'd shown up, no doubt about it.

"There's another," Simon had gasped in the foyer that morning, with Lansloet barely cleared off down the hall. At the time Sander hadn't had the slightest suspicion that before the day was out he'd be skipping town with his whole family in tow, but that was the thing about mornings—bloody things had a way of getting out from under a fellow. "God's blood, Jan, I found another child!"

"Shut it!" Sander had shoved him against the front door, and then waited. The house was silent. Because of course it was not like Jo or one of the servants was going to leap out and start accusing him of anything, but still: "Outside, cunt, outside. We'll take some air, we'll take some beer, and you'll tell me everything."

"Another one, Jan, another one!" Simon's voice kept leaping up and down, like a lapdog bouncing for treats. "Out at the warehouse. In the mud. Right by our dock!"

"If you don't lower it, you'll be lowered yourself," Sander cautioned, though the street was empty before them, and, yeah, behind them as well. It was a bit warmer that day, and positively blazing for January, which made the whole city stink like fresh shit and old fish. Goddamn Dordt. Sander directed Simon over the bridge, down Groenstraat, and up an alley; adding some time to their trip to the White Horse ought to give the loudmouthed cunt a chance to calm down. "Start at the bottom, I mean, and we'll see how high we get before I have to tell you to shut it."

"Went out to relieve myself this morn," said Simon, wringing his hands and shaking his head and nearly walking into the canted wall of the alley. "There was some drift caught in the mud and ice at the foot of the dock. It was too dirty to tell what it was, maybe a log, I thought, or some bundled-up garbage that went overboard. So I passed my water over it, as you do, as you do, just for a lark, and oh my dear Savior, Jan, as the mud burned away from my stream, I saw, I saw!"

"A dead kid?" Sander supplied, wishing that for once he wasn't so damnable wise, that he was wrong and Simon was distraught over something, *anything*, other than—

"I *pissed* upon it," said Simon, and released a deep, lung-rattling moan. Sander cuffed him. "A child, saints forgive me, I spilled the wine of my belly upon a child! Another headless, butchered child!"

"That wine of your belly's going to be a red when I'm done with you, Simon, you don't shut it. *Now*." Sander's mind turned over along with his guts. Another child. Another murdered child laid at his doorstep. What did this bode? Had Simon already gone to the militia, or—

"I didn't know what to do, I didn't, so I just, just, pushed it down with an oar, under the ice, and—"

"You *what*?!" They were halfway down the alley, and Sander was disturbed to notice the walls on either side were pockmarked with windows. From down here he couldn't tell if any were open. He pushed Simon against a wall and ground his weight into him, trying not to enjoy it too much and to stay focused on the task at hand. "Why in all the fuckwords in French did you do that?!"

"It was only sticking out a little," Simon said, as if that made everything better. "I was able to get it all under. You know how it is out there, the top of the mud is all wed with the ice now, thick as plates, except the slip in the marsh where we bring up the boats; I've kept that well loose all winter. That's where the child was, in the mud on the edge of the slip, so I could just give it a push down, out of sight under the top of the ice, and—"

"*Why*," Sander groaned. "Stupid, stupid, cunt, I asked why."

"You told me to," said Simon, but perhaps seeing from Sander's expression that this was not an acceptable answer in the least, added, "you said I shouldn't tell anyone until the ice melts, when—"

"That was the other one, Simon, the *other* one, the one that wasn't at *my* fucking *warehouse*," Sander hissed into the man's ear, feeling the same bizarre satisfaction at this exchange that he had upon trouncing Gilles back in front of the White Horse. "That one made sense to forget about, but this, this one, you . . ."

Sander trailed off, a thought coming to him. A sight arrived at the same time, though, from the corner of his eye—a hooded figure watching them from back the way they'd come. This took precedence over his musings, to say the fucking least, until he realized the man was just pissing against the alley wall, and then disappeared back onto Groenstraat. Simon was blathering on about how he didn't know why this situation was different, and yeah, that reminded Sander of what he'd realized before being distracted by the pisser. Simple goddamn Simon.

"It's not another body, *idiot*," Sander said with a sneer, turning back to the blathering Gruyere. "It's the same one. Somewhere between now and when we found it, the tide shook it loose from Trash Island and washed it over there, is all."

"No," Simon said with the certainty all fools possess for the wisdom of their folly, "it's not, it can't be, it—"

"It's another dead kid missing its head in the meer? Think, you clot, think, what makes more sense—two kids getting done the same way and dumped near our warehouse, or one getting tide-kicked less than fifty paces from where it started? I swear, Simon, you had me worried for a—"

"A boy," said Simon, his eyes suddenly fierce as they'd been on the steps of the Leyden church that Easter so long ago, before Sander had taught him who was the harder man. "This was a boy, Jan, the other was a girl. Or don't you remember? Too busy drinking nice wine and having nice parties to remember exactly what we found? I remember, Graaf, I do, because I sleep out there every night His Worship doesn't invite me in, like an abbot giving a bunk to a beggar, every night I'm out there and she's out there haunting me, all because you wouldn't let me tell the militia, you wouldn't, and now there's another. So now what? Now what do I *do*, Graaf? What?"

Sander hadn't the slightest idea, so he asked, sure, stupidly, but it had to be asked, "You're sure it's a boy? Even without a head?"

"Pretty sure I can tell the difference," said Simon, tapping his plain lead codpiece. "I pushed him under, but couldn't get him deep. You can still see the bump under the ice and mud, Jan, they could still see!"

They. Like a quarrel hitting its target, the old fear speared Sander through the heart. They might see, mightn't they? He didn't even realize he had seized Simon by the throat and was throttling him until the lad landed a lucky knee to Sander's codpouch, reminding him of the corporal world. How had things got this mixed up, Simon having proper gear to gird his junk but Sander wearing naught but thin leather over his tenders?

"—wrong with you?" Simon gasped as Sander released him and stepped back, wringing his own hands now. *That* was even worse than a dead kid or two popping up in the mud, losing himself like that. "Why?"

"Lost my temper," Sander decided. "Sorry, Simon, but Christ, why are you so thick? Why did you have to go and..."

"And what?" Simon said, rubbing his neck, making a big

show out of how hurt he was, the whinger. "You still haven't told me what I did wrong, or what I should've done different! You haven't told me anything, you've just, just…"

Simon looked like he might be about to cry. The goddamn child. And here Sander had been anticipating seeing him again, now that the gift he had spent all winter working on for Simon was finally finished. A few weeks after Christmas, sure, but good things took time. "Look, Simon, I need to think on this."

"First time you've done that, I wager," said Simon, and perhaps Sander inflated at this or something, because the smaller man immediately changed his tune. "I mean, sorry, yes, of course you do. I'll just go to the Horse, I was supposed to meet Braem there at noon anyway, and—"

"Come on home with me, Simon," said Sander, realizing just what a liability this stupid noble was—broke, desperate, and knowledgeable of a rather foolish decision Sander had made last autumn. If only he'd let Simon report the first body to the militia right when he'd found it, all this would be…well, all this would still be substantially fucked by the arrival of a second corpse, but it might not be as bad as it was now.

Or maybe this was better? Point was, keeping Simon close by was crucial until Sander could be sure what to do next, and keeping him away from his scheming brother was even more important. Fortunately, Sander knew just how to assuage Simon's fears, which were manifesting themselves at present in a torrent of verbal diarrhea about how he had to go to the tavern.

"Come on, Coz," said Sander, slinging an arm over Simon's shoulder and leading him back down the alley. "I still need to give you your Christmas present, it wasn't done last time I saw you."

"A present?" asked Simon, perking up. "What is it?"

"A cloak," Sander said, when they were back in the parlor and the gift was given. Normally he wouldn't have stated the obvious, but by the way Simon was running his fingers through the short fur and staring wide-eyed at the garment in his hands Sander thought he might be confused. "Had it made special and all. Something to keep you warm out at the warehouse."

"For . . . me?" Simon at last looked up from the mottled cloak, and Sander saw there were tears in his pretty brown eyes. Yessssss. Sander hadn't been sure if the spoiled little fop would appreciate the present, but apparently falling from his lordly status as brother to the interim graaf had humbled Simon more than he usually let on. "You made me this?"

"Well, I didn't," said Sander. "Had a woman make it up for you. Was harder than you'd think, finding someone on the island to do the job properly."

Simon swung it over his shoulders, trying it on. It was a little short, but available materials were what they were, and it looked good on the man, the dark patches of fur contrasting his light curls and mustache. He couldn't stop touching the thing, and swung it back off, holding it up to admire the play of firelight on the varying hues—it was almost piebald, as unique a cloak as any in Holland. Simon held it up and buried his face in it, rubbing the soft garment against his face.

"The whole thing," Simon breathed. "The whole thing's fur. I *cannot* believe it. The whole. Damn. Thing. This must have cost a fortune!"

"More than I expected," Sander admitted, which was uncouth, yeah, but if Simon was going to comment on the price, Sander wasn't going to play it down. That old bitch had charged him an arm and a leg for it, and even still balked at the task until he agreed to keep it a secret that she had sewn it, should anyone ask.

"What is it?" Simon asked, rubbing his cheek on it again. "It's so sheer. Otter?"

"Better." Sander had outdone himself. Here it came, the big revelation, the only thing that could make the gift better, more personal, more perfect. If he didn't get a dick-sucking out of this gift, Simon just wasn't a dicksucker, plain and simple. Which was all right, sure, Sander hadn't commissioned the piece in hope of sex, he'd done it because Simon was a friend, a real friend, and that's what friends did for one another. "It's rat."

"*What?*" Simon's face raced through a series of ugly contortions as he began crushing the garment between his lanky fingers. "You...what?"

"Rat," said Sander, his sails drooping a bit at this lack of good wind from Simon. "Our rats, Simon, all the ones we've pegged at the island. I saved 'em, skinned 'em, and had that made up. That's why it's not bigger, 'cause we stopped shooting out there after...Anyway, yeah, token of our friendship."

"You said you were taking them home for Jo's cat," said Simon. He looked on the verge of tears again, though not so comely a cry as he usually issued. This one looked...petty.

"You ever see a cat around here, dummy?" said Sander, feeling a heat spread through his chest. Simon did not like his present. "She had one years ago, sure, but left it with Primm when—"

Shit, fuck, whore's piss, what was Sander doing, spilling the beans like that? Simon had no idea they'd been to Dordrecht nearly a year prior to arriving there as graaf and daughter; the whole point, in fact, was that they were long-lost Tieselen relations who had never set toe in the city prior to meeting Simon at the church in Leyden. No matter, though, Simon was still biting his lip and staring at the cloak, not hanging onto Sander's every misstep. An easy fix, good lies being short and half-honest: "...When we first came to Dordt, she gave the cat to Primm, and we ain't kept one since."

"Rat fur," said Simon weakly, and lowering his face, he gave the cloak an exaggerated sniff. A moment of reckoning for Simon Gruyere. It was on him, now, what came next. Sander felt a well of warm, dark emotion yawn before him, felt himself rocking back and forth on the lip of the drop, wondered if Simon would push him over or pull him back.

Simon winced and bucked his head away, as if the cloak were

woven from wet hound hair, freshly dyed in dog shit. Of all the ungrateful vermin farted forth from Satan's asshole . . . the cloak didn't smell like anything, Sander knew, for he'd put it to his own nose time and again, just to be sure. It was a beautiful cape, a one of a kind labor of love, and this little cunt dared to act like he was above it?

"Never mind, then!" Sander ripped the cloak from Simon's fingers. "I'll keep it for myself, you don't want it!"

"I—" Simon gulped, clearly too out of sorts from the wine they'd just toasted with to even muster an obvious lie that might placate his master. "No. It's just . . . rat?"

"Our rats, Simon, our bloody rats!" Sander suddenly, stupidly, felt a knot of misery constrict his throat, the way Jan had once—hold up, was he, Sander, *crying*? What in all the angels' . . . the angels' . . . *fuck*.

"Jan, I'm sorry, I just wasn't . . ." Simon took a step toward Sander, extended a quavering hand. "Today, you know, I haven't been myself, I was so shaken up, I—"

"Just leave," Sander managed. Getting the words through his grief-clogged gullet hurt, but not as badly as the abject pity he saw on Simon's face. *Pity*, for Sander, the presumptuous ponce. "Go to the Horse, then. Go to your brother. Cut from the same bolt, you two—think you're better than us."

"No, Jan, that's not—"

A loud knock from the front door bounced into the parlor, arresting Simon's protests and aborting Sander's half-birthed sob. They both stayed still as the statues in the Saint Nicolaas Church, listening to creaking footsteps make their way from the kitchen down to the foyer. This was just perfect, another visitor, and after the squeak of Lansloet opening the door, Sander caught the unmistakable lilt of Count Hobbe Wurfbain. Of all the slippery cunts in the devil's whorehouse . . .

"Go down the White Horse, then," Sander hissed, the shell-in-the-bare-foot pain of his friend's cruelty swept away by a wave of alarm as he remembered why Simon had shown up in the first place—another dead kid in the meer. "Don't tell your brother nothing. Not yet. I'll be by later. Don't go no place else."

"Right, yes," Simon nodded, equally eager to be gone—there was very little love lost between him and the count, what with Hobbe's engineering the downfall of the Gruyere brothers. "If I just had some groots to keep Braem too drunk to ask any questions..."

"What questions—no, shut it, here," said Sander, fumbling with the purse at his belt. A rather brilliant notion had struck him, something entirely, wonderfully clever—they would get Braem Gruyere very drunk, then have Simon take him out to the warehouse to spend the night, as he sometimes did. Such slumber parties were in direct violation of Sander's orders that Braem not set a single foot on the warehouse dock, the rude whoreson, but he wasn't so thick a graaf as to think Simon obeyed him in every respect—and besides, he'd once surprised Simon for an early morning's ratting and found Braem asleep on a pile of Tieselen crate hay, so it went beyond suspicion into confirmed truth. That made it easy: get Braem drunk, get him to go out to the warehouse with Simon, and have those chumps "discover" the dead kid— Braem wouldn't have to fake his surprise at the find, Simon would have a corroborating witness, and they wouldn't be lying to the militia when they told them they'd found the body that very day. To top it all, there wouldn't be any worry, just yet, about having two dead kids found near Sander's warehouse, since the girl at Trash Island was still under ice and mud, and when she turned up that spring, she'd be farther from his place, not closer to it.

Of course, even with a second witness to the grisly discovery there was the chance the militia would try to pin the crime on those who reported it, as was always the way with corrupt fuckers. That was a substantial portion of the reason Sander hadn't wanted to cop to having found a body himself, after all, not wanting to have to look an experienced lie-sniffer in the eye and claim he'd never dumped a body in no watery grave outside of Dordt... but this way if anyone was snuffled on by militia swine, it would be the Gruyeres...

But what if the brothers rolled on him, what if pressure came down and Simon turned to what the cloak was made from? Shit, this plan was awful, what was he—

"—Thinking?" Who? Hobbe, standing there in the door to the foyer, Lansloet having let the count in without announcement, the traitorous eel. Why was Simon still fidgeting in front of Sander, pretending not to have noticed his old nemesis? Ah, money, yeah—Sander's hand was still buried in his pouch, and he pulled out a groot, offering it in what he hoped was a casual fashion to Simon, who took it in a manner that was anything but.

What was the last thing Sander had said to Simon? Had he told him the plan, ordered him to take Braem out to the warehouse, or had he just been thinking that? He'd been so lost in thought he couldn't remember, and now he couldn't very well say anything, not with Hobbe here.

And speaking of, the count said, "I say, are you all right, Graaf? You didn't respond to your man's announcement, nor my query regarding your faraway expression, and now you ignore me to pass coin to a peasant. Have I caused offense by arriving earlier than my footman gave notice to expect, to be treated so shabbily?"

Simon bristled at the peasant crack, but was far too puss to do anything about it. Quick, Sander, quick, before Simon ran off with his coin: "Now, remember, Simon, I shall join you shortly, and until I do, you will keep absolutely silent about everything we spoke of. *Everything.* I need to think, and so act as though I hadn't said nothing up until now, other than to keep quiet."

Hobbe seemed intrigued by this, Simon simply looked baffled. Sander threw up his hands like Primm would've—all this wheedling and plotting and scheming was utter bullshit. Life had been a lot easier when he could just order scrawny cunts like these two around and bottle anyone who lipped off, rather than having to kiss their mutton-buttons.

And on that very subject… Sander bowed to the bitchy noble, and said, "Apologies, Count, many apologies. I was discussing a…belated Christmas present with my man here. A matter of absolute secrecy, yeah?"

"That cloak? Handsome," said Hobbe, eyeing the fur hanging limply from Sander's hand before returning his bow. Striding over to the fire, he peeled off his gloves and waved one at Simon as he said, "Good day to you, Freeman Gruyere."

"Good day to *you*, Graaf," Simon said, bowing to Sander but not to Hobbe. That was why Sander liked the cheeky little cur, that sort of bad attitude. It was sexy, when it wasn't obnoxious.

Hobbe planted himself in Sander's lounger and put his feet up on the stool. With the count out of eyeshot, Simon made a motion with his fluttering fingers that was either an obscene gesture or confirmation that he'd understood Sander's message not to blab to Braem. Hopefully the latter. Then the Gruyere stalked out of the room, and Sander pulled up one of the remaining, substantially less comfortable chairs to see what the deuce Hobbe wanted.

III.

"Jan, Jan, Jan," said Hobbe after he'd sniffed and found wanting the half-drained glass of wine Sander had left on the tiled table set between the chairs in the parlor. The count must be headed somewhere nicer than Sander's after this, to go by the ermine trim and purple-threaded codpouch highlighting Hobbe's black silk ensemble. "What have I told you about fraternizing with the Gruyeres? They're stray poodles, and if you think they'll forget who reduced them to such just because you buy them the odd supper, then you're even sillier than I thought."

"Braem's a plaguebitch, you won't hear other from me," said Sander, relieved to be talking about a subject he felt confident to speak on. "But Simon's all right. No hard feelings there."

"No hard feelings? You cost him his fortune, man! You've taken his very title, reducing him from wealthy merchant and powerful city councilman to another bleary-eyed beggar getting by on the scraps of his betters—and you don't think he cultivates the *teensiest* resentment?"

"See, you're wrong on him being a beggar, too," said Sander defensively. It was one thing for a paragon of virtue like Sander to talk down to Simon, but quite another to have this bossy peacock running his gob about a good man. "Got him working at the warehouse for some time now."

"You *what*?" Hobbe seemed genuinely appalled, as though Sander had casually mentioned that he kept live eels in his bowels. "You two were quiet about that when last you let him dine here, with Laurent and myself!"

"Well, he needed a place to stay after that hertog…what's that big asshole's name…Von Wasser, yeah, after Hertog Von Wasser kicked Simon out, he didn't have no place to go, so I said he could stay in the loft out at the warehouse so long as he pitches in with the loading and all."

Hobbe's stiff expression softened, and he laughed long and hard. "Well, I suppose it's kinder to his pride than hiring him on as rat-catcher."

"Yeah, well." Sander squirmed in his chair, trying like Christ tried to save the wretched not to let his emotion get the better of him. Not so long before, he had been ready to sort Simon with his own two fists, but that was in the past, and there was only so much piss a man could be expected to swallow from a conniving, condescending winesack like Hobbe before they drowned or spit it out, damn the consequences. Sander relaxed himself by imagining Hobbe's stupid face bawling under an avalanche of fists. "Sure, Count, sure."

"In any event, this will be my last visit to the city until after Jacoba and her army have landed and the day's won—I anticipate there being no small emotion directed at any convenient Hooks once the war begins, and it will take some time for her forces to make it all the way out here. Hard to storm an island, even with our preparations, something she knows well from experience." Hobbe reached to the table and picked up a small, ivory-lined bell set beside the two glasses and wine jug. "I'll just have Lansloet bring us a better vintage while we chat."

"Yeah, fine," said Sander, his mind snagged on what Hobbe had said. Leaving town was not, come to it, a bad idea at all, what with a dead kid or two about to be discovered right next to his warehouse. If the Gruyere boys dug out the bodies and reported them while Sander was abroad, that would certainly prevent his being interrogated by the militia about the find—no, they'd deal with the whole mess while he was gone, and then when he came back he'd get the inevitable gossip on the affair, and maybe not even from nosy militiamen but old Eckert at the Horse, say, or Poorter Primm.

"—the coming battle at least gives the Tieselen family quite the local economic advantage, with all your competitors off to fight. Obviously Dordrecht has supplied far less men and money than they might, were they better recovered from the flood, but as it stands, any Cod who can afford it will be there in the flesh," Hobbe was saying, and Sander gave a knowing nod before realizing he might actually want to be abreast of whatever development Hobbe was on about.

"How's that, then?"

"Gloucester, Jan, Gloucester," said Hobbe, with obvious satisfaction that this further perplexed Sander. The name rang a bell, though a smaller one than that which had, at fucking last, succeeded in drawing Lansloet, whom Hobbe addressed as though the servant were one of his. Which, sure, he may well be planted by the count, or at least taking his coin in exchange for keeping eyes and ears on graaf and daughter; Sander wasn't thick, he knew the score, he—"Something a bit stronger than this brine, Lansloet, and with a good dollop more honey."

"Sir," said Lansloet, and he sounded like he meant it, talking to Hobbe. Rats, all of them.

"All right, then," said Sander, figuring he ought to return the favor of pissing Hobbe off on purpose—playing foolish always turned the trick. "Sure, Gloucester—moving into cheese ain't a bad idea, pairs decent with the wine, even if that Englander stuff gets a little rich for my bowel. You got us a good deal lined up for importation? We'll need new boats, the wine ones are only for river—"

"Humphrey, duke of Gloucester," said Hobbe, which annoyed Sander to no end—his cheese-monger fantasy had barely gotten in the water before this mussel interrupted. "Jacoba's new husband. He's landing, or landed, by now, down in Zeeland. We're on the cusp of real war, with our odds never better—a success here will signify the end of Philip and his Codpieces, and a victory for true Hollanders."

"So Jacoba and her new duke take Zeeland, they come up the Maas, and then I'll start getting invited to courts and feasts, neat as that?" said Sander. The open animosity most of his noble neighbors directed toward him couldn't be entirely the result of his personality—Jo was adamant that it arose from Sander's adherence to the cues Hobbe fed him, which, sure, ran counter to the common Cod interest. Yet between being unpopular with a bunch of rich Dordt assholes or unpopular with the one count who could expose them as frauds, well, that wasn't a hard choice at all. Or rather, it hadn't been… "Given the grief these sheepheads give this particular pillar of the community over letting the occasional wine-boat into the harbor, I don't see them spreading the city's legs for a countess they hate with passion and her Englanders, who they hate on principle."

"It wasn't so long ago that local sympathies lay with our dear Jacoba," said Hobbe. "In addition to those principled, if secret, allies we already have in Dordrecht, the wiser townsfolk will hang their cloaks according to the wind. They always do, and those who don't may well find themselves in a spot of trouble."

"Like the Gruyeres did when we came along," said Sander. A thought came to him, as thoughts were wont to fucking do ever since he'd shoved the raw feet of a madman into the soft boots of a graaf. "And if Jacoba and her duke don't win the day in Zeeland, what then? Am I in for a fresh load of moldy turnips thrown through my windows?"

"Still getting the new-noble treatment, eh?" said Hobbe. It had actually been some time since the last incident of vandalism, thank the saint of shitfree doors and shutters, whoever that was, but the thought that the dastardly hostilities might resume sat poorly with Sander. Much as he tried to ignore or correct it, the rejection he'd faced from the Dordrecht community was a constant irritant, like a bent eyelash. Hobbe was still talking some dumb shit, trying to play down the situation, but Sander finally pieced it all together and cut the crook off:

"Oi, that's why you're running off to Leyden, ain't it? Now that Jacoba's brought the fight home again, you don't want to be in Codtown if she loses." Made sense, actually, and wasn't too far from Sander's notion to skip Dordt until the inevitable dead-kids-at-your-place-of-business storm blew over—get out before the squall, and come back when it's calm.

"I'm departing Dordrecht, but Leyden's rather…*warm*, at present," said Hobbe. "Especially with Duke Philip spending entirely too much time there of late. Don't worry about me, though, I have my sanctuaries."

"So you hide out, and if the countess wins, you tell her you were just too far away to help in the fight, and if she don't, no Hook can prove you took her part."

"I swear, you are nothing like I'd been led to believe," said Hobbe. "Not just sound of pate, but smart as the nip of a horsefly!"

"That supposed to be a compliment or an insult?" said Sander. "Not a wise way of putting it, whatever the intent."

"Well, as I said, you *are* the smart one, Graaf Tieselen. Ah, there you are—thought we'd have to muster a search party!" Lansloet had returned with a bottle that looked far too dusty for Sander's liking—why didn't the servant ever bring *him* drink that well seasoned? Sander quickly helped the old bugger out by draining his half-finished glass and shaking the dregs from Simon's mug into the fire, where they hissed in a pleasing fashion. Lippy goddamn Hobbe, always treating Sander like some mutt or other such beast that was too dim to recognize when it was being openly mocked. One of these days, one of these jibes… "Yes, that's much better, capital refreshment. Now, where were we? Ah, yes, you were reiterating all my points for some uncertain purpose. Let's just move on to business, shall we? The ventures I have lined up for you while your peers are off playing war. First up, there's—"

"Where's the fight going to happen?" Sander said, illumination coming to him like the finger of God, well, fingering him. In the brain, like. He was suddenly as excited as he'd been that night in the street with Gilles. He might not feel much like himself on a day-to-day basis, but by all the heavenly Host he could force himself to surface when he put his mind to it, when he got a brilliant scheme like the one currently cooking in his skull-pot. What was the limit on pigeons you could bring down with one rock?

"Where?" said Hobbe, sipping the pricey wine he put away like it was water. "The first engagement, I suspect, will take place at a little port called Zierikzee, but after a victory there we shall—"

"*When*," said Sander, putting his glass down on the table. His hands were actually shaking, and he'd splashed some onto his white silk sleeve. "When's the fight going to be, 'tween Philip and Jacoba? I know you know, deep in it as you are."

"And I know that look upon your face or I'm a goose," said Hobbe, refilling his glass. "If the battle hasn't been joined yet, it surely will be soon—our English friends have already landed in Zeeland, bolstering the local Hook ranks to insurmountable proportions. But, *regardless*, you're not to get any further involved. If the will of God Almighty is that our fair land suffer further trials rather than immediate salvation, and our countess's force thus fails, well, as you yourself pointed out, it's one thing to be covertly funneling money to her mission and something else entirely to fight for her on the front line where everyone can see you. Willem Von Wasser and the rest of the councilmen suspecting you of Hook sympathies is manageable, but their *seeing you* in her ranks is most certainly not. I shan't allow you to ruin everything I've worked for on account of bloodlust—it's not as though your joining her army now will change the tide, formidable though your sword surely is."

"I'm not going to join her army, you boob, I'm going to join his," said Sander with a grin. His warm satisfaction at finally telling Hobbe where to stick it was only partially dampened by the count's confusion regarding being stuck.

"Whose army?"

"Our beloved Duke Philip's, of course," said Sander, the sheer joy of the moment making his arms tingle like they'd fallen asleep; like *he'd* fallen asleep. "I'm going to Zeeland, I'm kneeling in front of our Burgundian lord, and then I'm going to help him pound that Brabançon bitch of yours into a pancake, and her Englander bullyboys beside."

"No, you are *not*," said Hobbe without the faintest whiff of concern. "You're going to stay here, you're going to press that pretty gold ring of yours against the documents Laurent presents you, and that is all. If you attempt to do anything other than that—"

"You'll what?" said Sander, springing from his seat and planting his hands on the armrests of Hobbe's chair, getting good and properly in the count's face. In the cunt's face, rather. "Tell everyone I'm a fake? Have me arrested?"

"Initially, yes," said Hobbe, but was the wrinkled old pudding starting to blanch, maybe tremble a bit around the crust? "Once you've been unmasked and incarcerated, matters will worsen considerably for you."

"Can't bluff me," said Sander, breathing in the older man's face. It felt good, taking this tone with Hobbe at long last, finally letting it all out. "I've got just as much on you as you do on me—even if they did take you on your word, I'll call you out as a Hook, sneaking money to the countess every chance you get. You got my shorthairs, I'll allow, but I got yours, too—they take me down, I take you down."

"My dear Graaf," said Hobbe, and from the way those wispy storm clouds of his had come down low over his narrowed eyes, Sander could tell he'd genuinely gotten to the crooked count. "Every pfennig I have given to the countess's cause over the last two years has gone through you, courtesy of Laurent. Our mutual lawyer friend has, all told, no less than fifty incriminating documents tying you to Jacoba, but nary a one with my scent on it. I've been using you as a scapegoat, you dunce, something that should have been obvious from the very first sheaf, if only you could read."

"Makes sense," said Sander, because it did. He shrugged, but otherwise showed no reaction to the betrayal. If he hadn't been planning on pummeling Hobbe into a pulp as soon as their discussion was concluded, he might have been angered by this disclosure, but as it stood, he was relieved to hear it—for all of Hobbe's warts, Sander was somewhat fond of the man, and anything he said to further justify a beatdown put Sander that much more at ease.

"Of course it does," said Hobbe, leaning forward until their foreheads were almost touching. More of a fivehead in the count's case, with that receding hairline. "You have nothing but your word that I am anything but a loyal retainer of Duke Philip, and the word of a charlatan counts for precious little, I fear."

"Except folk here in Dordt know you're a Hook, even if they can't prove it—they've been looking for an excuse to string you up since the flood, if not before," said Sander, and rather than retreating, as Hobbe had no doubt hoped, Sander pressed in, nearly straddling the lounger and actually touching his brow to the count's. Hobbe didn't pull back, and Sander rocked his head against the count's in an attempt to further unnerve the fucker. "They'll believe I'm an impostor, sure they will, 'cause it's the truth. But they'll also believe me when I finger my accomplice, 'cause that's the truth, too—think any of your Cod friends forgot whose coach I got out of that first day, back at the Leyden church? Think they forgot who vouched for me when Laurent and his cronies were rigging it up to get rid of the Gruyeres and install Jo and me? Think they don't see you coming and going from my place oft enough they might mistake you for a resident? The truth, Hobbe, can be a right mean bitch, and all I got to do is loose her from her leash and your rich friends will do the rest."

Nothing but silence to that, and Hobbe slouched back in his chair, defeated. Nicely done, Graaf, *very* nicely done. Sander straightened up and cracked his knuckles, looking down at his defeated adversary. Maybe the count didn't need a beating, after all.

"You are making a *dreadful* mistake, Sander," said Hobbe wearily. "All I have done for you, all—ah!"

Sander had dropped into a crouch, grabbed one of the front legs of Hobbe's chair, and upended both man and seat backward. He was on top of the count before Hobbe could even decide between scrambling up or rising in a more decorous fashion. The heel of Sander's boot rested softly against Hobbe's throat, fixing the man to the floor. The steadily firming hard-on that act had stirred in Sander's pouch could plug up a well, or another such wide aperture—some things never changed. Time to lay some truth on this scheming asshole:

"My name ain't Sander, and it's you that made the mistake in calling me such. You done shit for me since day one; you've only done for yourself, and we both know it. You wanted a Hook you could push around on the island, someone with more coin and influence than that Zoete woman you run with, and if Jan had come back with the ring, it would've been him instead of me. Except he would've put you where you are a sight sooner than it took me to do it, on account of his not being half the cunt I've been down these days since you made me graaf. Well, I'm not your cunt no more, Hobbe, to slap about or finger my purse whenever you get the notion. Long as you acknowledge that, we'll be just fine, you and me. Just fine."

Hobbe might have tried to reply, but during his speech Sander had unconsciously begun pressing his foot down, and the count was apparently too dignified to writhe or seize the boot that was crushing his larynx. Instead he just lay there, silently being choked and staring up at Sander with eyes as cold and pale as snowmelt. Eerie, that was, and Sander removed his foot, but gave the old boy a light kick to the chin before setting it back on the floor beside its mate. "So what say you, Hobbe, are we sorted, or do I need to sort you a bit more?"

Hobbe took the hand Sander offered and rose to his feet, his back or knees or something cracking and popping as he did. Jesus, Sander hoped he hadn't done any permanent damage to the scoundrel, he was aged and all and—"Graaf Tieselen, I must regretfully take my leave."

"Yeah, sure," said Sander with a wink. "When the war's won and I'm settled back in here, you'll have to come and have a stay. Good Graaf Tieselen judges a man by his deeds, not if he's Hook or Cod. In the meantime, enjoy laying low in whatever burrow you've carved out and—"

"I will be staying in Dordrecht, after all," said Hobbe, his eyes flashing like a cat's from the firelight. Though the shutters were open, it had begun to snow again, rendering the parlor dim enough to make the effect good and spooky. "There is a matter of business that yet needs attending. You have, and I mean this not as a threat but as a statement of simple fact, absolutely *no* comprehension of the forces at work. Of the forces you upset with your proud, foolish resolution to bite at the teat that has nursed you. Even now I would hear an apology and a recanting of your behavior, but should you actually follow through with your boast of raising arms against our countess, well . . . your final decision is entirely out of my hands, of course, but I promise you this—you will make amends to me, and shortly, or you shall look back on this hour and regret it as you have never regretted anything in the sum of your days."

A pause, but yeah, no fucking apology for the count, and so he concluded his pretentious little speech: "In any event, I expect to see you again before very long, and, of course, your lovely daughter as well. Good day, sir."

"Now, Hobbe," said Sander, placing a hand on the count's bony shoulder and giving it a friendly squeeze. "You threaten Jo ever again, and I will pick you up, carry you to that hearth, and hold your face in the fire until you stop moving."

"I said *good day, sir*," said Hobbe, wrenching his shoulder free and trying to stride proudly to the door. Pride before a fall, and all, and Sander kicked the count behind the knee. Hobbe stumbled, but before he could regain his balance or topple forward, depending on nature's whim, Sander stepped quickly behind him and swung his arm in front of the man's face, catching Hobbe's neck in the crook of his elbow. He pressed the full weight of his body into the count's back; it made his erection falter a bit to be ground against so unappealing a posterior, but for the sake of effect Sander tried to keep it solid.

"Hobbe, Hobbe, Hobbe," Sander whispered in the count's ear. Up close the man smelled like garlic and aged Edam. "If you think I'm more concerned with keeping my station than getting my vengeance, you're even thicker than I am. You come at me, and I'll murder the world just to get at you. I'll burn this house, I'll burn Jo, I'll burn the money and boats and warehouses and dear old Simon inside it, just to put my hands on you."

Sander paused long enough for Hobbe to start to speak: "All right, you have made—"

"No, I haven't, because you still think you can talk to me like I'm some cunting coachman, like I'm old Lansloet." Sander ground his cock into Hobbe's ass even as he tightened his elbow, and to his satisfaction that got the count squirming, if only a little. "So we're of an understanding, I'll say it to you the once more—if I have to put my hands on your slimy skin again, I *will* make it worth my while. We both know what I can do, something you made clear way back in your carriage when we was first sussing out the terms of our arrangement here. So I've got a wee promise for you: You so much as give me a shitty look from now until the end of our acquaintance, *Hobbe*, and I will make it my life's work to take you apart, slow as possible, piece by piece. For days, man, days. Until the notion of dying and being cast into the pit for

Satan's eternal sport seems a comfort as warm as a kitten dozing in your lap. Now you get *the fuck* out of my house, and don't you dare knock at my door again until you've been invited. Count."

Sander relaxed his elbow but didn't drop it entirely, forcing Hobbe to duck out of the hold. The count did not look back as he hustled out through the parlor doors, and Sander smiled to see the man stumble on the stoop in his haste to be away. Yet as soon as the front door slammed shut behind the fleeing noble, the magnitude of his decision began to sink in—Hobbe was anything but stupid, and was like as not angry as a bee-stung hornet. Another reason to be out of Dordt, and as soon as possible—if Hobbe did try to expose them as phonies, he'd be wise to do it before Sander got a chance to leave town.

Hobbe would be making straight for Laurent's office, otherwise Sander would go and retrieve as much money as he could carry and simply quit the city for good, but in case Hobbe stopped by a gatehouse to fetch a militiaman or three before visiting Laurent for the inevitable pity party ... well, Sander would just have to take what he had around the house, and hope that further down the road Laurent was greedy enough to try and work both sides instead of simply backing Hobbe's play at ruining the Tieselen heirs.

As it stood, war was looming, which was a welcome distraction, and who knew, if Sander made enough of an impression with the local Cod nobles during the campaign, they might back him up upon his return to Dordt, even if Hobbe followed through with his threat. Maybe. Or maybe they would hang him and Hobbe both. Well, worry about how to get that shit off the shoe after it was stepped in. For now he had to get through the rest of the day, which, at a minimum, involved sending the Gruyere brothers out to the warehouse and getting himself in a boat directed toward whatever Zeeland isle was hosting the party. Zierikzee was the port Hobbe had mentioned, wasn't it?

But what of Jo—could he leave her in Dordt, with Hobbe furious and ready to strike?

Easy enough, he'd take her with him—after the coin he'd dropped on buying her gear and the smashed fingers he'd accumulated from her whaling on him with a practice sword, he was due a return on his investment.

But what of Lansloet and Drimmelin? He wasn't worried Hobbe would try to fuck with them, but he was definitely concerned that one or both of the servants he had inherited with the house would heed the count before they would answer to good old Graaf Jan. Leaving his home in the possession of people who might work with Hobbe to somehow betray Sander and Jo seemed exceedingly foolish.

Easy enough, take all the servants with them—surely the other campaigning nobles brought their own people to cook and clean for them, yeah? They had to. Better to leave the house shuttered and empty than in control of traitors, which he had always suspected Drimmelin and especially Lansloet of being.

So: book passage to the Rotterdam harbor, rally the entire household to immediately leave for war, send the Gruyere boys to the warehouse to discover and report the dead kids dumped in the mud, and, somewhere in there, grab a bite of dinner—in the madness of the morning he'd missed breakfast. Busy day for the graaf, but he'd had busier, and at least he had already taken care of the items "alienate your only noble friend who also knows your dirty secret" and "get your feelings hurt by your only other friend in town who doesn't appreciate a nice gift when it's in his own two hands."

Righting the upended lounger and wrapping his rat-fur cloak around his shoulders, Sander set off to find Simon Gruyere, his devious brother Braem, and, saints willing, a decent snack.

IV.

After a teary parting with Lijsbet at the Dordt harbor (the girls were cheerful and dry of eye, but Lansloet silently wept when he realized the young maid was being left to mind the house while he was forced to accompany his master), Jolanda, Sander, and the two older servants arrived in Rotterdam only to discover they'd missed the last fleet leaving for Zeeland by the better part of a week. Sander couldn't believe it, and kept saying so over and over, to no resolution. While Sander gnashed his teeth and rent his hair, Jolanda went to the harbormaster and appealed to the man's higher nature, as well as his thirst. Thinking it might help their heart-to-heart, Jolanda dredged up her old accent to pair with the Tieselen Red, and within an hour of arriving in the Rott she'd found them alternate passage to the islands.

The voyage across the meer and then down the Volkerak to the Grevelingen estuary would have been a mite cramped in the narrow, stunted sailboat even if it had just been the one-eyed captain, his son, and the four members of the Tieselen contingent. Instead, they were tacked in shoulder-to-shoulder, as the vessel was delivering a monk, a nun, and a pair of potted apple trees to the village of Ouddorp on the lonely, windswept islet of Goeree. It sounded like the setup to a bad joke, and so the voyage proved: they spent the bulk of the journey getting on one another's tits, literally as well as figuratively.

The awkwardness of the situation was amplified rather than mitigated by the merriness of the two clerical members of the crew, who, to extrapolate from their boisterous songs and less-than-surreptitious fumblings under each other's vestments after dusk, were in the process of eloping from their respective holy orders. The skeletal apple trees seemed dead, but the captain swore they would bloom again, and to Jolanda's surprise one did seem to be budding in all defiance of the season by the time they reached Duiveland. They skirted that isle's northern coast and carried over to the island of Schouwen, at which point the sea became so rough even the captain appeared olive around the gills. Arms linked to keep each other from falling overboard, Sander and Lansloet took to their knees at the edge of the boat, master and servant made equal as they prayed at the altar of Neptune. The ferocious wind carried their half-digested oblations up to paint the sail instead of letting them join the turbulent waters, leading the captain and son to curse like what they were.

As they drew near Brouwershaven, a port north of Zierikzee where the Rotter harbormaster had claimed the Hooks and Cods were engaged, the captain took advantage of a break in the gale to steer them into a small sound. There he deposited them on an ancient pier, having no intention of sailing his ship anywhere near what Sander had been asserting since Rotterdam was sure to be an epic, show-no-quarter-and-take-no-hostages battle. The tide being in their favor, it was a wobbly step rather than a desperate leap onto the pier. While Sander, Drimmelin, and Lansloet picked their way slowly down the rickety structure, Jolanda thanked the captain and his son profusely and offered the clerical couple the best of luck with their future together.

"It's easy to sail before the wind!" the nun called as the ship circled the sound and back out to sea, the reflection of the setting sun adorning the taut canvas like a great burning eye.

They marched west. Dark as it soon became on the pebbly beach, there could be no doubt they were heading toward a raging combat—the tumult could be heard from afar, and the sky above the town blazed as though someone had set fire to the curtain of night. As they reached a tent city on the strand,

Jolanda cringed to see this side of the encampment unguarded, all available men presumably engaged in the fight, and cringed again to hear the shrieks of pain emanating from the majority of the crowded canopies. Barbers emerged looking even more haggard than their wan charges, dumping out bowls of blood and hanging sodden, unrinsed rags out to dry before calling, "Next!"

As excited as she'd been on the ship and even as they approached along the beach, Jolanda began to feel her eagerness wilt at seeing man after man caked in burgundy sand, at hearing the clash of metal and bloodthirsty cries grow ever louder as they wove their way through the hospital tents. Looking around, as awed and curious as she'd been the first time she'd set foot in Rotterdam, she realized Lansloet and Drimmelin had dipped out at some point, but there was little to be done about that now. Who could blame them? They weren't warriors, like her and Sander, like all these half-murdered men screaming in the perpetual gloaming of tent-filtered lamplight…

Sander had never given her his helm—he'd forgotten it in Dordt, the dunce—but her hood seemed to offer her anonymity enough, for none gave her a second glance. Seeing one footless soldier writhe in the sand while two men tried to hold him still and a third pressed a red-hot iron pan to the ruined stump of his ankle, black fumes that stunk of burning hair belching from around the cauterizing instrument as the living meat sizzled, she supposed they had greater concerns. And so should she, Jolanda decided, telling herself to buckle down, to get mean…it was time to fight as she never had before, it was time to get crazy, it was time to abandon mercy, to kill and kill and—

—Feast?

Aye, that's what it was. They'd come to a break in the tents, but rather than a field of battle Jolanda saw the din was coming from dozens upon dozens of long tables arrayed along the strand. One of them was far enough out that the tide was lapping at the greaves of the men who refused to leave it, their bare white hands

tearing into cakes and breads a sharp contrast to the steel cara-
paces covering the rest of them. Pages hurried between the
makeshift kitchens erected beside bonfires and the tables, delivering great racks of pork or lamb or maybe both, whole salt-
roasted fishes, carafes of wine, and jugs of ale. Metal struck on
metal as knife met plate, tankard met tankard.

Sander stood beside Jolanda, the two of them in the border of
blackness separating the lamplight of the hospital tents from the
bonfire glow illuminating the bizarre fete. Jolanda thought
Sander looked as though he was going to be as sick as he'd been
on the ship, but instead he belched out a, "*What?*"

"Come on," said Jolanda, taking his hand. This was somehow
more intimidating than a battlefield would have been. She pulled
him forward, toward a cluster of red-and-white Dordrecht ban-
ners planted beside a table. "Let's find out what happened."

They didn't get ten paces into the firelight before the cry went
up: "Tieselen!"

"Jan Tieselen!"

"The Dordt Hook himself!"

"Graaf Tieselen!"

Jolanda and Sander froze as a good dozen of the yelling men
rose from their nearby table and turned to stare at them. The
biggest of them all, a burly, bearded giant, stumbled off his
bench and advanced on them, his spattered armor glowing in
the firelight, his eyes black as wounds. In one hand he held a jug
and in the other an entire leg of lamb, its bloody end dripping in
the sand. Jolanda recognized him at once, but before she could
give Sander a whispered reminder of the giant's identity, he'd
stepped forward and called, "What's all this, Von Wasser?"
Jolanda nearly cheered the minor miracle of Sander's remembering the hertog's name—they saw him at church every Sunday, but to the best of her knowledge in nearly two years they'd
never exchanged more than a dirty look. "What's happened?"

"I'd put the same to you, but I know a spy when I see one,"

said Hertog Willem Von Wasser, raising his voice to a triumphant bellow as he went on. "You tell your Leyden master his vixen got hounded this day, and with vigooooor!" He gyrated and thrust his hips in a lewd manner while delivering this last.

"I see that," said Sander, and Jolanda could scarcely believe how calm he was. If anything, he seemed dour rather than irate.

Jolanda heard feet kicking through the sand behind them and wondered if these drunk Cods were surrounding them, looking to be done once and for all with meddlesome Tieselens. When she spun around, however, she saw Lansloet and Drimmelin slinking over from the tents—apparently they, too, had realized no battle raged this night and were drawn to the smells of cooking food and warming campfires.

"He sees it!" Von Wasser howled, earning cheers from the scarlet-and-white-mantled group he had quit, but most of the other tables had gone back to their merrymaking and were ignoring the besotted giant. "At last, the Hook sees his ambition crushed, his traitorous—oof!"

Sander neatly seized the man by the beard and head-butted him in the face. Von Wasser stumbled back, dropping his jug and his lamb joint to put both hands to his face, and Jolanda felt the beach drop away beneath her, plunging her through a void of what-the-fuck: had Sander just killed them both? Great God in all his mercy, had Sander insisted they come to war as some sort of convoluted suicide plot? Had the madman panicked at realizing Wurfbain would come after him, and decided to end it all in one final glorious battle against whatever foe he could sufficiently antagonize into slaying him?

Before Jolanda could decide between drawing her sword and accompanying him to hell or fleeing back through the tents, every man at the table Von Wasser had left now rose as one and scrambled off their benches, advancing on the Tieselens. Sander dropped to a crouch just as the stunned, wobbling Von Wasser fell back, landing on his arse, but before the mob could charge,

Sander had straightened back up, having retrieved the hertog's leg of lamb. He directed it at Von Wasser's friends, most of whom Jolanda recognized from church as minor Dordt Cods, now that they were drawing closer between two bonfires. All of the other nearby tables had quieted at this display, and Sander issued what Jolanda was sure would be his final shit-talking:

"Alla you listen! With both ears!" Sander's voice boomed louder than the waves, crackled with the heat of the bonfires, and he waved the shank over the entire assembly as he pronounced his judgment. "My name's Jan Tieselen, and I'm graaf of Oudeland! I'm also the man bringing wine up to Dordrecht! Yeah, you heard—I'm out of Dordt, same as Von Wasser, same as all these mussels coming down on me!"

That got a few cheers from the observing tables, though Jolanda had no idea why. Sander waved the leg behind him, at her and the pair of cowering servants who hung back halfway between Jolanda and the tents, like spotted hares debating flight. He went on:

"I brought my daughter, Jolanda! And two servants! What spy brings his cook, pray?! We came to fight, damn your eyes, we came to fight! For Philip! For Holland! For Dordt!"

"He's a Hook!" one of the lesser local Cods protested, and a grumbling arose from the mass of men as though they were a pack of half-dozing hounds Sander was tiptoeing through the midst of. The mouthy one who'd started the muttering must be a younger son, if noble at all, for Jolanda didn't recognize him, but even the smallest adder could have killing spit. Before the complaints could rise to shouts or the Cods could resolve to charge, Sander began again, apparently shifting tactics:

"I come up in the East! But got to Dordt fast as I could! All you sheepheads knew my uncle...the graaf, the old Graaf Tieselen! Some of you must've been his friends! Just like some of you must've had your quarrels with him! Point is, you wouldn't have taken him for no cunt! You wouldn't have done him the way you done me!"

This earned Sander hisses, which was much more in line with what Jolanda had expected when Sander began his foolhardy speech. He flicked her a grin and then strode forward, to where Von Wasser still sat sprawled in the sand. A half dozen of the Dordt Cods began matching Sander step for step, closing the distance. Sander stopped before Von Wasser, staring down at him, and the hertog looked up, his face dark with blood or shadow, Jolanda couldn't tell which. Sander addressed him, but still his pronouncement carried back to her, and any who cared to heed it, she supposed:

"I come to Dordt! Wanted to live up to my family name! But Wurfbain got his teeth into me! That fucking fox! And being from stranger lands than these, I took him at his word! And not *one* of you mussels set me straight! Not one! You *knew* he weren't good for me! You *knew* he made me no good for Dordt! But you all just let me listen to him! Let me heed the council of a Leyden Hook! 'Cause no one had the grit to tell me I was a fool to listen to 'em! No one had the grit to tell me I was acting against my city! My people! My very *family*!"

Despite the popping of a dozen bonfires, the choir of agony behind them, and the crashing surf, it went very quiet as Sander surveyed the interrupted banquet, the line of men before him, and the sand-sprawled Von Wasser. Jolanda saw that other than the fallen hertog, nobody in sight was still seated, hundreds upon hundreds of men fanning inland to get a better look, standing on benches, tables, each other. Glancing over her shoulder, she saw that every break in the barbers' tents was clogged with faces— they were utterly surrounded, cut off from escape, save for the sea. There was a thought... she shuddered, and knew she would die on the sand before she'd brave those winter waters.

"But no more!" cried Sander, extending the sandy lamb joint to Von Wasser. The hertog took it, and Sander pulled him to his feet. They stood facing each other, close enough to bite each other's throats, and Sander went on, barking in the man's face. "I figured it out! I quit Wurfbain! He's wroth! Wroth as God! But I quit him! He threatened to ruin me! To ruin my family! Threatened I don't even know! And! I! Told! Him! To! Stuff it!"

Another nigh-sinister silence, and Jolanda knew they were good and truly fucked now—Sander hadn't been so mad after all, there at the end, he had tried to explain, but it was too little, too late. It would take more than loudly crashing a feast to convince every Cod in Holland that the Tieselens had changed their Hookish scales, and now—

—Von Wasser went for Sander, and Jolanda set her foot to charge, hand on her sword, and—

—Von Wasser threw his arms around Sander, and a great cheer went up through the crowd. They had bought it? They had really, truly bought Sander's mad story?

Aye, apparently they had, as the Cods of Dordrecht fell over one another to be the next to formerly introduce himself to the neighbor they had studiously ignored in public and certainly mocked in private. Much ado was made over Jolanda and her patchwork armor, and the confirmation that Graaf Tieselen had indeed brought two servants rather than squires or mercenaries made the nobles roar with laughter. This sat poorly with Sander, but there was no pleasing the dotty fool.

"Lady Jolanda," said a shapely silhouette standing between Jolanda and one of the bonfires, the voice frustratingly familiar. "How wonderful that you and your father have...come around. May I invite you to join my table?"

Squinting at the black figure, Jolanda had no better idea of who the woman might be. Anything beat hanging behind Sander, though, as Von Wasser and the rest clobbered his back and rode him for being such a no-good-stinking-Hook for so long—either Sander would pick up on their condescending jokes at his expense and fly into a rage, or he would take what they said as sincere compliments and become even more of a conceited doofus than usual. And so Jolanda curtsied to the mysterious woman, saying, "It would be my absolute pleasure, m'lady."

"Excellent," said the woman, and as she turned back to the feast, Jolanda saw her face in profile and gasped—it was Lady Meyl, the widowed mother of Willem Von Wasser and the richest woman in Dordrecht, if not all of Holland. Jolanda had only met her the once, at the Hooglandse Church in Leyden; every time she had glimpsed her in the Dordrecht markets and church she had prayed the noblewoman would say hello, maybe even invite her to her manse, but not once had the imperious old biddy acknowledged Jolanda's existence. Indeed, Lady Meyl was as skilled at avoiding your eyes with her own as Sander was at hitting your nerves, yet now Jolanda was following her to a royal table at an epic feast held beneath the winter stars on a wind-swept strand, the dowager's pale, pearl-laced gown trailing in the sand behind her like something from a dream...

Jolanda's initial disappointment that Lady Meyl simply planted her ample bottom on a bench rather than first introducing Jolanda to their tablemates was somewhat assuaged when she saw that there were no other ladies present, only a handful of noblemen clustered at one end of the bench. These braying fops were clearly as drunk as a brewer's fart. The seat was rough and frigid under Jolanda's arse, even through her reinforced leggings, and the nearly raw meat cooled within moments of being laid on the frosty plates. Ice crusts of wine spotted the board, with globs of frozen fat and cold-brittled bones strewn across table and bench alike. Jolanda's first feast was shaping up to be a lot like one of Sander and Simon's nights in, only outside on a beach in January.

"Well, well, *well*," said Lady Meyl, pulling a fur blanket off of a snoring figure on the bench beside her and swaddling herself in the bristly thing until only her sharp face poked out. She resembled an enormous hedgehog. "This is a pleasant surprise, having you and your father join us. It's ever so nice to see you again, Jolanda."

"Indeed, it has been too long," said Jolanda, taking a bite of the lamb a servant had brought her. Ravenous as she was, the bloody, gamy meat made her feel like a wolf. "I trust in God that all is well with you, my lady, both here and at home?"

"It is pure shit, is what it is," said Lady Meyl. She sounded tired, which, aye, made sense, late as the hour must be. "Between your father and that Van Hauer bitch, Zoete, Count Wurfbain has brought any substantial civic development to a standstill in Dordrecht. Now, now, don't protest, I heard the graaf's poetic speech and I'm *sure* that all is forgiven, but you asked if all was well with myself, both at home and here, and I am answering you in an honest fashion."

"I do appreciate your honesty, my lady," said Jolanda, breaking the plug of ice on a jug of wine and filling a goblet all the way to the top. Anything to get the taste of sheep blood from her mouth. "And it's true I cannot claim to understand all that goes on with my father's business and the politics of Dordrecht. But I am confident that from this day forth we will all enjoy a strong shift from whatever stagnation Wurfbain's plotting has inflicted upon our city."

"I'm *sure* you understand more than you let on, young lady," Meyl grinned, showing that she had very few teeth left in her dull gums. That explained the bowlful of meat slurry she kept stirring up, to keep from freezing, and the whistling sound that accompanied every one of her matronly exhalations. "Clever as you are, I wonder you let that Hobbe push your father around as long as he did."

"He doesn't listen to me," Jolanda said in her defense, to which Meyl responded with a burp. Recognizing this audience as an opportunity as exceptional as it was unexpected, Jolanda went for it before she lost her nerve: "Begging all your pardons if I am out of turn, my lady, but I know I may speak for my father when I say that we are in need of the counsel of a wiser, more experienced nobleperson now more than ever. We are not from Dordrecht, after all. Having fallen under the sway of Count Wurfbain, the dastardly Hook, we have little idea of what might truly do the most good for our adoptive city, and of course her citizens. If there was a learned Cod we could turn to for guidance, we—"

"Fie on Cods and Hooks alike," said Meyl with more passion than she had heretofore displayed. "If you *must* listen to a word I say, pray do it for the sense it makes rather than the party I supposedly belong to."

"You're not a Cod?" said Jolanda, confused and, truth be told, a little relieved.

"I'm a woman of Dordrecht," said Lady Meyl. "Whatever that means. As for Hooks and Cods and what have you, it's a plain fact that a divided city is a chaotic one, and having Wurfbain sticking his nose into our business is no good for anyone. As it happens, I counted Jacoba as a dear friend and one of the wisest young women I ever met. That was before all that bad business with her uncle, and now *this*. The only reason I came along with my son was that I hoped to have a chat with her, if she were captured, but she's slipped away again, and so it's a sore ass and numb fingers for no reason at all. *None*."

"When's the next battle?" asked Jolanda. "I mean, is it known, or do they figure that out later, or what? I gather we, er, the Cods won this one."

"There won't be, I don't expect," said Meyl, and yawned. "They trounced her good, this time—she'll recover her spirits, of course, she always does, but I can't imagine her new husband will be very pleased, having all his thousands of men hacked to pieces and shot full of bolts on the strand there. Sir Boomsma, that's one of Willem's friends, finally got to fire his precious cannon at the English, an occasion we'll never be hearing the end of. And so the war is over, my dear, but I still envy you your armor— it has to be warmer than my satin, mink pelisse be *damned*."

"Oh," said Jolanda, trying not to be too disappointed. "Jan— that is, my father—said the war would go through the spring and maybe the summer."

"Your father is an idiot," said Lady Meyl, though not unkindly. "Just like my son, there. I think they've taken to each other well enough—that's the rub, child, we should all be such marvelous friends, Hook and Cod, man and woman, rich and poor, if only we could laugh in each other's faces instead of behind one another's backs. Ahoy there, boy, bring me that plate. Yes, *you*!"

Jolanda was surprised to see Lansloet appear between them with a currant tart nearly as large as his frown. This was simply a fiasco, and Jolanda looked sadly out to the black sea. More to herself than Lady Meyl, she said, "I don't suppose most feasts are quite like this."

"No," said Lady Meyl, tearing into the sweet with her fingers and popping little bits of mushed-up tart into her maw. "They are, though not so whore-heartedly cold, obviously, and there are women in attendance beyond the camp sluts and we few stray ladies. When we're all back and settled, I'll have you and the graaf over and you can see for yourself that feasts are every bit as wretched in town as they are in country."

"Oh," said Jolanda, brightening. "That would be lovely!"

"No it won't," said Meyl as she stared off into a bonfire, the salty wind lashing fur around her features making her resemble a barbarian queen of old. "You'll see soon enough, my child, you'll see soon enough."

V.

Mackerel the Second was a gargantuan bay, and even after two days of travel the horse made Jolanda anxious—she'd been very much looking forward to having a real ride again, on solid ground, but now that she had a steed of her own, she found the creature alien as something from the sea. She had such fond memories of the first Mackerel, of learning how to control the beast under Jan's careful, quiet tutelage, but from the moment she'd mounted the horse Hertog Von Wasser sold her, she knew the equine was going to be trouble—there was no warmth in his titan's eyes as he surveyed her over his shoulder, only an emotionless curiosity, as if he were constantly reevaluating his initial assessment that riders did not make good eating.

She was doing better than Sander, at least—his horse threw him three times the first day. That it had only pitched him off its back twice on the second he viewed as a great improvement, and to his credit he never punched the animal, despite his threats. Jolanda recalled how adamant Von Wasser had been that Sander take that particular mount, whereas Jolanda was free to choose from the half-dozen animals made available by the deaths of their riders in the battle that Sander, Jolanda, and the servants had narrowly missed.

A great day for Holland and a great day for its steward, Philip the Good, whom Jolanda glimpsed once or twice through the throng of hangers-on that constantly swarmed him like ants upon a juicy bone. Duke Philip was departing for Middelburg, on the southern island of Walcheren, but before he and his retinue moved on, Sander was able to finagle a brief audience with

His Highness. It was barely long enough to get through the mandatory kneeling, groveling, and apologizing for missing the fight. Of course, to hear the ribbing Von Wasser and the rest gave him, the fact that Graaf Tieselen had shown up at all was seen as a great exceeding of expectations.

The night of their arrival in Brouwershaven, they all piled into the crowded hospital tents and slept amidst the injured and dying, lodgings being hard to come by in the Zeeland port's army-infested inns and houses. Despite the surprisingly warm welcome he'd received from the rich men of Dordt, the next morning Sander seemed eager to be off from his new friends, but not in the direction she'd hoped. Jolanda repeatedly tried to talk him into returning to Dordrecht, as being away from home just as Wurfbain must be plotting some revenge seemed the height of folly, but he would hear none of it, maintaining they stay away "until things cooled down," whatever that meant. At least their journey to Brouwershaven wasn't a complete waste, as Lady Meyl seemed as shrewd a woman as Jolanda had ever met, and winning new allies was never an ill venture. With Wurfbain gone from sole guardian to nemesis, Jolanda suspected they could do with as many of those as possible.

Since fleeing the endless revel of Brouwershaven was of paramount importance to Sander, Jolanda eventually coughed up the coin for two horses and passage off the Zeeland island, back to the mainland. A small mercy was that she convinced Sander to let Drimmelin and Lansloet find their own way home with Lady Meyl and Hertog Von Wasser's people, whenever they cleared off, rather than humping along on another horse. The triumphant hertog and his mother, being of one of the few old-money sheephead families to financially survive the flood, would likely stay in Zeeland as long as Duke Philip's court remained there, and so even if the two servants were colluding with Wurfbain, it wasn't as though they would beat Jolanda and Sander back to Dordrecht. The deciding factor for Sander had been that if the servants returned separately, he could charge them with delivering his plate armor, sparing him from wearing the uncomfortable suit on the road. For all the shit he talked about her armor being worthless, she certainly got a lot more wear out of her brigandine than he did from his steel shell. When pressed for where he meant to travel "until things cooled down," Sander would just shrug and mutter, "anywhere but here," and so Jolanda picked their course.

The boat that carried them and their horses from Brouwershaven dropped them off in Schiedam, and from there Jolanda figured she could add a few weeks to their ride home by detouring west and then north along the coast to Monster, and from there retracing the surreptitious route by which Jan had first brought her to Rotterdam. Such a delay would comfort Sander without letting him stay away from Dordrecht forever, as seemed to be his wish, and so toward Monster they went, without her telling him the reason. He never asked why she might have chosen that particular town to visit, a lack of interest in her motivations that annoyed her a bit, but he seemed to have fallen back into his old, worrisome, worrying ways, and so she tried not to take his self-centered demeanor as a personal affront. Not like the goddamn neuker took much notice of her personal affairs in Dordt, so why should it be any different here on the road?

Or rather, the strand.

"Cold as indifference on Christmas," Sander said when the wind died down enough for them to bandy a few words back and forth, like beggars sharing a mug of something hot. "Hate the sea like I hate all Hooks, I do. Let's cut over the dunes next break we get."

"No," said Jolanda. "I don't know the way from the other side."

"How you know where we're going from this side, then? It's all the same, sand on one side and water the other, and couple of half-wits betwixt the two—whatever you think you know or remember about coming to this place, you'll find yourself mistaken."

"No," said Jolanda, though not being a half-wit herself, she knew there was wisdom in what he said—for the past two days every stretch of beach they passed reminded her of home so keenly, she had to bite her lip and think of warmer things or give in to emotion. No, not home, but the place she'd grown up— totally different sort of thing. Still, she'd take them clear up to Amsterdam before she admitted defeat on something she should know as well as if a map of the place were dyed on the insides of her eyes. They would find it. She would find it. And then she would move on her father, make him an offer he couldn't pass up, and load up Mackerel II with enough purple to fill a dozen chests with groots, once she'd flipped the stuff. She'd keep a little for her arms, of course, be done with the woad once and for—

"Oi!" Sander was shouting to be heard over the steadily rising wind that was making her lean forward, mid-daydream, and close her eyes to slits for all the sand pelting her face. The eternal gray quilt was cracking on its clothesline to her left, ragged strips of dirty lace capping every wind-whipped wave, and she grinned despite the grit it bore into her gums. If this wasn't home, she didn't have one at all. "Oi, Jo, we got to get out of this breeze! I'm dying!"

She didn't even try to be heard over the wind piping between her teeth, echoing down her throat, filling her lungs with brine and the dust of shells shattering under hoof-fall. Home. The sea almost looked inviting, and for a moment that old madness seized her and she tried to steer Mackerel II to the dark border where the sea puffed out as far as it could before drawing back in, a panting, liquid Leviathan. Home.

The horse wasn't keen on braving the breakers, and truth be told, neither was she, so she let him drift back to the softer sand to their right, his head down, bearing into the gale. Jolanda told herself it was the season, that it was too cold to dive in, but the truth was she hadn't gotten in anything deeper than the Dordt baths since becoming a lady. The thought made her queasy, made her throat tight. Too cold, she thought, which it was ... but aye, that weren't the reason.

Keeping the reins in her left hand, she let her right swing down to the pommel of the sword Sander had commissioned for her after she'd finally bested him in a sparring match, what, over a year ago? Her Tooth, given to her their first Christmas together as father and daughter in the house on Voorstraat. It was a comfort, was a good sword, and she again regretted their tardy arrival at Brouwershaven—she had dearly anticipated the chance to use it.

Maybe it was for the best, though—she'd have an easier time meeting Lijsbet's eyes when they returned home, and what quarrel did she have with Englander arseholes that she didn't with her next-door neighbors? As in, arseholes were everywhere, and who knew, if Wurfbain came for them, she might have a chance to use the weapon soon enough. Wasn't there something Sander said about the best sword being the one you never drew? No, that definitely wasn't the sort of saying Sander would repeat, maybe it was Lijsbet…

"I said, you see that?" Sander had ridden up beside her, but she hadn't noticed for the wind in her ears and sand in her eyes. He was pointing ahead, and following his gloved finger, she made out a huddle of figures beside a beached boat far down the strand, where the dunes curved inland. "What's that?"

"Fisherboys," she replied, her heart hopping along with her tangle of escaped hair and slipping wipple—that bend in the beach was Snail Bay or she'd eat her veil.

"Who?" The wind reduced his bellow to a mutter.

"Fishermen!" Jolanda shouted back. "Fishermen!"

"Ask them if we're close!"

"Aye!" Though she didn't have to, not anymore—that was the cove where she'd learned to swim, the place she'd spent more time in than in her own home, baiting more traps than there were days in a year, bringing up more shellfish than there were numbers. It was the only place the snails dwelled, and from the first occasion she'd dove all the way down to their blind depths and felt them resting there on the bottom, she knew that it was a special place, reserved only for her. She hadn't been stupid enough to bring one of the rough-shelled creatures up with her, otherwise her father would have dispensed with the laborious trap-setting process and had her swimming down there every day. Much as she loved the water, doing a thing that pushed the shark's share of the labor from the shoulders of her shitbird brothers to her own knobby pair seemed stupid as sin, even to a child of her limited wits.

On autumn days, though, when the sun sank before the Vespers bell even pealed over the blackthorn from Monster, she would come running down the dunes and fling herself into the warm water—the rest of the time she stayed with the sea, but when her brothers and father were gone from the bay, she'd chance a swim, a dive, a prayer down there at the bottom where the shellfish crept and crawled. Home.

The fishermen had seen Jolanda and Sander coming and paused what they were doing, riders being a rare enough sight on that dismal spit to attract interest from its residents. The winter sky, rough slate as you'd find in any quarry, gave precious little indication of the hour, but to judge by the number of times Jolanda's arse and legs had gone from sore to numb to aching sore again, she'd put it somewhere near dusk—the men were home for good, then, if they had any sense. Most of the fisher-boys she had known had lived farther back behind the bay, if not in Monster proper, but there had been a few families on this side of the inlet, tucked up in the dunes. She was still trying to remember the names of the ones who'd lived around here when she got close enough to recognize Comijn amongst the men, the shittiest of her shitbird brothers.

Here it was, then—what she'd come for. The wind gave them enough respite for her to hiss at Sander, "Whatever's said, you keep shut and follow my lead, aye? Call me Lijsbet if you call me anything."

"Eh?" said Sander, raising a brow in obnoxious if unconscious imitation of Wurfbain. "Call you what, now?"

"Lijsbet Tieselen," she said, her heart trying to squirm up her gullet. "You're Jan, same as ever, but I'm Lijsbet. Don't fuck this up, or I'll make you sorry, Sander, I swear it."

"I told you all about me falling out with Hobbe, but you're playing games now, leaving me out the story?" said Sander, but didn't raise his voice. Good Christ in all his glory, there were the twins, and Jetse, and the youngest, Gerard, who had grown from perpetually snotty kid to equally drippy teenager—hang her from a hook if this pack of fisherboys weren't her shitbird brothers to a man!

"Later," Jolanda said, feeling her face go as dark as her glove-hidden fingers. "*Please.* Just let me do what I will."

"Long as it gets us out of this wind!" he shouted, though it hadn't really picked up enough to necessitate such volume. He gave her a wink, the blessed idiot, and she turned to her brothers.

"Ho there!" Jolanda called to her bedraggled family. Devil's hoof, but they looked bad—the few years had not been kind to the boys, each and all looking worse then she'd left them... although Comijn had at last grown into his bulbous nose. They lacked proper clothing for an amble on the beach, to say naught of braving the winter sea, most swaddled in ragged blankets rather than oiled cloaks. Jetse had one of their mother's old gowns over the rest of his kit, though it was thin enough that it took her a moment to even make out where halter ended and stained shirt began.

None of them answered Jolanda's greeting, save to look collectively at their feet now that Sander had thrown back his hood and let the wind carry his cloak over his shoulder, showing off his orange velvet doublet and the thick gold chain wound 'round his neck like the gaudiest noose. His stubbly face had erupted in pimples since they'd left Dordt, and his clothes were sandblasted to the point that he looked more dune than duke, but Jolanda knew her brothers had never seen a man dressed so fine; to think

Jan's ratty raiment had seemed impressive when he'd called on the Verf clan!

"The Lady Tieselen greets you, villains!" Sander said as they halted their horses before the grimy crew. From here Jolanda could see that the stringing rope in the bed of their boat had, at most, a dozen small fish along it. Small wonder they looked so hollow of cheek, if that was indicative of the general quality of their casting. "Is this how you honor a noblewoman who deigns address you?"

"Ya want us ta bow?" asked Comijn, looking up and staring dead at Jolanda. At first she thought he'd recognized her, was having a laugh, but then she saw he wore the same bulging-eyed, shivery expression he always donned when their father was taking out a bad snail crop on his brood—he was terrified.

"Of course you bow!" said Sander, and all five of Jolanda's brothers fell to their knees. She covered her smile with her hand—this was absurd. All that was missing was her father lined up with his shitbird offspring and she'd have done all that she needed to ensure happiness until the end of her days—if she got some kind of purple-dealing arrangement set up, then so much the better, but this, *this*, right here, was worth coming back to this dreary, colorless place.

Quick as it came, though, the pleasure turned, like a delicious morsel, once swallowed, revealing itself to be mere conveyance for a sizable hook now tugging at your guts, the line in your throat making you gag, but the worst, the absolute *worst*, being the knowledge that you took the bait of your own volition. Mind, the sight of her brothers' threadbare knees buried in the pebbly sand didn't make the animosity they had beat into her any less tangible, it wasn't as if she was going to invite them home to Dordt so that they could all live happily ever after, it was just...she knew how cold and coarse that sand was. More than one of these men had, in their youth, ground her face-first into it on account of some perceived slight or honest injury, and now that she was on her horse she was returning the favor ...

Except it felt awful instead of wonderful. She felt ... she felt like how she imagined Jan must have, watching her treading water out there in the dark sea, not knowing if she'd drown or come ashore and risk his mercy. Or how he must have felt when he'd put the noose 'round her neck, a detail of his murder attempt that she suspected he'd done just to somehow bother Sander. If this was a victory, then so was the kicking of smelly dogs, the pummeling of slow children, the killing of some moony mussel who stepped on your shoe at the market and didn't apologize.

She looked at Sander and saw him looking back at her, waiting for further instruction. What sort of fickle fate put her and that lummox on horses while leaving the rest of her kin to the sea? What made her trust and, aye, care for a murderous, stupid arsehole more than her stupid and arseholish but certainly not murderous brothers? The fate she was given, she supposed, and one to be carried through to its conclusion. She sat straighter on her horse, much as she longed to dismount and give her legs a rest.

"Stand, fishermen, stand," Jolanda said, waiting for one of them to meet her gaze—one with better eyesight or memory than Comijn evidently possessed. It had only been three years since she'd left, so one of them was bound to recognize her, and then she could leave again, be done with them for good. She had promised herself a hundred times she would someday come back and lord herself over these shitbirds, and by God she would see it through, even if it now seemed petty, vicious, pointless.

They stood, and she saw more than one wince at the exertion. She wondered how long they had been in the boat, which led her to wonder what they were even doing on this side of the bay. No harm in asking, and the more she talked, the sooner they'd find her voice familiar, peer closer at her, put it all together, and then ... what?

Only way to find out what lay ahead was to walk there, and so she did, asking, "What are you doing on this side of the bay?"

There was no answer from the downcast men until Sander cleared his throat, which got Jetse talking, fast and rough. By all the tongues of men and beasts, he had an accent on him, and Jolanda found herself struggling to understand her brother as he pointed to a faint path through the marram grass on the nearest dune. "Ma wiff und aye dwill dar, und ur bairns und hur mudder's well, und ma brudders thar drop me hare."

"You catch that, m'lady?" asked Sander, clearly enjoying himself. Such a goddamn bully, to take sport in the fishermen's obvious anxiety. She wondered how they would have reacted if Sander had kept on the plate harness he'd worn to Brouwershaven.

"Aye," she said, letting a bit of her own old accent creep in there. Anything? Nothing. "And the rest of you, what place do you call home?"

A pause, and then Comijn spoke up, though his eyes stayed shoe-fixed. "Me und the rest, we're in our fadder's house 'cross the bay."

"At least I can understand this one!" said Sander. "Oi, lad, there a town with an inn nearby?"

"Nay," said Comijn. "'Twas, but none run it no mur."

"Well, shit," said Sander, dropping the snooty lilt he'd adopted and addressing Jolanda in his normal tone. "I'm not sleeping on sand again. What say we take advantage of these gentlemen's hospitality?"

Jolanda felt dizzy, and hunkered down in her saddle. "Hospitality?"

"You'll lend us your roof on a cunting night like this, won't you?" Sander grinned at Jolanda's brothers. They were quaking, but from nerves or the rising wind, she knew not. Comijn quickly nodded, rubbing his hands together, but still not looking up. She remembered her brothers as being feral and fearless, even when

Jan had come to take her away, yet these men were as skittish and shy as beaten pups. "Settled, then—you know the way, I trust?"

It took Jolanda a moment to realize Sander was addressing her. "Oh. Uh, yes, I was told the purple-maker had five sons—are you his children?"

"Six," said Comijn. "Papa had six, but Pieter went way years ago."

"How didja know 'bout us?" said Gerard, wiping his nose on his sleeve and staring with obvious wonder at Jolanda's horse. "Can I...touch it?"

"You may," said Jolanda. "I know about you...as I have come to buy purple dye from your father. I was told the man with five sons in Monster brewed the dye, and I mean to offer him a very lucrative proposition."

"Danno whut one of thum is," said Jetse. "But na matter. Dye's gone, Papa's died, und I'm ta home, if iss right with you?"

"What?" Jolanda said, though she had made out enough to know she was too late. Monstrous as he'd been, it had never occurred to her that the old man might be mortal.

"Our fadder died a year back," said Comijn. "And we're out've purple."

Oh. Jolanda had nothing to say to that. When the silence grew long, Sander asked, "When'll you get more?"

"Mur purple?" That was Comijn, maybe, she couldn't see so well, the sandy gusts picking back up. "Never. Sir, I mean, never, sir."

Sander looked to Jolanda but she didn't want to ask, didn't want to know. Curiosity was for cunts; some questions didn't have a good answer...just shut it, Sander, she thought, and as if she'd said it aloud and he was being contrary, he said, "And why not?"

Gerard was beneath Jolanda, petting Mackerel II's neck, and she forced a smile. He stared up at her, too stupid or young to be as scared of the rich. No recognition on his wind-burned face, only the dullest of curiosities.

"Snails gone," said Comijn. "Ways back we come to catch less, then lots less, und now we ain't pullt none up in a year. Bay's got cold, too. Chill und hollow. No snails, no purple."

That stabbed her the way she ought to have been stabbed at hearing her da had died. What was wrong with her, sitting on a high horse above her family, hiding her tears behind veils of swirling sand and imported silk? And all for some shellfish destined for a hammer, instead of the man who'd birthed her, raised her, and, aye, smiled at her, too, from time to time—yet the thought of there being nary a snail in Snail Bay was the saddest thing she'd ever heard.

She needed to get her shit together; Sander was staring. She tried to think about it in hard terms—this explained why they were even leaner than she'd left them, why they were piling five men into a two-man dinghy. No purple, no Papa, no prospects. Except Jetse, she supposed, who'd married some poor girl, saints save her.

"Go home, iss right with you?" Jetse repeated, and aye, of course he wasn't waiting on his brothers for an answer, he was waiting for permission from Sander. From her.

"Go home, then, Jetse," she croaked, tired as she could remember feeling. He was off like a dune rat chancing an open patch amidst the blackthorn, not peering closer at the handsomely dressed stranger who somehow knew his name, not looking back at his brothers, away, away, away. If only it weren't so cold, she would insist she and Sander sleep in a bole in the dunes, or under an overturned boat, anywhere else…but it was too cold to sit outside on principle. "The rest of you go ahead, and make your home ready for us. We shall ride around the bay and arrive there soon. Take this for your trouble."

Sander groaned as she dug into her saddlebag and withdrew the largest of her three purses. Part of her still wanted to hurl it at their feet, where it could split like a honeycomb and spill its treasure across the sand and shallows, but instead she gingerly lowered it to Gerard, who took it with wide eyes and delivered it to Comijn. He received it with the same reverence possessed by those who held the Christling in the altarpiece of the Saint Nicolaas Church, and all four of the remaining brothers stared up at her now, too awed to simply fear her any longer. They might have stayed that way for a very long time if Sander hadn't barked, "Well, get on and ready the house, then! And see that most of that coin goes to buying us a decent supper and drink from that village of yours—I'll be well angered if there isn't a warm fire, a warm meal, and warm ale awaiting us!"

They didn't thank her, turning and shoving the boat off and squeezing in without a backward glance, away, away, away, across the bay. Sander and Jolanda watched them go, then Jolanda led Sander inland, along the shore of Snail Bay. Sander did not say anything, though he clearly must know what she was about now—though she didn't use her bedroom mirror in Dordt as often as Sander used his, the peacock, she had seen enough of her own nose and chin and ears in the fishermen to know that Sander must have recognized the same, even if all the talk of purple hadn't been enough to clue him in. At least he held his tongue, for once.

It was very dark by the time they had circumvented the inlet, passed through Monster, and found the trail through the dunes to Jolanda's ancestral home, the cloudy night sky and wind-cast sand doing precious little to aid them in their search. When they arrived at the black hovel, Sander kept avowing Jolanda had led them astray, that this couldn't be the place, but even without the shallow impressions in the stained sand where the purple pots had rested or the familiar angles of the listing shack, she would have known it by the smell—even after all these years, it reeked of piss and sea-rot and too many people in too small a space.

"Don't see a fire going," Sander finally said after they had stood there in silence for a while, staring at the desolate house. "Think they're back in town, getting food and all?"

"I suspect they're halfway to 'S Gravenhage by now," said Jolanda.

"What's that, a better provisioned village?"

"It's a woodland where they can hide out. They've nicked off with my money, Sander."

"Nah, not those boys—they were shitting their breeches, no way they'd be so bold!"

Jolanda closed her eyes, listened to the wind squealing through the chinks in the driftwood walls, and imagined she could hear it groaning through the empty cauldrons that used to rest out here, in the shadow of the blackthorn. They must have sold off the purple pots once they realized the shellfish weren't coming back. Sander was cursing now, but she simply smiled and went to the door—at least this way she could set the place aflame when they left in the morn.

Home.

Februari 1426

"Everything, However Finely Spun, Finally Comes to the Sun"

I.

Home.

Sander hadn't believed he'd ever think of Dordt that way, but here they were, back on Voorstraat, and damned if it didn't feel like the end of a journey. That was a new sensation, it was, the sense that the road actually stopped at a certain point, that you could quit it as long as you wanted instead of just until the search party passed by or you got kicked out of the tavern. As they approached through the gloaming, snow again powdering their crowns, Sander saw light spilling through the shutters of the parlor window and let out a long, happy sigh. Much as he'd feared Lansloet and Drimmelin returning before them and conspiring with Hobbe, over the last few weeks of awful, drafty inns with awful, nasty food, he'd been even more scared that the servants might *not* beat him and Jo back to Dordt. Duke Philip must have drawn his court away from Zeeland, and once that happened, Von Wasser and the rest of the Cod locals would've been eager to be home to crow about their victory.

"Happy?" Sander asked his moody compatriot. Even burning down that hovel at the beach hadn't cheered her up, angels only knew why. When he'd finally called her on the fishermen being her kinfolk, she'd fessed readily enough, but not provided more than a sour "aye." Probably raw they hadn't recognized her, but what did she expect? It wasn't like she was merely dressing a mite differently these days; she looked totally unlike the rabid little bitch Sander had met in Rotterdam, ten years older instead of three, human instead of monster. "To be back, I mean?"

"*Yes*," Jo said with more passion than he'd heard from her all trip.

"Me too," said Sander, slapping her back, and that finally knocked a smile loose from the grump. She swung back on him, and then they were capering in the street, no longer caring if slush got into their boots, for they would be shed soon enough, bare feet propped in front of a warm fire. Sander let her land a good smack to his cheek, and his pratfall turned genuine as the icy cobble rebuffed his heel. She laughed like old to see him go ass-first into a filthy brown snowbank between their stoop and their neighbor's, but stopped cawing soon enough as he fumbled together a snowball. By the time he had it packed, though, she was up the stairs and through the front door.

Sander sat there for a while, closing his eyes and letting the dirty snow soak through his surcoat and hose—weren't so long ago he would've been sitting here because he was a drunk idiot without anywhere better to go. Yet now he could stand whenever he wanted and go inside a graaf's house and wring out his clothes and warm himself before a ball-sweatingly hot hearth. How about that?

Eventually picking himself up and tossing the snowball aside, he'd stepped onto the stoop when something caught in his eye, like a fleck of sand. Turning to look down the lane, he saw a figure standing in the middle of the road half a dozen houses down. That put the shudders on a fellow, no doubt. Sander squinted, but could make out nothing beyond the obvious—it was somebody tall wearing a hood. Huh. Sander licked his lips, and quick as it had come, the chill inspired by this peeper warmed off, and he resolved to give the nutsack a wee lesson in the propriety of staring at one's betters.

"Jan!" Sander nearly jumped out of his skin as Jo shouted in his ear. He hadn't heard the front door open; lazy broad probably hadn't closed it after her. He scowled at the girl, too surprised to immediately scold her for creeping up on him. "Look!"

Jo was still in her brigandine, which must stink like a pig's crooked dick by now, but she had her cloak off and was holding it out to him for inspection. Fuck that, he had bigger fish to fillet, and—shit. He'd only looked away for the moment, but the peeper down the lane had vanished. *Hell* no. Sander took off after the cunt, ignoring Jo's shouting, but when he reached where the dastard must have been, he couldn't find any tracks—the center of the lane was a shiny, cobbled creek instead of snow pack. Sander kept running, hoping to spot a fleeing shadow in one of the alleys or at the intersection with Visstraat, but nobody was about, despite the hour—it was mostly dark, yeah, but this time of year that was still early enough. There should have been people out; it was like the whole shitty town was working together to help the plaguebitch get away.

"Shit," he said, spinning around in the intersection. He thought of the night Jo had seen someone watching her window from the street, thought of what he and Simon had found out in the meer, thought of how nobody had been minding the dark warehouse when he'd had the Rotter boatman swing by there on their way back into the city not an hour ago. He thought of Hobbe, like as not eager to make a move on him and Jo, if he hadn't already. "Shit!"

"What is it?" said Jo, catching up to him. "Where are you going?"

"Nowhere," he said, not wanting to scare her. "Thought I... forgot something, is all, but the boatman'll have pissed off back to the Rott by now."

"The harbor's the other way," said Jo, glancing back toward their house.

"All the more reason to forget it," said Sander, and seeing she still held her cape in both hands, he hoped to distract her by asking, "What've you got there?"

"My cloak," said Jo, falling for Sander's ploy like the dullard she was. "It's...look, what do you think that is?"

"Eh?" Sander squinted at the blue cloth, reached out and brushed a dark stain with the back of his fingers. A bit came off on his skin—cold, wet, brown. He sniffed it, licked it. "It's blood, yeah?"

"Aye," said Jo. "That's what I thought."

"How'd you—" Sander began, worried this was going to be some kind of talk about her monthlies or busting her maidenhead on a horse or something, the stain being right there on the back of the garment and all.

"It's Lijsbet," said Jo, which was hardly an improvement to talking about cuntblood. "I gave her the cloak before we left."

"Oh," said Sander, because, yeah: *oh*. "Well, where's she, then?"

"I don't know," Jo snapped, like it was his doing. "She...I don't know, I ran inside, and was in the kitchen before I saw you weren't after me. Drimmelin's in there, and she asked what happened to the cloak, and I said *what*, and she said it was hung up all muddy and when did we get back, and so I went and found this on the peg and took it out to you and then you ran off."

"So they're back, then," Sander nodded. "Wondered if it was just Lizzy, when I seen someone was home."

"I gave it to her," Jo said, plaintive.

"Well, let's go find her, then," said Sander, and figuring a lie couldn't hurt, added, "And yeah, might not be blood at all, just some mud, like Drimmelin said."

"You said—"

"Everything tastes like blood, chapped as my lips are," said Sander, because sure, a few more lies on the stack wouldn't topple it. "You haven't looked upstairs for her, nor the attic, nor asked Lansloet or Drimmelin where she might be, yeah?"

Jo didn't answer, spinning on her heel and dashing back up the street. Sander wondered if she was as sure as he that Lizzy wouldn't be found asleep in Jo's bed, nor straightening up the attic nor sweeping the snow in the courtyard nor anywhere else in the house. He hoped she was, of course, hoped he'd walk in the door and they'd be laughing it up. Oh, how he hoped…

After giving the crossroads a final scowl, Sander took his time walking back—not so eager to be back inside after all. When he reached his own stoop, he could hear raised voices from within. Nobody was watching him this time, but he still paused in the doorway, wondering what he'd find in the kitchen, where it was Jo doing the shouting. Was it too much to ask to come home to a quiet house? Apparently.

Sander kicked the door shut with his heel as he strode in, and making out Lansloet's quiet protests during a lull in Jo's storm, he sighed and took off his damp, freezing leather cloak and unbuckled his scabbard, hanging them both up on their pegs. The surcoat was shed next, but he was out of hooks and so he just dropped it on the floor. Looking through the open parlor doors to the crackling fire in the hearth, he sighed again—if he had to re-don his wet boots he'd just become depressed, and so he left them on, pausing only long enough to bolt the front door before heading down the hall.

"—was here!" Jo said, looking back and forth between Lansloet and Drimmelin, who stood on opposite sides of the table where the cook had laid out a goose stuffed with jellied pike and almonds.

"Lansloet, Drimmelin," said Sander, leaning in the kitchen doorway. "A welcome sight, a fire in the parlor and a bird ready for the roasting. How, I wonder, did you know we'd be back to enjoy such finery?"

There was a pause while Lansloet and Drimmelin pushed at each other with their eyes, and Jo scowled at Sander for interrupting her interrogation. Lansloet eventually piped up when it became evident the cook wouldn't. "We knew Your Worship would crave something of substance upon his return, and we thought it better to err on the side of having a hot meal prepared and our master absent than risk a late-arrived lord with nothing suitable in the pot."

"And if we didn't make it, you'd find a way to see the food wasn't wasted, yeah?" said Sander. He was going to take great delight in sacking these two, as soon as he got to the bottom of more pressing matters. "Where's Lizzy?"

"Like we told the young miss, we don't know," said Drimmelin hastily. She looked sallow and shaky—concerned for the maid's safety or guilty for her part in whatever had befallen the girl?

"Why not?" said Sander—whatever their answer to the next, he'd see that they were well searched before they quit his house, lest one have an extra key secreted somewhere. "She let you in, didn't she?"

"As we told the Lady Jolanda," said Lansloet, not trembling in the slightest, "we arrived to find the door unlocked, a fire in the hearth, and several candles burning around the house. A most irresponsible situation, you will agree, and one that ought to be addressed when next you lay hands on the girl."

"She's not stupid," Jo said. "Somebody was here, as I put to these two, but it can't have been her—she wouldn't leave the fire going, or use our candles."

"Or perhaps she did, and eloped with her beau upon hearing our approach," said Lansloet. "Girls, you know, are like that. The kitchen shutters were open, were they not, Drimmelin?"

"They were," said Drimmelin, but Sander thought it might have been, "they were?"

"Why would—" Jo began, but Lansloet talked over her, the steely-eyed steward meeting Sander's gaze.

"*Girls*, sir, are like that. I presume you gave her a key and instructions to mind the house in our absence?" Sander nodded once, and Lansloet continued. Jo looked as though she might leap upon the servant at any moment. "An honest mistake, then, on your part. The girl has a lover, and as soon as we are gone, she pokes a broom through the window to signal him inside. Thereupon he enters your home, and the two of them take full advantage of your larder and cellar. We did find several empty wine bottles and cheese rinds, did we not Drimmelin?"

"We did," said the cook, but again, that doubt: was it a question or an answer?

"You're lying!" Jo said, striding to Lansloet and seizing his tunic front. She stood a head and a half shorter than the servant, but he somehow seemed dwarfed by the furious young woman. "You tell another lie and I'll bludgeon you, you scheming cunt! They did it, these greedy arseholes, they ate and drank and lived it up on our fortune, and now they're trying to pin it on Lijsbet!"

Lansloet said nothing, looking plaintively over Jo's head at Sander. Drimmelin intervened, and Sander thought her too flustered to be lying. Maybe. "But it *is* true, m'lady, m'lord—the house was in a proper state when we came home this morning. We spent last night in Rotterdam with Lady Meyl and Hertog Von Wasser's people. Ask the lady or the hertog you don't believe us, Graaf Tieselen, I beg you! Mud and dirty dishes everywhere, what Lansloet and me spent the day cleaning. Begging all your pardons, we thought...we thought..."

The cook had gone the color of the diced garlic peppering the raw bird—perhaps recognizing her own goose was destined for the same fate, now that she'd run her mouth. Sander crossed his arms and said, "You thought what?"

"We thought Your Worship and my lady Jolanda had returned before us and made the small mess," Drimmelin said, not meeting Sander's eyes. "But that you were out upon the town when we come in. We spent the day restoring the house, thinking you'd be home again any moment, but then my lady burst into the kitchen, giving me a fright, and ran out again, and—"

"Shut it," said Sander, although not cruelly. "That's not what you said when I asked about the goose, is it, Lansloet? You said you'd err on the side of us coming back, but weren't sure if we'd be home or not. Said you thought we might still be on the road, didn't you?"

"If I may be so bold as to request you release me, dear lady," Lansloet said to Jo, who unhanded him in disgust and stamped around the table to a jug of wine on the far side of the bird. She hoisted the clay vessel in both hands and took a chug on it while Lansloet addressed Sander. "With all due respect, Your Worship, what I said was that I preferred to have a hot meal for you in the event that you returned rather than risk a cold oven upon your return. I was referring to whether or not you might be dining on trenchers at the White Horse, or at another gentleperson's home, or some entirely other location, but, and I feel this is important to clarify, another location here in town. As Drimmelin said, we had every reason to think you'd returned."

"The house is wrecked so we did it, eh?" said Jo, thumping the jug down on the table and wiping her mouth on her sleeve. "That your every reason, Lansloet?"

"In addition to my lady's cloak hanging by the door, there are a gentleman's boots with fresh mud upon them beneath it. These boots bear a striking resemblance to those Our Worship wears upon his feet at this very moment, as you will surely agree once you inspect them for yourself," said Lansloet. Tone was everything with the old stoat, and Sander marveled at Jo's restraint in not giving him the jug full in the face. "Your unexpectedly late return to the city leads me to conclude that the girl, Lijsbet, had a male friend installed in the house while we four were away, and upon Drimmelin and my entering the house this morning they fled through the kitchen window. I would be very surprised if we see her again."

"Out the window into the canal?" said Jo. "That makes a lot of sense, Lansloet. Nice offer, but we're not buying."

"I assure you, my lady, a desperate criminal has very few compunctions against getting her feet wet, once caught in the act." Was Lansloet giving Sander a knowing look there? Memories of

Sneek welled up, welcome as a gut-ache at the start of a feast. "Perhaps they kept a boat moored beneath the window, and if not, there is enough of a ledge for an enterprising thief to creep along the rear wall of the houses until a suitable alley or pier presented itself for a drier escape."

"Bullshit!" Jo cried. "She wouldn't!"

"Quite the mystery," said Sander, hoping that his face wasn't betraying how intensely anxious all this was making him. The last person in the house he would have expected to betray or take advantage of them was Lizzy, but that certainly seemed to be a possibility now. She might even have been working with Hobbe all along—hadn't Jo said the maid was adamant she not be made to go to war against Countess Jacoba?

"My lord," said Lansloet, and now the servant actually looked nervous or excited, his eyes darting back and forth from Jo to Sander. "I wonder if I might venture to provide a final piece of information, one that might, perhaps, shed some small light upon the maid's accomplice?"

Even Jo seemed curious as to this, and Sander nodded, trying like Satan tries to tempt the righteous to unravel the knot before him.

"This afternoon, not an hour before your arrival, there was a knock upon the door." Lansloet seemed to be trying to smother a smile or else hold in a fart. "When I answered, it was the freeman Braem Gruyere."

"Braem?" That was queer—that cunt knew better than to call on Sander without invitation, which, yeah, hadn't been given yet, nor would it ever be, so long as Sander was graaf and Braem was a bitch. Forever, in other words. "By himself?"

"Yes, my lord," said Lansloet with relish that was nigh obscene. "He seemed surprised to see me, I must say, although I cannot imagine who else he might be expecting to answer the door at *your* house. Sir."

"So Braem and Lizzy...No." Sander nodded, putting it

together. Whether or not it was true would be proven in time, but this was certainly what Lansloet was implying: "Simon. Braem was calling 'cause he thought Simon was inside with Lizzy."

"Upon being greeted by me, he became flustered, and when I inquired as to his purpose in calling, he stammered something about how Your Worship should do well to meet him at the White Horse upon your return, an urgent matter, but I'm sure I don't—ugh!" Lansloet fell back as Jo caught him in the jaw with the goose, the leg she'd seized it by tearing free from the momentum of the greased-up poultry and sending the rest of the bird ricocheting away. The servant hit the wall and Jo hit him again, this time rapping his nose with the drumstick.

"Liar!" Jo struck again with the goose leg. "Shameless, dastardly liar!"

Recalling the incident after the fact, Sander would chuckle to himself at the memory of Lansloet being battered by a dismembered bird, but in the moment, he was thinking too hard on all the possibilities at work and was simply annoyed by Jo's interruption. Hauling her off the servant, he caught the drumstick across the cheek as Jo turned her weapon on him. He snapped at it, catching the raw leg between his teeth and clamping down. Once disarmed, Jo calmed substantially—perhaps the sight of Sander with goose blood and fat running down his chin was fierce enough to put the fear of a beating into her, or perhaps she was simply as tired as he was after weeks on horseback and boats.

"He's lying," Jo protested as Sander spit out the drumstick and carried her from the kitchen. "She wouldn't!"

"Let's hope not," muttered Sander, though in regard to Lansloet being a liar—given the scenarios an ominous cloak, a trashed house, and an open window left them, he'd prefer Lizzy be just another lousy cheat in a city full of them rather than a victim herself. Sander had always liked the lippy maid, but even if he hadn't, Jo was fond of her, and that would've been enough for him. Glancing back down the hall, he saw Drimmelin kneeling over the fallen Lansloet, but then she straightened back up—she'd been retrieving the bird. Sander called behind him, "See that's cooking before it gets any later!"

"It's *bullshit*," she said. "Lijsbet wouldn't, not with *Simon*. She . . . do you think she's all right?"

"I'm sure of it," said Sander, though a particularly gruesome thought had entered his imagination—what if the girl had been wearing Jo's cloak, and an assailant mistook the maid for her mistress? If Hobbe had hired an assassin and the poor servant had suffered for it, he would see Count Wurfbain chained out at Trash Island, a fancy target for graaf and daughter to hone their shooting.

Having carried Jo all the way down the hall, he deposited her at the foot of the stairs and knelt to inspect the foreign pair of boots that indeed muddied the floor beside his discarded surcoat. A man's, sure enough, and a cut similar to his own. "I'll just be out to check the Horse and see if Braem's about, and if so, I'll have the truth out of him before that goose loses its blush."

"Good thinking," said Jo. "Let's go by the harbor on the way, see if the warehouse boat is moored or missing. I didn't think to check when we were coming in."

"You're minding the house," said Sander, and before she could protest, he lowered his voice and added, "in case she comes back, or Simon, or someone else. I don't trust neither of our loyal servants, nor should you. Until we know who we can trust, any one of them might be working for Hobbe, and I'd rather not leave the house in their hands."

Jo bit her lip, and saints pat her pate, her hand had dropped to the hilt of the sword she still wore on her belt. Her mostly leather armor might do fuck-all in a real melee, but right now he was a wee bit jealous of her having something more substantial than a doublet and hose in which to face unknown foes. That said, he wasn't yet such a ponce that the likes of Hobbe Wurfbain or

Braem-fucking-Gruyere would spook him into donning his plate before going down to the goddamn pub—assuming those miserable servants of his had even followed his instructions and brought his armor back from Brouwershaven. No time to worry about that now.

"Be careful," said Jo as he opened the door, which was, yeah, sound advice in the fairest weather, and it looked like both snow and wind had picked up since he'd gone inside. Never even got the chance to take his wet boots off.

"You, too," said Sander. "Lock this behind me, and don't let anyone inside other than Lizzy. And only then if she's got a damn fine tale to tell."

II.

Crossing the Visbrug, Sander realized he'd neglected to re-don either the heavy cape or surcoat he'd ditched upon first entering his house, his soft azure doublet scant protection from the wind that now howled through the narrow avenue. Snow was blowing in his eyes, and he hurried down Groenmarkt to where Vleeshouwersstraat cut over Varkenmarkt, which was the long way to the White Horse, but he needed time to think. Vleeshouwersstraat was narrow enough to restrict the snow even as it channeled the wind, and coming out of the alley, he cursed—he'd meant to run by the old harbor, as Jo suggested, but he'd sooner kiss the devil's cock than retrace his steps now. No matter, he'd go that way on the return, assuming he didn't find the answers he sought at the tavern. Of course, getting answers required questions, but he'd figure those out just as soon as he was out of the harsh night.

Angling across town, he saw few people on the streets, the wind too stern, the snow too thick—even the militia would be tucked into their gatehouses, he supposed. Which made the fact that a hooded figure had followed him for three turns now all the more obvious. Sander's hand fell to his waist, but his sword was back at the house, hanging up beside his cloak, and he almost laughed at his folly. He quickened his pace, making for the alley just ahead that cut between the White Horse and the neighboring bakery. The backdoor to the baker's house lay just inside the alley's mouth, and he could flatten himself in the doorway, get the drop on this git, sword or no—the day he needed tools to take down a single man was the day he deserved what he got. If it was someone Hobbe had hired, or—

"Graaf!" came from just ahead, and peering through the churning snow, he saw Braem Gruyere had stepped out of the White Horse. Trying to be nonchalant about it, Sander glanced over his shoulder, but his shadow was gone, swallowed by the night city. Goddamn Gruyere. Braem was wearing a sackcloth suit of a considerably poorer cut than the richly colored outfit he had flaunted at court when Sander, Hobbe, and Laurent had stripped the Gruyere brothers of their rightful inheritance. The man looked haggard, which was a rare state for the proud if disenfranchised pretty boy. "We've got to talk, Jan."

"'Bout you skulking around my place without invitation?" said Sander. "Wager we do. See, where I come from—"

"Please," said Braem. How'd Lansloet described him, flustered? That was an understatement; the lad was positively losing his shit. "Everything's moving too fast. Simon's been arrested, and they mean to hang him. You need to help."

"Eh?" Sander squinted, looking for a break in the man's bullshit. Simon, arrested? "Let's get inside, have a drink and you tell me all—"

"No!" said Braem. "No, they, they have spies everywhere, we can't be seen together. For you as well as Simon and I. Come on, let's go to the south gatehouse, they're keeping him there, I'll tell you as we go. Pull your collar up, you won't need to talk, just listen, please listen."

"Right," said Sander, leading the man directly into the alley he had originally made for. Braem seemed less drunk and posturing than usual, which made his raving all the more odd, and—

Shit. Sander sighed, realizing Braem meant to lead him into an ambush. Simon might have truly forgiven Sander and Jo for taking his house and property—maybe—but this sad little dandy had certainly never accepted Count John's wisdom in awarding the Tieselen estate to Sander. Hell, Sander wouldn't have let that shit slide if he'd been in the Gruyere brothers' position, so he should have expected something like this—the only question now was if Simon was in on it. A bad question, a very, very bad question, but one that came to mind now that Sander was being led away from bright lights and witnesses by the shifty Braem.

"The Hooks are behind it," said Braem, slowing his pace. It was blatant what he was doing, but Sander slowed as well. By the faint light that seeped down into the alley and reflected on the snow, Sander saw that Braem was wearing a sword, not something the man was in the habit of doing but a welcome sight nevertheless—this confirmed the cunt's intent, and if Braem had a sword, then Sander was never a few quick movements away from having a sword. Sander focused, making the pommel look more and more like her, like his queen, his mistress. It was her, he thought, she'd found him again . . . but she hadn't, it was just a plain sword, and he grunted, trying harder to make her appear.

"They've been replacing real nobles to put their own . . . *impostors* into power." The words left Braem in a rush, like oats spilling from a cut feedbag. "I thought you were one, which is the whole reason we did what we did, but I see now that you're not, you can't be, you're as real as me or Simon. Impostors, they're impostors, but not just that, no no, something much worse is afoot. Something too horrible to even . . . Lord Above, I've seen it with my own eyes and I don't know what to make of it, what to make of all their plotting, all the *eels* . . . We need to free Simon and get to my friends, our friends, before they kill him, or you. They've done it all wrong, they've made it look like Simon's the killer, that he murdered the kids, but you and I know better, the kids were put out there to set *you* up, and now that he's been arrested, we—"

"Shut it, shut it—who arrested Simon?" Sander interrupted, the pieces not fitting together.

"The militia, of course," said Braem. "But we both know

who's feeding the orders, don't we? *They* are, who else? It's like this..."

Sander had been a breath away from snapping Braem's neck at the mention of impostors uprooting real nobles, but then Braem saved himself by saying he didn't suspect Sander. Then Braem had mentioned the murdered kids, and for a minute Sander thought Braem might be telling the truth, that Simon's reporting the dead kids in the meer turned out to be every bit as bad an idea as Sander had thought, with the lazy militia blaming Simon... but this was just spooky, all this talk of conspiracies, eels, and sundry craziness.

A different Sander might have taken the bait, might have been intrigued by what Braem was ranting about, but Sander was a goddamn graaf, and not a fool one at that. Yet Braem clearly thought he was the sort of nutter who'd buy into inscrutably complicated plots and—

Despite his intention to play it cool, Sander groaned. Simon had betrayed him.

There. Braem was still talking and talking, feeding out his overly complicated line about the militia having arrested Simon, but Sander was no longer listening to his lies, instead turning everything over in his mind. It all fit now, and Sander felt his heart sink at the treachery. Simon wasn't locked up in the gatehouse, he was the plaguebitch who'd been tailing Sander, like as not the same plaguebitch skulking outside Jo's window all those months back. Like every good lie, there was a grain of truth in Braem's tale, and the honest kernel here was that the headless kids were planted out there to blame Sander, to get him hanged for murder so his enemies could steal his title and house ... Ruthless. Simon had been the one to find the girl, after all, and had called Sander over—he must have thought himself so cunning to plant her out there, to act disgusted by what he'd found.

But Sander had been too sly to report finding the dead girl, or to go out and have a look at the second corpse Simon had told him about, and so the Gruyeres were running a different game now—get Sander to the gatehouse, where some bought militiamen were ready to throw chains on his gullible ass and then execute him as a child-killer.

Not a bad plan, Sander had to admit. The more he thought about it, ignoring Braem's prattling about eely Hooks and honest Cods and the murdered children, the more Sander realized that Hobbe had no doubt played a hand in the setup—these greedy Gruyeres would roll over and do whatever the count ordered, so long as they had their precious inheritance restored. And after all Sander had done for Simon, too...

"So that's the long and the short of it," said Braem, stamping his feet and making a big show of rubbing his hands in his eagerness to be off again. Giving the second man, who yeah, sad to say, was probably Simon, time to circle around to the other end of the alley. Would Simon reveal himself, or was he going to hang back, thinking himself unseen, until they reached the gatehouse? Sure, that was it—if Sander told Braem to fuck off and tried to break away, then Simon would jump in, and they'd cut him down. A dead child-killer was even better than one who'd protest his innocence, after all, and—

Lizzy. Mother of Christ in all her pregnant glory.

The thought of dead kids had brought to mind a certain young woman's bloody cloak, and Sander felt his disappointment in Simon's betrayal turn to something harder. One of these two assholes had mistaken her for Jo and murdered her, or maybe they'd sought to have a third headless corpse to hang on Sander's stoop. Hell, maybe she was just tending house at Voorstraat when they'd broken in, meaning to have a sip of Sander's wine while he was off at war, and they'd needed to keep her quiet. That would be just like these Gruyere fuckers, too impatient to wait until they'd gotten Sander hanged for crimes he didn't commit before sticking their grubby hands into his pie...

And what of the other two kids, the ones without heads? Had

Braem lured them into an alley like this one and hacked them up for the sole purpose of framing Sander?

Had Simon?

"Jan, *please*," said Braem. "Haven't you heard a word I've said? We have to go, now, we have to free Simon! I have a friend at the gatehouse who will take him out the side, onto the dock, and once he's in the boat, we can all go to see my friends. *Our* friends."

Some plan! Braem was even dafter than Sander had previously suspected if he thought a scheme like that would appeal to Graaf Tieselen—yes, yes, Braem, let's go see your mysterious friends this very night, all because of some mad story you've spun that's too stupid to even make sense of. That they would think him to be so utterly foolish, so utterly mad, as to fall for such a line...but that was all right. They'd underestimated him, to say the least, and he tried not to grin as he at last resumed walking, letting Braem lead him through the dark alley.

If Simon was indeed the man who was tailing him earlier, Sander would do just fine; two on one wasn't even something he'd take a wager on, it'd be good as thieving...but if they'd hired some other muscle, if there were more men waiting, he might have to think on his feet. The end of the alley was coming up, and Sander slowed again, which agitated Braem.

"Hurry!" said Braem. "They only arrested him because you were out of town. You're their real target, you're the one they want to replace with...one of them, one of those—"

"Easy, Braem," said Sander, growing disconcerted by Braem's intensity and the unexpected development of having some of his suspicions about the dead kids directly confirmed. Then again, a coating of truth helped sweeten the poison lie, didn't it? If Simon really was following them, Sander would have to drop any pretense at buying their shit and seize his warehouseman—he could beat the truth out of him, if it came to that.

But then why wait? Giving Braem a final chance to come

clean while they were still alone might save some serious blood-shed, and so Sander said, "Look, you're full of shit and we both know it. I won't fall for it, and—"

"I'm not!" protested Braem, glancing to the mouth of the alley, so close, shining like a slice of moon in the darkness. "Please, listen—"

"No," said Sander, his bile rising at this caitiff's denial in the face of an outright calling of his bullshit. "You listen, Braem—I don't care if that ponce Hobbe put you up to this or if you two set it up yourselves, but if anything's happened to Lijsbet, then you and Simon—"

"Who? Never mind, it's not important, what's important is that we get Simon free—he was never involved, it was all me," said Braem, his cheeks going dark as the shadows, and Sander felt relief flow through him to hear the admission of guilt. Braem's voice rose to a desperate cry as he grabbed Sander's arm and tried to pull him out of the alley. "They *showed* me things, when they caught me, they told me things and *showed* me things, and I still haven't reported in. I knew they were watching her house and I dared not call attention, but we have to stop them, we have to—"

"Shut it," Sander growled, realizing that Braem's shouting must be some signal, that he was muffling the footsteps coming from behind them down the black alley, or from the street ahead. "Shut it, *now*!"

"You don't trust me, that's fair, but you trust Simon, so let's go to him! Now! If you want to protect yourself and Jolanda, Sander—" Sander went cold as the dead at the use of his real name, and Braem froze in mid-sentence, presumably seeing something in Sander's expression that knocked him clean off his bluff. The shoulder of a figure waiting for them at the end of the narrow passage appeared around the corner, then ducked back. The obviousness of the ambush was simply pitiable, but that didn't stop a hot burst of excitement from flooding Sander's heart. *Finally*, a part of him thought, and the rest had to agree as Braem went on, "That's right, I know everything, and so do you, don't you? About what happens when Sander is unmasked for—"

Sander tightened his hand around Braem's fingers and yanked him backward, the traitor's feet slipping on a patch of ice and sending him sprawling onto his back. Sander let go of Braem's hand as soon as the man lost his footing, and before Braem could move or even squeal, Sander raised a foot and stomped his throat. There was a wet cracking noise and ebon liquid ejaculated out of Braem's mouth, then a shrill, high-pitched whine began to rise from his ruined throat. Sander gave him another stomp, relieved he'd left on his heavy boots instead of changing into something dry but lighter, and Braem went quiet.

The assassin, be he Simon or simply some hired thug, must not have heard, for nobody appeared in the mouth of the alley. Perfect. Sander knelt and drew Braem's sword. Sander's sword. He had her now, his pounding heart finally convincing his skeptical mind—it was her. His cold-numb hand instantly warmed at the touch of Glory's End, and a smile crossed Sander's face as he advanced. He should go back the way he'd come, try to lose whoever it was waiting for him out there, but his fury at Simon's betrayal was burning through his arms, his legs—Braem was one thing, that was to be expected, especially since Braem was the older brother and thus had more to gain, just as he'd had more to lose when Sander and Jo usurped the Gruyeres. But to have Simon use Sander in such a craven fashion, to know that the friend for whom he'd made the finest cloak in the land had killed children just to get some dirty groots . . . it would not stand.

Sander leapt out into the street, the point of Glory's End already jabbing at where he had seen the shadowy figure lurking. There was no one there. Looking up and down Wijnstraat, he saw nothing but white snow gusting through black night, the stuff coming down so thickly that what firelight might have come from the upper-story windows failed to reach the cobbles. There were footprints in the powder, however, and he followed them half a block before he heard voices ahead, militiamen singing the same ruddy song they always did on especially cold nights when they didn't want the bother of dealing with troublemakers and preferred to warn them off with their off-key caterwauling rather than risk catching any crooks unawares.

Shit on all the saints. Sander quickly doubled back the way he'd come, but didn't let himself run, staying to the shadows on the southern side of the street. The Graaf Jan Tieselen had fluttered off to roost on some quiet rooftop far above murder and betrayal, and down here in the streets the old Sander did what he did best—he fled, taking a surreptitious route to shake any pursuers. Cutting up 'S Heer Boeijenstraat, he was almost to Grote Markt Square when he heard the squeak of a boot stepping in a snowdrift he'd just passed. Excellent. Never looking over his shoulder, he crossed the empty square, entering the alley to De Waag. As soon as the alley's shadow fell over him, he stepped into an alcove where the wide corner building met its narrower neighbor. He waited there for a good long while, the sweat beginning to freeze in his whiskers and eyelashes, but no pursuer appeared.

Keeping to the wall, he crept the few paces back to the square and peered into the snowy clearing. Nothing but the statue in the snow, and—

Sander's balls shot up into his guts, was how he'd describe the awful, icy sensation that came with his remembering that there wasn't no damn statue in Grote Markt. Some cunt was standing stock-still in the snow, and Sander got the shivers something bad that the figure was staring right at him. Right, time to sort out Simon or whatever goon the Gruyeres had hired to—

But before Sander could step from the mouth of the avenue and confront his pursuer, the man suddenly raised an arm over his head and hopped in place, violently cocking his head to the side as he did. Then he began to shudder, and through the flurries billowing down, Sander could make out teeth flashing wet and white and shiny as the snow between them.

The man was pantomiming being hanged.

That was goddamn *sinister*, was what that was. Sander found himself backing away along the alley wall until he could no longer make out the edge of the square, and then he turned and fled down De Waag, toward the sanctuary of his manse.

A spooky cackle echoing behind Sander might have somehow made it better, would have let him know someone was fucking with him, but the silence that enveloped him as he at last stood panting on his doorstep was like the quiet of being underground. Of being underwater. Giving the street a final glance, he thought he might have seen a silhouette walking down the lane toward him, but he didn't give it a second look, instead banging on the door for the two or three beats it took for Lansloet to flip the peephole open, and then the door. Staggering in and nearly bowling the old servant over, Glory's End still gripped in his trembling hand, Sander kicked the door shut and threw the bolt. He put his frosty brow to the hard wood and closed his eyes, trying to still the painful throbbing in his chest, behind his eyes. Home.

Wait, Lansloet? Where the fuck was Jo? Sander spun around, ready to hew the traitorous servant to the spine, when he saw two figures backlit in the doorway to the parlor. He dropped the sword with a cry. The weapon clattered on the ground, and Lansloet hurried wordlessly back down the hall to the kitchen, from whence the aroma of cooking goose wafted like a pungent belch.

Lizzy was standing beside Jo in the mouth of the parlor, close enough that he could reach out and touch the maid. Both women looked scared, but sure, that might have had something to do with Sander's appearance, for the first words out of Jo's mouth were, "Good God, what's happened?"

Sander just stared at Lizzy, at Jo. This was…good. Very good. Sander laughed, a somewhat maniacal laugh, admittedly, but a laugh nonetheless. When he could speak again, he said, "Nothing. Misunderstanding, was all."

"My lord, I have terrible news," said Lizzy breathlessly, as though she'd been the one harried from pillar to post across a snowy city. This only brought on another laughing fit. Jo was looking frightened for him, Lizzy was looking frightened *of* him. He got himself back under control—what in all the angels' blessings was wrong with him, laughing at a time like this?

"Good to see you, Lizzy," Sander said, trying hard not to look down at his boots to see if he'd tracked Braem's blood inside. No, it would have come off in the snow. It would have, it would, it would, it would.

"It's Simon," said Lizzy. "He was arrested the day you left. They say he's killed two kids. They're going to put him to death."

"Oh," said Sander. "Shit."

III.

The day after Jolanda and Sander returned to Dordrecht, things worsened considerably. Disobeying Sander's orders to remain around the house in case he needed her for "something urgent-like, which, sure, will probably happen soon, so yeah—stay in today," was never a question for Jolanda. Simon might be flaky, but he was a friend, and the Tieselens didn't have a great many of those. Sander should be beside her, marching up the street in ostentatious attire to demand his employee's release, but instead he was lying in yesterday's clothes on the floor of his parlor, too drunk to stand. It was barely noon. Jolanda sighed as the hem of her gown was run over by the wheel of a cart running perilously close to her and the other pedestrians edged over to the side of Voorstraat. Another day she would have had words for the driver, but she was trying like the devil tries to enter a wager to maintain her ladylike equipoise as she approached the old harbor gatehouse where Simon was being held.

God's wounds, was she tired, though. Lijsbet had kept her up chattering in bed, and even after the servant dozed off, Jolanda's mind wouldn't stop turning over what she'd learned. Lijsbet had been distraught to distraction over the state of the cloak Jolanda had given her—the maid apparently came home to find a cat had gotten into the courtyard and mangled a cock, and putting the bird out of his misery resulted in a bloody mess.

Much more troubling than a stained cloak, however, was Lijsbet's guilty admission that she had spent the last several nights with an aunt across town rather than sleeping alone in the Tieselen manse. Jolanda didn't fault her maid for leaving the house unattended, but the question of who had broken in the house persisted. The only possible clue Lijsbet provided was that once or twice she'd seen a handsome, brown-haired man lurking in the alley when she'd come by to check on the house, as she swore she'd done every day. Whoever the intruder might be, he must have trashed the parlor and left his boots the night before Lansloet and Drimmelin returned, for the place had been in normal order when Lijsbet departed for her aunt's apartment that final afternoon.

The thought of someone Jolanda didn't know lurking in her house, eating her food, maybe even sleeping in her bed, was about the eeriest thing she could think of, and didn't exactly help her fall into a restful slumber her first night home. Much as Jolanda tried to push it away, the memory of that figure in the snow staring up at her window kept worrying at her, and several times before dawn she wriggled out of her snoring maid's arms and crept to the cracked window to check the street below.

At least she had a decent theory come morning: Wurfbain had set Simon up to hurt Sander and get them back under his thumb, and the man who had broken into their house was likely Simon's brother, Braem, who was beaver-haired and, if you didn't know what an arsehole he was, handsome enough in the face. Creeper that Braem was, he'd probably been spying on their house for ages, to God knew what end—he must've been the cunt that Jolanda caught staring at the house that night. When Sander, Jolanda, and the servants had left town, he'd seized the opportunity to sneak in and live it up like old times. If Lijsbet only came by once a day, it would've been easy for him to figure out her routine and clear out when she came by . . . or, even more unsettling, hide somewhere in the house while the maid checked in. And all the while his own, decent brother was locked up in a cell, awaiting the gallows. Despicable.

Jolanda intended to go straight to see Simon after getting

dressed, but Sander had rebuffed her at once. That was unexpected. She told him as much, and he started in with his noises about how she needed to stay inside and steer clear of associating with Simon, especially with Wurfbain looking to get back at them for Sander's disobedience. When she'd pointed out that Simon's incarceration and impending execution were certainly the result of Wurfbain's framing the innocent man in order to strike at Sander, the dirty git had just belted back another glass of wine and slurred that nonsense about urgent business needing attending around the house.

So Jolanda had a busy day ahead of her. Visiting Simon and hearing his side of things came first, obviously—Lijsbet knew he'd been arrested, and why, and what would become of him, but nothing beyond the obvious gossip. After that, Jolanda would go to Lady Zoete's house and see if her gentleman caller was in—assuming Wurfbain hadn't run off back to Leyden and was willing to talk, she'd see what sort of bribe or other arrangement it would require to call him off, get him to clear Simon. Sander would be furious if he found out, but then she had no intention of telling him—Jolanda had held private conferences with the count in the past when the matter was important and Sander had proven either incompetent or unwilling.

If that didn't work, Jolanda would have to go to Lady Meyl and tell her everything. Well, not quite everything, but enough to solicit her help. Simon Gruyere was down on his luck now, to say the least, but a few years ago he'd been a respected Cod noble... Hell, now that she thought of it, Jolanda was pretty sure Simon had stayed in the manse of Lady Meyl's son Willem until he and Simon had suffered some falling out, so maybe Jolanda could mend old wounds and solicit Hertog Von Wasser's help, even if his mother wouldn't.

Jolanda almost hoped that Wurfbain wouldn't compromise, now, so that she could put him in his place. She flirted with approaching Lady Meyl and Hertog Von Wasser first, but quickly decided against it. Edifying as it would be to call Wurfbain out, if for some reason the local Cods were reluctant to throw down against the Hook count, then she'd have good and well fucked any chance of then approaching Wurfbain…

All these machinations gave her a headache. She turned down the old harbor channel that exited the city beside the gatehouse, and comforted herself with the one small certainty the day offered: If nothing else, Simon would know where to find his creeper brother. She could hardly wait to lay hands on Braem, though it bore returning home to change out of her noble-lady dress before going to stomp him into gruel, the dirty—

There was a thought. Jolanda stopped walking. Lijsbet had said the bodies of two children were recovered, and Jolanda had assumed that Wurfbain had arranged for it to look like Simon was responsible. That someone had originally murdered two children was not terribly surprising to Jolanda, but what if Wurfbain wasn't even involved? What if Braem, creeper that he surely was, had killed the kids for some twisted reason of his own, only to have his brother be blamed instead of him? Or even worse, what if Simon really was involved, what if the two brothers were murderers?

No, she was certain that regardless of whether Braem or Wurfbain were to blame for the killings, Simon was innocent… but then she had been every bit as sure of Jan's pure intentions, right up until he'd tried to murder her, hadn't she? What was wrong with men? With her, that she kept getting mixed up with people who'd do in a kid the way she'd do in a shellfish? Once Simon was free, or hanged, she'd be better off quitting Dordrecht, quitting her ruse, just taking what coin she could and starting over somewhere, letting her arms fade once and for all, never seeing Sander or Simon or Wurfbain or anybody from here ever again. Better to run away than to look at something awful. If only she hadn't burned the shack in Monster, she could have gone back there, seen if the snails would return to the bay…

It was overcast and cold enough that the morning frost still lingered on the lip of the old harbor canal. They kept the ice in the channel well broken up, though, otherwise the whole city would be trapped—Jolanda looked down to where the gatehouse abutted both town wall and canal, looked past the stubby dock protruding from the building to where the raised iron gate afforded her a clear view of the gray plain of the Maas beyond. Oh, to just follow the canal back to the harbor, hop in the Tieselen boat, and row back down and away, out of the city, out of the flood...

She shook her head. Mooning in the street could wait until she'd cleared up the sundry messes they'd returned to—of all the idiotic developments, to have Simon pinched for killing kids...

Other than the placard bearing the begriffined city crest that hung from the second story and the bars in the windows, the gatehouse could have been any bleak building in Dordrecht. There not being any sort of bell, Jolanda knocked on the dark wood door. It opened on the oldest man she had ever seen; he might have been Lansloet's grandfather.

"Yes, my lady?" he rasped. She had thought his eyes were closed, but apparently not, or maybe the skin had worn thin enough over the years that he could see without cracking them.

"I am here to visit Simon Gruyere," she said, hoping that would suffice. Miraculously, it did.

"This way, m'lady," said the living prune, ushering her in. It was dim, the window barely letting any light at all into the wide room. There were two doors leading off and a ladder dropping from a hole in the ceiling; other than a table, some crates, and shelving cluttered with jars and jugs, the room was barren and dusty as this old guard's pate. If she had known how ill attended the gatehouse was, she might have stormed the place instead—somehow she didn't think this sterling member of the sheephead militia would put up much of a fight.

The old man led her to the second door—the first must open directly onto the dock in the channel, she figured—and swung it open. It wasn't even locked. The hallway beyond was short enough to seem totally pointless, until she nearly kicked over a chamber pot, and then they came to a second door, this one with a heavy bolt on the outside but no actual lock. This was just absurd. "Ho, lad, your lady friend's arrived."

Curious, that, but Jolanda knew better than to pipe up until Simon called through the small barred window set at the top of the door, "My dear, dear lady, when I received word of your impending visit, my heart was buoyed, yes, buoyed upon a—I say, Jolanda?"

"Hey there, Simon," Jolanda said as Simon's mug appeared in the small window. "I'm so sorry we didn't come sooner."

"Dearest Cousin Jo, rest assured that I am innocent! But fear not, for I shall be delivered from this barren cell, this stinking hell!"

"Jolanda. Cousin Jo." The militiaman smacked on the words, as if they were crumbs of stale cheese he was trying to mash up with his gums. "No, there's been a mistake. He's not to see anyone, is the prisoner. Come with me, lady."

"There has been a mistake," said Jolanda, fumbling in her kidskin bag for her purse. "But one we can fix with a groot, I should think. I only need speak with him for a—"

"I won't be bribed," the old man said haughtily. "I'm not some blackguard, some brigand. I'll drag you out, missy, you don't leave now."

"Tell Jan!" Simon called as Jolanda let herself be led back up the hall by the dotard. "They won't let me write to him, and Braem never showed—God forgive him, my own brother must be in league with them! Jan must come here! I must speak with him! I did everything right, but they won't listen! Send Jan!"

"Who was the other lady?" Jolanda called back over the old man's protests that she be away at once. "Who's coming to visit you?"

"If you can believe it, it's—" but the old man shoved Jolanda out of the hallway and slammed the door behind him, muffling the rest.

"*Enough* of that," the guard snarled. He probably thought he looked menacing instead of comedic, the shriveled-up shrew. "Get on out, you, get—don't come back."

There was a moment where the old man's life was a groot spinning through the air, equal odds of cross or crown. In the end it was his age that saved him—if he hadn't been so damned old, she would have at least popped his chin for taking such a tone with her, but the last thing she needed was to accidentally kill a militiaman, and she wasn't going to gamble on the number of punches he could take without collapsing into a heap of dust.

Walking back up the canal toward the harbor, Jolanda chewed her lip. That had been odd, to say the least—what had Simon meant when he said he'd done everything right? And the thing about Braem not showing up, or his being in league with a mysterious *them*? And who was Simon's impending visitor, the lady the old guard had initially mistaken Jolanda for?

Lijsbet had known Simon was arrested, but said she hadn't been to see him. That left all the women in Dordt, and to hear him boast, Simon was popular enough with noble ladies and common girls alike. Some clue, that was... what woman might fit into Jolanda's theory that Wurfbain had framed Simon?

Lady Zoete. That made sense—Wurfbain wouldn't want to visit Simon himself, he'd send someone else, like his mistress. But to what end? To make Simon an offer, to get him to point the finger at Sander—we'll let you out if you say it was Graaf Tieselen who did it, not you. That made some kind of sense... made even more sense, come to it, than just framing Simon to annoy Sander. Except Simon wasn't going along with it, Simon was loyal to the end, Simon—

"Excuse me!" The man she'd bumped into raised his palms as he danced around her. "Mind your step, girl. Carefully."

"Sorry," said Jolanda as the man hurried along his way, but

she hadn't taken three steps when her knees turned to aspic. She was suddenly shaking so badly she couldn't walk, and dropped to a crouch in the middle of the street. Too scared to breathe, she looked back over her shoulder, but the man was already gone. If he had even been there at all, she told herself, which of course he hadn't. He couldn't. He wasn't, simple as that.

Jolanda forced a laugh, but knew better than to try to stand immediately. Just for a moment, she'd thought the man she'd run into was, well, Jan. And not Sander, whom she called Jan, obviously, but the real Jan, the one she'd...the one who...Jan. Dead Jan, back from the swamp, smiling even as he scolded her for bumping into him.

Ridiculous. She wasn't Sander, to be acting the loon like this. Jolanda stood up, wiped sweat from her face with an equally damp sleeve. Jan was dead, and not a little dead, but butchered, chopped to pieces, food for eels for going on three years...

All thought of paying Wurfbain or Lady Meyl and Von Wasser a call forgotten, Jolanda hurried back toward Voorstraat, doing all she could to keep certain thoughts, certain memories, way down in the deep where they belonged. Dreaming while she was awake, was all, like Sander had said. She kept glancing over her shoulder, making sure she wasn't being followed, making sure he wasn't there, but aye, of course he wasn't, he was back in Oudeland, another skeleton at his father's table, another—

"Shut it," she muttered to herself. "Shut it, shut it. Shut. It."

But of course she couldn't. Memories of Oudeland assailed her, memories of how she had come to find the ring that had been the source of so much trouble, of what she had seen when she had taken that final dive into the flooded manse, when she had swam through the kitchen door and saw what lay beyond. She had told herself often enough that was all it had been, a dream, even with the ring she had taken away from it, and Sander's telling her about how you could dream when awake had made it even softer to sleep on, that thought...but that was before she bumped into a ghost in broad daylight—it was happening again, obviously, this dreaming-when-awake business.

The memory of the hooded figure watching her window from the snowy street came to the surface as she reached Voorstraat, and she broke into a trot, slipping over the icy cobbles but staying upright. That hadn't been a dream, not a waking one nor the regular kind, and gazing back through the haze of her mind to that night, she saw the silhouetted features of Jan beneath the hood, the snowlight flashing on his handsome, upturned face. If there was a comfort to be had in knowing you were mad, Jolanda could not see it.

Taking the stoop in a bound, green velvet gown flapping like a sail in a squall, the Lady Tieselen fled inside her house and did not emerge again that day. When Lijsbet came to her bedroom after supper, Jolanda let her maid under the covers but pretended to be asleep, not trusting herself to keep it together if she started talking. Better to push it all down, let it sink under, the way she was sinking into the pallet as Lijsbet droned on and on. The maid sounded like the fisherboys shouting at Jolanda as she swam from them, voices garbled by water and waves, and then the surface closed over her, the tide spinning her 'round and 'round until she settled facing the bottom, everything dim and cool.

She found her brother Pieter down there. She had no idea how he might look now, or even what he had looked like when he'd left home so very long ago, but it was surely he. It should have been a good dream, then, for she missed him even down all these days, but it wasn't.

He was in the dining room from her other dream, the waking one she had suffered in the flooded Oudeland manse. They had candles burning down there in the meer, the table set with putrid food, the poses of the seated corpses so identical to how real nobles sat at supper that when she'd first attended one in Wurfbain's Leyden manor, she had nearly fainted from the shock of it, the vision from the sunken house somehow forgotten until that very moment. Count Wurfbain and Lady Zoete had turned to acknowledge her and Sander when they'd joined the table, but thankfully the drowned Tieselens had done no such thing when she swam through the kitchen door and saw them arrayed at their board. She'd already found the one corpse in the kitchen, but seeing all these dead folk sitting there as if the flood had never happened would have been bad enough even without the eels.

The drowned graaf and his family had worn them in place of clothing. It was nauseating, seeing the swarming black ribbons coiling around one another and the bones of the Tieselens to make doublets and gowns and even feathers in hats and hairpins for veils. She had known then that she was dreaming despite being awake, and so hesitated in the doorway for only a moment before swimming to the table, and the man who sat at its head.

A beard of eels curling down through his jawbone, a glint of metal on the finger of the hand that rested around the stem of a black goblet. Floating over the table, she saw the wine that filled it was a mass of tiny red eels, and she nervously expected them to explode from the glass as she wrested his skeletal hand free. Instead she knocked the goblet over and the thin coils of the elvers spread across the tabletop like liquid, running in rivulets that only broke the illusion of wine when they reached the edge of the table and ran off it in long threads rather than individual drops.

There was the ring, cold and heavy in her palm, and as soon as it was there, the shadow of the great catfish passed over the open window. Jan must have swum through that very window on his first attempt to find the ring, when it was still too muddled with silt to see his family as he passed them, blindly seeking access to the second floor and the bedroom where he believed the ring to be. So close, Jan! In this dream Jan did swim past her, then, into the kitchen, and she made for the window just as she had on that day when he had tried to murder her, when she had found what Sander was made of.

She went to pop the ring into her mouth, to better swim with open palms and keep the prize tucked beneath her tongue until the catfish would spook her into swallowing it. As she raised her hand to her lips, however, she felt not the metal band but something cold and slimy squirming in her fist. Try as she did to keep it trapped, the young eel wriggled between her fingers. She chased it, but then Pieter was there, rearing up from the murk just as the catfish had, and the elver-ring swam directly into his needle-ridged maw. She twisted away, through the water and the nightmare and the memories, but could not awake, much as she wanted to. As in life, so in dreams.

IV.

If I think of anything else, like, I'll look you up," said Sander as the sheriff in charge of the city militia offered him a bow on the stoop. The sheriff was just how Sander always pictured sheriffs when he heard the word—big, cow-faced plaguebitch with a mustache like a woolly caterpillar and a squint you couldn't slide a sheaf of vellum through. Lansloet stood at the ready to close the door, as though this were some welcome guest being shown out and not a rat-eyed chiseler working an angle.

The sheriff said something about that being very good and all as he left. As soon as Lansloet had the door closed, Sander let out a bottled breath in the servant's face, the vintage of which must have been impressive indeed, for the normally unflappable Lansloet coughed into his spindly fist. It was the second morning after Sander had slain Braem—the day after the dirty deed, Graaf Tieselen had not left his manse, but now Sander was itching to be away from the oppressively cramped quarters.

"Who saw Simon with the kids?" Jo met him in the hallway, but Sander pushed past her.

"Shouldn't eavesdrop," he muttered. "Some sheephead fishermen, nobody we know."

"Wurfbain's friends, I don't doubt, and how does that prove anything?" Jo said, following him. "So what if some fishers saw him with 'em while they were alive? Simon's a creeper, no question, but he's no killer!"

"No," said Sander. "He's not."

Sander hadn't tried to hide Braem's body or anything, yet the sheriff had only brought news of Simon's impending execution, with no mention of the condemned man's brother having been found murdered in the street. Why not? No man could walk off a stomped stump, no way, no how, and the odds of nobody noticing a dead man in the mouth of an alley after two nights and a full day between them seemed pushing reason harder than a man had to push to pass piss through a morning cockstand. No, the militia must have found the dead Braem and suspected Sander, but not having enough to go on, were trying to trick him into letting something slip to the sheriff.

"Let's go and see him," said Jo. "They'll let you into his cell, they have to!"

"Nay, going to see Primm," said Sander, the commission he'd ordered from the fat man suddenly seeming like a vital addition to the household instead of a fun toy he could pick up any old time. He tried very hard to avoid thinking of how Simon had helped him pick out the wood for that particular arbalest. Much as he wanted to visit the incarcerated Gruyere, how would it look for him to associate with a reviled, doomed child-killer, especially with Hobbe like as not looking for a means of discrediting the Tieselens? According to the sheriff, there was no question as to Simon's guilt—a boatload of fishermen had detoured by the Tieselen warehouse to see about buying a cask, only to discover Simon up to his knees in the mudflat, a headless boy half-buried before him.

Poor cunt was doubtless trying to retrieve the body to turn it over to the militia, but luck of the luckless, got rumbled midway through—where had Braem been during all that? Sander had told Simon before the brothers had dropped everyone off at the Rotterdam harbor to pretend to find the body only when Braem was with him, so he'd have someone to back him up if the militia tried to pin the crime on him...little late to ask Braem now, Sander thought ruefully, and what could he himself do for Simon?

Bust him out, a part of Sander suggested, spring the fool…
but Sander throttled the thought. Simon had brought this on
himself by being an impatient fusspot, and so he'd have to stew
in his cell until Sander thought of a way of freeing the idiot that
didn't involve jeopardizing both himself and Jo. They were far
too vulnerable to try anything rash to save Simon before Sander
could figure out what exactly Hobbe was plotting. Then there
was the question of what exactly Simon had told the militia since
his arrest, what he might say if prompted…

"You going to let me tag along, or am I confined to the house
again?"

"Nobody confined you," said Sander, having wandered back
through the kitchen to the dining room, where his interrupted
breakfast awaited.

"I did as you told and stayed inside yesterday," said the girl,
looking a touch more sheepish than usual for some stupid reason. She'd been acting strange ever since they got back to Dordt,
and hadn't said a word at supper the night before. Odd, but now
she seemed back to her annoying old ways, or close enough.
"What's going on? You think I'm too thick to see how queer
things are?"

Sander had hoped she was that thick, but that was the problem with the little bitch, too clever where it inconvenienced him
and too dull when he needed her sharp. If she'd been smarter,
she would have cottoned on to Sander faster, forced him to talk
sooner. Now that she had called him out, how much to tell her?
Not about Braem, definitely not that, but maybe something…

"Get your shit on," he said, looking down at the hard bread
and harder cheese on his plate. Everything might be totally
fucked, they might have to be out of the city by nightfall. The
uncertain situation with Hobbe was one thing, but now that
Simon was nabbed and might well finger Sander as an accomplice if a certain count leaned on him heavy enough… Then
there was Sander's actually having murdered someone in the

city, and the militia staying mum on it... You didn't need to be as quick on your toes as Sander was to see it might be time to cut their losses. "Wear your armor. Big cloak, something with a deep hood."

"We're going to see Simon before coming back here," said Jo as she turned to leave. "You don't have a choice on that."

"We'll talk about it when we're out," was the biggest bone he was willing to throw her, but it was enough to get her moving.

Sander sat back down at the table, dunked the bread into his wine, and sucked on the ruddy rye. If they were to just make a break for it, this very day, how much could they pack up without being obvious? He'd stop by Laurent's office, see if that scoundrel would still work for him, even after Sander's severing ties with Hobbe. If anyone knew a good way of transforming weighty metal wealth into the sort of words on vellum that Sander could trade for coin somewhere else, it was Laurent. Of course Hobbe wouldn't stand for Sander's maintaining the part of noble after their falling out, of course Sander had put himself in a precarious position by bumping Braem, but there might still be time, there might...

But what if the situation with Braem was different than how Sander had initially seen it? Braem had said spies were everywhere, that Sander shouldn't be seen with him, and even to the end Braem had been a Cod loyalist, whereas Hobbe was as Hook as they came... What if the spies Braem had feared were Hobbe's? If the count caught wind of Braem's murder, would it restore his faith that Sander was a better Hook than a Cod, that he might still be useful? Or at least convince him that Sander could now be blackmailed if necessary? Not like Hobbe had a lot of better options, one of the two legitimate heirs to the Tieselen wine importation business being dead and the other condemned to the same, and so if he got rid of Sander now, he was as good as out of Dordt politics... might be worth trying to patch things up with Hobbe, rather than just abandoning a king's ransom on account of the Old Sander rising to the surface, making Graaf Tieselen nervous...

And what about Hertog Von Wasser? He was a powerful man if ever there was one—should Sander risk turning to him for help with clearing Simon's name and combating Hobbe's schemes? Or would that be even worse, exposing his weaknesses to a man who had, up until a fortnight ago, wished nothing but the very worst for the Tieselen family?

Then there remained the question of who was watching Sander from the Grote Markt the night of Braem's murder. Gilles had done a similar impression of being hanged when they'd first met at the White Horse, and so he came to mind first. Even if the Frenchman hadn't pissed off back to grapetown like he'd claimed, though, he was a sight stockier than this cunt had been. A wee bastard could bulk himself up with extra clothes and all, sure, but Sander had never heard of a trick that let a big man look markedly smaller.

What about Hobbe, then? One of his men? It hadn't been Simon, that much was sure—Braem had been honest about his brother being locked up...What else might the deceased Gruyere have been telling the truth about?

Being so confused made Sander want to puke. He closed his eyes, trying to find a loose end amongst the knotted possibilities in order to start unraveling the scheme, to find out if he was part of the hunting party this time or if he was the quarry—at present he was doing a merry jig on the safe side of the gibbet, but it was his fault Simon would be fitted for a hemp necklace before very long, and who knew, he might soon be joining the Gruyere in doing a different sort of gallows dance. Again his thoughts turned to somehow busting Simon out...

"Are you neuking kidding me?" said Jo, and blinking at her, he saw she was ready to go, her conspicuous brigandine attire smothered under a hooded canvas cloak—one of his old jobs, if he wasn't mistaken.

"Nay, I was just…won't be a tic," and Sander was out of his chair and up the stairs, telling himself nothing was fucked, everything was good, he had friends now, Von Wasser and the other Cods he'd met at Brouwershaven, and the old broad Jo had dined with…

Or if not friends, people who found him and Jo useful.

Or who *might* find them useful…

The cold truth was that Sander was out of his depth and needed help, and between his choice of Hobbe or a Cod, he'd take the Cod. His odds weren't much better with Von Wasser, maybe, but at least this way he'd have a decent shot at fucking Hobbe over even if he doomed himself in the process.

Pick up the commission from Primm, then head straight to Willem's manor, which was somewhere along the harbor. So yeah, go to Von Wasser, offer Willem the exquisite new crossbow as a sort of princely friend-making gift—much as it would pain Sander to give the weapon away without having used it—and then tell the hertog how Count Hobbe Wurfbain was out to get him, that the dirty, lying Hook would do anything to get at the Tieselens…Now, *that* was a plan!

The streets were shallow canals from the snowmelt, and the sun had brought out crowds of women and children tired of being cooped up by a winter that couldn't make up its mind whether it wished to be brutal or mild. As a result, Sander had to abandon any hope of staying on the edges of the roads where he might keep his boots dry and instead plowed through the wet, dragging Jo along after him. She was nattering about the importance of visiting Simon immediately, but he was too busy keeping an eye on the faces drifting past them, all of which looked vaguely familiar. That one there was definitely a graafling made destitute from the flood, just as the Gruyeres had been, and had he been eyeing Sander a little too long? Was he the one from the square? Had his family been Hook or Cod before the flood?

And why were there so many more cats out than usual? A

clowder of the mangy strays crept along curbs and atop walls behind them... Sander must be losing his shit, because if put on the spot by a bishop, he'd admit to suspecting that *they* were watching him as well. That was just crazy... wasn't it?

"*Sander*," Jo hissed. "We're here."

"Huh?" Looking up, Sander saw they'd almost passed Poorter's door. Glad to be out of the watery streets with all their potential assassins and spies, strange human and stranger feline, Sander hot-footed it up the stairs and banged on the door. Silence. Sander knocked again, and finally came the sound of bolts being slid back.

"What?" The door had opened barely a crack, Poorter clearly aiming to keep them out. Fuck that.

"Here to get that piece you're making me," said Sander, trying to keep the edge out of his voice. "Thought we might have a blather while we're here."

"I'm sorry, Graaf Tieselen," said Poorter. "The commission isn't ready, and at present I find myself—"

"Come on, cunt," said Sander, his smile positively stinging now from the effort as he put his hand on the side of the door. "I'm not going to—"

"*Later*," Poorter whined. "Please, I...I've got a woman here and—"

"Ah, I getcha," said Sander, pretending to be put at ease by this and taking his hand off the door. A cloud had passed over the sun, and he was able to make out Poorter a bit better through the gap between wall and door. Unless he was mistaken... "Got something on your nose, old boy."

Yes. Instead of lifting his right hand, which was definitely bandaged, Poorter took his left off the inside of the door to gingerly touch his face. As soon as he did, Sander threw himself into the door, not giving a pike's tooth if anyone in the street saw him forcing his way inside. Poorter was neatly knocked back and then Jo was right there, closing the door after them as they slid inside fast as good luck slipping through your fingers.

Poorter lay on his back, bleating like a birthing sheep, and between his bruised, swollen face and cloth-wrapped hand Sander supposed he wasn't putting on a show for once. Jo locked the door behind them as Sander bounded over the prone artisan and ran to the kitchen. He hadn't forgotten his sword this time, and not that piece of shit he'd taken off Braem—that one had gone straight out his bedroom window and into the canal—but his real girl, Glory's End herself, honed and hard for him. How she'd gotten from the Oudeland bog to his bedside scabbard warranted no scrutiny—she always found her way to him when he needed her.

The kitchen was empty, as was the closet privy, and Sander went from window to window to make sure no one was in the chink of a yard between Poorter's place and the neighbor's. When he got back into the workroom, Poorter was up on a stool, talking to Jo.

"—comes around occasionally, but never close enough for me to grab her," Poorter was saying. A tremor passed from ears to asshole, Sander suddenly wondering if they were in on something together, Jo and Poorter, but then he realized they were talking about that damn Muscovite cat they'd brought back from the meer. Hobbe had forbidden them from taking the creature with them to his estate in Leyden, and though Poorter had offered to mind her until they returned to take their somewhat-less-than-rightful place in the Tieselen house, he had let the cat out while they were in the country. The cat was long gone now, but Poorter always fed Jo the same line about it showing up for food from time to time.

"Why you think she wants to be grabbed?" said Jo, though Sander remembered her telling the big man to do just that on numerous occasions—if she'd finally come to terms with the murdered Muscovite's cat being lost to her, then so much the better. Or maybe the puss was one of the beasts following them in the street? Would the cat appreciate Sander's bringing her back from the swamp-sea, or would she resent his killing of her former master, back when the Muscovite had hit Jan with an oar? Had this drowned world gone so mad that on top of corrupt counts and conspiracies Sander now had to fear revenge-minded tabbies? "Just put out the leftovers and leave her alone."

"Of course, Lady Tieselen," said Poorter, rolling his blood-shot eyes.

"Who did it?" said Sander, and before the fatty-tats could start in with his lies, Sander slapped him hard in the face, sur-prising him so much Poorter didn't even think to fall off his stool in exaggerated pain. "Who roughed you up, cunt, and why? It's got something to do with us or you wouldn't be acting so fucking goofy, would you? Who did it?"

"It's got nothing to do with—" Poorter began, and this time he did fly from his seat as Sander backhanded him. Poorter may have actually landed on his hurt arm, it was hard to tell if his screech was manufactured or not.

"I'm not of a mood, Primm," growled Sander. "I'm a mad-man, as you well know, and if you don't spit, I'll stomp the pud-ding out of you!"

"Who did it, Primm!?" shouted Jo, following Sander's lead and getting in the fallen fat man's face. "Who?!"

Glaring up at them, Poorter looked anything but intimidated. He looked, well, pissed. "Friends of yours, apparently, you god-damn frauds! Stern helpers of Count Wurfbain, making sure I wasn't approached by any Cods curious about your credentials, and that I knew what to tell them if I am in the future!"

That…that made a kind of sense—Hobbe wouldn't want it getting out that he had knowingly installed two impostors, and Poorter was another loose end in that regard. That Hobbe hadn't ordered his bullyboys to kill Poorter outright boded well for everyone's prospects, Sander figured. Before he could weigh it further, though, Jo had snatched a gorgeous, cherry-butted crossbow off the table and brought it down with both hands onto the edge of a workbench. The delicately curved lath was smashed and unmoored, its whipcord string snapping across the room, splinters exploding into the air, and Sander and Poorter both stared at Jo in mute horror. Though her hands must be agonized by the reverberations, she held tight to the battered weapon, and, straightening up, hurled it into the wall. Sander flinched as it connected, the stock cracking like thunder.

"What?" said Jo, meeting Sander's eyes. "He's lying. Gonna play us, he's gonna get punished."

"My commission," Sander said quietly, kneeling to pick up the remains of the bow from where it had landed beside the bench. It was just as he'd imagined it; no, better. Pass a bolt clean through a rat, feathers and all. Poorter sat up on the floor and all three of them appraised the broken weapon in silence.

"Oh," said Jo. "I'm . . . I'm going to check the loft."

"Sure. Said he had a woman in here," said Sander, straightening back up and pointing the broken bow at Poorter. "Wouldn't be lying to his friends, would Poorter Primm?"

"I told you—" began Poorter, but Sander cut him off with a snap of the lath across the shoulder.

"And I told you to tell me who did it, fat man," said Sander. "I'm good and mad now, so I'd talk fast, I were you."

Poorter wouldn't talk. Or rather, he did, but he talked too much for it to be honest, giving them too many details, too many names, things they'd have to investigate before being sure if he was lying. If his information didn't check out and they needed to come back, good luck getting Poorter to open his door again. Then there was the matter of the open window in the loft, which Poorter claimed was for fresh air, and the two mugs on the kitchen counter that Jo noticed after poking around the rest of the house, which he chalked up to good old-fashioned slovenliness. Still Poorter stuck to his story of Hook thugs making sure he stayed straight, or at least dependably crooked.

Except why would Hobbe think Poorter was a potential liability? At this point, nigh on two years recognized as noble, the only way anyone was going to start investigating whether or not Sander and Jo were legitimate was if Hobbe himself called their legitimacy into question. So why lean on Poorter, give the crossbow-maker the heads-up that people were going to be asking questions about Sander, and order him to keep up the lie? Wouldn't Hobbe need witnesses willing to confess to the deception, rather than loyal conspirators to the fraud?

One thing Sander had to come to terms with, he knew, was never figuring out half of what Hobbe was scheming—the count was too damn fox-pated. Poorter, on the other hand, was not, so focus on him. The only two options here were that Poorter was lying about who beat him, and why, or he was telling the truth. If he wasn't lying, fine and good, and damn Jo to the Belgians for ruining that cherrywood rat-sticker, but if Poorter was playing them, that meant someone had more than beat him blue, they'd put the fear of the Lord into him—why else act so shady about it, and why else risk the wrath of him and Jo, known nutters? Yeah, that was the worry—someone had scared Poorter so bad he wouldn't squeal even when his precious workshop was in danger, Jo wrecking a couple more pieces before Sander called her off. Poorter had either cracked at the start of their interrogation or else he never would.

After visiting Poorter, Sander decided to wait until he'd had a proper think before paying Von Wasser a call, and, yeah, Simon, too—he was starting to feel like a massive shit for not going to his friend sooner, consequences be dry-fucked. Before visiting anyone, though, he took Jo down to the market at Scheffersplein for poffertjes, a few enterprising sorts having set up stalls in what amounted to one big, slippery, witch-titted-cold puddle. Jo kept apologizing about the commissioned crossbow, but he wasn't listening, instead scanning the crowd for shadows they might have acquired as he chewed on dough and powdered sugar. Problem was, the sun was bright enough that folk were using their hoods to keep the glare out instead of the wet, and so there was an abundance of suspects. He was starting to lose himself. Again.

"Sander," said Jo, and the queerness of her using his real name got his attention. He was about to bawl her out when he saw how ashen she'd gone, sweat-browed and shaking. "Can I go home?"

"Yeah," he said, wiping crumbs from his mouth, "something wrong?"

"Sick," she said, her eyes darting over the crowd like a hungry wasp. "Please?"

She didn't look well, and he reckoned she must have had too much wine the night before, goofing off with Lizzy. It happened, wake up fine, and an hour later—

Jo threw up all over their shoes. Shit. She squatted down, the flow of people around them giving her a slightly wider berth as she retched. Sander sighed, hating these sorts of situations more than he could bear—just what they needed, attracting attention, and fucking great, here was some nosy biddy getting involved.

"She's fine," said Sander, putting himself between Jo and the old woman, who gave Sander the stink-eye as she stepped around them and ordered her poffertjes. Real nice, sick girl puking up her all and this whore not even checking to see if she was all right before stuffing her own gob. Sander hated this place, wanted to see it burn, but just as he was about to tell the old woman off, Jo had staggered upright and tugged on his sleeve.

She seemed to improve after he got her out of the square, the shade of Groenmarkt refreshing after the blinding sunlight shining off wet cobbles. Things were looking up now that they were out of the crowd. Then, only a few houses down the lane, Sander glanced over his shoulder and saw they were being followed by that same cunting hooded figure from the other night.

Except it was the middle of the damn day, and a nice one at that, so they weren't being followed, it was just some bloke walking the same street as them. Not a crime, that. Except what if he wasn't some random sheephead?

"Shit," Sander muttered, his foot sinking in a pothole and saturating his boot with ice water. This was just what they needed—all his old suspicions coming back, and with a vengeance. People couldn't walk the street now without Sander's thinking they were after him?

"Sander," Jo said, her voice scratchy from the puking. "I didn't listen to you."

Some surprise, that, but what in particular? "How's that?"

"I went out yesterday, tried to see Simon." She looked as though she might spew again at any moment. "After, I started doing it again. I'm going mad."

"No, you're not," said Sander, trying not to lose his temper with her. Do that, and he'd never get the truth out of her. "You went to see Simon, then what?"

"I'm doing it now," Jo gagged, as if the words were noxious. "Happened after I saw Simon, and it's happening now. Dreaming while I'm awake."

Brisker than the wet boot, that. He tried to steer her along faster, taking them to where an alley ran over to Buddingh' Plein—it was the opposite of the way home, but if they were being followed he wanted to throw whoever was after them. The only time she'd claimed to see something that wasn't real was in regards to a creeper outside her window, but what he hadn't told her then and wouldn't now was that he didn't think she'd been dreaming, awake or otherwise; he'd just told her that to put her at ease. What the hell had she seen here, and yesterday, apparently, to put her in this state? What was wrong with her? Was the madness he had suffered after escaping Sneek returned, and catching?

"Seeing things that ought not to be there, you mean?" said Sander, tugging her into the alley and quickening their pace as they wove around heaps of filth and debris. Militia ought to stave in some heads, goddamn peasants cluttering up the thoroughfare with stinking sacks of garbage and piles of broken roofing and all. "It'll pass, Jo, it will, just lean on me and don't let it get to you. Pretty normal, when you're sick."

"Thank God..." she said, her voice so small they near-drowned it completely with their splashing through the snow-melt. Maybe not just theirs, but he wouldn't look, he weren't so green as that. Another alley T-boned this one, cutting between two dilapidated houses, and Sander took it, dragging her after him.

"Dead quiet, Jo," he whispered, pushing her forward and flattening himself against a wall. "This goes queer, you run home and..."

And what? If something happened to him, what was she supposed to do? Hobbe had talked a lot about marrying her off, but she hadn't wanted that, so Sander had never pushed it. Should have, maybe. Would Hobbe try to get rid of her once Sander was gone? Could he afford not to? Jo was harder than Sander was, no way she'd do Hobbe's bidding, the little idiot...

Someone was coming quick now, splashing along, back the way they'd come. Not trying to be quiet, trying to catch up. Glory's End called to him, but it was too late to get her out without making noise or maybe flapping his elbow 'round the corner, spoiling the ambush—shouldn't have been worrying about the girl at a time like this. Come to that, he shouldn't have gotten fat, gotten sloppy, gotten old. Right, and the sun shouldn't rise on a cloudy day for fear of getting rained on. The wet footsteps didn't slow as they reached the corner, and Sander sprang.

His eyes were at the man's chest and shoulders, seeing where his arms were, seeing what he was holding. Nothing in the left, but a dagger in the right, tucked half-under his cloak. That was good. Meant Sander had his man, all right, didn't have to go easy. Of course, it would've been better if the cunt had been holding a sword—harder to get stuck with a sword this close up, but beggar's choices and all. Sander's right hand was on the man's wrist even as the dagger was coming up. Got you, Sander thought, *got you*. Crushing the knife arm into the man's chest,

Sander rabbit-punched the back of his hand. The man dropped the dagger. Perfect.

Jo screamed. Shit. Should've known there would be more, but checking on her would mean looking away from the cunt he was currently driving into the alley wall with all his strength. He had the one hand pinned to the man's chest and felt a sudden chill at not knowing what the other was doing, but then it was punching at Sander's stomach and he relaxed—punch away, little man, so long as there weren't nothing sharp to go with it. Just as he slammed the thug into the side of the building, Sander finally got ahold of the asshole's other wrist, arresting his weak blows. The same thug who'd followed them from the poffertjes stall, like as not, and Sander reared his head back to butt this bastard into nightmareland. Before he could slam his forehead into the bridge of the goon's nose, however, Sander caught sight of brown hair, brown eyes, and stumbled back, wringing his hands like a man realizing the rope he'd just picked up was actually a live snake.

Behind him Jo had stopped screaming, her breath coming in stuttering gasps, and Sander bumped into her as he backed away from the handsome man. Sander pushed her down the alley without turning, trying to find something to say. The man pulled his hood the rest of the way off as he advanced on them, rubbing the back of his head where it had connected with the wall.

"Good to see you, too," said Jan, smiling at them from the shadows of the alley.

"Run," Sander finally managed, spinning away from the ghost or devil or whatever blighted thing had crawled from their past to torment them. Jo couldn't look away from the phantom, and Sander scooped her up as he broke into a run. She weighed hardly anything—certainly less than guilt.

"See you soon!" the specter called after them as they flew from the dim alley into the blinding sunlight. "Soon!"

V.

This must be how Sander felt all the time, Jolanda thought as they both pretended to have an appetite at supper. Or how he used to feel, anyway—ever since becoming graaf, he'd seemed progressively saner. When she'd seen Jan watching her from the crowd in the square that morning, the effect had been immediate, visceral—she was frankly surprised she hadn't pissed herself, but now, hours later, it wasn't any better. No, it was worse, much worse, she and Sander occasionally darting glances at one another over their herring, only to pretend they hadn't made eye contact. Even Lansloet and Drimmelin seemed concerned by the strangeness of their behavior.

They had hid in the Great Church, which was perpetually under construction, until a carpenter ran them off, whereupon Sander had led them on a frantic race to the harbor. When they'd set out that morning he'd brought only enough coin for their poffertjes, however, and their own small rowboat was currently engaged in ferrying out to the warehouse the man Laurent, in Sander's absence, had hired to replace the incarcerated Simon.

After Sander nearly assaulted the third boatman who laughed at his offer of a promissory note in lieu of money, Jolanda finally convinced him to go home. He'd insisted they only run in to get money for the crossing, but once they were inside, he showed no interest in leaving—perhaps it was his returned suit of plate that convinced him to stay, Von Wasser having had it delivered while Jolanda and Sander were paying Primm a visit. Sander suited up right there in the parlor, and the weight of it seemed to somewhat squash his panic. He sat down in front of the fireplace with his sword across his knees, a bottle in one hand and a poker in the other.

Lijsbet was out, having asked and received permission to baby-sit her nephews that evening, and without anyone to confide in even if she'd been of a mind to, Jolanda retreated to her bedroom. Rather than hiding under her covers, as she had fully intended when running up the stairs, she paced the small room, fingers unfurling and curling faster than her eye could follow. They had both seen Jan—that couldn't have been a dream... Could it? You couldn't share a waking dream any more than you could the regular kind... Could you? Jan, stalking them through the streets of Dordrecht, showing up just after everything soured with Wurfbain, just after Simon was accused of murder...

She tried to make sense of it all, but each time she seemed on the cusp of revelation, the memory of Jan's mangled corpse lying in the bottom of a rowboat rose up to distract her with its horrific certainty—no man could recover from such wounds. If it were possible that he could, then anything could happen, even the other things she'd seen in the flooded Tieselen house, things she had rejected so thoroughly as to put them entirely from her mind, except for the odd nightmare. There was a reason she hadn't been able to bring herself to eat eel since that fateful day...

Eventually both nervous nobles relented to Lansloet's quiet insistence that they come to supper, though Sander wouldn't take off his armor, and Jolanda put on hers before joining him. Her embroidered suit of brigandine and plain leather might not look as impressive as his plate and chain, but it was a hell of a lot more comfortable at the high table.

"An impostor," Sander finally said. She nodded enthusiastically. "A con, is what it is. Someone trying to... chisel something."

"Wurfbain's doing," Jolanda suggested. "He knew Jan from before, didn't he? And he'd know how we'd react to seeing him again."

"Of course Hobbe did it, of course," Sander nodded so vigorously his visor slipped down and he had to knock it back up. It was the first time she'd seen him actually wear the ridiculous helmet that went with his armor. "Who else, though?"

"Primm?" Jolanda suggested. "He was worried, too worried, when we talked. He's hiding something."

"Maybe, sure, but I meant who is... the impostor?"

"Braem Gruyere?" She took another long guzzle of wine—it wasn't doing her anxious stomach any favors, but was taking some of the mystery out of Jan's reappearance. It hadn't been him. It *couldn't* be. "He's got brown hair and eyes, like Jan, and is pretty enough. And he's got a reason to help, wanting his house back. That's it! Wurfbain got some actors or someone to make Braem up, disguise him somehow, make him look—"

"Braem's dead," said Sander, not looking so lively himself.

"What?" Jolanda put her glass down, wondering just what else this stupid shitbird had been keeping from her. "When? What—"

"Other night, I went out. Seen him outside the White Horse. Ever notice every town has one? Place with that name, I mean. Easy to draw on a board, I guess." Sander was staring at nothing, and Jolanda realized he wasn't calm so much as totally out of his head on fear and drink.

"And what happened to Braem?" she prompted when he didn't go on, instead idly picking the pale flesh from his fish and dropping it into a flaky pile beside his plate.

"Tried to lead me into a trap. Said spies were after him. Hooks. Said there was a plot. That he'd been in on it, but decided to get out." Sander blinked, shook his head, and drained his cup.

"And then he was killed? Simon said something about Braem never showing, he must have been planning to help, but somebody killed him before he—"

"No. Aye. I mean, I. *I* killed him. Braem. He was leading me into a trap, so I took him out."

"What?!" Jolanda couldn't believe it—despite her counsel to stay clear of the Gruyeres, Sander and Simon had been fast friends following a run-in at the White Horse one night after Sander became graaf. Sander had never warmed to Braem, admittedly, but the idea that he would do in the brother of one of his only friends, and be so nonchalant about it…but then he hadn't done anything to help free Simon, had he? And Sander had been much closer to Jan than he ever was to Braem, and that hadn't stopped him from murdering Jan…Jan, who had come back…Jolanda felt dizzy, and like a desperate fish trying to escape a weir trap by wriggling deeper into it, she sipped more wine. It looked like blood.

"—off his head." Sander had removed his helm and was looking away from her, barely speaking above a whisper. "So I stomped 'em. Other cunt got away. And now he's trying to scare us. Wurfbain knows what we did, who we are, and he found someone who looks like Jan. Simple."

"Simple," Jolanda said numbly, and in the quiet that followed this agreement they clearly heard the groan of the front door swinging open. They waited, neither moving, both listening. Feet padded across creaky wood, then went silent at the worn hallway carpet, and resumed their soft footfalls across the tile. Lansloet appeared from the kitchen, and he looked even less happy than he had about serving his masters in full armor.

"A Sander Himbrecht to see you," said the servant, as though it were the sort of thing you could just say like it was no big deal. Jolanda looked desperately at Sander, who looked into his empty mug, frowning. "Sir?"

"What the devil, man?!" Sander exploded, hurling the cup against the panels that cordoned off the parlor. "Send him in! He's always welcome here, isn't he?! We don't keep old friends waiting!"

Lansloet narrowed his eyes and nodded, then turned and was away. Sander's face had gone the color of his wine, and he was sweating onto his plate. Jolanda wanted to excuse herself, wanted to flee, wanted to at least ask Sander what she should do when the ghost—*no*, she firmly corrected herself, the imposter, when the imposter joined them, for who else could it be? She suddenly imagined a second Sander walking through the door, and laughed. It was a mirthless, shrill sound, like a crow being tortured.

"Mind the rug, sir, there's been an accident," came from the other side of the parlor panels, and then the partition opened as Lansloet ushered in their guest. The old servant closed the panels behind the man rather than staying to clean up the broken crockery.

"Well, then," said Jan Tieselen, looking back and forth between Jolanda and Sander, an amused expression on his winsome face. "This is a little cozier of a reunion, isn't it?"

"Sander Himbrecht," said Sander, staggering up and motioning toward a chair set in the middle of the rectangular table that he and Jolanda sat at either end of. In rising, he nearly knocked over his naked sword, which was propped against his seat. "Welcome to my home. I am Graaf Jan Tieselen."

"Charmed," said Jan, but he was staring at Jolanda. She should have brought her sword, too, but Drimmelin had convinced her to leave it in the kitchen. She glanced at the door. Jan was pulling out a chair instead of pointing his finger and screaming and erupting in hellfire, so that was something. Maybe it was just a plan to trick them... "How *have* you been, Jo?"

"Good," she tried to say, but couldn't hear her own voice. She tried again, and squawked something that sounded close enough.

"Excellent," said Jan, reaching across the table and taking Jolanda's mug from in front of her. "Do you mind?"

She shook her head. Jan picked up the jug and filled his cup, casting a sideways glance at Sander, who stood at the head of the table, his arm still extended in welcome. It would have been comical if not for obvious reasons. This close it was undeniable— not an impostor, not a grift, but Jan himself.

"Sit down, Sander," said Jan. "The sooner we get this explained, the sooner we can get to the fun stuff. Can't have you running spooked from your old partner Sander every time I come around, can you?"

Sander's shaky shrug implied that no, they really couldn't have that, and he collapsed back into his chair. Jolanda had the bread knife in her lap, both hands tight on the handle. All of Sander's creepy fucking ghost stories came back to her, and she hated him more in that moment than she'd ever hated Jan, even as he was murdering her in the meer—it was Sander's fault the specter had come. He'd been the one to insist they leave the corpse in the flooded manse rather than the graveyard proper for fear of a fish, after all, and how could you expect a dead man to stay quiet if you dumped him in a haunted house instead of hallowed ground? Thank you, Sander, for putting such thoughts in her head...

"May I?" said Jan, and Jolanda realized he was motioning toward her barely touched plate. She nodded so hard she hurt her neck. He took it, and set in with relish.

"I can't tell you how good it is to be home," he said after putting away most of the fish in silence and licking his fingers. "Catch is good, and our wine's damn fine, if I may boast. And of course the company is top-notch. Confession time: I may have let myself in and kept your bed warm for a couple of nights while you were off playing knight and squire in Zeeland, but it's better to be here on the up and up."

"You..." was all Jolanda could get out. "You..."

"You had the right idea," said Jan, wagging a fishbone at Sander. "Killing me and taking my place. That's some foresight I didn't anticipate, but then I never gave either of you enough credit, did I?"

"It wasn't like that!" Sander suddenly wailed, standing back up so quickly his greaves rattled the whole table, and before Jolanda could move, he'd charged Jan. He tipped his sword over in the process, and threw himself on his knees at Jan's side, pitching his head onto the surprised man's lap as he wept and gibbered.

Jan cocked his head, and pulled an exaggerated long face at Jolanda as he picked up the unused knife beside his plate. He pantomimed stabbing Sander in the back of the neck with it as he made the ludicrous expression at her, or maybe it was a jerking-off motion—at this point, nothing seemed too absurd. Then he put the knife back down and stroked Sander's hair, cooing to him, "It's all right, Sander, it's alllllll right. I'm home now, that's what counts."

Jolanda closed her eyes and told herself it was a nightmare, and that she would soon awake. It was like she was underwater again, drowning. Except she wasn't, she was here, dry and alive, and she forced herself to breathe. This was really happening, which meant she had to do something, since Sander obviously wasn't going to. Confront the ghost, then: "You here to kill us, Jan?"

"Sander," said Jan, holding a finger in front of his ripe lips. "You must call me Sander at all times. Spies everywhere, my lady."

"Don't know why I even ask. You'd just neuking lie about it," she said, her long-pent fury making her forget her terror. "You were killing me! Arsehole!"

"I'll allow, I was a ruthless man," said Jan, pouring another glass of wine. He was drinking pretty quickly if he actually intended more roguery than giving himself a proper slant. "I did mean to kill you, you're quite right, and I would have, if my true love here hadn't betrayed me."

Sander howled at this, his face still buried in the modest tan tunic that cascaded over Jan's hose. Jolanda stood up, stabbing the bread knife into the table. It stuck quivering in the oak, and never taking her eyes off Jan's, she barked, "Stop your goddamn simpering, Sander! Think he wouldn't have killed you next?"

"I wouldn't have, as it happens," said Jan, gently raising Sander's head by the hair. "But we had a different sort of relationship, didn't we? And shouldn't you be better at calling him Jan by now? Clean up, love, and go back to your seat."

Sander took the proffered napkin and returned to the head of the table, giving Jolanda a dirty look as he went. That stupid, drunk, guilt-addled shitbird was skulking the way he had back before everything happened, when they were three schemers holed up in Primm's workshop. Had he gone off his head again? Looking back at their guest, she had to wonder if she'd gone off hers as well. A disturbing thought came to her, and she peered closer at Jan—he didn't just look good, he looked better than he ever had before, cleaner, without a blemish on him.

"Are you . . ." She wasn't sure if such a thing were possible, and she knew she couldn't believe him regardless of his answer, but it had to be put out there, for her and Sander's benefit. "Are we . . . did we . . . are we dead?"

"What?" This truly seemed to nonplus Jan. "You?"

"Hell," said Jolanda. "Is this it? Are you a devil? *The* devil?"

Jan was giving her the sort of friendly, curious expression one offers an animal that has performed a clever trick. "That's a funny thing to think, isn't it?"

It was. No, not funny, stupid—but what other possibility was there? "Like, I never came back from the meer. I drowned down in that house, which is how I saw what I seen down there, with the eels. Or I got out the house, but that great fish ate me. Or when you . . ."

"Or when I first met you, on the strand," Jan said helpfully. "Perhaps you drowned in the sea and everything after was but a dream, a vision, a hell designed to make you suffer more by offering you fortune, happiness, hope, only to take it all away. Perhaps that. And perhaps Sander met a similar watery end somewhere, and ever since he's wandered through this same hell. Two damned spirits, ignorant of their fates and condemned to play out some ghoulish tragedy."

"Jesus *Christ*, have mercy," Sander gasped from the end of the table. Jolanda saw he was whiter than the flakes of fish he'd heaped on the table, and his fists were clenched so tight in front of him that blood had begun to drip from his hands onto his doublet—she was always on him to pare his nails back, but did he listen? He was saying other things, but not in a voice they could hear, the shock in his face unlike anything she had seen, even when he'd encountered Jan back in the alley that afternoon.

"I'm *fucking* with you!" Jan suddenly cried. "Calm down before you give yourself a fit!"

Sander licked the froth from his lips, but didn't relax his hands. Jolanda began backing toward the kitchen, saying as she went, "Wine. Need more wine."

Jan made another incredulous face at her, motioning to the half-full jug, but she didn't acknowledge it, didn't acknowledge anything until the smooth door bumped into her back, and then she was through. Drimmelin fell backward from where she had obviously been eavesdropping, and Jolanda shook her head at the cook, at herself, at the whole impossible day. This was what happened when you told yourself nothing could be worse than the day before—there was always something beneath you, Sander had told her often, always a worse horror to rise up.

"Mistress, I…Lansloet told me to, but I'd only just, and I didn't…" Drimmelin began, but perhaps recognizing the I-couldn't-give-a-fuck expression on Jolanda's face, she brusquely brushed her hands on her apron and turned to the larder. "Lansloet had to go out, is all, to check on that sick brother of his, so I'll just see to getting more wine in his stead."

Drimmelin hastily departed, leaving Jolanda wondering just how much the nosy cook had heard. Enough to damn them, or just enough to confuse her? Then again, what proof did Jolanda have that the cook was actually as clueless as to their ruse as she always pretended—what if she was just another one of Wurfbain's spies, playing along with the deception? What if all the servants were in on it, Lansloet and even Lijsbet? She knew Lijsbet was at her aunt's, again, and now Lansloet was supposedly out visiting an ill relation he had never mentioned, but what if all the servants were lying about their destinations? Jolanda felt her guts knot like a tangled net.

No matter, Jolanda told herself, no matter at all—so what if everyone was in league with Wurfbain? There was a much more immediate problem right behind her, and it was time to tend to it. She returned to the dining room.

Jan had scooted his chair close to Sander, and they were talking in low voices, Jan's hands resting on top of Sander's. Jan looked painfully sincere about whatever he was saying; Sander simply looked pained. Jolanda quickened her pace, her throat going tight at the memory of the cord around it, and whatever else she might have said or done or thought was washed away in a flood of bile and blood. *This* was how it felt to be Sander.

"Ah, Jo—" Jan began as she strode up to him, but whatever fucking rot was about to spill from his trap was interrupted by her fist. He fell out of his chair, Sander standing and shouting at *her*, of all neuking people, and she booted Jan in the crotch before he could rise.

"Ball-washing poot!" she shouted, trying to land another kick even as Sander stepped between them. She stubbed her toe on the greave covering Sander's shin. "Wrong with you?! This, cuh, cuh, cunt! Tried to kill me! Kill *you*, motherlicker! Hear me?! Fucking kill *you*!"

Sander carried her purposefully from the room, ignoring the blows she rained on him as she raged in his arms. He lugged her all the way to her bedroom, Drimmelin clicking her tongue as they passed the cook in the kitchen. Sander heaved Jolanda onto her bed and stood over her. She tried to rise, but he slapped her back down, his palm smacking dully against the steel plates riveted inside her leather doublet. She lay there panting, knowing that what strength her ire had granted her was now gone, rinsed off by the confusion his actions doused her with.

"Why?" she demanded. "Why, why, why you always side with him?! He's a goddamn ghost haunting your stupid arse and *still* you suck up! You worthless poot!"

"That word don't usually sound so nasty, coming from you," said Sander, and she thought he must be angry, too, his eyes red and wet as the inside of an undercooked chop. "Got to find out what's happened. This ain't natural."

"You think?" Jolanda cackled, a mean, hurtful sound. "You neuking think, idiot? Why don't we kill him 'fore he kills us?"

"I already did that, remember?" said Sander, his shoulders slumping. "Go to bed, Jo."

"He'll kill you," Jolanda said miserably. "He'll kill you, you fucking idiot! Trust him, don't trust him, he'll kill you, you don't kill him first!"

"That'll make us even, at least," said Sander, his back to her. "Go to sleep."

Rich, that. After he was gone, she locked the door, then realized her sword was still in the kitchen. Shitfuck. At least she had her blunted practice blade, which could do the job if she tried hard enough.

Packing didn't take long, even in the dark, but after that all Jolanda could do was wait. She wouldn't leave until Lijsbet returned, so that they could go together—Sander was a lost cause. As it grew later and later and still her maid remained absent, though the front door opened and closed several times, Jolanda began to imagine all the horrible fates that might have befallen her handmaid, and an already worthless night grew ever more dire. Several times she made ready to throw open her door and murder Jan again, see if it took the second time, but could never bring herself to follow through with it. As long as she stayed in her room, he could be killed or she could escape, but if she left the stronghold, she might forfeit both possibilities for a grimmer fate.

At last she hauled a chest in front of the locked door and slept with her back to it so that if someone forced the door, she'd be roused. Her brigandine was too uncomfortable to find rest in, though, and so she had to change into her warmest shift before being able to nod off, and even then her sleep was fitful. Near dawn she awoke to someone whispering her name through the keyhole, but it wasn't Lijsbet, and the male voice was too faint for her to tell if it was Sander or Jan. Hell, at this point she couldn't even ask and expect to know who was out there from the answer, could she?

Bad night, but the morning would be better.

Except it wasn't, not really.

VI.

That night back in Jan's arms Sander expected to die a dozen times—and that was before the phantom even put its warm hands around Sander's neck. The tenderly brutal fucking Jan administered was what fully convinced Sander that this was his old partner, more than his face or voice or familiar mannerisms. Nobody else made Sander die that sweetly, nor brought him back so delicately.

Sander had found a bit of sport here and there since becoming graaf, but having Jan back in him was…well, there wasn't nobody that set Sander aflame like that, neither before nor since they'd first thrown down on each other. It was tight like the first time he'd had someone in there, but with none of the pain. No, that wasn't right, because the pain was there, hell, the pain was what made it so sweet—it was the pain without the, whatsit, discomfort. As if that made any sense. Point was, taking Jan to the root in one agonizingly slow go while the smaller man drooled onto Sander's cock and then worked it in his noble-soft fist was worth anything that might come later, and when he felt those spunk-sticky fingers at his throat, the fire burning up his backside could incinerate the whole world…

Yet for all the, well, perfection of it, the experience was a strange one.

No, not strange—bizarre, appalling, nightmarish. This was a man he had murdered, after all, yet Jan's flawless, toned body offered not a single scar to let Sander pretend that his lover had only been hurt and hadn't, you know, fucking died back in the meer. He *had* died, Sander had killed him. Just not good enough.

If there had been any niggling doubts as to Jan's authenticity, they were assuaged by the medallion bouncing against his sweaty chest as they made love, the medallion Sander had taken from that cheeky warden way back when. The last thing Sander had done before shoving Jan through a hole in a mud-and-reed-covered roof was to kneel over his corpse and tie the pendant around his flayed neck. Christ's crown, he'd thought it would help Jan find peace down there in the dark water, a guardian saint 'round his throat in lieu of a decent Christian burial...

Sander came back to himself from the fever-dream of their coupling on the chill tile floor of the kitchen. What in all the devil's schemes was he doing, fetching cheese and more wine for his fuckmate in the dark of the night, as if he had a mundane paramour awaiting his return and not some monster that wore the face of a dead man? He barely made it to the latrine before puking into the pot, and he lay on the tile, shivering, until Jan's silhouette appeared from the blackness and helped him back to bed.

"Will you?" Sander asked the darkness, Jan's heavy legs woven between his, as welcome and familiar a sensation as a cool pillow squeezed there on a warm summer night.

"What?" said Jan. His voice was sluggish with drink, his breath pungent with cock. What was most queer about his reappearance was how jovial he seemed—this was Jan when he was between schemes, content to drift straight for a while instead of looking for an angle. Sander's favorite, amongst Jan's many, mostly inscrutable, moods. He was going to snore tonight, Sander could tell from his voice, but that was all right. Sander might snore, too, who could tell if he snored? How did—Jan's fingers tugged on his hair, just hard enough to make him flinch. "I said, what?"

"What?" Sander snuggled tighter against the ghost.

"You said *will you*. Will I what?"

"Will you?" Sander remembered then, and shuddered. "For what I did out there, will you...are you going to kill me?"

Jan was quiet. Sander imagined if he opened his eyes, he might catch a glimmer of Jan's teeth shining in the dark, a glimmer like you'd see from a patch of moonlit rushes out in some dismal swamp. Jan's lips settled on Sander's, and they kissed.

"I already have," murmured Jan, and Sander smiled in the blackness. This was worth it. Anything was. Sleep took him, as it takes us all eventually, whether we wish it to or not.

The problem with dreams is they sometimes get weird and bad instead of staying nice, and even if they don't, right, you still wake up, wondering why you'd thought *that* was such a good vision in the first place. The wake-up for Sander, or maybe the turning point from sweet dream to fucked-up nightmare, came when he started out of his empty bed, sweaty blankets swaddling him like a winding sheet. Twisting around, he saw the room was empty, save for himself and the usual clutter. Except for the familiar dull aching in his posterior and throat, he could almost dismiss the previous night as one intensely bizarre dream.

No such luck. It was all real, it had all happened, and now Drimmelin was pounding meat down in the kitchen, making Sander's headache pulse in time with the knocks. She'd woken him up with the racket, and provided a welcome irritant to focus on, rather than the fact that he'd been up all night fucking an unquiet spirit. Clenching his hands into fists, he bawled, "Shut it, cook! Quit that racket!"

She did not, and so he stomped on the floor. To no avail. Cupping hands to mouth, he directed his next holler to the heavens. Or rather, the attic: "Lansloet! Lansloet, shut her up!"

Nothing but the banging. Which, yeah, wasn't coming from the kitchen beneath him, but the front of the house. It couldn't be someone knocking, not this loud and early and insistently. Could it? He didn't pull up so much as fall into a pair of hose, and hauling on a shirt, he stumbled down the hall without even taking his morning shit. That first one after a serious fuck could be intense anyway, so no harm in putting it off. The knocking was even louder out here in the corridor, and he yelled again, "Lansloet! Lansloet, you cunt, get that!"

Nothing but the banging. He detoured into Jo's room, which was open, and made straight for her window to have a peep at who was out there making the ruckus. Cracking the shutters just enough, he saw…the tops of three heads he didn't recognize. Men's heads, if he had to guess, but a fat lot of good *that* did. Turning to Jo's bed, he hissed, "Get your ass up and ready, we're out of here. Never thought I'd see the day, but the game's got too bent even for—Jo?"

Talking to an empty bed. Christ's crotch, what a morning. She better be out with that Lizzy and the rest of the servants, because if there was a single cunt in the house ignoring the racket, he'd…where could everyone be? He stomped down into the foyer, and the oddness at last maneuvered its way past the phalanx of headache, hangover, and his general morning irritability—where in the name of God could everyone be?

He felt a chill all the way to his marrow, and the pounding at the door filled him with a dread unmatched in all his days… except for last night, granted, where his dead lover had returned, but that had all worked out for the best…Hadn't it?

Sunday.

It was neuking Sunday, and everyone was at church. Everyone except these nutsacks knocking at his door, and Sander threw open the door to let them know exactly what the Graaf Tieselen thought of rude bastards skipping the service to harass dozing lords in their own homes.

The sheriff and two militiamen. Huh. Last time the sheriff had visited, he'd come alone, not flanked by a man-ox and a wee scowler with a shitty little crossbow aimed at Sander's face. This looked like some straight-up bullshit of the Old Sander variety.

"Sheriff," said Sander slowly, palms up so the twitchy one with the bow wouldn't get the wrong idea. Wait a tic, where the shit was his ring? He never took the thing off, yet there was a pale band of skin instead of gold around his greasy ring finger, just where—Jan.

Mother*fuck*.

"Graaf Tieselen," said the sheriff, looking a good bit softer than he did alone, overshadowed as he was with the beefy militiaman beside him. Big man was carrying a maul, like he was come to help raise a barn instead of... what the shit *were* they doing here? "We're here to... we have news."

"Oh." News was all right, or could be. "What sort of news?"

"Your man Simon..." said the sheriff, and was he looking away on purpose, not meeting Sander's eye? "He dead."

Sander blinked. He tried to ask "What?" but nothing came out. The whole world tilted, but the doorframe caught Sander as he pitched to the side. There was some mistake... Sander was going to get Simon out, they'd said he wouldn't be killed for at least another month, plenty of time to spring him. Christ have mercy on the humble sinner, Sander hadn't even worked up the stones to visit the man yet... or had what happened after Sneek happened again, his losing track of time? Had he been asleep for weeks, months, and missed any opportunity to save his friend? The sheriff had been talking this whole time, and Sander shook the tears from his eyes, the quills from his heart, and got out the word he'd choked on: "What?"

"I said he implicated you, my lord," said the sheriff, and by the way the cunt looked at Sander's bare feet instead of his face, Sander knew he was about to get fucked in a rather epic fashion. "Before he hanged himself in his cell, he swore that you were the one who—"

If that militiaboy's bow had been one of Poorter's instead of some piece of shit, Sander would have been deader than a thrice-stuck rat, but even at such close range the weapon missed Sander completely. Credit to the lad, who fired as soon as Sander jumped back in the doorway and slammed the door, but quick reflexes are no substitute for quality materials. The bolt had flown into the parlor, but Sander made straight for the kitchen, where he'd seen Glory's End waiting the night before—when he'd gone to fetch the snack for Jan he'd wondered what she'd been doing on the table there, but now he knew, yes he did, and these militia mussels were—whoa!

Sander didn't even realize he'd slipped until he came back to himself, lying flat on his back with what felt like a walnut pushing out of the back of his skull. He must have only been out for a moment, for he heard the front door opening down the hall, the sheriff bawling and a bell ringing. Sander scrambled up only to slip again, his bare feet unable to get traction on the slick tile, but he caught the edge of the table and evened out, upright and ready for what came next. He was soaked to the skin in whatever the goddamn cook had spilled; he'd ring her out, leaving the kitchen a bloody—

Bloody was right. The window was still shuttered but enough light snuck through that he could see he was covered with the cold, wet liquid, the floor suddenly feeling tacky beneath his toes instead of slippery. No time to suss this out, where the devil was Glory's End? Popping the shutters open, he saw his sword was missing, but at least he knew where all the blood had come from.

He'd always distrusted Lansloet, but it seemed that suspicion had been unjustified. That, or the traitor had gotten what he deserved. Except no, Sander corrected himself, nobody deserved that, he was just trying to make himself feel better about seeing his servant flayed and—

Christ's mercy, no, there was Drimmelin as well, her head sheared clear off and resting on her prone back and—

"Murder!" the sheriff cried from the kitchen doorway. Behind him the massive militiaman had doubled over, puking his belly up like a kid on his first proper drunk.

"It's not what it looks like," said Sander, but the sheriff wasn't paying him any mind, gaping at the two mutilated corpses. Fuck it. Sander was up and crouched in the windowsill in an instant.

Looking down at the canal, he grinned—funny how you always end up right where you start. A bowstring twanged behind him, these chumps unaware he was blessed lucky where such things as bolts were concerned, and the day he got took down by—

—No, shit, they had him, a quarrel sticking his left buttock and sending him toppling out of the window. Warm as the last few days had been, the water was cold as a lover's betrayal, and as soon as Sander surfaced, he realized just how fucked he was—it was too cold to breathe, say naught of swimming. For a moment he considered letting the icy water take him down to the well, with all its Belgians and sundry mysteries, but then the big militiaman was poking his long maul down from the window, and Sander seized it, letting himself be pulled out of the canal like a dead rat skimmed from a barrel of beer. Once they had him back in the kitchen, the three men proceeded to give Sander the worst hiding in a life full of positively epic beatings.

Ah well, he thought as he lay sprawled in the blood of his servants, boots and fists and weapon-hilts pummeling him into a pulp, *the rain that falls today doesn't fall tomorrow.*

VII.

When Jolanda crept out at dawn the morning after Jan's reappearance, she had intended to return as soon as she had made sure their boat was safely moored at its bollard in the harbor, but after confirming that the vessel was present and ready for a rapid departure, she lost…well, not her nerve, but her ability to just walk back into the quiet house as though everything were normal. After starting awake in her gloomy room she had been in such a hurry to get away, to be anywhere else, that she hadn't even put her armor back on, instead creeping from her room and down the stairs in the shift she'd slept in and the first gown she tripped over. The dress was far too ostentatious for a walk to the harbor, but so it went.

Now, with the prospect of returning to the Jan-haunted house on Voorstraat, she wished she'd taken the time to both arm and armor herself. She had the dagger she always kept in her bag, sure, but why hadn't she secured herself in the leather and steel suit? Come to it, why hadn't she brought everything she needed to make away and never look back? It wouldn't take much, just a few changes of clothing, the coin she and Sander hadn't spent returning from Brouwershaven, and her sword.

Because she wouldn't leave Sander to Jan's mercy, was why. Because she wouldn't quit the city without first warning Lijsbet to steer away from them, to quit the Tieselen house and stay with her aunt, with anyone. Once upon a time Jolanda would have been able to just run, but no longer…yet she couldn't go back to the house, not yet. She needed time to think, a place to rest until she was even *capable* of thinking straight; she needed friends she'd never made, sanctuaries she'd never secured.

Where to go? She considered Poorter Primm's, but now had some idea that the violent visitor he had been so reluctant to admit to hosting may well have been Jan, and she would have been wary of sleeping with only Primm watching over her in the best of times. Lady Meyl, then, but that would involve some sort of explanation as to why she was seeking refuge from a woman she'd met all of twice, and after a mostly sleepless night Jolanda was ill prepared to concoct some plausible excuse, let alone offer the truth, which was pure madness—Jan's impossible reappearance complicated matters that were far from simple to begin with. She ended up just walking around the brightening city, unsure what to do next, until a hullabaloo of whistling and bell-ringing and shouting drew her back toward Voorstraat. Once there, the crowd quickly validated, if not her worst suspicions, then at least some fucking dire ones indeed.

"It's Graaf Tieselen, they've arrested Graaf Tieselen!"

"Hang the Hook!"

"Killing kids with that Gruyere man of his!"

"Killed his servants!"

That last accusation was the hardest, and by the time Jolanda had worked herself through the mob, toward her door, she was crying. Just as she was about to address the militiamen barring the stoop of her house from the more mischief-minded members of the crowd, a hand fell on her shoulder and a familiar voice whispered in her ear.

"Don't go, mistress, the folk'll be mad for your blood, they realize who you are." Lijsbet steered Jolanda, too exhausted and relieved to even speak, back through the crowd. When at last they reached a less-thronged alley, Lijsbet threw her arms fully around her mistress. When Jolanda finally broke the embrace, she saw that her servant was also weeping. "Is it true, Jo? Did the graaf...are Lansloet and Drimmelin..."

"No. I don't know," said Jolanda, her voice breaking. "I don't know, but he wouldn't. I'm so tired, Lijsbet—is there anywhere we can go?"

"I…" Lijsbet pursed her lips, nodded to herself. "Right, so I need to come clean—I wasn't staying with my aunt when you were gone, nor minding my nephews last night… You know my husband left me, and he's not coming back—I mean, if he did, I wouldn't have him, I'd run first, I would…"

"Lijsbet," said Jolanda wearily. "What are you talking about?"

"I've been lying about where I've been off to," said Lijsbet. "I've got a fellow I've been spending time with, a…a Jew, m'lady. I know I should have told you, but I… well, I didn't want you thinking less of me. I promise I never shirked in the house on account of him, I'd only see him when I was dismissed, and—"

Jolanda sucked her teeth. "I'd have thought you'd know better, Lijsbet, than to get mixed up with some horned cheat. I didn't know there were any in the city, seducing innocent girls with their spells and—"

"M'lady, that's the veriest nonsense," said Lijsbet shortly. "I'm sorry to correct you, but it is—why I didn't say anything before, I *knew* you'd act like this. He doesn't have horns, nor a tail, and he doesn't cast spells—he's a cobbler, and—"

"Lijsbet," said Jolanda, offering her maid a watery smile. "I'm fucking with you. The graaf's the one who told me all that, and I shouldn't need to tell you what credence I give his tales. Can we stay with your Jew, is that why you brought him up?"

"Yes," said Lijsbet. "Yes, of course, I'm sorry, it's just what people think about him, you know, and I'm just flustered, too— you and the graaf acting so queer ever since you came back, and I've been worried about Simon, and so I've been with my Solomon, he takes my mind from it, and if I hadn't spent last night with him, I might…like Lansloet and Drimmelin. Jan might've—"

"Lijsbet," said Jolanda. "Not another word about it. He—" Jolanda's skull ached as she forced herself to call Sander by his hated persona—"Jan didn't kill them. Somebody's after us, after Jan, and me, and Simon. Now, can we please get out of here?"

"Of course, of course," said Lijsbet, and they were moving off down the alley. "You can stay with us there long as you need. His mother's gone to Tilburg to visit her sister, so it's just us, and he's got a secret loft where he does his praying, so even when the shop's open, you'll have a bit of privacy. It's tight in there, nothing like you're used to, but it is what it is."

As it turned out, Jolanda stayed with Lijsbet and her surprisingly kind Jew, Solomon, for close to two weeks, never leaving the tiny house and rarely leaving the secret loft with all its candles and suspicious-looking scrolls. It was in the leather-stinking loft that Jolanda grieved for Lansloet and Drimmelin when it was confirmed that both servants had indeed been murdered, and where she wept for Simon when Lijsbet brought word of his confession and subsequent suicide. The loft was also where Jolanda plotted to somehow avenge him, not believing either of these claims about the dead, disgraced Gruyere. Over the din of shop noise, she also tried to figure out a means of helping Sander, now held in the same cell Simon had been locked in, and after many a lip-gnawed, leg-cramped night, she started to put together a plot.

When she finally left Solomon's house, Jolanda went to Laurent's office, thinking that if anyone would take a bribe to help her, it would be the lawyer. After expressing concern for her and her family, Laurent genially informed her that a distant cousin had arrived to take over affairs while her father was awaiting trial, and if she hadn't yet seen him, she should return home at once. She took the advice—Jan had certainly wasted no time in installing himself, which backed up her theory that he had set all this up with Wurfbain.

And so she returned to the house on Voorstraat where she had spent the last two years. Its glazed brick facade no longer looked so grand, its profile so tall and lordly—it seemed to squat there, squished between its neighbors, the pigeon-steps of its triangular roof the wedge that had pushed it up from the bowels of the swamp like a stinkhorn emerging from a rotten log. This could be the last time she ever set foot in the place, the last time she ever laid eyes on the familiar foyer, the narrow stair, her bedroom. That thought was what finally propelled her up the stairs—be done with it, and be away.

She went to the door and tried her key. The lock had been changed. *Cunt.*

She knocked. After a long wait, she knocked again. And again.

Finally, the door opened. A short, thin man she had never seen before peered out at her like a wary turtle having a look outside its shell and not at all pleased by what it had found. Ants, maybe. He had on the same plain gray livery Lansloet and Drimmelin had worn. A fortnight after the two servants were murdered, and here was a new one dressed the part—if this wasn't her home, damn it, if she were just some passerby asking directions, she should never have suspected that this turtle was a new addition to the house.

"Yes?" said the servant.

"I'm here to see..." Jolanda paused, unsure if Jan had slipped on yet another alias despite Lansloet's referring to him as Sander when he'd introduced the unwelcome guest—who would want to be *Sander*? She pushed her bulky, ugly cloak farther back to showcase her somewhat filthy grass-green velvet-and-satin gown, hoping her obvious money would outweigh her vagueness. "The master of the house. I am... his relation. Jolanda Tieselen."

"Please," said the servant, standing aside and ushering her in. He was nervous—competent, but not yet used to nobility, she guessed. "Graaf Himbrecht is in the parlor, if you will..."

The man blanched and froze. Definitely new to all this— Lansloet let people in without asking all the time, but that had clearly been his rebellious streak; he'd known better, he just liked getting on Sander's tits. Jolanda never thought she'd find herself half-smiling, half-choking up at the thought of Lansloet, but he—

She had to stay focused, and gave this fellow a reassuring smile as she whispered, "Don't worry, I won't tattle that you told me he was in without asking. Go on and make sure it's all right. It will be."

He relaxed, giving her a grateful nod as he went down the hall to enter the parlor via the kitchen and dining room, rather than through the doors beside them—an old trick to make the narrow house seem larger than it truly was. As soon as he went into the kitchen, Jolanda took the stairs, bracing her palms against the walls to keep her footfalls as quiet as possible. Her room was open, praise the goodness of God, so she had slipped inside and locked the door behind her before the servant even returned to the creaky floorboards of the foyer. Wriggling out of the cloak, she began to strip.

The room was as she had left it two weeks before—apparently Jan hadn't made time to get rid of everything belonging to the former tenants. She retrieved the pieces of armor she'd scattered across the floor when blindly shedding the suit the night Jan came home, and laid them out on the bed. Quick, quick, quick, she thought as she pulled the leather chausses on—her wearing the padded leggings all over Creation after Brouwershaven had loosened them a bit, but it was still a battle to get into them. She was topless, still buckling the plates of the poleyns over her knees, when she heard the slat of the lock pop open—she knew it was easy enough to do with a thin piece of metal. Such as a dagger. She snatched up her sword, her Tongue—she had left it in the kitchen her last night here, she remembered, but it had been waiting for her on the bed, right beside her blunted Tooth.

Instead of the servant who had admitted her, Jan stood in the doorway. In one fist he held two mugs by the handles, in the other a small knife. The cups made her more nervous than the weapon—those, and his smile. He didn't feign embarrassment at catching her half-dressed; on the contrary, he stepped into the room and bumped the door shut behind him as he eyed her bare chest.

"You've filled out nicely, Jo," he said, and she told herself to swing on him. She would have, too, if Sander hadn't fucked himself quite so tremendously and needed her to find a way to free him, or, or, or . . . "What do you say we have a tumble, for old time's sake?"

"Stay where you are," she said, impressed with how steady her voice was. He looked more handsome than ever, but then they said the devil was a gentleman. They also said he was a cunt. "I'm dying for a pretext to cut you down, and you so much as—"

"*Pretext*," said Jan, pulling a face. "My, you've taken to being a lady, haven't you? Certainly explains how Sander was able to get away with it, having you to help. I underestimated you, Jo, I—"

She whipped the sword through the air between them, breaking the clay mugs in his hand and skimming the hair off his knuckles. He stopped advancing at that, scowling down at the wine that had exploded all over his hand and shirtfront. He backed away, tossing the jagged, wet mug-ends onto her bed. She grinned, doing her best to look as wild as she must have when he'd first found her on the beach. "Don't you know 'bout staying clear of lady-chambers, poot? Get to fuck, and when I'm dressed we'll have a blather, aye?"

He nodded, and she saw she'd taken more than hair off the edge of his fist—a thicker vintage was blurring with the wine dripping from his hand. The devilry in his eyes was still there, but he didn't let any dribble out of his mouth, silently exiting the room. Only when she heard him on the stair did she resecure the latch, put her sword down, and finish dressing. Her hands were shaking so badly she had to wait a spell before lacing up the leather half-sleeves of her vambraces, but she was proud of herself, and knew Sander would be, too, when she told him. First she had to spring him, though.

Picking out several sets of her warmest clothing rather than her handsomest, she packed the gowns, pelisses, and shifts into a large satchel, but when she went for the most important component, she felt herself shrivel inside—her money pouch was gone. She and Sander had spent a bit while traveling to and from Monster, and she'd given a full third to her shitbird brothers, but there had still been so much left... except it wasn't where she'd left it secreted in her chest. After checking the room twice over, she confirmed it wasn't anywhere else. Miserable thieving neuker had the whole Tieselen fortune at his disposal, and he still tossed her goddamn chambers...

The cloak went over her brigandine armor, then the satchel went over her shoulder, and then a sword went in each hand, Tooth in her left, Tongue in her right. The twin scabbards on her hips made the bulky cloak poof out behind her, but she had more important things to worry about than how ridiculous she might appear to those expecting more elegance from the Lady Tieselen. Important things like burning this whole fucking city back into the meer, if that was what it took to free Sander and her from its sucking clutches.

Coming down into the foyer, part of her cautioned against engaging with Jan—the front door was right there, she could be away down Voorstraat and never look back. It wasn't like she'd never been skint, she could get by without the money Jan had stolen, and who knew if she could even expect him to turn it over... but no. Leaving would mean never having all her questions answered, never figuring out how a man could return from the grave. She wasn't afraid of no plaguebitch, ghost or no. She wasn't. Licking her lips, she turned away from the door, advancing down the hall.

Entering the kitchen, she found the turtleish servant sitting on a stool in the corner by the cheese barrel. He gave her a dirty look, but dared nothing more, and she gave him a bright smile in return. This energized her a bit—it was fun, falling back into bad behavior. She wondered if Sander had missed it as much as her, not giving a flea's weight what any random dickskin thought of you. Kicking the kitchen door open, she found the dining room empty, but the gate-section of the partition was spread, and she could see her prey in the parlor.

Jan sat in Sander's chair in front of the empty fireplace. There weren't even ashes in the grate. His right index finger was bound in dark cloth, and in his left hand he held a new mug. He was looking up at the uncannily lifelike painting of Christ that Wurfbain had convinced Sander to purchase, the one she'd petitioned him to take down any number of times.

"Who did this?" Jan asked, not looking away from the pallid savior lurking above the hearth.

"He's a court painter," said Jolanda. "Another goddamn Jan, I think they said he was called. Eyck, maybe, Jan Eyck. Reckon his name was part of the appeal for Sander, but I gather Wurfbain wanted us to buy it to piss off the local Cods, since most've 'em couldn't afford a fancy picture by one of Duke Philip's favorites."

"Oh," said Jan. "I wondered if it was someone on the island. I've never seen anything like it. Won't you join me beneath his loving gaze, dear lady, or are you intending to skulk over there indefinitely?"

Jolanda approached Jan, but even if he had set out another chair, she wouldn't have sat. Not on her life. He didn't have a weapon in hand or sight, though, and to prove she didn't have any more concern of him than he did of her, she sheathed both swords.

"Will you marry me, Jolanda?" he said lazily over the sound of metal sliding home.

"Well, I weren't doing nothing else this afternoon," she said, careful to keep herself from talking too properly. She ought to be stupid for him, or at least rough enough to be shapeable. She shifted her arm, her satchel uncomfortably pressing her armored doublet into the skin.

"I'm serious," he said, looking up. "It would save us both a lot of trouble."

"You would have killed me, he hadn't stopped you," Jolanda said, wishing it could be a question.

"I'm a changed man, Jo, though obviously I don't expect you to believe that immediately. In time, though, I think you will come to understand."

"Smell like the same turd we left bobbing in the swamp," she said.

"If that were true, I might have tried some lie about how I never really meant to hurt you back there, how it was all some trick to betray Sander that went horribly, horribly awry. But you're right, of course, I did mean to murder you." He flexed his bandaged finger with a wince, the binding darkening as he did so.

"But only because you'd never felt that way 'bout a lass before and was all mixed up, aye?" Jolanda rolled her eyes.

"No," said Jan, "though that does sound like something I'd have said before, doesn't it? No, I was going to kill you because you were dangerous to me alive. You'll see the wisdom in not leaving witnesses to my plotted deception, I think. Now, however, it's changed, and you're much more useful as a crony than a corpse. We were all quite worried about you, by the by, disappearing after your father's arrest—so happy you're safe. Laurent cautioned that even unwed you could complicate my claim, being a closer blood relation to the soon-to-be-departed Jan Tieselen, but I'm sure that you and I will be able to work something out. I hope Hobbe and the rest appreciate the humor in all this—I, the actual son of the actual graaf, having to assume the identity of a cousin twice-removed."

"Laurent's supposed to be our lawyer," said Jolanda. "Why's he helping you?"

"Plenty of reasons. I've known him a lot longer than you have, don't forget, from before I even dreamed I'd have to resort to such measures to become graaf—my father introduced us when you were still learning not to eat birdberries. Wurfbain wasn't the only one who assumed treachery when you and Sander came back with the ring instead of me, and like Wurfbain, Laurent's been only too happy to shift allegiances, now that I've miraculously returned and pledged fealty to both lawyer and count's respective causes."

"Meaning money," Jolanda sneered. "Like the groots you nicked from my room."

"Jo, I just want us to be friends again," Jan said, and she might have laughed at the absurdity of it if he hadn't looked so earnest. She'd forgotten how honest he could make himself appear. "I am...I was a monster. I was...like a windfall apple, shiny and appealing without, spoiled and mealy within. I exploited you, I exploited Sander, and for that I'm sorry."

"Which is why you murdered all those people, those kids and our servants, and pinned it on Simon and Sander?" said Jolanda, disquieted to find herself actively enjoying this exchange. She had figured this cunt's scheme out during the first hour of her long fortnight of sitting in a loft and thinking, thinking, thinking, but she mustn't let herself get cocky.

"Did you put it together all on your own?" Jan sighed. "I really didn't expect Cousin Simon to take the fall, nor could I predict Braem's being murdered, baselessly, at the hands of our Sander, gentle lamb that *he* is. Certainly simplifies things, I'll admit. Did you know Braem was trying to help you two when Sander murdered him? It's rather a funny story."

Jolanda couldn't imagine that it was, but since Jan was showing his hand without being prompted, she didn't interrupt. That was basic Karnöffel, right there.

"Braem always was the smarter one, to hear father speak of my cousins, which is odd—usually younger sons are sharper, because they have to be, but that certainly wasn't the case with the Gruyere brothers. No matter. Braem suspected skullduggery from the first and, aided by that meddlesome Meyl bitch, he'd

spy on Hobbe whenever he came to town, hoping to prove the
count had planted you. Hoping to find evidence of the truth, in
other words. Cousin Braem never could prove it, but he did
stumble on something quite a bit more alarming after Simon
was arrested—me.

"We caught him spying, but since there were already quite a
few corpses floating around Dordt, we tried to bring him into the
fold rather than dispatching him outright. We all shared a common enemy, after all, in you and Sander, even if we had slightly
different ideas about who should succeed you. We almost convinced him, or he played it well enough at least, but the…*particulars* of my resurrection, as well as certain particulars regarding
the true nature of Count Hobbe Wurfbain, well, let's just say he
didn't have the stomach for it. That he managed to give us the
slip only for Sander to slay him like a dog is…well, it's ridiculous,
but, as I think I mentioned, rather perfect—now we don't have to
worry about either Gruyere, or, for that matter, Sander."

"But you didn't have to come after us at all," said Jolanda,
keeping to solid ground rather than the slipperier turf he was
baiting her toward with all his *particulars*. "You'd just showed up
and asked, we'd have given it all back to you, left Dordt and never
come back. No, I think you liked killing our servants and those
kids, setting us up, plotting with Wurfbain to do us in."

"Well…yes," said Jan, grinning at her. That dug in like leech
teeth, that truth, and she felt any doubt over her plan melt away
like frost weeping off the porridge pot on a winter's morn.
"Mind, Hobbe took more convincing than you might expect—
he wasn't happy to see me when I arrived in Leyden last summer. My not being dead complicated things—you can't imagine
how much it hurts, to hear your old friends and accomplices
describe your being alive as a complication."

"I think I might," said Jolanda.

"Well, maybe you do," Jan allowed. "But Hobbe of all people
quickly realized what had happened, how I had returned, and

since the two of you had already caused him quite the headache, reverting to the original plan of my being in charge of—"

"What's that mean, 'him of all people' knew why and how you come back?" Jolanda demanded, disappointed with herself for asking, furious with him for making her. They were falling back into their old pattern, her questioning, him enlightening. "Suppose you tell me, *of all people*, just what the shit is going on? You're not dead, you're not a ghost, you're the same old mussel you always was, but Sander hacked you up in front of me. How did you... resurrect, like you said, from that?"

"That's a bit of a secret," Jan said, leaning forward in his chair and leering at her. "One that not even those who learn of it often care to remember, as evidenced by dear Sander, or Braem's poor reaction to discovering it. It's difficult to explain, but if you really want to know..."

"I do," said Jolanda, not at all sure that she did, wondering what he meant about Sander...

"Very well. It's all very Christian, but then we're as Christian a land as you'll find—the miracles of Lazarus and the Savior all rolled up with the Deluge of Noah. So I shall do unto you as was done unto me, and then you'll know, simple as that—how does that sound?"

"Why don't you just tell me?" she said, incensed with herself for letting him get under her hide the way he had. Terrible as the idea of Jan cheating death surely was, she was suddenly convinced this wasn't Jan at all, this was someone else entirely. Someone, or aye, laugh it up, *something* else. Funny, she had found succor in the idea that this Jan was an impostor but an hour before, yet now the notion seemed infinitely more diabolical than his simply returning from the dead.

"Marry me, Jo, and never think of it again," said Jan, and this time, bizarre though it was, he seemed to really and truly mean it. "Marry me and be safe. Your only other option is to go where I've gone, and, between you and me, I don't think you'd like that."

"You can still let us go," she whispered, hating her cowardice. "You can. We both loved you, Jan, we both trusted you—and you can trust us."

"I wish that I could," said Jan, sounding as though he was trying to convince himself as much as her. She knew from experience what that sounded like. "Hobbe won't hear of it, even if I thought it was wise. But I'll tell you what, Jo—I think I will take you where I've been, and that way you can decide for yourself what it all means. Just like me, just like Sander."

"Sander?" Jolanda wanted to bludgeon him into silence, wanted to do something, anything, that would shut him up.

"As I said, he doesn't even remember," said Jan. "I do, however, and so does Hobbe and our confederates. Or rather, Sander doesn't remember much—he's never mentioned Belgians to you? Nothing about eels?"

Belgians were, of course, Sander's personal bugbear that he occasionally invoked, but it was the comparatively mundane mention of eels that set her teeth to aching. Sander never mentioned eels, never even had them served at his table, but that had always sat fine by Jolanda, after what she'd seen in the sunken house. The house where they had deposited Jan's corpse…

"No? I asked you a question, Jo, don't tell me you picked up Sander's bad manners from association with the mad bastard?"

Jolanda decided, emphatically, that she didn't want to know what Jan was implying, didn't want to hear anymore. One thing she *had* acquired from spending so much time around Sander was his chronic nasal drippage, and producing something solid, she spit it in Jan's face. He went quiet, but only, she suspected, to prevent it from getting in his mouth. "Shut it, you godless poot, just shut it."

Using his sleeve to get the mess off his upper lip, Jan said, "You asked, I answered."

"Let me ask you this, cunt—why are you doing this to us?" Jolanda was losing her temper again, knuckles itching for some sport. "We loved you! We loved you, and you made us do what we did, and now you're back and you said you were sorry, that you're changed, but I don't believe you! I don't, 'cause you're the same as old, gloating over your secrets, hinting at your wisdom! You ever love anyone in your life, you cruel bastard, or are people just a means for you?"

"No, I..." Jan shook his head and took a sip of his neglected wine. "I never meant to betray Sander. We would be living here together, he and I, if not for you."

"And who got the ring, eh?" Jolanda saw it shining on his uninjured hand, wondered if he'd stolen it or simply asked Sander for its return. She couldn't stand how smug he looked, refusing to even rise at being spit on. "Who near-killed herself diving for a piece of jewelry?"

"It was never even necessary," said Jan, holding his splayed fingers up to admire the band, and that more than anything sealed it for her. Before he could say another word, she was on him, riding man and chair backward, but to her frustration he made no effort to defend himself, even when she broke his nose. Such a cunt. He damn sure came alive when she went for the ring, but by then it was too late for rebellion—she was atop him, her knee grinding into his throat, and only when he went limp and unclenched his fist did Jolanda remove her leg so he could breathe. Aye, killing him here and now would be sweet, but for all she knew, it would just get her hanged by the militia and then he'd come back again, yet another in an endless row of Jans, numerous as angels in a church window.

"You won't mind I take it back, then," Jolanda said as she removed the ring and got off him, wiping her split knuckles on his bloody, wine-stained shirt. A pendant had slid out from under his collar, the dull necklace hanging down behind his head like a cut noose. He just lay there, staring up at her crook-nosed and curiously sheepeyed, serene as a swimmer drying out on some warm shore. She righted the chair, then went to the kitchen just as the new servant rushed in to check on his master.

At least Jan hadn't moved the beer and mugs, and she stood in the kitchen drinking two pints in quick succession before going back down the hall to the foyer. She paused by the coat pegs, considered what she saw there, and then removed two hanging cloaks—the sky blue cape Jan had given her and the short fur mantle Sander had made for Simon. She jammed them into her satchel, spit on the floor, and opened the door.

Out on the sun-sparkling cobbles of Voorstraat, Jolanda stood and considered the fate that had brought her here. Flexing her bloodied hand and admiring the gold ring resting in its palm, she smiled to herself and set off toward the harbor. No time for more questions meant no time for more answers, thank all the saints who love us.

Time to go mad.

Shrovetide 1426

"Every Herring Hangs by Its Own Gills"

I.

Sander was noble enough to have luxuries like a frypan for the smoky little fireplace and a barrel of wine in his cell, but obviously not so much of one as to be allowed to stay in his house until they hanged him. Or chopped off his head or something, if he was really unlucky. Which obviously he was.

Who was that buddy of Hertog Von Wasser's the guard had told him about? Brilling? Belding? Beiling. Some knight or noble on the wrong side of things in the Hook and Cod squabbles, he'd been given a month or year or something to live at his home and get his affairs in order before they buried him alive, but then, he hadn't murdered any servants. No, none of the real richboys would do anything that strong, but Jesus, being buried alive seemed about as bad an end as you could find, even if you went looking for such a thing.

Thing was, Sander couldn't die. Ever since the militiamen dragged him out of the river and worked him over, he was having a right bastard of a time keeping things straight in the old brain-tankard, but that was a point he was sure of—he couldn't die yet. He knew what was awaiting him, down there in the dark, and he wanted fuck-all to do with it—Belgium was hell, right, and he'd be damned before he went there.

Rather, before he went there *again*, permanent-like. Avoiding that end wasn't as simple as they made it sound, neither, getting talked at by a priest; confession might not cut it, bad a life as Sander had led, and with nary an honest telling of his sins in all that time—no, what needed doing was to lead a good long life yet, before he went back down there. No guarantee he could avoid it altogether, but that was all the more reason to put if off as long as possible.

Hence the Hand of Glory. The door was a thick oaken thing with bolts on the other side keeping him in, so without a lock for them to worry 'bout him picking, he'd been able to set everything up. Tin cup for a mold was no problem, and he was allowed to cook his own chow, even in prison—weren't that something sick? All those honest souls slaving away just to lick rancid oats off their dirty fingers come mealtime, and here in lockup he still had his Shrovetide pancakes served up with his private cutlery. Fooling the guards into thinking he was trying to hide a knife, he'd finally given up the blade and kept the spoon instead. Amateurs. The wall of the gatehouse had given the latten ladle quite the edge, and he had his wee hearth in the cell, which was an old sleeping chamber, like as not, so yeah: Hand of Glory.

Or whatever that Frenchman Gilles, had called it—Glory something, and it was made from a hand, so yeah, Hand of Glory. Gilles had been too sweet-looking for witchery, you'd have thought, the sort of handsomeness you didn't usually put with badness, but Sander had run with Jan long enough to recognize when good looks were being put to misdirection for some inner scheming. Funny how the world tells you all you need, even if you don't ken the import at the time, and—

"Are you listening to me?" Hobbe snapped his fingers in Sander's face.

"Nay," said Sander, blinking away his plan. "Said they were letting me out?"

"Of course not," said Hobbe.

"Then what I care to hear it?" Sander would have throttled his double-crossing visitor to death, but the guards might respond by simply braining Sander and saving the city the trouble.

"It's about those papers I brought you yesterday," said Hobbe, shifting in his chair. Sander would allow the two seats in his cell weren't as comfortable as he'd like. His ass was still so swollen from where the quarrel had struck him that sitting was a torture to rank up with the ordeals the martyrs suffered. The real bad ones. "I know you were too busy then, but have you had a chance to sign them?"

"Nay, and I won't until you tell me what they say," said Sander. "We both know you're lying 'bout them being for Jo's benefit."

"I swear, Sander, I'm not," said Hobbe. "I know you and I have had our differences, but I'd still rather see Jo inherit the business and deal with her than with whatever inevitable relation of the Gruyere brothers comes slithering from the fens. If you had married her off, as I suggested, we wouldn't be having this conversation."

"I told you, Jan's back," Sander whispered, glancing nervously around the windowless cell. "He was the one who did Lansloet and Drimmelin, he was the one who did the kids, who made Simon hang himself. He's back, and he's pretending to be me, and he'll try to get at Jo, if he hasn't already. You have to watch out for him!"

"All the more reason to sign the papers," said Hobbe. "Jo's been staying with Zoete and me ever since your arrest, but if this impostor you keep talking—"

"He's not an impostor, he's bloody Jan! Back from the grave! Back from Belgium!"

"Indeed," said Hobbe firmly. "You'll be executed before the week is out, Sander, and if you haven't signed these—"

"What?" said Sander, paying more attention now. How long had he been locked up? Of late Sander had been having a devil of a time keeping track of little things like time and space. He hadn't even started on the Hand of Glory yet... "You said you could delay it. You said you could work something out, that—"

"—That was before Simon's confession, the one that implicates you, was made public." Hobbe rubbed his temples. "Bribes won't delay the execution now, nothing will—Dordrecht won't be appeased until you die, and publicly. They'd have come for you in the night already if I hadn't exercised my influence, had honest militiamen stationed here instead of Cod stooges."

"I can't die," said Sander, his hands shaking. Hands of Glory. "I can't. Oi, give me that dagger of yours and I'll sign, you swear it'll do Jo good."

"You have my word," said Hobbe, eyebrows reassuringly flat.

Sander nodded, sharply, and the count drew his ornamental knife, offering it pommel first. Sander staggered over to his cot, his ass afire, and stashed it in the hay. Then he took the quill from the pot and scratched his X on the bottom of the greasy vellum document Hobbe had brought the day before. Sander must've already sealed the thing at some point, because there was the Tieselen crest in a blob of wax right next to his mark. When had he done that? He'd lost the ring, of all the foolish . . .

"Sander," Hobbe said kindly, and Sander realized he'd been drifting off again. Looking up from the document, he repeated that simple truth in a mad world:

"I don't want to die."

"Come now," said Hobbe, blowing on the wet ink. "You're a versatile fellow, I'm sure you'll find a way to manage it when the time comes. Always easier the second time around, Your Worship."

Sander stared at Hobbe. What the shit did that mean? Before he could find his voice, which he seemed to have misplaced, or calm his heart and stomach, which seemed to be trying to trade places, Hobbe stood to leave, the vellum held open in his hands to keep it from smearing.

"Farewell, Graaf Tieselen," Hobbe said, a bit more cheerfully than Sander thought the bleak situation warranted. "You had me rather worried at the onset, you know—I wondered if your being shat from a ewe in a ditch had infected you with some idiotic sense of duty toward your fellow peasants. I actually had a nightmare on one occasion that you ruined the whole business by shifting your fortune into draining the polders outside Dordrecht, to create honest work for all those poor souls made destitute by the flood. It was *quite* the relief to wake up and find you every bit as selfish as a born prince."

"What?" Sander still hadn't wrapped his stiff mind around what Hobbe had said about his dying twice, and now it rather sounded like he was being insulted. Maybe? "I mean, I hired Simon, helped him in a tight spot. Yeah?"

"How charitable that you found a place in your heart for a fellow noble while ignoring a whole city's worth of desperate paupers, people who no doubt grew up in conditions every bit as miserable as your own. In fact, you might have even known some of them personally—didn't Jan say you hailed from somewhere out in the Groote Waard? I wonder why ever you left the cheerful farms and fragrant fields!"

"Never you mind that," Sander muttered, the circumstances regarding his flight from his childhood home being a topic even less desirable than his imminent execution, his apparently un-Christian administration of his estate, or that unsettling crack about managing to die better the second time 'round.

"A happy chance that you did, whatever the motivation," said Hobbe, and seeing the ink had dried enough to get a move on, get a move on he fucking did, the ponce. "I'm ever so pleased to have known you, and *especially* pleased that we could come to this ultimate understanding. And *if* I might offer a parting suggestion, from one friend to another, use your bedsheet to effect what Simon did—it shall spare Jolanda the pain of witnessing your execution, and prove less excruciating for you than a quartering. Guard! I'm ready! Good day, Sander, you won't be seeing me again."

Then he was gone, leaving Sander to stare down at his grimy, ink-damp hands. Except for the yellowish band on his left ring finger where the Tieselen seal had rested for those too-brief years, they weren't very calloused or scarred, the way you'd expect those of a peasant's son to be. For all the dirt and grease and dried blood adhered to them, they were the smooth hands of a gentleman.

It wasn't until the door was again bolted that Sander remembered what the count had said about Jo staying with him and Zoete. What was that idiot doing, running straight to Hobbe after all Sander had done to keep her safe? There wasn't any time to lose, he needed to bust himself out, and fast. Sander turned to his wine—hidden somewhere in that barrel was the nerve to cut off one's own hand, and he was just the cunt to dive in and find it. At least the count's dagger would make better work of the job than a sharpened spoon.

II.

When the knock came, Poorter Primm jumped in his chair. He always did—would that he lived in happier times, when patrons bought expensive crossbows by the bushel, so that an honest businessman could react with joy, or maybe even ennui, at a knock upon his door. Granted, over a year of steady commissions in preparation for the resumed war with Jacoba and her Hooks, Poorter had grown almost comfortable with callers, but given that the last two times he'd opened up he'd received horrendous beatings and the ruination of several exquisite pieces, Poorter knew he could be forgiven for falling into old, anxious habits. Poorter never had a problem forgiving himself.

He rose from his seat in front of the hearth and toddled across his workshop, scratching Beatrix on the head as he passed the table where she snoozed. That Jolanda girl had called her something else, something dreadfully foreign, so Poorter had given her a much better name. As a rule he detested cats, but Beatrix was the exception—her limp kept her from running around knocking valuable parts over, and she was skittish enough that whenever visitors called she would vanish, like a conjurer's trick, and not reappear for days. Ah, and there she went as the knock came again, the cat not even waiting for him to open the door before shooting up into the loft and out the window he left cracked for her. Farewell, Beatrix, he thought, as he stared at the ominous door.

There was no real need to be wary, he told himself—the mad graaf was incarcerated and awaiting execution, his faux daughter missing ever since the arrest and thus presumably taken care of, and after the rather intense pummeling he'd given Poorter when last they'd met, the returned Jan had promised that they were now square, so long as Poorter kept his mouth shut. Those three were the whole reason Poorter had come to fear guests, after all, and now he was free of them. At worst it was some besotted Shrovetide revelers banging on every door they passed, and at best it could be a noble or three coming by to compliment him on how true his bows had fired at Brouwershaven. Nobles, he told himself, loaded patrons, and with a prayer he opened the door.

A noble lady and three attendants. Poorter blinked at them, and tried not to grin. Unless he was very much mistaken, he'd sold this grande dame's son half a dozen of the most lavish bows he'd ever set to lathe. She'd better not be here to try to get some of the money back, there was no way that was flying with Poorter. He bowed, and said, "My lady, to what do I owe the honor of this visit?"

"Do you always conduct business on your stoop like a pimp, or shall we move inside?" said the commanding crone, advancing on him before he'd even stammered an,

"Of course, my lady, of—"

"Lady Meyl," said she, striding into his shop and making straight for the fire. "I am not *your* lady, Primm, I am *the* Lady Meyl, and I trust you know what that means?"

"I do," said Poorter, though of course he didn't, beyond it meaning she was a heinous noble who was bossing him about simply because she could. Hertog Willem Von Wasser had been a good bit more cordial than his mother.

The last of her footmen closed the door behind him and bolted it, which seemed a touch odd, and taking in his visitors a second time, Poorter's heart began to sink. Rather than furs and pearls, Lady Meyl was wearing a voluminous plain brown cloak, and her three attendants wore the same, as well as swords—hardly handmaids attending their lady on a shopping spree.

Lady Meyl had taken Poorter's only chair and nodded at the

stool beside his suddenly shaky knees. "Bring that over here, you treacherous hog, and let us see if you truly comprehend what you have done. It may mean the difference between a painful lesson and a fatal one—a fool I can abide, but never a clever man. Fortunately for you, I have it upon very good authority that you are the former, and thus *potentially* useful."

Poorter felt light-headed. He was only going to the window to let in some air, but one of Lady Meyl's thugs moved between him and the curtains. A hand fell to a pommel. Oh dear. Poorter took the stool, nearly dropped it, and carried it over to the hearth, wondering just how deeply he had stepped in it this time.

"My lady, I assure you that the price I gave your son was fair," Poorter began as he sat. "I am aware that the cost may seem high, comparatively, but the difficulty in attaining quality metals and unwarped wood on this isolated and damp island is, I assure you—"

"That's right, you're a bow-maker," said Lady Meyl, which did not put Poorter at ease. "It was all my son talked about on the way to Brouwershaven. If you make it out of this, Primm, I expect you will find a rather dependable patron in Willem—my son loves toys every bit as much as he evidently enjoys breaking them. I suppose he gets that from me. Bring me your finest working example, if you please."

"Of course, my, ah, Lady Meyl," said Poorter, wondering just what the blazes was going on. Poorter took a moment to weigh whether to give her a genuinely impressive crossbow to show off his skill or a lesser model, in the event that she intended to have it smashed before him by way of intimidation. Why, *why* did everyone always take it out on the bows? He quickly chose a midrange selection, and took a knee before the tarpan-faced old woman, holding it up as he explained, "The stock is beech, which, yes, is common enough, but the inlay is—"

"Load it," said Lady Meyl, her eyes as cold as Poorter's guts felt.

"I—what?"

"With an arrow, Primm, with an arrow," said Lady Meyl impatiently, but that hadn't been what he was unsure of. He heard the sound of a boot shifting on the floor just behind him, and already being good and well poached at this point, he did as she asked. It was hard, with one arm still in a sling from the drubbing Jan had given him when he'd tried to escape through the kitchen window upon seeing a ghost at his door, but Poorter soon got it strung and nocked. He was about to straighten up and retrieve one of the unfletched shafts that he'd yet to fix a head to, when one of Meyl's men helpfully handed Poorter a dove-feathered frog-crotch bolt. Well. That was just wonderful. He fit the quarrel into place, fingers trembling, and looked up to see Lady Meyl extending her hands to accept the weapon.

Shoot her and run, thought Poorter as he offered up the bow, die with honor, you sheep! "Be *very* careful, the metal bar on the bottom will fire the bolt as soon as you apply pressure, and it really doesn't take much to—"

"Be very careful, *Lady Meyl*," said the sinister dowager, taking the crossbow and turning it to face Poorter without even pausing to admire the filigree on the trigger plate. "Now, then, Master Primm, shall we talk of Jan Tieselen, Sander Himbrecht, Hobbe Wurfbain, and all your other friends?"

"I…" Poorter thought he might be sick, and didn't trust himself to rise from the crouch he still held beside her chair. From this end his beautiful bow looked terrifying. "What…ah, what about them?"

"Poorter Primm, I said that I might abide a fool—*not* an idiot." Lady Meyl narrowed her blue eyes at him. "This weapon is quite heavy, so I suggest that you expedite this by answering quickly and honestly, and not asking questions of your own, which is a loathsome habit. Do you understand?"

Poorter nodded, because you couldn't provide any faster an answer than that. Everything might be fine, this might be totally unrelated to the various frauds and impersonations that had been plotted under Poorter's roof, this might have nothing to do with—

"Sander Himbrecht isn't really a noble, is he?" said Lady Meyl, and Poorter gave up. He fell from his crouch onto his knees, awkwardly clasping his hands together before his breast as she drove the blade home. "You know it, I know it, Hobbe Wurfbain, Zoete Van Hauer, and Jan Tieselen all know it—he's a fake."

"It wasn't my fault," said Poorter. "They made me, they did, I never—"

"That was not the question I asked," said Lady Meyl. "But while we're on the subject, who *made* you? Lie but once and you're a dead man, Primm—we know everything, we just wish to hear it from your lips."

"Sander, Sander did, and that little bitch, and, and, and…" Poorter Primm hung his head. "And Count Wurfbain."

"Exactly as we suspected," said Lady Meyl, pushing the point of the crossbow directly into Poorter's forehead, the brass stirrup on the end cool against his sweaty brow. "I can expect that you'll put your signature to a full confession, one that names the perpetrators of this fraud, from architect to impostor? A confession that leaves no doubt as to the depth of this deception? Now, now, do not weep, Master Primm, do not weep. I mean it, do not *dare* shed a tear in my presence, or I shall stick you like the rat that you are. You don't wish to wind up like your cohorts, do you?"

"Of course not," said Poorter, trying to keep it together. "And what about…you said…you mentioned Jan?"

"Jan is a friend," said Lady Meyl. "He shall be well looked after. You, Master Primm—"

—They were going to hang him, they were going to have him ripped limb from limb, they—

"Are going to be let off with a slap on your prodigious rump. You shall make minor financial restitution to the city, per annum, in exchange for this cooperation, but otherwise life will go on for foolish, foolish Poorter Primm," said Lady Meyl, at last lifting the crossbow away from his face. He looked up to see her nodding at one of her men. The thug removed a roll of vellum from beneath his cloak and spread it flat on Poorter's table while a second removed an inkpot and quill from the folds of his. Poorter tried to stand, but his legs were still too weak. The third man, considerate fellow that he was, seized Poorter by the ample armpit and hoisted him upright.

At last Lady Meyl began properly examining the bow in her hands, and Poorter scanned the document held open before him. He had learned letters out of necessity arising from the sundry crossbow manuals he'd acquired over the years, but didn't put the skill to use often enough to be particularly competent. When he'd finally picked over the document twice, he licked his lips, looked to where Lady Meyl sat, the grande dame again watching him with the bow leveled. This didn't make a lick of sense, even he knew it read all wrong, and—

"Something amiss, Master Primm?" asked Lady Meyl.

"May I…may I ask a question?" said Poorter.

"So long as you're quick about it," said Lady Meyl.

"How exactly did you come to discover the plot? Not that ours were any match for your wits, my lady, it was always a question of time, not—"

"A servant recognized his name," said Lady Meyl. "Sander Himbrecht is indeed of Dordt blood, it seems. He was born and came of age in the Groote Waard, but frequented our fair city often enough to gain a certain reputation. He, like his father before him, was a thief and a swindler, up until the day he became something much worse—a killer."

That certainly sounded like Sander, so why was the confession saying that—

"He murdered his own father," Lady Meyl continued. "He drowned him in a well. His neighbors saw, or saw enough, and came to the Dordrecht militia for assistance when they were unable to catch this Himbrecht on their own. They never caught him, though my sources in the militia say they suspect he returned here from time to time. He's something of a menace beyond our borders, as well—a sheriff from some remote Frisian village journeyed here seeking justice a few years ago. Apparently our Sander killed a man in their town, Snell or Snuck or something, and when they arrested him for the crime, he claimed to be a rather important member of the Dordrecht community, so they had better let him go."

"Did they?" asked Poorter, not having heard this version of the story Jan had told him after Sander temporarily disappeared prior to the scheme really taking off.

"Of course not. They tried to hang him, but he escaped, murdering a priest in the process, and several of their militia. They searched for him, but when nothing came of it, the sheriff came here to report the incident and see if our militia might know where to find the knave. We could not help them . . . until now, that is. He'll swing for them yet, and I daresay they'll be sure to do a more thorough job of it the second time around."

"I see," said Poorter, because he got that part of the confession, that all made sense—sending Sander up to Sneek to be hanged seemed fine and good, even if Poorter suspected the people of Dordrecht would be angered to miss out on the public execution of their notorious child-killer. "It's just . . . I don't understand what I'm signing, my lady. Lady Meyl."

"There's no *shame* in being illiterate," said Lady Meyl, but she sounded as if there decidedly was. "It says what everyone already knows—that Sander Himbrecht killed the children found in the meer, but was clever enough to pin the deed on Simon Gruyere. Yes?"

"Yes?" A very queer thought came to Poorter, but before he could follow it and see where it led him, Lady Meyl was talking again:

"Sander Himbrecht is in league with Count Hobbe Wurfbain—I cannot speculate as to which one found the other and proposed such an evil plot, as the fellow I had investigating the matter was recently assassinated in an alley by persons unknown. The important fact, as that ever-so-confusing confession makes abundantly clear, is that they worked together to murder orphan children, who were then dumped like refuse into the meer."

"Gruesome," said Poorter, which earned him a scowl from the lady with the crossbow. He decided to let her finish before supplying further commentary.

"Himbrecht and Wurfbain had the goal of framing someone for the murders but their target was not, as it happens, Simon Gruyere. They were actually hoping to accuse Graaf Jan Tieselen, but when the graaf and his daughter unexpectedly left the city to join Duke Philip's army at Brouwershaven, the conspirators must have grown impatient. The corrupt militiamen in Wurfbain's pocket thus accused the Gruyere boy, obviously hoping to coerce him into implicating Graaf Tieselen. I visited this Simon in his cell, and he swore to his innocence, as well as that of Jan Tieselen."

Poorter couldn't have interrupted even if he wanted to, his throat tightening, his innards knotting. Lady Meyl thought . . .

"Sander Himbrecht then went to the Tieselen house on Voorstraat to call on the graaf and his daughter, who were *most* upset at his arrival. A Tieselen servant named Lansloet, whose acquaintance my own dogsbody had made while we were all returning from Brouwershaven, knew the villain at once—this Lansloet was a sheephead from birth, and beyond merely recalling the name of a wanted man, thought he recognized Himbrecht's face from its regular appearance in the stocks. Seeing the graaf's obvious distress at Himbrecht's presence but knowing, as we all do, that Graaf Tieselen can be too proud to ask for help, this brave servant came straight to me, wanting the graaf's friends to know a murderer was loose in his master's house. Good that the servant did not take this information to the militia, but then he is local, and so must know how cheaply our sworn protectors can be bought."

Poorter was accustomed to being the smartest man in the room, but since he was usually lording his wits over a cat, it wasn't always the most rewarding experience. To his increasing delight, Lady Meyl continued.

"I chose to send the servant home and wait until the morning to act on this information, to catastrophic result: all in one night Wurfbain, Himbrecht, Zoete, and their confederates gained access to the Tieselen house, murdered that loyal servant Lansloet, *and* the cook, kidnapped the Lady Jolanda, who has been missing ever since, and finally assassinated Simon Gruyere in his cell, making it appear to be a suicide and forging a confession that implicated Jan Tieselen. I immediately presumed they were holding Lady Jolanda ransom to exact a similarly fraudulent confession from her incarcerated father, whom I have not been permitted to visit despite my efforts, and lo, this very morning their lawyer Laurent announces that a new document has come to light! Can you guess what it says?"

Poorter had his suspicions, but she still had his bow, and so he stayed mum.

"This document, signed and sealed by Jan Tieselen himself, confirms the existence of a heretofore-unmentioned cousin named Sander Himbrecht. It is worth noting that this brazen, lowborn impostor installed himself in the Tieselen house a week ago, not even waiting for this ridiculous letter to be forced from the true graaf's hand. It further goes on to state that the Lady Jolanda Tieselen is to *marry* this Cousin Sander, or else forfeit any claim to her father's fortune. I have the worst suspicion that the poor girl will turn up any day now."

Lady Meyl seemed about spent, smacking her thin lips as she concluded. This all made a great deal more sense now, Poorter thought as he gave the confession a final skim and picked up the quill. "Expertly deduced, Lady Meyl. And so by putting feather to confession I give justice wings, so to speak, and you will in turn arrest the, er, fraudulent parties?"

"Do you take *me* for a fool, sir, to wait on your dithering to act?" Lady Meyl elegantly rose from the chair, accidentally firing the crossbow in the process. The bolt flew into the ceiling and hung there, quivering, as Poorter completed his belated crouch. As if it had been intentional, she dropped the spent bow on the empty chair and began walking to the door.

"I had my son and his men arrest Sander Himbrecht hours ago, and by now the fraud is on his way to Sneek in chains. He is a born liar, to hear Willem tell it, and my son knows a tale when he hears one. He gets that from me. I should like to execute the scoundrel here, rather than giving the Frisians the satisfaction, but it simplifies matters if the third new graaf on Voorstraat in as many years simply vanishes. Imagine the ignominy of a public unmasking and execution—I should be mortified, as should any decent citizen of Dordrecht, to admit that even for a fortnight a common cutthroat was able to pass himself off as noble."

"Brilliant," said Poorter, and meant it. Now there was no chance of Jan coming after Poorter for throwing him and Count Wurfbain under the cart with this confession. "And the rest?"

Lady Meyl frowned. "Wurfbain, Laurent, and Zoete must have caught wind of my movements, for all three are missing. If they're hiding on the island, we'll find them, even if we have to search every house, and if they've fled, well, then we'll just have to come up with another means of catching them. In any event, each and every one of them is finished in Dordrecht once you sign that."

"Ah, yes, of course," said Poorter, dipping the quill, shaking it off, and then scrawling a "PP" on the bottom of the vellum. "But what of, ah, the Tieselens? I trust you've freed Jan, and located his daughter?"

"Not yet," said Lady Meyl, nodding at one of her silent men, who leaned over Poorter's shoulder and blew on the ink. "But we've had several informants report seeing the Lady Jolanda flee from the house on Voorstraat not an hour before we arrested Sander Himbrecht—he must have been keeping her captive in her own home, only to have her break away. She's a wise child, and I anticipate that once she calms down, she'll head straight to my estate for asylum. Once she does, I shall take her to release her father—I want her to be the one to let him out."

"But will the people stand for it?" asked Poorter. "I mean, the graaf is accused of killing children, and his own servants—what will people say if he's released without so much as a mutilated face or a flogging? I thought you meant to keep all the Wurfbain and Sander business quiet, so as to spare yourself embarrassment, and—"

"Spare us *all* the embarrassment of your continued prattling," said Lady Meyl. "Tieselen is as innocent as he is foolish, which is to say absolutely—I am an excellent assayer of character, and that man is no more a killer than Sander Himbrecht is a nobleman. This beleaguered city has suffered enough tribulations without another honest son being cut down by forces beyond his control—it is time, at last, for the flood to recede and the sun to return." Something about Poorter's expression must have prompted her, for she added, "And even if he was guilty as the devil, so what? It's only a couple of servants, which were his, and a few homeless brats—the *people* of this fair city you're so concerned about upsetting kill just as many of those beggar-orphans through neglect each winter. We'll simply hang those militiamen who were in Wurfbain's employ and announce that Graaf Tieselen's confession was a forgery—I think Jan shall be only too happy to agree with such a course, don't you?"

"But why the confession, then?" asked Poorter as the document was rolled up and returned to its carrier. "If you're not keen on making it all public, why have me sign it?"

"It is still possible we can come to some sort of arrangement with Wurfbain, when we catch up with him," said Lady Meyl as she walked to the door. One of her men unbolted it for her, and a second stepped out before her, peering up and down the road before nodding her ahead. It was growing dark. "Your cooperation may help secure *his* cooperation, and next thing you know all is forgiven and we're making small talk at a feast. One has to have faith in one's fellow man, Poorter Primm, and not just in his propensity toward folly."

"And Jo, er, Lady Jolanda, you're certain she'll come back?" Poorter said, following the lady out onto his stoop. He knew he had nothing to fear from the feral strumpet, but had still been more comfortable with the idea of her being held for ransom than he was with her running around unaccounted for, with no way of knowing that he hadn't been actively working against her. Well, that he wasn't anymore, at least.

"I certainly hope she turns up promptly," said Lady Meyl, pulling her raised veil back down over her face. "And if she doesn't tonight, I'll go and release her father in the morning myself. In the meantime we'll let him enjoy his last night as a doomed man—teach him a jolly good lesson regarding the recklessness of trying to handle affairs by himself instead of asking the assistance of his betters. Good evening, Master Primm."

"And to you as well, Lady Meyl," said Poorter with a bow, and by the time he'd straightened, she and her men were half a block away, mingling with the thickening mob of Shrovetide merrymakers. Even still, he whispered when he added, "You horrible, horrible woman."

Going back inside and bolting the door, Poorter went to stoke the fire that had burned low during the visit. Although he'd been trying to ration himself, Poorter decided to splurge and dropped two logs onto the coals—it wasn't Lent yet! He set to rubbing his hands together over the hearth. They were still shaking! What a day, what day, he thought, and hearing his cat bump the loft window farther open, he called, "Beatrix, Beatrix, you're so fat, go and eat a skinny old rat."

Poorter chuckled to himself. Nothing better than chiding a cat, except, perhaps, somehow dodging the gallows despite one's numerous, blatant crimes. The logs were starting to catch, and he turned to retrieve the bow Lady Meyl had been playing with from the chair. As he did, he saw a living shadow step from the loft above and drop down onto his worktable, landing in a crouch.

That put the ice in a fellow's soup, all right, and Poorter raised the bow instinctively to his shoulder. "Another step and you're dead!"

It was unloaded, but this rogue didn't know that, and—

The intruder flew across the table, a sword in one hand, his face masked. Poorter tried to fire, the way you might in a nightmare, as if prayer was enough to arm an empty bow. It clicked impotently and then was battered out of his hands by the assailant, and the last thing Poorter realized before the sword came down on his chest was the identity of his assassin.

III.

The rowboat bumped loudly against the side of the old harbor channel. Jolanda was in the Tieselen dinghy, but that it was her family's vessel wouldn't make much difference if she were discovered mooring it against the canal wall instead of at its post in the harbor from whence she'd nicked it. It being Shrovetide, such mischief in of itself wouldn't land her in exceptional trouble, but the contents of the boat might raise some very awkward questions. She lassoed the cable over a bollard jutting out of the cobbles and tied it on, then hopped up beside it—ever since the flood the waterline was barely half an ell below the city streets.

Here's how it would go: She'd hurry down the road to the gatehouse where they were keeping Sander and bang on the door. Seeing she was a woman, they'd open up, and she'd force her way in, hopefully before they saw she was armed. Then she'd put down whatever chump they had manning the gatehouse while the militia patrols were out keeping order, or taking part, at the sundry revels in the downtown market squares—that ancient guard who'd been minding Simon, with any luck. After that, it was as simple as releasing Sander from his cell and getting his help to raise the gate that cut the channel off from the river after dark. The gatehouse was built into the city wall itself, so even if they were seen fleeing the building, it was only half a block back here to the boat, and then the night currents would take them between gatehouse and Great Church, out into the Maas. From there they'd gain the meer before anyone could pursue from either harbor, assuming anyone in the city was sober enough to attempt it.

A perfect plan.

"Hoy, you can't moor there!" came a voice from the direction of the gatehouse, and that was that—she'd thought she was far enough away up the unlit street to avoid detection, but apparently not. The man was walking quickly toward her from the gatehouse, his lantern bobbing. He was alone, which was something.

"Can you help?" she called, hoping her voice wasn't as loud as it sounded. With the whole of the city living it up across town and the Great Church yet again shuttered for construction, the gatehouse behind him and his lantern were the only nearby lights save the stars and moon above. "I just need a quick hand."

"What's that?" he said, seeming to relax at the sound of a woman's voice. "You can't moor here, I said. Why you leaving the harbor this time of—"

The militiaman paused, not five feet off—bastard must've caught a glimpse of her armor under the cloak. Might've been better to go naked under it, freeze them up like the fisherboys with the unexpected sight of some tit instead of a shiny embroidered doublet with gilt buckles, but it was too late for such thoughts. He was stiffening, raising the cudgel in one hand and the lantern in the other, and meaning to raise the alarm besides, no doubt. Brought this on himself, then.

Jolanda surprised even herself with her speed, so his gasp of shock was certainly warranted as she leapt forward and struck him in the throat with her sword. It had the desired effect of bringing him down, but he let out a howl as he fell, lantern and club flying into the air. Before they landed, she cracked her weapon into the side of his head, which silenced him, but it was a sight too fucking late for that to make much difference. Her last thought before the lantern exploded on the cobbles in an orange fireball was that she should have used her Tongue instead of her Tooth—if someone was going to die, better him than her.

The street beside them was blazing with spilled oil, which was about as tremendous a fuck-up as she could have managed. Nothing for it but to run. So she ran.

Straight at the gatehouse. Shouts were rising on both sides of the channel—it seemed that this part of town was not wholly abandoned after all. The gatehouse door opened, and closing the distance, she threw her practice sword at the figure that appeared in the doorway. He fell back with a cry, the sword missing his head by centimeters, and she hurled herself through the entrance, drawing her real sword as she stormed the room.

The closest militiaman was perhaps sixteen years old, and he dropped his pike with a scream as she fell upon him. She supposed the charcoal she'd rubbed on her face made her resemble some wrathful Black Pete crashing the wrong holy day to the poor kid, and at the last moment she diverted her sword, driving her shoulder into his chest instead of her blade. He fell backward, bashing his tailbone on the edge of a table and pitching to the side as his wail became a gasp. From the corner of her eye she caught sight of the two other men in the room moving toward her, and she spun to face them.

One was the dried-out old herring who'd been minding Simon, thank all the saints, but the other was a serious hoss, two meters tall with a flat, scarred face like a shield that had proven its worth. Both held pikes, and they stepped forward in tandem, jabbing their weapons at her. She darted forward, battering the ancient guard's point aside and narrowly avoiding the bigger man's as she slid between the spears.

The old man dropped his pike and fumbled with the sword on his belt, but the lummox brought his spear back over his shoulder. It looked like he meant to swat her with it, as if the pike were a broom and she a bold mouse. The room was a small brick box with barely enough room for the table the boy had fallen over, however, and so as the big man swung his pike back around, its tip caught in the shelves lining one wall and stuck fast.

Jolanda only dimly recognized this as her sword arced down and hacked into the old man's foot. It split his shoe from the toe halfway to his ankle, and he toppled with a howl even as she was flicking the sword up, underhanded, toward the big man's knee. Her tutor's favored style of combat was the cut-and-run, so called because you cut some ball-washer's legs and then ran before the rest could catch you. Though this was only her second time drawing real blood with a real weapon, she couldn't argue with the result.

And yet. Rather than going down when Jolanda's sword hacked into the side of his knee, the hoss went berserk. He snapped the head off his pike as he jerked it free from the shelving, then whipped her shoulder with the thick wooden shaft. The shelf his weapon had broken off in came down beside him, jugs of lantern oil shattering and splashing across the floor as Jolanda went tumbling from the blow. She did as Sander had taught her, rolling even farther from the big man than the impact would have taken her and coming up in a squat to launch herself at him.

Except she'd dropped her sword, and her back was to the wall. Shit.

Before she could orient herself in the small room, the hoss was on her again, his broken pike discarded in favor of a chair that he wielded in an identically maladroit, clublike fashion. His trouser leg was bloody and he was moving clumsily, but nowhere near so bloody and clumsily as she would have liked or expected from the wound she'd given him. She scuttled away as he smashed the chair against the wall where she'd been moments before, the room a blur of too-bright light after the dark street and canal, a riot of crashing and cursing after her silent boosting of the boat from the harbor.

Behind the big man someone was up and moving—must be the kid, because there was the old-timer between her and the lummox, still lying on the floor and moaning as his cloven shoe spurted bright red jets. She felt sick to her stomach, and prayed the senior didn't die.

The big man lurched at her again, and she danced around him, the ruined chair coming apart even as he swatted her with it. Sharp, stinging lines of pain flared along her already sore shoulder as the seat struck her, and then the boy was beside her, swinging his sword at her neck.

Fuck that. She ducked low, plowing into him again as she rabbit-punched his side three, four times in quick succession. He was going down, but she caught his arm.

His young, slightly doughy face tilted up in what might have been a smile as she arrested his fall, but then she had the sword out of his hand and let him topple. A hand as wide as a pancake clamped onto her shoulder and spun her around, straight into the sword the big man now held in his other fist.

She parried it away from her face, his sword point nicking her cheek and ear and skewering her oversized hood. Better that than her head, and in deflecting his blow her own blade ricocheted straight into his bull neck. Not hard, but then a throat wasn't too hard, neither.

The sword bounced off his neck, and with horror she realized the weapon she had taken from the youth was her edgeless practice sword, whereas the big man had retrieved her real blade from the oily floor. The hoss froze, perhaps unsure if he had been killed and definitely unsure what to do with his overextended sword arm, and Jolanda snapped her Tooth back, dull or no, and stabbed him in the throat with its blunted point. His face contorted, his hand slipped off her shoulder, and, ruthless, admitted, she repeated her attack. He collapsed, making horrible gurgling noises as his eyes rolled back in their orbits.

The boy was up a third time, and his pike with him. Enraged at his idiocy in not staying down, she ruthlessly beat the weapon out of his hands and then set to teaching him the utility of sitting some fights out. She only stopped when he began to cry, his mangled hands covering his face like a broken mat of woven reeds. She would have liked to tie him up or something, but it sounded like the whole city was shouting outside the gatehouse— they were so fucked it was almost unbelievable. This was more like it, a real Sander scheme.

"Stay where you're at or I'll kill you all," she addressed the weeping boy, the hobbled old man, and the unconscious hoss as she traded her Tooth for the Tongue the big man had taken. "I mean it."

None answered, and so she kicked the front door shut and bolted it, noting as she did that a crowd gathered in the street. The lamp oil fire near the boat had been mostly extinguished, but beyond the creek of flame that still licked along the cobbles she saw the silhouettes of fingers pointing in her direction. Let them point, stupid goddamn shitbirds. Dordrecht had never been for her, and she would have liked to see the whole awful place burn down to the water.

The winch that raised the gate must be up the ladder, on the second floor, but first she had to get Sander. She went down the short passage leading off the main room, surprised he hadn't talked some shit—he should've woken up from the fracas and started heckling her by now. She could see faint light spilling through the small window set in the cell, so what the good goddamn was he doing?

"Sander!" she said, reasoning it was a little late to worry about raising awkward questions in Dordrecht if the guards heard her calling him such. "Sander, get the fuck up! We're out!"

She yanked the bolts open, her shoulder a pulsating reminder that she'd been slapped across the floor by a giant's pike. If he was too drunk to walk, she'd bloody—

—Blood. Everywhere, pooling on the floor, dripping off the edge of the bed where he lay, soaking through his shirt—the only thing not bloody was his face, which was the pastel white of fresh cheese. He was stone dead, his dangling, nearly severed right hand only attached to his wrist by maroon threads of sinew and skin. Jolanda felt the strength pour out of her in one rush, like beer from a busted barrel, and she fell into a squat.

"I'm sorry," she whispered to her bare feet, having left her shoes in the boat so she could move more quietly along the empty street. It was supposed to be empty, anyway, but then, that hardly seemed to be the biggest flaw in her plan now. She was too late, always too late, always thinking she knew better than everyone else and being dead wrong about it, always too late to help—if only she had told Sander straight away that she'd snuck out and seen Simon in this cell, together they could have busted him loose instead of fucking about with Primm that morning. They could have saved Simon, skipped town before Jan revealed himself in the alley, before they had murdered Simon...

They? Now she really was thinking like Sander, but it seemed like he hadn't been so mad after all. They had murdered Simon, and made it look a suicide, and now they'd murdered Sander and made it look a suicide. They hadn't been smart about it, though— if anyone would have hanged himself, it was Sander, not Simon, this was so obviously a murder made up to look like suicide—

"Uhhhh!" said Sander, jerking upright on the bed and flapping his arms around. The movement detached the hand completely, and it flew from its wrist and slapped onto the ground in front of Jolanda. She fell back with a scream, and Sander vomited all over himself. Scrambling up, she stared in horror as he finished retching and wiped his mouth with what appeared to be a leather belt wrapped 'round his blackened stump. Only then did he take notice of her. "Jo?"

"Sander!" she said, rushing over to him. "What the neuking hell, why, what, what, Sander, what?! What's happened?!"

"I made. Ugh. A Glory Hand," he said, hunching over and dry-heaving. The belt on his wrist was a tourniquet, there was a blood-covered dagger on the floor between his feet, and beside that lay a flapjack pan caked with a circle of burned flesh where he'd tried to cauterize the stump—that was probably what had knocked him out, the agony of searing his own living flesh and bone. Goddamn madman had done this to himself. She forced herself to breathe, to think, to act.

"We have to go," she told herself as much as him, stabbing her sword into his knotted, sweat-moist blankets and tearing a wide swath of linen free. She could do this. She could. "Let me see your hand."

Chriiiiist. It made her want to puke, that gory, half-cooked stump with its core of black and yellow bone, like a roast not properly butchered, but she made herself bind it, carefully. He jerked it away the first time she got the cloth on it, but the second time she touched it, he passed out again, which made the task a sight easier. She could do this. She would do this.

Right. No time, no time at all, the gatehouse would be surrounded by the roving militia patrols, if it wasn't already. Time to go. The wound was as bound as it would get, and she slapped him until he shook his head like a confused dog roused from a nap, blinking at her. He let her help him up, and to her relief he seemed able to stand on his own, if only just. The only thing he said as he limped out of the cell was, "Get my hand."

"We have to go, Sander," she said, hating him so much for being so goddamn mad but grabbing the appendage anyway.

"Even if I die, it'll getcha out," he said, giving her the craziest expression yet in a friendship full of crazy, crazy expressions. "Hand of Glory, Jo. Gilles. Yes."

"Gotcha, Hand of Glory," she muttered as they gained the hall, wondering just how the hell she would get the canal gate raised without his help.

Returning to the main room, she saw the militiaboy unsuccessfully trying to unbolt the door with his broken hands. She scared him off it with a shout and he returned to cowering beside the table. The other two guards were laid out where she had left them, the floor puddled with oil and blood, and she picked up one of the upended chairs and helped Sander into it. Sheathing her Tongue and retrieving her Tooth, she deposited both the dull weapon and Sander's severed hand into his lap.

"They try anything, kill 'em," she said for the whimpering boy's benefit.

"Glory's End!" Sander gasped, reverently touching the pommel of the practice sword. "You found her!"

"Christ alive," said Jolanda, realizing she would like as not be dead before the night was out on account of his moony mind and self-mutilation. No way they were getting out of here, she thought as she scrambled up the ladder to the second story, no way she was getting the gate up by herself, no way at all. Because she neglected to bring up the lamp that hung over the table, it should have been too dark for her to see on the second floor, but through the window came light aplenty from the street below.

She went to the wall and peered out rather than stepping up to it all easy-like. Someone still caught sight of her shadow, though, and a bolt sailed up and through the open window, embedding itself in the rafters above her. It had come from the large crowd advancing along the canal toward the gatehouse. At least four or five of the militiamen who'd been keeping order downtown led the mob, with maybe thirty figures behind who were probably curious, drink-emboldened citizens. God's fucking wounds. Jolanda ducked past the window to where a great wooden disk protruded from the wall, like an oversized spinning wheel. She pulled one of its raised knobs with all her strength, but it didn't budge.

Well. This was to be expected—it must take at least two men to move it, which was why she'd only seen the old man when she'd visited Simon, the other two being stationed up here. She tried pushing the wheel the other direction, even though she knew nothing would come of it . . . and it shifted, rope or chain on the other side of the wall groaning. Well.

Jolanda laid into it, digging her bare toes into the splintery wooden floor, and though it made her bruising shoulder howl, she fought the wheel into turning, a ratcheting noise rewarding her labors. Trading off from one knob to the next as she pushed was the hardest part, and then, just as she thought she had it, her big toe slipped and skewed itself on a sliver of floorboard. She released the wheel, the splinter snapping off in the wound as she hopped about in agony. Thank all the whores in Sodom, the wheel didn't fall back near so far as she'd expected, and bracing herself on her good foot, she returned to her trial. Finally she'd pushed it as far as it would turn, and though no real time at all could have passed, she was drenched in sweat.

She didn't risk the window, knowing full well what she would see, and as she went down the ladder, she heard them banging at the door. She peered around as she descended, keeping her splinter-spitted toe off the rungs, and saw that Sander had almost reached the door. Stupid goddamn shitbird.

"Sander!" she shouted, and he paused, looking at her in confusion. The practice sword was in his left hand, and his right was held between his teeth. Jesus. "Get away from there!"

He tried to answer and his hand fell out of his mouth, which distracted him from whatever nonsense he was trying to spout. The crow and the cheese, that one. The banging was growing louder, waves of shouts breaking against the door, but Jolanda's attention was captured by the room's only other exit: a small wooden door set in an alcove beside the table. It must open onto the small dock where those entering the city might pause their vessel long enough to bribe the militiamen rather than dealing with the harbor's excisemen. An idea took hold like a polecat on a rat, and as she dropped off the ladder and sat heavily on the ground to remove the splinter from her toe, a smile spread across her charcoal-blackened face like a wedge of moon breaking through a midnight cloudbank.

IV.

The girl, Jo, had come for him, but Sander couldn't really figure out why. He'd always been a shit to her. He tried to tell her that, tell her she shouldn't have come, tried to give her his hand so she could make the Hand of Glory, get herself out, at least, before Jan and his Belgians broke down the door. She wasn't having any of it, shoving the bloody hand into the waist of his hose and slapping him hard across the mouth. He grinned at her little love tap, but then she slapped him three more times, shouting something, and each blow brought him a little closer to the surface.

"—to listen!" she was saying.

"Been listening," he said, or tried to say. His tongue felt numb as his hand. The one he'd sawed off with Hobbe's dull knife— would've been better using the spoon. "Belgians, Jo, out there. You need—"

"Please, Sander," she said, her voice cracking. Her face was all black, he saw, except where it had dripped off in stripes under her eyes. Was she some devil, too, was that why she was all blacked up? Of course not, the Belgians were out there, and she'd stopped him from opening the door, hadn't she? She was on his side. Why was she crying? "*Please.*"

"Yeah, sure," he said, unsure what he was agreeing to. "Sure."

"Sure what?" she said, not crying after all. Who was crying? He looked around—there were a couple of cunts he must have put down lying there, cuntlike, and a third, who was curled up under a table—he was the crier. The Hand of Glory was working like the charm it was, keeping these ball-washers in dream-town. Where was he? In a dream? Was it Belgium? Was Belgium hell? Probably all of that, sure.

"Sure," he said, then hung his head, caught in a lie. "I don't know, Jo. Whatever you said."

"Here," she said, leading him to a door. It made him dizzy to look at the whorls in the wood. He didn't like it. Led somewhere nasty, somewhere dark. Somewhere Belgian. The girl was unbolting the door, and he would have stopped her if he didn't think the effort would make him fall, and he really didn't want to fall, not here, where he might not find the surface again. "See the water?"

"Ugh," said Sander, the crack she had opened in the door revealing a small dock surrounded by black liquid, lights from somewhere beyond shining on wet wood, wet water. Last place he wanted to go, that. She poked her head out, looked around, and jerked back inside as several bolts whizzed down and stuck in the dock.

"Good, they can't get to it from the street. I'm going out front," she told him, leading him away from the door onto the water and past the rattling shutters of the barred window, toward the other door, where the Belgians thudded the wood with their flat paddle tails, ululating beyond it for Christian blood. Why the fuck would she go out there? They'd rip her to pieces. "I'm going for the boat. You have to bolt the door after me, Sander, do you understand? *You have to bolt the door.*"

Well, obviously. "Uh-huh."

"Good," she said, and he was relieved to see her smile. She was cute when she smiled, girlish in a way she'd maybe never truly been, at least as long as he'd known her. "Then you go to the canal door, and look out until I come along with the boat. Then you jump in and we float away, understand?"

That didn't sound so good at all. He frowned, tried to tell her it was a bad idea, and found he was crying after all. Jesus, Sander, buck up!

"You have to, Sander," she said, taking off the black blanket she was wearing over her like a cloak. Or was it a cloak? A big one, yeah. She kept talking as she began to unfasten the armor he had given her, taking it off because she was going to die. She paused, her brigandine half-undone, and snapped her fingers in his face, like she was goddamn Hobbe or something, the little bitch. The flash of anger brought him back up for air, and she came into clarity as he blinked away the tears. Why the hell was she stripping? He'd thought by now it was well understood he didn't go in for cunt.

"Of course you don't," she said, smiling again, and he wondered what other thoughts he might've unintentionally voiced. She was somehow getting her fingers into his pants from across the room, but then he saw his own bloody stump jutting up from his waistband and felt his heart stop. What in all the heresies of the pagans had he done?

Well, sure, he'd chopped his hand off. Christ's weeping eyes, was that wise? Would he bleed out? Had he already, was he dead in his cell and this was all a death dream, like had happened the last time he'd died?

No. He hadn't died, ever, and he wouldn't here. The girl was still talking at him as she got her doublet the rest of the way off and started working on the buckles fixing her knee plates on. She meant to go out, past the... whoever was out there, to a boat. That made sense. Boats were how you got away from Dordt these days. Fine. But if the... whoever was out there, banging on the door, if they tried to stop her, how could she hope to reach the vessel?

He'd have to go instead. His fist tightened around Glory's End, felt her familiar throb. This *was* a dream, then. Relief warmed him like a pair of freshly pissed pants on a cold night in an alley, and he took a step for the door when Jo put herself between him and it, all naked and spooky-looking.

"I'm going for the boat," he said.

"No, I am."

"All right," he said, relieved. Dream or no, he was exhausted and wanted to fall back under.

"You lock up behind me, aye? And wait by the other door. With this." She offered him a bulging satchel. No, it was her blanket, cloak, whatever, with all her armor bound up in it. He reached for it with his stump. Frowned. Offered her Glory's End.

"She's seen me through every hell," he said solemnly. "Now she's yours."

The brat rolled her eyes, and he had half a mind to split her head, but she took the sword before he could decide if that was warranted or not. He accepted her bundle. She stood on her tiptoes and kissed his cheek. Why in Christ's name was she shaking so bad as she turned to thc door? Awe at the weapon he'd given her, no doubt. She weren't so foolish as he'd thought, then, bony-assed chit.

She was motioning him over against the wall next to the main door, and he followed her lead. She slid the top bolt out of the lock, quiet as she could, then knelt and did the bottom one. Only the middle bolt kept the beasts at bay, but rather than springing it she reached over and pulled open the portal of the tiny peep-window set in the door. Soon as she did, the crew out there quieted down, the silence spreading backward from the door like a dropped mug of wine soaking across a rug.

"I'll come out!" Jo shouted so loud it made Sander wince, her face pointed at the hole in the door but not in front of it, like, where she might get stuck. Smart enough, Jo. "I'll come out, you all just back away!"

The riot started up again, banging the door even harder, the shouts waking up the sleeping angels, no doubt, but then she roared again, and again they quieted down. Cowardly mob of nutsacks. "I'll burn it down!" she hollered. "Back off! Twenty paces! I'll burn it! Kill these three watchmen!"

Again the banging stopped, the silence spread, and she edged over toward the peep-window. She darted a peek before they could pop her, and seeing the grim smile on her face, he reckoned she liked what she saw. Mind, they'd shoot her soon as she stepped out, and there'd be men on either side of the wall, clear out of her view from the peephole and ready to pounce, and her nakedness wouldn't distract them for more than a moment—she would've been a sight better served with her brigandine. Before he could tell her any of that, though, she'd thrown the last bolt, wrenched the door open, and slipped out, pulling it shut behind her.

Shit. He dropped her bundle of armor and went after her, but the quick movement made him swoon in front of the door and he barely found the wherewithal to knock the top bolt in place while he got his bearings. He was right beside the peephole, and leaned into the door for a better look, his blazing forehead pressing against the oak. This was stupid, they would catch him like this, but he was too tired to move, and besides, they seemed busy enough with the girl for now.

Sander had been correct about men lying in ambush on either side of the door, then—two of them. One now lay screaming in the street but the other was right in front of Jo, the sneaky bastard having the drop on her and—no, Sander saw, that wasn't right at all, this second man was limp as a pickled herring, and only upright because Jo had a hold of his hair, her arm quivering from the strain of holding him aloft. Her bare back filled most of the window, but past her shoulders and those of the man she hoisted up, Sander saw the crowd maybe ten paces off, and then he heard a chorus of bowstrings strumming like the harps of angels. Jo dropped the man she'd been shielding herself with, his back festooned with shafts, and Sander tried to laugh, but only a wet cough came out.

She charged them before they could reload their crossbows or move on her, and as usual he was impressed with her grit. They weren't Belgians, like he would've fought, but, mundane men or no, there was a whole host of them, with cudgels and pikes and shining blades. The naked girl was among them, Glory's End whistling through the air, but instead of severing limbs and spraying blood, as the sword would have for Sander, she deigned only to bludgeon the men's limbs and weapons as Jo pushed through them.

Then, suddenly, tragically, impossibly, they were driving Jo back instead of letting her through. Maybe six or eight men lay clutching themselves on the cobbles, but there were at least twice that many pressing forward, and more behind them. Sander tried to warn her, tried to tell her what to do, but as quickly as she had joined the battle, she left it, fleeing back toward the gatehouse. They followed, and bows were raised, and she looked over her shoulder, which, what the fuck, never look over your shoulder, especially when you're running along a—

—Canal swallowed her. Sander blinked, not believing it could have ended this way, but there was the mob drawing up short at the icy ledge, those with lanterns waving them over the water, those with bows firing them into the channel. Stupid, stupid, stupid girl—first and last thing he taught her was mind the goddamn canals, especially when you're running.

"Ball-washers!" Sander howled at them. "Plaguebitches!"

That got their attention. A few lingered, waiting for her to surface with lanterns and bows at the ready, but most of them charged the door. He fumbled the middle bolt locked just before they reached the gatehouse, and slammed the hinged portal covering the peep-window back into place. They were beating on the door again, and he resumed his position of leaning against it, as if that would help. It smelled like oil in here; maybe he should burn the place down. That would learn them.

The door thudded again and again, and Sander smiled at the thought of drying out in front of the hearth with Jo. He'd had his fill of the wet and the cold. He closed his eyes, rallying the strength to go over to where the lamp hung from a chain over the table and dash it against a wall or something, or maybe just break it over his head like some drunkard smashing pots against his skull for a laugh, or—

Huh. The banging on the door had stopped, though they were still shouting. Not at him, though. He put his ear to the oak:

"—boat!"

"—bitch!"

"—back!"

Huh. Sander opened the peep-window, wondering if this were a ruse and he was about to get his eye tickled with something sharp, but too curious to care.

No, not a ruse. The men's backs were to him again, and the crowd on the edge of the canal was dispersing, and with the quickness, members of the militia and men and women and kids in their nightclothes all shoving one another aside to flee the channel. Strange. In one of those peculiar little gaps of silence in the cacophony of cries, Sander heard a bowstring snap. One of the men closest to the gatehouse pitched over, a fountain of black flying up from where the quarrel had stuck in his throat. Huh.

Was someone calling his name? It certainly sounded like it, an angel whispering over the battlefield, a mouse murmuring in an avalanche. *Sander*, it said, *Sander*, then something else? *Run*, maybe? Well, that—

—Ah. Jo was floating along the edge of the water, a vengeful ghost, and one possessed of a magical weapon to match Glory's End. It was a crossbow, but one that never emptied—the spirit need only kneel for a moment, as if in slack-assed prayer, and then the bow was nocked and loaded again. She had almost reached the side of the gatehouse, crying his name over and over again, and he stared in awe at the phantom. It had been so long since his dreams had been anything but nightmares that all he could do was ogle the spectacle as she shot down one plaguebitch after another. This was great!

"Sander!" She was nearly screaming it now, "Sander, run! The canal! Sander! Get in!"

Ah. He saw it now—she was standing in a boat that drifted down the channel. That was...pretty smart, he had to admit, and nearly tripping over the balled-up cloak full of armor, he lurched over toward the door in the alcove. The crying lad had buggered off somewhere, but as Sander rounded the table and opened the canal door, someone very large moved to snatch him.

He turned, swinging his stump at the man, too tired to explain why, no, he wasn't up to a tussle at present, and inadvertently knocked the lantern from its ceiling hook, onto the table. That sheriff's pet giant who had worked Sander over back on Voorstraat was right fucking here, somehow, his neck all black and blue and his face all red with fury, but instead of laying into Sander, the big baby fell back, scared. Damn right, he was scared.

No, shit, it was just that the lamp had broken, a column of fire shooting straight up to the ceiling, and then Sander's legs caught flame as burning oil flowed off the table, all over him. Tired or no, he found his strength then and pitched himself through the door, slipping on the dock and falling into the water. It was fucking cold, too damn cold, and he was too tired to think, let alone swim, so it was time to...

Someone had him by the hair, and suddenly dead sober and aware he was back in the well, Sander screamed underwater, kicking for the surface. He came up and clobbered Jo with his stump-hand, which crippled him with pain and nausea. It felt like someone was hammering an icicle into his fucking arm bone, and he blacked out which, sure, was probably for the best.

Ash Wednesday 1426

"Who Knows Why Geese Go Barefoot?"

Out on the meer the mist did not rise with the sun, and midday found Jolanda rowing just as blind as she'd been before dawn. She tried not to look over her shoulder at Sander, because at any given moment he appeared dead and she couldn't stop propelling them along to check for breathing every few strokes. She ought to cut off his scorched hose to see if his legs were all right, but at this point it wasn't like it would make a whole hell of a difference—she inspected his stump-bindings whenever she took a break, but beyond that she didn't know what to do with the mutilated idiot.

Hauling him into the boat despite his best efforts to drown himself had resulted in all of the gear she had packed becoming soaked, and to top it all he'd left her armor in the gatehouse, though his severed hand was still safely jammed down his hose. Typical Sander.

Jolanda locked the oars and let them drift as she stretched her deadened arms, the sweaty woolen gown she'd put on after rebinding his wrist even damper from her exertions than it had been from the splashing canal water. As if the release of the oars was a river lock dropping to loose a torrent, soreness flowed through her, washing away the numbness and flooding her body with a hundred tiny agonies. She had started to pass out at the oars, which was no good, and had all sorts of pressing needs roiling through her innards, and so she took the gown back off, and, never having put anything on underneath it, jumped overboard into the frigid bog.

The water proved warmer than the air, and just as her head went under, her feet sank into mud. Kicking free and up, she hung onto the side of the boat as she relieved herself, trying very hard not to think about giant catfish. It finally sank in that her plan had worked despite Sander's madness, that they had a satchel of clothes and blankets and a smaller bag stuffed with the cheese-heavy contents of Poorter Primm's larder, as well as a dozen of the fat man's finest crossbows.

Despite Poorter's general priggishness, she hoped she hadn't hurt him too badly when she'd smacked him with the practice sword—she'd been expecting him to give up without a fight, but he'd surprised her by pulling a bow and she'd had no choice but to swing on him. He'd gone down after the first blow and let himself be tied up, and only spoke to fruitlessly protest the gag that she shoved into his mouth. She supposed he recognized her despite the charcoal disguise and felt betrayed, but the double-dealer deserved a lot worse than she'd given him—just after scaling his roof she'd seen several hooded figures leave his house, no doubt Wurfbain's people checking in on their chum.

But Jolanda was done worrying about Poorter and who he might be plotting with. She was done with all of them, for better or worse, now that her plan had worked. She'd nearly abandoned it altogether, panicking at the last moment and going to Lady Meyl's estate to throw herself at the woman's mercy, to tell her everything, but the servant who answered the gate claimed that his mistress was out. That dogsbody had been just a little too insistent that Jolanda wait inside for Lady Meyl, and Jolanda rediscovered her resolve, running all the way through the crowds from Meyl's house to Primm's.

There she went, worrying over Dordt business again, when she was done with it forever. At least she and Lijsbet had enjoyed one final afternoon of cards and wine in Solomon's loft before Jolanda set upon the bloody path that took her from the house of the wealthiest noble in Dordrecht to the loft window of one of the city's shadiest artisans, from there to a midnight harbor, and then, at long last, escape. Between mist and meer the odds of their being found by any pursuers were dwindling by the moment. Wonderful.

Getting back into the rowboat proved a good deal more difficult than quitting it, and for a terrible moment Jolanda thought she was going to tip it completely as she hauled herself over the side, but then she was in and the rocking vessel settled. She sprawled amidst the crossbows, and with the same pulse of ice water you feel in your stomach at noticing a spider crawling across your face, she saw that one of the weapons was still nocked and loaded and pointed straight at her. If she'd bumped it hard enough to trigger the long tickler...

Slowly sitting up, she took the bow and unloaded it, then set to unstringing all but two of the weapons. Useful as it might be to keep them primed and loaded as she had while taking the gatehouse, it seemed unlikely they would need them in a similar state of readiness anytime soon, and seeing Sander try to move amongst them would be like watching a blind kitten cross a field of rabbit snares.

She yawned, wondering what time of day it was, and looked at Sander. He might yet live. The boat was much smaller than the one they'd taken out to Oudeland, and maneuvering around her unconscious shipmate to get at the wee anchor was near-impossible.

To hell with it. She cleared a space for herself in the belly of the dinghy, her aching back actually warmed by the few centimeters of water pooled beneath her, and fell immediately into something resembling sleep. She woke every few moments or hours, it was hard to tell, and at one point fought a tightly knotted bag into giving up one of its blankets. The mist thickened, and she did not dream.

It was well after dark when she started awake with the panic of one who knows she's overslept, and after rubbing her raw arms and blinking away the sleep-crust she saw that Sander was sitting up in the boat, munching an orb of Edam as if it were a sourdough boule. He crumbled her off a chunk of the cheese, and she took it gratefully. They ate in silence, save for the friendly lapping of black water against their boat.

"Do you think we died?" Sander said at last.

"What?" Good to see he was his old self, but the question nevertheless gave her the creeps. "When?"

"Whenever." Sander might have shrugged, it was hard to tell from his night-vague profile.

"I wish I had've," Jolanda said. "Which makes me think no, we're both still here."

"Where?"

"The meer."

"I don't want to die," said Sander. He sounded tired. "I know nobody does, but just thinking about it makes me sick. Sick. I can still feel my hand."

"Why did you take it off?" she asked as she pawed through the food satchel. She found a bottle, and pulling the stopper out with her teeth, guzzled until she coughed. Her throat burned like it had after Jan had tried to kill her out here.

"Hanged man's hand," said Sander. "Remember what Gilles said? You render the fat into a candle, and it helps you sneak past people."

"And you were going to make a candle in your cell?" The wine was so good it made her eyes fill, and she offered him the bottle.

"It would've worked!" His defensiveness made her think, at last, that he would indeed recover from his self-inflicted wound, that everything would be all right. Sander was Sander. "I was just resting my eyes, you came in."

"Aye," she said. "Sure."

"It's true!" She heard the bottle gurgling, and then he handed it back, panting. "Would've gotten loose, fixed 'em all. Burn the whole eely city. You take care of Jan and Wurfbain, or we need to go back for them special?"

"I ran, Sander," she said, bristling that her rather daring jailbreak was now deemed less than sufficient. "I got gear together, I broke Jan's nose, and I got the hell out. Gave Poorter a good working over before I left, too. He's been keeping shady company; friends of Wurfbain, I expect."

"You know about them?" Sander asked, excited. "'Bout the Belgians, you know?"

"What?" Same old Sander, all right. "Again with the Belgians?"

"What I call 'em," he said, and began blathering about plots and conspirators and monsters coming out of the water. She was done listening to the explanations of madmen and ghosts, and took the opportunity to get dressed. Making interested noises at appropriate-seeming lulls in his rant, she rose into a crouch and felt through the bags until she found a vair-lined pelisse, and then pulled on a cold, damp gown and, after wringing it out, a beaver mantle. She felt even chillier with the clothes on, but the fog finally seemed to be clearing, showing the side-lidded eye of the moon and the glittering freckles of night. She got back onto the rowing board and set to moving them along again as he prattled into the mist.

"—not hell, but like, somewhere different, yeah? No eel so small it doesn't dream of being a whale, right, so why not dream smaller, dream of being a man?" A final slosh from the bottle as he drained it, but that bit gave Jolanda pause.

What if she hadn't dreamed it all as she half-drowned in pursuit of the ring, what if there had been eels down there? What if those Tieselen corpses dressed in sharp-toothed ribbonfish had been real? It wasn't as if she'd ever heard the explanation for Jan's miraculous reappearance. In spite of her resolution to remain ignorant, to kill any curiosity that might crop up in her breast, she wished she'd paid more attention to Sander's ramblings . . . but he'd now gone as dry as the bottle.

To the saints' ears with her worries—there would be time enough for all that lunacy later. Unless there wasn't, which was fine, too.

"Sander, are you up?" she said after hours of silence, mostly to keep herself awake at the rowing board.

"Uh," he said from the black prow behind her.

"Did I ever tell you about my brother?"

"Nay," he said, or something like it.

"His name's Pieter. He ran away when I was little. I always wished he'd taken me with him." The mist had returned as she'd rowed, muting even the oars. She did not speak for a long time, but when she did, she whispered it, almost as afraid of Sander's hearing as she was of his not.

"Pieter run off, and when Jan bought me and took me away, I expected to see him everywhere. Pieter. The world was so small for me, I couldn't imagine I'd go long without bumping into him. But I never did." Something scratched at the bottom of the boat. A reed-bed, most likely.

"I'm not stupid. He might've died a day out from the hut, or maybe he lives still, rich or poor, content or hungry, someplace far from here. Or near. Maybe he was one of those men of the militia I put down. I didn't want to kill anyone, Sander, but I think I might've, getting you loose, even with a dull sword." Jolanda flinched at the memory of that young man in the gate-house wailing as she broke his hands and fingers. She'd let him live, but then the whole damn place had been aflame when Sander fell out of the door and off the pier. Even if the boy made it out, what if his hands never healed, what if he couldn't so much as pick up a mug? She repulsed herself, and took her mind off it with the resumption of what she'd been saying.

"Anyway, each and every time I heard I was to meet some new person, be it a stableman to take a horse or a count of Holland or whoever, every time, I half-thought it might be Pieter, and wouldn't that be grand? Wouldn't we recognize each other, like in a tale?" She thought of her other brothers then, but let them float away as she continued.

"But we never saw each other. Or if we did, we never knew

it—how would we? I was stupid, is what I'm getting at, because even though I knew I'd never see him again, I couldn't stop hoping for it, dreaming about it. Sometimes I'd even tell myself you were him, or Jan was, and something had happened where none of us remembered.

"Like with the cat. Margareta, remember her? The Muscovite's cat we brought back with us, but Poorter let go 'stead of keeping for me. Well, when I was planning all this, I was sure she was going to hop in the boat just as I was leaving, aye? And I'd know her down all these days by a limp in her hind leg, from where you said Jan threw her? I was dead certain that she'd be in the boat when I got to the harbor, and even when she wasn't, I thought she'd show up, by the gatehouse or something, and even as I was pulling your charred ass out of the drink, I checked the dock there to see if she was waiting. But she wasn't. It was just us."

Sander snorted, snarled, but before she could whack him with the oar for being a bitch, she realized he was snoring. Well then. She rowed them deeper into the night, wondering what would become of them—they must gain a shore eventually, and what then? Would Sander recover from his injury, or, more likely, would he die sometime in the days to come, leaving her as alone as she'd ever been? Would she ever return to Dordrecht, to avenge the deaths of Simon and Lansloet and Drimmelin, to repay the crimes of Wurfbain and Jan and Poorter? Would she ever see Lijsbet and her Jew again?

Or perhaps they would never come to shore, perhaps this meer stretched on and on forever, with only catfish and churchyards to break the monotonous gray waste. Perhaps militiamen were just behind them, and if she set down the oars for an instant, they would be overtaken—she imagined them hanging her from the boughs of the dead tree in Oudeland, where she should have died all those years ago, and rowed harder, her shoulders cramping. If they explained it all to her before slipping on the noose, if they could somehow make sense of all the murders and dead men coming back and what she'd seen haunting the Tieselen table in the flooded house, would that somehow make it all worthwhile?

Would it be worth dying to find out the truth?

Of course not. Which was why, assuming Sander ever woke again, and assuming they were not caught and turned over to the Dordrecht militia, she would concoct some story for him about Wurfbain and Jan and the rest being undone before they'd left the city, so they need not ever return, not for revenge, not for their stolen fortune (which had never been theirs to begin with), and not even for illumination—better to be blind than to see hell, or some such silly Sanderism. Perhaps they would live another fifty years or perhaps they would hang from a soggy gallows in the morning, but they would never hear a single answer to any of their myriad questions, so long as she could help it.

The meer and the mist took their little boat, as night-waters will take any who seek such dubious sanctuaries, and Jolanda felt a weariness in her throbbing limbs that she hadn't felt since the height of snail season as a girl. Gazing down to where her dark hands gripped the wooden shafts, she offered a prayer that she live long enough for the dye to fade once and for all, to see if she really had skin under all that purple.

Locking the oars at last, she picked her way between the crossbows and dug out Sander's gamy severed hand from beneath the bags. Then she returned to the back of the boat and felt around until she found the gap between rowing board and hull where she'd wedged Jan's ring before setting out from the harbor. Pulling it free almost cost her a fingernail, but finally she extracted the small gold band. Holding it up and peering through it, she looked all around, taking in fog and bog and hollow boat—the whole of her topsy-turvy world.

Then she shook her head, slid the ring onto the waiting finger of Sander's clammy, dead hand, and cast it into the night. Jolanda wondered if hand and ring might spiral forever through the swamp-vapors, never descending into the water nor rising up into the sky, suspended for all time between heaven and earth, an eternal wheel spinning ever onward through the changeless twilight...

She heard it splash into the meer, where it would no doubt make a hungry fish quite happy.

Jolanda turned away from the gray, mist-kissed water and made ready to rest. Rolling up the small fur mantle Sander had commissioned but apparently never delivered to Simon, she gently lifted the madman's heavy head and wedged the garment between brow and prow. Then she withdrew the stained cape Jan had given her when they had first come to Dordrecht and lay down beside Sander, resting her neck against the shared, bristly pillow. It was as cramped as her communal childhood bed, between his bulky body and the gunwale of the boat, and he stank even worse than rotting sea snails. Still, Jo smiled to herself as she stretched her blue cloak to blanket them both, two fools under one hood.

Bibliography

In addition to the following texts, I am deeply in the debt of several individuals who assisted me with various aspects of this project. First among these is Ekaterina Sedia, who aided with a rare instance of non-Dutch translation, proverb hunting, and general wisdom-acquisition. Then there are the generous folk at the Erfgoedcentrum Dordrecht (the city archives and heritage center), the Nationaal Park De Biesbosch (especially Daniel—bedankt again!), and the Biesbosch Museum Werkendam, who took the time to assist a blathering Yank who barged in with a hundred esoteric questions of dubious import. I would also be remiss if I didn't mention the youthful tutelage I received from Edgar and his mother Monique Wurfbain, Headmaster Himmel, Albert and Anika and their daughters, Michael and his family, Martin and his, a certain crew of role-playing students at the International School of the Hague, and especially my classmates in Poeldijk for all helping me along in my Dutch education. Penultimately, I must offer many, many thanks to Willem Valkenberg and Joyce Himbrecht for all of the above, as well as a thousand things besides—suffice to say, I owe them for putting up with me as an adult of suspect maturity in general as well as for their assistance with this book in particular. Finally, a rousing proost for Travis, Ari, and Riley of Amsterdam, and the staff of the Dordrecht Stayokay Hostel, for hosting me when I was researching this novel—the ability to relax and rest are crucial components of a successful investigation, and never was I so relaxed and rested as when I was in their company.

Adamson, Melitta Weiss. *Food in Medieval Times*. Westport, Conn.: Greenwood Press, 2004.

Baaij, Hans, ed. *Rotterdam 650 Years: Fifty Years of Reconstruction*. Utrecht/Antwerpen, The Netherlands: Veen, Publishers, 1990.

Blok, Petrus Johannes. *History of the People of the Netherlands, Part II: From the Beginning of the Fifteenth Century to 1559*. London: G.P. Putnam's Sons, 1899.

Borchert, Till-Holger, ed. *The Age of Van Eyck: The Mediterranean World and Early Netherlandish Painting 1430–1530*. London: Thames and Hudson, 2002.

Boswell, John. *Same-Sex Unions in Premodern Europe*. New York: Random House, Inc, 1994.

Breazeal, Sean. "Medieval Denominations." *Medievalcoinage.com*. http://www.medievalcoinage.com/denominations/index.htm.

Brown, Andrew, and Graeme Small, trans. and eds. *Court and Civic Society in the Burgundian Low Countries c. 1420–1530*. Manchester: Manchester University Press, 2007.

Bullough, Vern L., and James A. Brundage. *Sexual Practices and the Medieval Church*. Buffalo, N.Y.: Prometheus Books, 1982.

————, eds. *Handbook of Medieval Sexuality*. New York: Garland Press, Inc, 1996.

Cartellieri, Otto. *The Court of Burgundy*. New York: Barnes and Noble, Inc, 1929.

Crossley-Holland, Nicole. *Living and Dining in Medieval Paris: The Household of a Fourteenth-Century Knight*. Cardiff, U.K.: University of Wales Press, 1996.

Dean, Trevor. *Crime in Medieval Europe*. London: Pearson Education Limited, 2001.

Epstein, S. R., and Maarten Prak. *Guilds, Innovation and the European Economy, 1400–1800*. New York: Cambridge University Press, 2008.

Erfgoedcentrum DiEP. http://www.erfgoedcentrumdiep.nl.

Firebaugh, W. C. *The Inns of the Middle Ages.* Chicago: Pascal Covici, 1924.

Friedlænder, Max J. *From Van Eyck to Brueghel.* London: Phaidon Press, 1956.

Gathercole, Patricia M. *The Depiction of Architecture and Furniture in Medieval French Manuscript Illumination.* Lampeter, Wales: The Edwin Mellen Press, 2006.

Geerts, L. C. *The Dutch History Pages.* http:geerts.com.

Goubitz, Olaf. *Purses in Pieces: Archaeological Finds of Late Medieval and 16th-Century Leather Purses, Pouches, Bags and Cases in the Netherlands.* Zwolle, The Netherlands: Stichting Promotie Archaeologie, 2007.

Griffis, William Elliot. *Brave Little Holland, and What She Taught Us.* Cambridge, Mass.: The Riverside Press, 1894.

"History of Art: Masterpieces of World Literature—Netherlandish Proverbs." *A World History of Art.* http://www.all-art.org/world_literature/proverbs1.htm.

Hyatte, Reginald, trans. and ed. *Laughter for the Devil: The Trials of Gilles de Rais, Companion-in-arms of Joan of Arc (1440).* London: Associated University Press, 1984.

Kagay, Donald J., and L.J. Andrew Villalon, eds. *The Hundred Years War: A Wider Focus.* Leiden, The Netherlands: Koninklijke Brill, 2005.

Kittell, Ellen E., and Mary A. Suydam, eds. *The Texture of Society: Medieval Women in the Southern Low Countries.* New York: Palgrave Macmillan, 2004.

Leggett, William F. *Ancient and Medieval Dyes.* Landisville, Penn.: Coachwhip Publications, 2009.

Lesaffer, Randall. *European Legal History: A Cultural and Political Perspective.* New York: Cambridge University Press, 2009.

Mahmood, Cynthia Keppley. *Frisian and Free: Study of an Ethnic Minority of the Netherlands.* Prospect Heights, Ill.: Waveland Press, Inc, 1989.

Mane, Perrine, and Françoise Piponnier. *Dress in the Middle Ages.* New Haven: Yale University Press, 1997.

Muusers, Christianne. "Middle Dutch Cookery Books in Manuscripts." *Coquinaria.* http://www.coquinaria.nl/kooktekst/index.htm.

Netherton, Robin, and Gale R. Owen Crocker, eds. *Medieval Clothing and Textiles, Volume 7.* Woodbridge, U.K.: The Boydell Press, 2011.

Nijsten, Gerard. *In the Shadow of Burgundy: The Court of Guelders in the Late Middle Ages.* New York: Cambridge University Press, 2004.

Pollmann, Judith, and Robert Stein, eds. *Networks, Regions and Nations: Shaping Identities in the Low Countries, 1300–1650.* Leiden, The Netherlands: Koninklijke Brill, 2010.

Power, Eileen. *Medieval People.* New York: Methuen and Co, 1924.

Roberts, Keith. *Bruegel.* Ann Arbor, Mich.: Phaidon Press Limited, 1971.

Roodnat, Wim. *De Sint Elisabethsvloed: Hoe Het Water Geschiedenis Schreef.* Dordrecht, The Netherlands: De Stroombaan, 2007.

Schama, Simon. *The Embarrassment of Riches: An Interpretation of Dutch Culture in the Golden Age.* New York: Alfred A. Knopf, Inc, 1987.

Scott, Margaret. *Fashion in the Middle Ages.* Los Angeles: The J. Paul Getty Museum, 2011.

Sensfelder, Jens, ed. *Crossbows in the Royal Netherlands Army Museum, With a List of Names and Marks of European Crossbow Makers, Bow Smiths and Bolt Makers.* Delft, The Netherlands: Eburon Academic Publishers, 2007.

Thoen, Erik, and Leen Van Molle, eds. *Rural History in the North Sea Area: An Overview of Recent Research, Middle Ages–Twentieth Century.* Turnhout, Belgium: Brepols Publishers, 2006.

Vaughan, Richard. *John the Fearless: The Growth of Burgundian Power.* New York: Barnes and Noble, Inc, 1966.

_____. *Philip the Good: The Apogee of Burgundy*. New York: Barnes and Noble, Inc, 1970.

Winwar, Frances. *The Saint and the Devil: Joan of Arc and Gilles de Rais, a Biographical Study in Good and Evil*. New York: Harper and Brothers, 1948.

...And sure, maybe just the once: *Wikipedia* (http://www.wikipedia.org/).

Acknowledgments

On New Year's Eve, 1992, I traveled with my family to the Netherlands, where we lived for the better part of a year. We rented a small house in the outskirts of Poeldijk, a village bordering Den Haag, where I attended public school, ice-skated, played football, rode a bicycle everywhere, and fell into both love and canals with an alarming regularity—in other words, I went as native as my atrocious language-acquisition skills would allow. To this day, Holland holds a unique place in my increasingly evident bosom, and this work represents my clumsy, stuttering attempt to share my affection for the people, land, and culture I hold so dear. Also, my fondness for jenever cannot be overstated.

It's worth noting that in this text I've taken some liberties where specifics of the Dutch language are concerned—this may not be the usual place you'd expect to find such a confession, but it *is* called an acknowledgments page, and it certainly bears acknowledging! This was done in an effort to prevent confusion on the part of my English readers, hence variant spellings of groot/groote/grote, depending on whether I was talking about a coin, a region, or a market. Another example is my concurrent use of both "count" and "graaf," which amount to the same title, and "hertog," which is essentially Dutch for "duke"—this was likewise done so as to better differentiate characters, and I hope in attempting to spare puzzlement for some I have not inflicted it upon bilingual others.

In the past I've made the mistake of trying to individually

thank people in this space, which invariably leads to my inexcusably forgetting to include dear, dear people without whom the work would not be possible. The resulting emotion is, as the technopeasants say, the suck, and so I'll simply say thank you to everyone who's helped, and to everyone who's read, which amounts to the same thing—it's a strange, wonderful feeling to run across a random review from a stranger posted in some far-flung corner of the Internet, and exactly the sort of thing that rejuvenates me when I've been on a self-loathing bender and am in desperate need of random cheer. Thank you again, everyone.

extras

about the author

Jesse Bullington's formative years were spent primarily in rural Pennsylvania, the Netherlands and Tallahassee, Florida. He is a folklore enthusiast who holds a bachelor's degree in history and English from Florida State University. He currently resides in Colorado, and can be found online at www.jessebullington.com

Find out more about Jesse Bullington and other Orbit authors by registering for the free monthly newsletter at www.orbitbooks.net

if you enjoyed
THE FOLLY OF THE WORLD

look out for

THE FALLEN BLADE

by

Jon Courtenay Grimwood

1

Venice, Tuesday 4 January 1407

The boy hung naked from wooden walls, shackles circling one wrist and both ankles. He'd fought for days to release his left hand, burning his skin on red-hot fetters as he worked to drag his fingers free. The struggle had left him exhausted and – if he was honest – no better off than before.

"Help me," he begged, "I will do whatever you ask."

His gods stayed silent.

"I swear it. My life is yours."

But his life was theirs anyway; even here in an enclosed space where his lungs ached at every breath and the air was sour and becoming sourer. The gods had abandoned him to his death.

It would have helped if he could remember their names.

Some days he doubted they existed. If they did, he doubted they cared. The boy's fury at his fate had become bitterness and despair, and then turned to false hope and fresh fury. Maybe he'd missed an emotion, but he'd worked his way through those he knew.

Yanking at his wrist made flesh sear.

Whatever magic his captors used was stronger than his will to be free. The chains with which they bound him were new, bolted firmly to the wall. Every time he grabbed a chain to yank at it, his fingers sizzled as if a torturer pressed white-hot irons into his skin.

"Sweet gods," he whispered.

As if flattering the immortals could undo his earlier insults.

He'd shrieked at his gods, cursed them, called for the aid of demons. Begged for help from any human within earshot of his despair. A part of him wanted to return to shrieking. Simply for the release it would bring. Only he'd screamed his throat raw days ago. Besides, who would come to his grotesque little cell with no doors? And if they did, how would they enter?

Murder. Rape. Treason ...

What else merited being walled up alive?

His crime was a mystery. What was the point of punishment if the prisoner couldn't remember what he'd done? The boy had no memory of his name. No memory of why he was locked in a space little bigger than a coffin. Not even a memory of who put him here.

Earth strewed the floor, splattered with his own soiling.

It was days since he'd needed to piss, and his lips were cracked like dry mud and raw from where he tried to lick them. He needed sleep almost as desperately as he wanted to be free, but every time he slumped his shackles burnt and the pain snapped him awake again. He'd done something wrong. Something very wrong. So wrong that even death wouldn't embrace him.

If only he could remember what.

You have a name. What is it?

Like hope and freedom, this too remained out of reach. In the hours that followed, the boy hovered on the edges of a fever. Sometimes his wits were sharp, but mostly he inhabited a blasted wasteland inside his own skull where his memories should be.

All he saw in there were shadows that turned away from him; and voices he was unable to hear clearly.

Pay attention, he told himself. *Listen.*

So he did. What he heard were voices beyond the wooden walls. A crowd from the sound of it, arguing. And though what he heard was little louder than a whisper it told him they spoke a language he didn't recognise. One voice snapped out an order, another protested. Then something slammed into the wall directly in front of him.

It sounded like an axe or a hammer.

The second blow was even harder. Then came a third, his wooden world splintering as sweet air rushed in and fetid air blew out. The light through the narrow gap was blinding. As if the gods had come for him after all.

2

Late Summer 1406

Almost four months before the boy woke to find himself trapped in an airless wooden prison, a young Venetian girl hurried along a ramshackle *fondamenta* on her city's northern edge. In some places in that strange city the waterside walkways were built from brick or even stone. The one here was earth, above sharpened logs driven into the silt of the lagoon.

After sunset everywhere in Venice was unsafe, particularly if you were fifteen years old, unmarried and out of your area. But the red-haired girl on the *fondamenta* hoped to reach the brine pans before then. She planned to beg passage on a barge carrying salt to the mainland.

Her burgundy gown was already dusty and sweat stained.

Despite having walked for only an hour, she'd reached another world entirely. One where silk dresses attracted envious glances. Her oldest gown was still richer than the *campo gheto*'s best. Her hopes of passing freely ended when a small group of children stepped out of the shadows.

Opening her cloak, Lady Giulietta yanked free a gold locket from around her neck. "Take this," she said. "Sell it. You can buy food."

The boy with the knife sneered at her. "We steal food," he said. "We don't need your locket for that. Not from round here, are you?

Giulietta shook her head.

"You Jewish?"

"No," she said. "I'm—"

She was about to say ... something stupid, knowing her. It was a stupid kind of day. Being here was stupid. Stopping was stupid. Even treating his question seriously was stupid. "I'm like you," she finished lamely.

"Course you are," he said. On either side, others laughed. "Where did you get this anyway?"

"My m ..." She hesitated. "Mistress."

"You stole it," a smaller boy said. "That's why you're running. Nasty lot, the Watch. You'd be better coming with us."

"No," Giulietta said, "I'd better keep going."

"You know what happens if the Watch take you?" a girl asked. She stepped forward to whisper in Giulietta's ear. If even half were true, someone of Giulietta's age would be better killing herself than being captured. But self-murder was a sin.

"And if the Watch don't get you, then ..."

The youngest shut his mouth at a glare from their leader. "Look around," he snapped. "It's getting dark. What have I said?"

"Sorry, Josh."

The older boy slapped him. "We don't use names with strangers. We don't talk about ... Not when it's almost nightfall." He switched his glare to the girl who stood beside him. "I'm going to cut him loose. I swear it. Don't care if he is your brother."

"I'll go with him."

"You'll go nowhere," Josh said. "Your place is with me. You too," he told Giulietta. "There's a ruined *campo* south of here. We'll make it in time."

"If we're lucky," the girl said.

"We've been lucky so far, haven't we?"

"*So far, and no further,*" said a shadow behind them.

Old and weary, the voice sounded like dry wind through a dusty attic.

Unwrapping itself, the shadow became a Moor, dressed in a dozen shades of grey. A neatly barbered beard emphasised the thinness of his face and his gaze was that of a soldier grown tired of life. Across his shoulders hung a sword. Stilettos jutted at both hips. Lady Giulietta noticed his crossbow last. Tiny, almost a toy, with barbed arrows the size of her finger.

With a sour smile, the Moor pointed his crossbow at Josh's throat, before turning his attention to the young woman he'd been following.

"My lady, this is not kind ..."

"Not kind?"

Bunching her fists, Lady Giulietta fought her anger.

She'd become used to holding it in in public, screaming about her forthcoming marriage behind closed doors. She was two years older than her mother was when she wed. Noble girls married at twelve, went to their husband's beds at thirteen, sometimes a little later. At least two of Giulietta's friends had children already.

She'd been whipped for her refusal to wed willingly.

Starved, locked in her chambers. Until she announced she'd kill herself. On being told that was a sin, she'd sworn to murder her husband instead.

At that, Aunt Alexa, the late Duke Marco III's widow, had shaken her head sadly and sent for hot water to which she added fermented leaves to make her niece a soothing drink. While Uncle Alonzo, the late duke's younger brother, had taken Giulietta aside to say it was interesting she should mention that ...

Her world became a darker, more horrid place. Not only would she marry a foreigner she'd never met. She'd be taught how to kill him when the bedding was done. "You know what they expect me to do?"

"My lady, it's not my place ..."

"Of course not. You're just the cur sent to round up strays."

His eyes flared and she smiled. He wasn't a cur and she wasn't a stray. She was Lady Giulietta dei San Felice di Millioni. The Regent's niece. The new duke's cousin. Duchess Alexa's goddaughter. Her whole life defined by how she was related to someone else.

"Say you couldn't find me."

"I've been following you since I saw you leave."

"*Why?*" she demanded. Only in the last half-hour had she felt herself watched. She couldn't believe he'd let her travel right across Venice by herself, knowing he would stop her before she could escape to the mainland.

"I hoped you might turn back."

Rubbing her temples, Giulietta wished they'd sent a young officer she could shout at, or beguile with her charms, meagre though they were.

"How can I marry a man I haven't even met?"

"You know ..."

Giulietta stamped her foot. She understood. All daughters were assets. Princely daughters more than most. It was just ... Maybe she'd read too many poets. What if there was someone she was *meant* to marry? She regretted her words the moment they were spoken. The Moor's quiet contempt for her question ensured that.

"And what if he lives on the world's far edge or is not yet born? What if he died centuries ago? *What if he loves someone else?* Policy can't wait on a girl's fantasies. Not even for you ..."

"Let me go," Giulietta begged.

"My lady, I can't." He shook his head sadly, never letting his crossbow's aim stray from Josh's throat. "Ask me anything else."

"I want nothing else."

Atilo il Mauros had bought her her first pony. Dandled her on his knees. With his own hands he carved her a bear fighting a woodcutter. But he would return her to Ca' Ducale because that was his duty. Atilo did his duty without fear or favour. It had made him the late duke's favourite. And earned him Alonzo, the new Regent's, hatred. Giulietta had no idea what Aunt Alexa thought of him.

"If you loved me ..." Her voice was flat.

Lord Atilo glanced at the bow he held, looked at the ragged thieves and shifted Giulietta out of their hearing, without letting his aim waver.

"My lady."

"*Listen to me.*" She felt sick in her gut. Tired and fed up and close to tears. "King Janus was a Crucifer. A Black Crucifer."

"I know."

"And I had to learn it from servants' gossip. They're going to marry me to an ex-torturer, who broke his vows of poverty and chastity. Who abandoned *the purity of pain*." Her lips curled in disgust at the words.

"To become king," Atilo said simply.

"He's a monster."

"Giulietta ... The Germans want Venice. The Byzantines want it too. The Mamluks want your colonies. Even my people, the Moors, would happily see your navy sunk. King Janus was Black only briefly. Cyprus is an island we can use."

"*Use?*" she said in scorn.

"Venice's strength rests on its trade routes. It *needs* Cyprus. Besides, you have to marry someone."

"It might as well be him?"

The Moor nodded, and she wondered if he could read the fury in her eyes. Anger kept her fear at bay. Her fear of what being bedded by a Black Crucifer might involve.

"My lord," Josh interrupted.

Atilo raised his bow. "Did I tell you to speak?" His finger began tightening on the trigger.

"*Let him speak.*"

"My lady, you're in no ..."

"... position to demand anything?" said Lady Giulietta bitterly. She'd never been in a position to demand anything as far as she could see. At least not since her mother was murdered. Giulietta was a Millioni. A princess. She had one of the most gilded childhoods in Venice. Everyone envied her.

She'd swap all of it for ...

Lady Giulietta bit her lip so hard it bled. There were days when her self-pity nauseated even herself. This was turning out to be one of them.

"Let's hear what he has to say," she suggested.

Atilo lowered his tiny crossbow. A nod said the boy was reprieved, for now. "This had better be good."

"We should get off the streets, my lord."

"That's it?" Atilo sounded astonished. "That's your contribution? You're a split second away from death. And you think we should get off the streets?"

"It's almost dark."

"They're afraid of the Watch," Giulietta said.

She wasn't surprised. *Beat you and violate you, smash your face and twist your arms if you don't do everything they want.* That sounded as if the girl spoke from experience.

"Not the Watch," the younger boy said dismissively. "We ain't afraid of them now. They don't go out after dark."

"They're the Watch," Giulietta said.

"Got more sense," he told her. "Not with what's out there."

"And what is out there?" she asked. Perhaps the small

boy didn't see Atilo's warning scowl. Perhaps he wasn't bothered.

"Demons."

"No," his sister said. "They're monsters."

"Atilo ..." She shouldn't be using his name like that. Not without "my lord" or whatever title he held since the Regent had stripped him of Admiral of the Middle Sea, which had been his position under Marco III ... The late, and very lamented Duke Marco III. Since his son, Marco IV, her poor cousin, was a twitching simpleton.

"What?" His tone was sharp.

"We can't just leave them."

"Yes," he said. "We can." Atilo stopped at an owl's hoot, his shoulders relaxing slightly. When he hooted back, the owl hooted in return. "It's you we can't leave." There was bitterness in his voice.

"But you would if you could ... ?"

"I have fifteen blades out there. The best I've trained. My deputy, his deputy, thirteen others. Good soldiers. If half come through this alive I'll be grateful."

Giulietta didn't recognise him as the old man who had carved her a wooden toy as a child. This was the Atilo people saw in battle.

"Are we heading for safety?"

He turned, looked at her. A hard glare that softened slightly. "There is no safety tonight, my lady. Not here and not now. The best I can do is hope to keep you alive."

"And the children?"

"They're dead already. Leave them."

VISIT THE ORBIT BLOG AT
www.orbitbooks.net

FEATURING

**BREAKING NEWS
FORTHCOMING RELEASES
LINKS TO AUTHOR SITES
EXCLUSIVE INTERVIEWS
EARLY EXTRACTS**

AND COMMENTARY FROM
OUR EDITORS

With regular updates from our team,
orbitbooks.net is your source
for all things orbital

●

While you're there, join our e-mail list
to receive information on special offers,
giveaways, and more

●

Find us on Facebook at www.facebook.com/orbitbooks
Follow us on Twitter @orbitbooks

imagine. explore. engage.

orbit

www.orbitbooks.net